Five-Minute Mysteries Reader

Five-Minute Mysteries Reader

by Ken Weber

AN IMPRINT OF RUNNING PRESS
PHILADELPHIA • LONDON

Printed in the United States

9   8   7   6   5   4   3   2   1
Digit on the right indicates the number of this printing.

Library of Congress Cataloging-in-Publication Number 98-70172

ISBN 0-7624-0215-6

Cover illustration by Paul Zwolak
Cover design by Toni Renée Leslie
Typography: Adobe Garamond

Published by Courage Books, an imprint of
Running Press Book Publishers
125 South Twenty-second Street
Philadelphia, Pennsylvania 19103-4399

Dedicated to a very patient family

Contents

1   A DECISION AT RATTLESNAKE POINT   *11*

2   SOMETHING SUSPICIOUS IN THE HARBOR   *15*

3   IN SEARCH OF ANSWERS   *18*

4   A SINGLE SHOT IN THE CHEST   *22*

5   THE CASE OF THE STOLEN STAMP COLLECTION   *26*

6   NOT YOUR AVERAGE HARDWARE STORE   *29*

7   MURDER AT 249 HANOVER STREET   *34*

8   HEAD-ON IN THE MIDDLE OF THE ROAD   *38*

9   A 911 CALL FROM WHITBY TOWERS   *42*

10   THE CASE OF THE KRAMER COLLECTION   *46*

11   WAITING OUT THE RAIN   *50*

12   A ROUTINE CHECK IN THE PARKING LOT   *54*

13   AN ANSWER FOR KIRBY'S IMPORTANT NEW CLIENT   *58*

14   TWO SHOTS WERE FIRED   *63*

15   NORTHERN FARMS LTD. VERSUS
     DOMINION SPRAYING COMPANY   *67*

16   AN UNLIKELY PLACE TO DIE   *75*

17   TO CATCH A MANNERLY THIEF   *79*

18   TRACING THE COURIERS FROM DEPARTURE TO ARRIVAL   *83*

19   NOT ALL LOTTERY WINNERS ARE LUCKY   *87*

20   SPY VERSUS SPY   *91*

21   THE SEARCH FOR OLIE JORGENSSON   *96*

22   MURDER AT THE DAVID WINKLER HOUSE   *100*

23   INCIDENT ON THE PICKET LINE   *104*

24 FOOTPRINTS ON THE TRAIL *107*

25 A VERY BRIEF NON-INTERVIEW *111*

26 MURDER AT 12 CARNAVON *116*

27 THE CASE OF QUEEN ISABELLA'S GIFT *123*

28 QUITE POSSIBLY, THE ANNUAL MEETING OF THE AMBIGUITY SOCIETY *128*

29 THE CASE OF THE MISSING BODY *131*

30 THE CASE OF THE MARIGOLD TROPHY *134*

31 THE COFFEE BREAK THAT WASN'T *138*

32 WHO SHOT THE CLERK AT HONEST ORVILLE'S? *141*

33 SPEED CHECKED BY RADAR *146*

34 WHERE TO SEND "THIS STUFF HERE" *151*

35 A WITNESS IN THE PARK *154*

36 AN URGENT SECURITY MATTER AT THE UN *158*

37 THE BODY ON BLANCHARD BEACH *163*

38 ESTY WILLS PREPARES FOR A BUSINESS TRIP *168*

39 THE CASE OF THE BUCKLE FILE *172*

40 WHILE LITTLE HARVEY WATCHED *177*

41 THE MURDER OF MR. NORBERT GRAY *181*

42 A HOLDUP AT THE ADJALA BUILDING *185*

43 FILMING AT L'HÔTEL DU ROI *188*

44 WHETHER OR NOT TO CONTINUE UP THE MOUNTAIN *192*

45 NOTHING BETTER THAN A CLEAR ALIBI *194*

46 GUENTHER HESCH DIDN'T CALL IN! *198*

47 RIGHT OVER THE EDGE OF OLD BALDY *201*

48 SUNSTROKE, AND WHO KNOWS WHAT ELSE! *204*

49 SHOULD THE THIRD SECRETARY SIGN? *207*

50 A SUCCESSFUL BUST AT 51 ROSEHILL *210*

51   THE CASE OF THE BODY IN CUBICLE #12   *213*

52   THE CASE OF THE BROKEN LAWNMOWER   *216*

53   A QUIET NIGHT WITH DANIELLE STEEL?   *219*

54   VANDALISM AT THE BEL MONTE GALLERY   *222*

55   LAYING CHARGES TOO QUICKLY?   *227*

56   TAKING DOWN THE YELLOW TAPE   *232*

57   PROBLEM-SOLVING IN ACCIDENT RECONSTRUCTION 101   *236*

58   BEFORE THE FIRST COMMERCIAL BREAK   *239*

59   MORE THAN ONE ST. PLOUFFE?   *243*

60   WHEN THE OXYGEN RAN OUT   *247*

61   THE TERRORIST IN FOUNTAIN SQUARE   *251*

62   A MATTER OF BALANCE   *255*

63   PAYING ATTENTION TO ESME QUARTZ   *259*

64   INVESTIGATING THE FAILED DRUG BUST   *262*

65   A SURPRISE WITNESS FOR THE HIGHLAND PRESS CASE   *266*

66   THE LAST WILL AND TESTAMENT OF ALBION MULMUR   *269*

67   WHAT HAPPENS IN SCENE THREE?   *272*

68   ALMOST AN IDEAL SPOT FOR BREAKFAST   *278*

69   INVESTIGATING THE EXPLOSION   *282*

70   SOME UNCERTAINTY ABOUT THE CALL AT 291 BRISTOL   *285*

71   THE CASE OF THE MISSING CHILD   *288*

72   A CLEVER SOLUTION AT THE COUNTY FAIR   *292*

73   EVEN BIRDWATCHERS NEED TO WATCH THEIR BACKS   *296*

74   TWO EMBASSY CARS ARE MISSING   *299*

75   A MOST CONFUSING ROBBERY   *301*

76   TRANSCRIPT (COPY #1 OF 4)   *305*

SOLUTIONS   *315*

1

A Decision at Rattlesnake Point

THE CABLE SCREAMED OVER THE large pulley at the end of the mobile crane, launching a massive assault on the morning quiet. The arm of the crane was fully extended to reach over the brow of Rattlesnake Point, for the body had to come up from two hundred feet below. It was the distance more than the weight that made the equipment work so hard.

As he talked to Trevor Hawkes, the young doctor from the medical examiner's office watched the big machine with a wary eye. Perry Provato had ridden down and then back up via the crane within the past hour, and he was not at all impressed by what he saw, now that he was watching from the top.

"It's like I said, Trevor," he pointed sideways with his thumb at the body that was now coming over the edge of the cliff. Trussed up in a rescue basket, it bounced and swayed at the end of the cable like some macabre yo-yo that had got stuck on the way to the spool. "Like I said, I might do a bit better at the morgue this afternoon, but I'll take bets that the death took place six to eight hours ago."

Trevor nodded and looked at his watch. "So . . . 'tween one and three A.M. Makes sense." He motioned to the crane operator and then pointed to a clear spot beside the guard rail. "Highway patrol reported the car at, let's see, 4:46. Then . . ."

He waved frantically at the crane operator. "No! No! This side! Over here!" he yelled, pointing with both arms to the spot beside the rail.

"So," he said, his voice returning immediately to normal, "first light was 5:20. Patrol confirmed a body down in the scrub about ten minutes after that. And you went down, what? About eight o'clock. An hour ago, right?"

"Yeah, eight," Perry replied. "Never done that before. Go down on a cable, I mean. Can't say I want to again either! You just stand on the big grab hook and hang on! I mean, even the dead guy gets strapped into a basket.

"And what a mess when I got down there! He's a big guy. Not lanky like you, but a big one. Just think of the acceleration by the time he hit!"

Perry shook his head; his adrenaline was still pumping. "I remember this sicko physics teacher we had in high school. Liked to give us problems with falling bodies. She should try this one!"

Trevor looked at the body, lying finally where he had directed. Despite Perry's comment, it appeared remarkably intact. After a two-hundred-foot fall, all the parts were still there. In fact the face was almost unscathed. Only the big belly seemed pushed oddly to one side, and the suspenders on that side had come off. Trevor could see the neck was broken, likely the spine, too, in several places.

"One thing, Perry, before you go. In your, uh, your uh, uh . . ." Trevor was trying to find the right word. Perry was so young. He settled on "*experience*" anyway. "In your experience, uh . . . well, there's a note on the driver's seat in the car there." He knew that Perry was looking at the silver-gray Lincoln Town Car behind them. It was parked in perfect parallel on the verge between the road and the guard rail. "Can't be sure, of course, till we go inside, but my guess is it's a suicide note. Now, what makes a guy do himself in like that when there's . . . ?"

"You mean," Perry took the lead, "why didn't he just let the car run and go to sleep? Or overdose? Or something softer like that? I dunno. I guess some of them just want to be more dramatic. I know that some jumpers do it because they really want to punish themselves. But it's a lot quicker the way he did it! Then there's always the . . ."

The rest of what Perry had to say was erased by the scream of the cable. Both men looked to see Trevor's rookie partner, Ashlynne Walmsley, on her way over the brow of Rattlesnake Point. Unlike the other passengers so far, it was clear she was enjoying herself completely. Ashlynne waved a camera at Trevor as soon as the operator set her down.

"Lots of shots," she said. "Covered everything."

Trevor pointed to the body. "Get a couple there," he said, "then the car from several angles. And . . . just a minute!" He knelt beside the body. "Make sure you witness this." He patted the dead man's pockets and then reached into one of them and extracted a small ring of keys. "Just in case some jackass lawyer ever wants to know in court where we got these."

"Trust me," Ashlynne said and began snapping shots of the car.

Trevor, meanwhile, waved goodbye to the retreating Perry and went to the driver's door of the Lincoln. He inserted a key and turned it sharply. All four door locks popped open simultaneously, along with—to his complete surprise—the trunk lid. He reached for the door handle, then shrugged and went to the back of the car instead. Except for a CD player and a small rack of discs, the cavernous trunk was empty and very clean. With his pen, Trevor spread the discs apart and craned his neck to read the titles only to bump into Ashlynne who was peering over his shoulder.

"George Strait, Randy Travis, Dolly Parton," she read aloud. "Reba McIntyre. All country. Well, he's consistent anyway. Kitty Wells! Who's Kitty Wells?"

The question made Trevor feel his age so he ignored it. "Time to go inside," he said. "There's nothing here. You go to the passenger side and open up. Just witness what I do. I got a funny feeling we're going to have to explain a lot about this one."

"You mean," Ashlynne asked, "you think it's fishy that a guy would park his car so neat if he's going to jump? And lock it, too? And take the keys?"

Trevor didn't answer. He simply walked around to the driver's door and opened it after Ashlynne had done as she was instructed. The paper on the seat was of a standard memo-pad size. Again using his pen, Trevor turned it over. It was a note. It said simply:

Try to get me *now*.

A.

"Want my flashlight?" Ashlynne asked when she saw Trevor tilt up the steering column and bend himself in to look under the seat.

He just shook his head.

"Then is it okay if I see where the radio stations are pre-set? And, uh, like, Trevor . . . shouldn't the fingerprint people be here?"

Trevor Hawkes maneuvered himself back out of the car and stretched his long frame. He looked over at the crane operator who had sidled as close as he dared to the body.

"Good thinking on the radio stations," he said finally. "And yeah, you're right. Let's give the forensic bunch their shot. There won't be any prints though. Whoever murdered this guy isn't that dumb."

What has finally convinced Trevor Hawkes that this is a murder case?

2

Something Suspicious
in the Harbor

SUE MEISNER BROUGHT BOTH OARS forward into the little rowboat and drifted until the boat bumped against the huge freighter. It was especially dark down here on the water between the two big ocean-going ships. She felt as though she were in a tunnel, with the superstructure of *The Christopher Thomas* looming over her and the even bigger Russian ship alongside, completing the arch. Still there was enough light from the city to see the mark from early this morning, the little paint scrape where Sue had bumped against *The Christopher Thomas* the first time.

That had been with the police boat though, and Sue had been acting officially, as a constable with the Metropolitan Toronto Police marine unit. However, there was nothing official about this trip. It was anything but. She was in restricted waters to boot. Tiny, privately operated rowboats were not welcome in the main channel of Toronto harbor, and Sue knew if she were caught there, it would be hard to imagine what would be worse: her embarrassment or Inspector Braemore's wrath.

That was why, at sunset, she had taken the ferry from the city over to Ward's Island, collected the rowboat, and then pulled her way across the channel in the dark. By staying close to the piers along Cherry Street, she'd reached *The Christopher Thomas* undetected. So far anyway.

Sue shifted on the seat to relieve her sore back. The movement caused the little craft to rock, and it banged hard into the side of the freighter. The rowboat was aluminum, and to her, the sound in the tunnel between the two larger vessels was like a gunshot. But she knew it wouldn't be heard on deck. With the racket up there and in the hold, especially from the noisy diesels powering the loading winches, there wasn't a chance even for normal conversation, let alone picking up a sound from the surface of the water.

The crew of *The Christopher Thomas* had been loading big containers full of automobile engines for several hours already when Sue and her partner had made their official visit that morning. The two officers were responding to a tip. Sue had taken the call herself right after coming on duty.

"Something crooked in the harbor," the caller had said. "On *The Christopher Thomas* and maybe that Russian one beside her— the *Potemkin* something. You people should go check." Then the caller had hung up.

Inspector Braemore had not been very impressed. It was his opinion that some disgruntled sailor wanted to harass the shipowners and was using the police to do it. And Sue's visit this morning, if anything, seemed to confirm that, for they'd seen nothing amiss. She and her partner had circled the ship inside and outside. There were no safety violations, no evidence of contraband, not even a suggestion of drug use in the crew's quarters. *The Christopher Thomas* appeared to be just a freighter being filled with cargo by a busy crew that did not want two police officers getting in their way.

It was Inspector Braemore's I-told-you-so expression that had got Sue's dander up. It explained why, later in her shift, she had stood on the nearby ferry docks for half an hour and watched the loading through binoculars, and why she'd checked the ship's papers twice with the harbormaster. And it also explained— or so she told herself—why sore back and all, she was sitting in a tiny rowboat in the smelly darkness of Toronto harbor long after sunset.

"Well," she said out loud, "at least, it's paid off. At least now I *know* there is certainly something crooked going on. Tomorrow morning there's going to be another inspection so we can find out just what it is!"

What has led Sue Meisner to the conclusion that something crooked is going on aboard The Christopher Thomas?

3

In Search of Answers

EVERY WINDOW IN THE LITTLE studio was open as wide as possible in a vain attempt to catch whatever tired breeze might limp by from time to time. Inside, however, this arrangement produced no results. The air in the place had been hot, wet, and motionless all day. Still, at least one of Celeste Wyman's questions was answered: namely, why had Virgil Powys left every window—and the door, too—wide open when he supposedly dashed back to his house? In this heat wave, it made sense. No one was closing windows these days.

There was an answer, too, for another of Celeste's questions. Why wasn't the place air conditioned? By visiting the studio personally, by actually coming to the scene of the crime, so to speak, Celeste could see that an air conditioner would be intolerable. Too noisy. And it would box the place in. One of the studio's charms was that, despite the tight quarters, the number of windows created an impression of space. Powys claimed he had claustrophobia. Celeste certainly didn't, but she could sense what the effects would be if the sight lines were blocked.

She sat down at the table that served as a desk and looked out the large window across the room. Beyond it, over the alley and on the other side of a line of mature oak trees, traffic from Bronson Avenue superimposed its noise over the buzz and beep and chunter of the computers to her right. Side by side, on a counter that ran the length of the one wall without a window, sat a 486 tower, a Gateway 2000 4DX2, and beside it, a much more modest 386 desktop. Celeste leaned a little closer to the 486. Sixteen Meg RAM, she figured. Clockspeed of sixty-six megahertz. Powerful. A lot more powerful than its immediate neighbor.

The machinery made a sharp contrast to the Chippendale reproduction table at which she was sitting, but both the table and counter shared the disarray of the studio. Stashed in every available space on the counter was a flotsam of envelopes jammed with material, the lot held in place by a Gordian knot of wires and cables and power bars that only an original installer could ever untie. On the nearest edge of the table, pens spilled out of a pewter beer stein and trailed across to a pewter envelope holder lying empty on its side. On the left edge, irregular stacks of medical reference texts were interspersed with piles of dictionaries and manuals.

Celeste lifted a heavy metal stapler from the pile of papers on the crowded working surface in front of her. The first page, and then the second, the third, and then the fourth, when she looked further, answered yet another question. Powys was obviously one of those types who worked things out on paper first and only then went to the keyboard. It was not what she would have expected. Someone with his expertise, his passion for computers, seemed more likely to work "cold," right on the keyboard with no intermediate steps.

Virgil Powys had a reputation as a computer *wunderkind*. He'd started with IBM three years ago, and after two revolutionary patents, jumped to Apple for six months and then to Wang for two before going freelance. But he wasn't doing well at freelancing. He was brilliant but erratic; he needed the discipline of an organization around him, but with his reputation for instability no one would touch him anymore. Nevertheless, when Celeste's company, Hygiolic Incorporated, retained him six weeks ago, they thought they'd made a steal. This morning, "steal" suddenly had a whole new meaning.

Celeste Wyman was Director of Research at Hygiolic. It was a company specializing in the development and production of highly advanced and complicated drugs and medicines. For months the company had been on the verge of an historic medical breakthrough. By means of computer models, they had developed—theoretically—a vaccine to protect against common cold viruses. The trouble was no one could put all the strands together; there wasn't anybody in Celeste's department who could do it. And the board of directors had so severely limited access to the models for security reasons, that, in effect, Hygiolic had been going nowhere with what could be the biggest thing since the Salk vaccine.

Yesterday, Powys had called to say he'd done it. This morning he called again, this time to say he thought the work might have been pirated, that while he'd been out for just minutes, someone had been into the studio and into the program.

Celeste leaned back in the chair and stretched, idly running both index fingers against the flyscreen behind her. There were so many questions. Should she call the police? Not yet. Find out more first. Is it possible that Powys himself was stealing the program? That this whole break-in thing was a red herring? Not likely. It would be too hard for him to sell it. Oh, there were companies that would grab it first chance. But from Powys? No. Too easy to trace.

She leaned forward again, and put her elbows on the table. Did whoever had been into the system actually steal Hygiolic's big discovery? Yes. At the very least that had to be assumed. Espionage in medical research is as vicious as in warfare.

But then there were the truly niggling questions. Was Virgil Powys in cahoots with whoever did the pirating? Why, especially if he had put audit controls in the system that could tell him if someone had been into it, had he not encrypted the data? Used code? Powys's explanation was that Hygiolic was pushing so hard for results that using an encryption scheme good enough to protect against even a run-of-the-mill hacker would have slowed him right down. Reasonable enough, Celeste knew; she had been one of the ones pushing.

But then, at the very least, why hadn't he protected his system with a password? The answer to that was on the wall. For the third or fourth time in the past half hour, Celeste looked up at the wall above the 386. In large block letters she could see "HYGI-SNEEZE" written on the wallpaper with a felt-tipped pen. She shook her head. He had used a password all right! But then, hanging it out for all to see was something she did herself. So did others in her department. Not on the wallpaper though.

A noise from behind her made Celeste turn. Through the open door she could see Sean, her assistant, leaving the back door of the house and making his way across the lawn to the shed where Powys had built the studio. She counted Sean's steps: twenty-five. About twenty seconds, she calculated. Another ten to come up the stairs. Powys had said he'd gone back to the house to go to the bathroom, so that would be about thirty seconds each way. Allow, say, five minutes in the bathroom. Then he got a phone call. Long distance, he'd said, so that would be easy to verify. The call took about five minutes, supposedly, according to Powys, he was out of the studio for ten or eleven minutes. Enough time for a pirate to dash in and copy everything? No, not at all, no matter how good. Not even if he knew where to go and how to get in.

So, was Virgil Powys out of the studio for longer than he had said he was? No doubt about it. And was he out for a longer time because he had arranged to be? Well, Celeste thought, maybe it is indeed time to involve the police. They're probably better at finding out that kind of information. At least she knew that Powys needed to be questioned.

Why is Celeste Wyman certain that Virgil Powys was out of the studio for longer than the time he claimed to be?

4

A Single Shot in the Chest

BRIAN BRETON HELD HIS TONGUE as long as he could.

"For heaven's sake, Roly!" he finally blurted. "Doesn't it bother you to be playing with evidence like that?"

Roly Coyne lowered the binoculars for just a second, looked at them as though he were seeing them for the first time, and then put them back to his eyes.

"C'mon," he said. "What do you mean *evidence?* Who cares! This case is open and shut. At least as far as you're concerned. You got a body. You got a shooter. You got a confession. What more do you want? This case is, like *closed.* I mean *shut!* 'Sides, that's the ten o'clock class across the street there. I'll bet half the guys in our building are doing what I'm doing right now."

What Roly Coyne was doing, along with—according to him— half the guys in the building, was focusing a pair of binoculars on an aerobics class across the street from the morgue.

"You see, this ten o'clock bunch," Roly went on with unconcealed delight, "it's the one with all the chicks from the college up the street."

For the first time since Brian Breton had slipped into the office five minutes ago, Roly turned his back to the window and faced him. "Here, see for yourself."

He handed the binoculars to Brian. "C'mon, take a look!" he

insisted. "You never seen a spandex parade like this! Not over in the coroner's office anyway!"

"Aw, Roly, get off it!" Brian was annoyed. "It's bad enough being here without your juvenile nonsense." He used the opportunity to take the binoculars out of Roly's hand. "Besides, these are no good to someone like me, with glasses, without those little rubber cups on the eyepieces. Anyway, forget this and let's get down to the cooler. I want to get this over with."

Roly sighed. "Okay, Breton." He swiveled back to the window for one final, drooling stare. "You want to take any *terribly important evidence* down with us?" Without taking his eyes off the window he waved his hand vaguely at a table in the corner to his right. "It's all over there."

Brian had perused the evidence before, while Roly was studying aerobics. In addition to the binoculars Roly was using, there was a well-worn pocketknife with one of the blades broken off, a few coins, some wooden matches, a very dirty handkerchief, three fence staples, a bent nail, and—this one really caught Brian's eye —a World War I issue Ross rifle with the name MANOTIK burned crudely into the wooden butt.

"No," he said to Roly. "The evidence can stay here so you have something to play with when the aerobics class is over. Now let's go!"

Roly swiveled frontwards again. "All right, all right." Reluctantly he got to his feet. "Actually, this one shouldn't be so bad for you. Just your average dead body with a hole in the chest. I don't see why it always makes you sweat so. You don't have to kiss him! Anyway, you should have done this before I washed old Manotik. I bet he never had a bath in twenty years! Did he *stink* or what!"

"Roly! Just let's go." Already Brian was feeling sick to his stomach. After thirty years as an investigator with the coroner's office, he still had nightmares after a visit to the cooler, the refrigerated room full of slabs in sliding cabinet drawers where bodies were stored. Whenever he could, Brian ducked out of his obligation to examine cadavers, and in the case of old Manotik he was very tempted.

Manotik was a hermit who, for as long as anyone could remember, had lived in a swamp north of the city. The problem was, he was a squatter. Manotik had never owned the swamp. Three years ago, a company called Nucleonics Inc. had moved in, drained off all the water, built a complex of modern buildings, then surrounded the property with a huge chain-link fence and patrolled it twenty-four hours a day with armed guards. In a humanitarian gesture it soon regretted, Nucleonics granted Manotik a small piece of land next to the fence. It was from this base that the old man launched his campaign of harassment. At least the company *believed* it was the old man. His guilt had never been established.

At first, the problems were annoying but manageable. The Nucleonics property was plagued in turn by an infestation of snakes, then rats, and then skunks. But one night a section of fence was dynamited. A week later it happened again. Then the worst step of all: on six different occasions over the past two months, rifle bullets had winged through the windows of the Nucleonics executive suites. When a secretary was badly cut by flying glass, the company doubled the guard. It was one of the new guards who had shot the old man.

"His statement is pretty simple, isn't it? The guard's, I mean." Roly was repeating what Brian already knew as the elevator creaked its way down to the cooler. "He sees the old guy at the fence with the rifle poked through it, sorta hangin' there in the chain link. But shoulder level. And he's got those binoculars focused on the exec suite. The guard shouts at Manotik and the old guy grabs the rifle, so boom! The guard offs him. I'd say the plea'll be self-defense."

Brian wasn't listening. They had crossed the short hallway into the cooler and he was bracing himself. Roly, meanwhile, seemed to get cheerier.

"Number 42," he said, "right here." He rolled out the slab and grabbed a corner of the cover sheet. "And now! For your viewing pleasure . . . Ta-da!"

Brian gagged. "God, Roly," he muttered, then forced himself

to look at the scrawny white form that had once been Xavier Manotik. Roly was right about the bullet wound, an almost harmless looking hole in the chest. The rest of the body looked so clean and untouched. So did the face. Well, almost. Roly may have scrubbed it, but years of dirt still marked the ridges on the old man's forehead and darkened the cleft in his chin. Only the nose seemed really clean. It was a long, thin nose with calloused indentations on both sides of the bridge, and creases leading down from it toward the mouth, the kind of creases that come from years of frowning.

Brian leaned closer to see the stubble on the old man's cheeks. Despite his distaste for this routine, he never failed to be fascinated by the fact that body hair continued to grow after death.

"Hey, you startin' to like this or something?" Roly's voice intruded. "Seen enough or what?" Roly wanted to get back to the aerobics class. "Let's go up and you can sign off."

"Not yet, Roly. Not yet." Brian replied. "There's something about that guard's story that smells as bad as this place does."

"What do you mean?" Roly asked.

What does Brian Breton mean? What's wrong with the guard's story?

5

The Case of the Stolen Stamp Collection

IN THE DOORWAY OF MIKA FLECK'S office stood a very nervous young man in a blue delivery uniform. Miles Bender was waiting to be summoned, and he wasn't the least bit comfortable about the idea.

Mika's opening statement didn't help either. "Come in here and sit down, young man," she said without looking up. "For heaven's sake you're going to wear out the rug with your fidgeting."

Miles shuffled across the floor to the only chair that was empty of books and files and all the paraphernalia of an extremely busy office. "It didn't get there, did it?" he said as he sat down. "The shipment. Like, the stamps?"

Mika looked over the top of her half-glasses, freezing Miles Bender in mid-squirm. "No," she said. "It did not. The first bonded shipment that Acceleration Courier Service has ever failed to deliver." She pushed up her glasses and looked through them. It didn't make Bender feel any more relaxed. "And I don't suppose you're surprised to know that collection is worth over half a million dollars. That's why we had a police escort."

"I know it was valuable." For the first time, Miles Bender

stopped squirming. "I know that. But how can you blame *me* if the cops stole it. I mean—they looked like cops anyway."

Mika spread her hands on the desk and spoke more softly. "Okay. Let's go through it again. You say two policemen took the stamps. Just like that."

"Not just like that." Miles was beginning to whine in spite of Mika's obvious attempt to be more gentle with him. "I mean, they were cops! Look, it was standard procedure. All the way to the border, like, there were these two Vancouver city cops, one in front and one in back just the way we're supposed to do it. And at the border the two American cops took over, the ones from Bellingham. Motorcycle cops."

Miles Bender was becoming more confident as he sensed his side of the story was finally being listened to. He leaned forward in the chair. "I mean, there was no reason to be suspicious; you wouldn't have been either. They had real police bikes. Real uniforms—the boots, the gloves, the sunglasses, everything!"

Mika opened her mouth to speak, but Miles kept talking. "I mean they even *acted* like motorcycle cops. You know, sort of strutty and cocky and . . ."

"According to this report," Mika broke in, "you got a good look at them."

Miles took a deep breath. "At *one* of them, yeah. When we stopped on the highway and they made me get out. The one that put his bike in the van and, like, got in to drive, he got pretty close."

"According to your description," Mika said, "he is about your height, but heavier. Bit of a beer belly. Blue eyes and a reddish moustache. Maybe 35 to 40 years old."

"Yeah!" Miles Bender was enthusiastic in his agreement. "And the cut, the nick on his cheek? They got that on the report there? Like maybe he cut himself shaving?"

Mika nodded and then looked up from the report. "And you say all this took only a couple of minutes. They stopped. You stopped. They ordered you out, and then one of them put his bike in the van, and they took off leaving you at the side of the road."

"Exactly! That's it exactly!" Miles was excited now. "I mean, like, by this time I know they're not cops but, I mean, like, what am I gonna do?"

Mika cleared her throat. She was looking over the top of her glasses again. "For one," she said, "you're going to tell us where they took the stamps. Depending on how well you do that, we'll work out the next steps later."

Why is Mika Fleck suspicious of Miles Bender?

6

Not Your Average
Hardware Store

"SO YOU THINK THAT'S WHY we were handed this one?" Gordon Pape's question was rhetorical. He really didn't expect an answer but got one anyway.

"Figure it," Hugh Furneaux said. "Why else would the agency bring us this far north? It can't be any other reason. They've more than enough bodies up here for this kind of work."

"This kind of work," on this particular morning, was a repossession. Gordon Pape and Hugh Furneaux worked for SIMM Resolutions, a collection agency. "Field operatives," they were called in the agency's pretentious terminology, the ones who actually went out to face the locked doors, the insults, the angry dogs, the tears, even on occasion—and by far the most disturbing—sad, silent acceptance. All in order to repossess unpaid merchandise.

"My God. Look at it!" Hugh Furneaux exclaimed. "He must be a character all right."

The two operatives had pulled off the road to park in front of an ugly cement-block building. Its large yellow and black sign proclaimed it to be:

"A Real Man's Hardware Store."

Hugh scanned the shopworn banners in the display windows that flanked the front door. "Hard to believe there aren't some feminists out picketing here," he said. "I could see their point, too!"

The banners, all of them as dusty as the goods in the display windows, each supported Wilfrid Norman's idea of what a *real* hardware store must be, or a real *man's* hardware store at any rate.

"Real Men Don't Buy Teacups," one said.

Another offered:

"You Want *Seven* of Something? Ask Us!"

And directly underneath:

"No Pre-Packaging! We Sell You What You Want!"

Still another announced:

**"If We Ain't Got It,
      Then It Ain't Hardware!"**

The "**ware**" had partly torn off from the end of the last banner and hung away from its host sentence at an awkward angle.

"You know," Hugh observed to his partner, "it may not just be that we're strangers. This guy could be very hard-nosed. Did you see the shepherd running loose out back in the storage area? I'll bet he didn't come with a 'Good with Children' guarantee. Wonder if there's any of those loose inside?"

Gordon Pape was about to reply but then paused. He was looking at the Christmas lights that hung from the fluorescent fixtures just behind the windows. In mid-July. Apparently Wilfrid Norman's sole concession to the festive season was to plug and unplug an extension cord.

"I was here once," he said absently. "Needed a new handle for my splitting maul up at the cottage."

"Your *what?*" For the first time since they'd pulled in, Hugh took his eyes off the front of Norman's hardware store and looked directly at Gordon.

"A spli . . . Never mind. Not important," Gordon said. "The point is, the guy had one here. In stock. Actually he had about half a dozen! You just don't buy that kind of thing in a typical hardware store anymore. That's one of those crummy special orders that takes forever and gets surcharged to boot, all because some bean counter has told the owner his inventory has to roll over a certain number of times a year."

"And the whole place is like that," Gordon continued. "Full of everything you'd never get anywhere else. It's dirty and it's dusty and it's scattered all over the store. There's bins, barrels, shelves. Don't know how anybody can find anything, but they do. Well, anyway he does. Norman, I mean." He paused reflectively for a moment. "It's really your good old-fashioned hardware store. Everybody for miles around knows it."

"That's what I meant about why we were asked to do this," Hugh commented. "All the SIMM people up here must know him. That's why we're here to pick up—what is it anyway? It's a computer isn't it?" He reached into the back seat for a clipboard. "Yeah. Kirznet Cash Flow Control System."

He looked out at the display windows again. "Somehow it just doesn't seem to fit in there, does it?"

Gordon chuckled. "Probably why he hasn't paid for it."

"Well, pay or not," Hugh opened the car door, "let's get it over with." He was halfway out the door and then sat down again. "By the way, I make it 9:15. Is that what you've got? Awfully late for an old-fashioned hardware store to still be closed."

"That's true," Gordon replied, a note of concern in his voice.

The two men got out and stood beside their car to take in a wider view. The area was very quiet. There was no one else around.

The "Real Man's Hardware Store" had no sidewalk in front of it, just a small parking lot, empty this morning. There were no adjacent stores either; the building was separated from the edge of town by a small field.

"This isn't a holiday or something, is it?" Hugh looked at Gordon as they approached the front door. "Don't they have a half-holiday or something like that in these little towns when everybody closes."

"Not in the morning," Gordon said, somewhat distractedly for they'd reached the door and it was definitely locked.

"Wow! Look at that latch!" Hugh said. "This has to be the last store in the country with a thumb la . . . Oh, oh! Look there."

"I see it—him," Gordon answered.

On the floor inside, just a few steps from the door, the body of a man lay face down at an angle slightly oblique to the door. Hugh and Gordon moved to the display windows on either side so they could peer in.

The body was that of a man at the far end of middle age. They could see white hair protruding over the edge of a baseball cap, some of the tufts leading to the back of his lined neck. He wore a red smock, the kind one might normally expect on a hardware store clerk.

The position of the body seemed peculiar. It lay in a very wide pool of blood that seemed to have congealed at the edges now. The man's legs were crossed at the ankles as though he had tripped himself and fallen that way. One hand, his left, was in the pocket of his shiny brown pants. The other was in the small of his back, palm upward. In the wan light from the fluorescents left on for nighttime security, both Hugh and Gordon noted its soft, clean, whiteness in contrast to the menace just above it. For there, inches above the hand, thrust deep into the man's back, was a black-handled knife, a multi-purpose sportsman's knife, probably one from the store. It appeared as though the victim's last living effort had been to try to pull it out.

Neither Hugh nor Gordon felt an urge to rush. There was no question the man was dead and had been for some time.

"I'll call," Hugh said, pulling himself back from the scene. "Do they have 911 here?"

"They must," Gordon replied. "Wouldn't matter anyway. Everybody knows Wilfrid Norman's place."

"Sure, but that's not Wilfrid Norman," Hugh said over his shoulder on the way to the car and the cellular phone.

Gordon Pape has been to Wilfrid Norman's store before, and might recognize the hardware man, but how does Hugh Furneaux know that the dead man is not Wilfrid Norman?

7

Murder at
249 Hanover Street

AS SHE PULLED OVER TO the curb, Janet Dexel cocked her head a little closer to the portable radio on the seat beside her.

"The wettest first day of October since records were started in 1826," the announcer was saying, "and the outlook for the next several days is more of the same."

Janet snapped off the radio and peered almost gloomily across the sidewalk at 249 Hanover Street. "A perfectly miserable day," she said out loud to herself, "and now a perfectly miserable night and a perfectly miserable place over there to go with it all."

Certainly, 249 Hanover Street was not inviting. Although the brick pillars supporting the heavy gates, together with the wrought iron fence, would never keep out any determined intruder, they said "You Are Not Welcome" in a most effective way. If the message failed here, at the edge of the property, then the double doors under the dimly lit portico at the house itself took a second stab at it, for their design repeated the warning that visitors to 249 Hanover Street would not be pleasantly received.

Janet groaned as she forced herself out of the car into the pouring rain. She drew her heavy rain cloak tight around her shoulders and stared at the big house for a few seconds before walking back to an empty squad car parked at the curb behind her. She leaned in and switched off the flashing red lights, then made a note of the car's number before turning to walk quickly through the open gates. Staff Sergeant Janet Dexel hated fuss. She especially disliked police operations that attracted attention unnecessarily. Someone in her unit was going to get a dressing down as soon as she had the opportunity, and at the moment, the odds favored tonight.

Rain began to fall even harder so she broke into a run for the last few steps up to the double doors. Once inside, the sight of Chesley Barron-Ripple, or rather, what had been Chesley Barron-Ripple, quickly took her mind off the bad weather and the fool who had left the lights flashing. Two of her officers stood over the body. Neither was enjoying the assignment very much. One of them held a handkerchief over her nose.

Chesley Barron-Ripple was attracting the kind of attention that would have embarrassed him beyond measure had he been alive. An assistant from the medical examiner's office was snapping picture after picture of him where he lay on a priceless, silk-on-silk handwoven rug. Behind the police officers, a pair of ambulance attendants, looking far more at ease than anyone else at the scene, were holding a body bag like a pair of Boy Scouts about to fold the flag at the end of the ceremony.

One of the policemen, the younger one, almost stood at attention as he addressed his boss. "The lab people have all gone, Sergeant," he said. "Except for him." The policeman nodded at the photographer. "And he's almost finished—*Aren't you?*"

It was clear to Janet that everyone wanted to get this part of the investigation over and done with.

"We're waiting for you to give us the clear." It was the other officer. She was speaking through her handkerchief. "Detective Andrew is in the next room with the three . . . uh . . . I guess they're suspects, aren't they?"

"Oh? Suspects?" Another thing that bothered Janet was having her officers jump to conclusions. Especially if there were media people nearby. One positive outcome of the heavy rain, however, was that the situation was free of the press, at least so far.

"Well, I mean . . . I don't know if they're suspects. They're . . . they're . . . they've been *detained* by Detective Andrew."

The officer appeared relieved that she'd found the right word.

"There are three people," she continued with more confidence now. "There's the part-time handyman. And Barron-Ripple's daughter, and . . . and . . ." Her discomfort had returned. "And the *butler*, Sergeant Dexel."

Before Janet could reply, the younger policeman spoke again. "He said he was the butler, Sergeant, but I think he's really a kind of valet or personal servant. Anyway, he's got an alibi. He went to his sister's in Kennebunkport on the 30th. Been there for two days. Actually, all three have got alibis like that."

"I see," Janet Dexel said, searching her coat pockets for a tissue to pat the droplet of rain on her eyelash.

"Yeah, the daughter, Sergeant Dexel," the policewoman was still talking through her handkerchief. "She's . . . well . . . her alibi's pretty solid. She's been drying out in a clinic for the past month. Got back this morning. When she got home here she saw the butler . . . uh . . . valet, I guess, standing on the portico. Seems neither of them had a key so they sent for the handyman. He lives over in Lower Sackville."

"And what's *his* cover?" Janet wanted to know.

"Sounds reasonable enough," was the answer. "He comes once a week unless there's something special to do. Tomorrow's his day, and he missed last week. Says his wife and two neighbors can back it up."

"I see." Janet nodded at the body and then at the two ambulance attendants who still held the body bag stretched out. "I guess you can move him out of here now." To the police officers she said, "You two tell Andrew to advise that butler or valet or whatever he calls himself of his rights and then bring him downtown. I'll meet him there. Shouldn't be too hard to break up his story. You were right about 'suspect.' Just don't say it. Leave that kind of talk for the lawyers."

What is Janet Dexel's reason for suspecting the butler rather than the daughter or handyman?

8

Head-on in the Middle
of the Road

JUDGE ELMER GRIEB OF THE Superior Court sat on the edge of an old wooden chair in his private office, elbows on his knees, chin in his hands, staring at the brown medicine bottle on his desk. *Karlsrhue Pharmacy,* the label said. *Take two tablespoons as required. DO NOT EXCEED RECOMMENDED DOSAGE.*

Elmer had already exceeded the recommended dosage. Three times. He was deep in thought, and whenever His Honor pondered over a case, he invariably reached into the bottom right-hand drawer for the helpful brown bottle from Karlsrhue Pharmacy.

The stress of making decisions in civil law suits had taken its toll on Elmer over the years. By his own admission, his nerves just weren't what they used to be. But he had a very low opinion of tranquilizers, indeed anything that came in the form of a pill. And years of listening to the so-called expert testimony of psychiatrists had entirely wiped away any faith he might have had in their powers. So, every morning of a day when he was about to endure the stress of handing down a decision, Judge Elmer Grieb turned to his own, oft-proven therapy. He filled a brown medicine bottle with homemade wine. Dandelion wine. His mother had taught him how to make it. According to Elmer's theory, the powerful amber liquid not only calmed his nerves and cleared his head, it was even a cure for his troublesome arthritis. And if the truth were known, it probably explained why he suffered far fewer colds than the rest of the population! Still another plus was that the stuff actually looked like medicine and tasted even worse, useful qualities in case any of the court staff got curious.

Earlier this afternoon, for two long and uncomfortable hours, Elmer had been formally and officially perched on the Superior Court bench feeling very much in need of his medicine. Over this time he had listened to the testimony of four witnesses: the two plaintiffs, the defendant appearing on behalf of Carrick Township, and the driver of the Carrick Township road grader. The case was one of those percentage-of-blame lawsuits that always made His Honor uncomfortable because he did not like to play Solomon.

It was a car accident case. Both plaintiff and defendant admitted to some blame. At issue was what percentage for each. Cases like these sometimes took Elmer a whole bottle of medicine to think through.

Several months ago, the two plaintiffs, traveling in separate cars at midday with no other traffic nearby, had run head-on into each other at the crest of a hill out on the tenth side road of Carrick Township. At the scene of the accident the police had decided that since both drivers were smack in the middle of the road when they hit, they were mutually at fault. Hence no traffic charges were laid, and neither driver had been able to attack the other's insurance company. However, the two had now joined forces and, together, were suing Carrick Township and the township road foreman, Peter Hesch, on the grounds that it was road repairs to the hill in the week before their crash that had made it necessary for both of them to drive in the center. The two wore neck braces, and both produced medical certificates attesting to whiplash and other possible, as yet unknown, damage. They had managed to look seriously injured in the witness box.

When it was his turn to testify, Peter Hesch, the road foreman, acknowledged that yes, there had been road repairs on both sides of the hill the week before. It was a steep hill, he explained, and usually after a wet spring the hill was pretty rutted and full of pot-holes. It was a repair that the township carried out just about every year during a spell of nice dry weather, he said. But then Peter Hesch managed to get the plaintiff's lawyer all stirred up when he added, somewhat gratuitously, at the end of his testi-mony, that the two drivers had to be pretty stupid because "any damn fool should know you slow down and pull over when you get to the top of a blind hill."

At the reference to "blind hill" the plaintiff's lawyer had prac-tically danced with glee and took almost an hour of court time establishing that on this particular hill on the tenth side road, it was impossible for a driver on either side to see a car on the other, until he reached the very top.

The fourth witness was Harvey Speelmacher, driver of the township road grader. To Elmer's considerable relief, Harvey's time in the witness box was brief and uneventful. Testifying in a case three years ago, Harvey had got very excited, and Elmer had to adjourn for twenty minutes while the cleaning staff scrubbed wads of tobacco juice off the sides of the witness box.

This time it took Harvey barely a few minutes, a calm few min-utes, to say that three days before the accident in question he had spent the morning with the township grader smoothing out the surface on both sides of the hill, the last step in the road repair. Then for no apparent reason at all, he added that he knew right well what day he had done it because it was his wife's birthday, August 9. He had booked off during the afternoon so he could take her fishing over on the South Saugeen, "bein' the weather'd been so nice and all."

After Harvey's testimony, the lawyers for both sides had sum-marized with surprising quickness, the plaintiff's counsel arguing strongly that because the hill was a "blind hill," Peter Hesch and Carrick Township were at least eighty percent responsible if not one hundred percent.

The gist of the argument from the defendant's counsel was that it was the two plaintiffs who were eighty percent responsible for what they had done to themselves, since common sense and safe driving obliged them to slow down and keep to the right in a situation where it might be a bit difficult to know what was coming from the opposite direction.

Elmer had recessed after that and directed everyone to return in one hour, at which time he would hand down his decision. That was eight tablespoons ago, and although he wasn't bothered by his arthritis anymore, he still had to go back into court and give his decision.

He reached for the bottle and the spoon one more time. This was definitely a ten-tablespoon case. What bothered Judge Elmer Grieb so much was the failure of the township side, the defendant, to bring up the most obvious counterpoint to the "blind hill" argument. And quite frankly, he didn't know what to do about it.

What is the important point that the township side has failed to bring up?

9

A 911 Call from
Whitby Towers

BEV ASHBY WAS SO DISTRACTED by the size of the crowd gathered
on the sidewalk that at first she didn't hear the concierge shouting
at her.

"They're up there!" He was bent over the driver's door, yelling
red-faced at the closed window and gesticulating wildly at the
building across the sidewalk. "Fourth floor! But you have to walk
'cause the elevator's been down since yesterday!"

It wasn't until several hours later that Bev ruefully acknowledged, yet again, that maybe it's true what they say about cops:
they just stick out. For the life of her she had no idea how the
concierge had identified her, first as a police officer, and second,
as the detective sent to investigate the incident. She was dressed
in civvies, the car was unmarked, and she had used neither siren
nor light. And there were several other cars at the curb that were
clearly sent there by a police dispatcher. Yet the concierge had run
out the revolving doors of Whitby Towers directly to her.

"Your uniformed people are up there! Two of them!" Bev had
her window rolled down, but now he was yelling even louder.
"And the chauffeur saw him do it!"

His shouting increased the size of the crowd and drew their

attention away from the incident that was entertaining them in the middle of the busy downtown street. A noontime fender bender had developed into a slugfest between the two drivers involved. Both were now draped over the hoods of their respective cars in handcuffs.

Bev had to push the concierge back to get out of the car. He was still waving his arms and sputtering.

"I'm the one that called 911," he said into her face. "The chauffeur saw him doing it from down here on the street! Hanging himself! Yelled at me to call and then ran for the stairs!" The young man wasn't shouting anymore, but he was still wound up enough to draw even more of the crowd toward them. Bev took him by the arm and forced her way through the gawkers toward the doors of Whitby Towers.

"Shouldn't this be *your* job?" she said over her shoulder. "I mean, you're the one supposed to be breaking trail, aren't you?"

"Yes, Omigod! Look, I'm sorry! This is only my second day. And I . . . like . . . I've never called 911 before! And I . . ."

Bev pushed through to the revolving doors with the concierge in tow. Once inside, the plush quietness of the lobby calmed him with dramatic suddenness.

"Fourth floor," the concierge said with professional detachment. "Number 411. The stairs are over there behind that pillar. We're very sorry about the elevator problem."

Bev nodded. "I'll be back down in a while to talk to you. Just don't leave, please."

By the time she reached the fourth floor she was puffing a bit. She wondered how the occupants of Whitby Towers were tolerating a two-day elevator failure. It was an expensive building and even though "Towers" was an enormously pretentious title—the place had only six floors—a lot of money was needed for the rent here.

Suite 411 was easy enough to find, for a uniformed officer was standing in the hallway outside the door. He tipped his cap with his index finger as Bev approached. "Body's inside, Lieutenant. We have not cut him down; we've only been here," he looked at his watch, "seventeen minutes now. Chauffeur's in there with my partner."

He held the door open for Bev so she could see the entire tableau before taking a step. Suite 411 was a luxuriously appointed studio apartment. What marred the sight of the deep pile rug and highly polished reproduction furniture was the body of a silver-haired man, in excellent trim, hanging from a thin nylon rope, an overturned chair at his lifeless feet.

"His name is . . ." The patrolman started to speak, but Bev cut him off with a shake of her head. Twice she walked slowly around the body and then expanded the circle to walk around the room. Everything was in perfect order as one would expect at Whitby Towers. Well, not quite everything. The telephone wire was cut. Actually, not cut. Torn. That had taken strength. There was something else, too. Bev bent over in front of the balcony doors. What was it on the floor there, one end of a shoelace? No. Nylon rope. Looked like the same stuff that was around the dead man's neck. With a pen, she spread the drapes just enough to follow the rope to about knee level where the other end was clamped between the doors.

Nodding to herself, Bev looked up at the uniformed officer. "Now you can tell me his name," she said to him. "On second thought," she turned to the chauffeur, "you go first. Let's start with your name."

"Sandford Verity." No hesitation. He responded as though he'd anticipated her question. And he didn't talk the way Bev thought a chauffeur might, but then, she had to admit, she didn't really know any chauffeurs. Maybe they all talk this way! "What happened is very simple." He continued as though he were in charge. "My firm is Brock Livery Service. We pick up Mr. Seneca every day—that's his name: Audley Seneca—at 11:50 and take him to wherever he directs. It's a standing, daily order. Yesterday and today I came up here to his suite, because of the elevator situation, instead of meeting him in the lobby. You see, he has a prosthesis, an artificial leg actually, and the stairs are somewhat of a problem for him. This morning when I arrived I happened to look up.

Thought maybe he might be watching that altercation on the street. That's when I saw him on the chair there, the rope around his neck. Of course I ran as fast as I could. Told the concierge to call 911. But I got here too late. The door was locked. What I should have done, I realize now, was get the concierge to come with me. With a master key. But then, after a crisis is over, one always thinks of things one should have done."

"Agreed, Mr. Verity," Bev said and turned to the uniformed officer. "Would you go down to the lobby," she said, "and bring the concierge up here? There's quite a big hole here in the story of Mr. Seneca's alleged suicide."

What is the "big hole" to which Bev Ashby refers?

10

The Case of the
Kramer Collection

GEORGE FEWSTER WOULD NEVER HAVE admitted it to anyone, but had he learned how to use a modem and a fax machine when they first came on the market, he'd have taken early retirement even earlier.

It wasn't really early retirement in his case, as he was quick to explain to anyone who raised an eyebrow. It was more a second career. Instead of Professor of Archaeology at Simon Fraser University, he was now George Fewster, Consultant in Archaeology. The change in job description may have introduced a tad of uncertainty into his cash flow, but that was more than compensated for by what he had done this morning, as he did each morning. That was to walk past his car, where it sat silently in the garage, pause to marvel at the birds squabbling busily around the feeder, and then go into the little office he'd built for himself some distance from the house. There, perched on the lip of a small mountain meadow with the town of Banff to his left, Mount Rundle to his right, and the Bow River down below, he could be warmed by some of the most beautiful scenery in the world. Or, especially in autumn after the leaves had fallen, he could peer around a corner of his house and feel sorry for the commuters heading out to the city. He could even work, if he was disposed to—and he was, most of the time.

This morning for example. During the night, his modem had brought in a report from the Museum of Civilization in Ottawa that he'd been awaiting for over a month. When he got his computer going and brought up the *KRAMER* file, he was rewarded with a screenful of information.

The top of the screen read: *Contents of Kramer Estate Collection.* A short personal note followed:

Dear George,

You're going to have fun with this one. It's a weird conglomeration all right. Some of it is just collectibles, hardly even rummage-sale quality. But every once in a while, as you'll see, there's a real gem. There's also some very interesting Arctic exploration stuff, if it's genuine. And quite a few coins. I think these might be very valuable. Anyway, have fun.

Sincerely,
Myrna.

The *Kramer Estate Collection* had been offered to the museum—for a price—some six months ago by a couple from a small town in the Eastern Townships of Quebec. George had the name written down somewhere. So far, the museum had been able to establish that the collection was put together quite a few years before by one Francis Kramer, a successful but extremely eccentric prospector whose final years had been spent in the Thirty Thousand Islands area of Georgian Bay, where he'd held a running battle with the local bylaw and health authorities because he insisted on living in a dry cistern.

But the Museum of Civilization didn't really care about Kramer's lifestyle; it wanted an evaluation of his collection, and that is what George now turned to on his monitor.

Under the personal note from Myrna, the screen said *Group One*, then it gave more information that went like this:

These items in Group One, George, will not appear to need your attention at first glance. They are mostly old magazines, some of them are nicely dated though. There's a Reader's Digest *from 1922 and an 1890 edition of the* London Times. *A really exciting piece is a 1728 issue of the* Saturday Evening Post. *A genuine fraud, so to speak!*

George pressed PAGE DOWN on his keyboard. He wanted to get to the coins, but something in Group Two caught his attention. Group Two was a list of material that Myrna had called "Arctic exploration stuff." Most of it described artifacts from expeditions to the Arctic: items like the compass used by Robert Peary in 1906, Otto Sverdrup's toiletry kit, and a tin of brown beans retrieved from a cache set up by the Rae expedition in 1854. What twigged George, however, was the description of a tract. *On the Origins of the Blond Eskimo,* the title read. *By Vilhjalmur Stefansson.* George made a note to have that one couriered to him right away and then kept pressing PAGE DOWN until the screen finally showed *Group Three: Coins.* This is what he wanted to see above all. There was another note from Myrna:

Can't wait till you come to Ottawa to see these face-to-face. This is where the real value is, I think.

There are two Washington half-dollars, 1792, in mint condition. Wait till you see them! And an Upper Canada halfpenny from 1883 that looks so good you'd swear it was never in circulation. There are several of this type. But probably the most valuable are the three really old coins in the collection. From some time B.C.

There's a silver stater from Syria. It's fifth century B.C. The British Museum paid $4,000 for one of these last year and this one's in better condition, I'm told. The other two are Roman coins. They're both silver, too. One's from early in the reign of

Caesar Augustus. Stamped 22 B.C., but unfortunately the pro-
file of Augustus is not very good. The other one is about two
hundred years later; you can't see the date, but the profile of
Emperor Hadrian is as good as a contemporary issue!

There's more in the collection. A whole bunch of beaver nick-
els from the thirties with George VI on them, and some of those
funny blackout nickels from World War II, but they're probably
not of much interest to the museum.

George leaned back in his chair and stared at the screen for a
few seconds. Then, impulsively, he turned the computer off without even getting out of the file. He was disappointed.

Before this report had come in, he had looked forward to a
trip to Ottawa, even if it meant he would have to join the commuters on a drive to the city. Now he knew the trip would likely
be unnecessary.

What is wrong in the Kramer Collection that has left George Fewster
so disappointed?

11

Waiting Out the Rain

MICHELLE LINK SAT IN ONE of the two window booths at Kline's Soda Shoppe with Julie Varughese and two of their classmates from Memorial Junior School. All four stared gloomily at the rain pelting down on the street outside. They had headed straight for Kline's right after school, beating the crowd so they could get their favorite booth. It was a perfect location. In the corner at the window, the booth gave them a sweeping view of everybody in the little restaurant—more important, they could see who came in *with* whom and not be too obvious about it. As well, if the patrons failed to stir up any interest, they could usually find something diverting out on the street.

Not today, though. Except for two older ladies who had come in for tea, Kline's was unusually empty. So was the street. The rain had begun to fall the instant they arrived, hard enough to discourage any of the regulars from Memorial Junior and, except for two pedestrians who had taken shelter in the doorway of Vex's Pharmacy across the way, hard enough to pretty much empty the street, too. Now, two Cherry Cokes apiece later, and having exhausted the day's school stories, the four friends were bored and quite ready to leave, but the rain was not yet prepared to let them.

The only distraction, and the only person who seemed to be enjoying the weather, was a little boy standing in the gutter just off the sidewalk a few feet away from Michelle. He couldn't be more than three, Michelle calculated, watching him stand there in the water that sluiced down the gutter around his bright blue rubber boots, splashing up against and almost over the toes where someone—an older sister, Michelle speculated—had painted a large "L" on top of one and an "R" on the other with pink fingernail polish.

Through Kline's screened door, Michelle could hear the boy's squeal of delight as a candy-bar wrapper floated up to the toes, then made a complete circle and carried on between the boots. She followed the progress of the wrapper for a few feet and for the first time noticed the woman on the edge of the sidewalk. Must be the kid's mother, her speculation continued.

The woman was not watching her son—if it really was her son. She was standing under the awning at Whippany Appliances next door, listening transfixed to the radio bulletin booming from the store. Whippany Appliances was advertising Motorola, their new franchise brand, and a big cabinet model standing just inside the door put the news out onto the street.

Michelle could hear it from the restaurant:

" . . . from General Eisenhower's headquarters in England a confirmation that five divisions are involved: two American, two British, one Canadian. Early reports indicate that German troops have fallen back from the beaches at all five landing areas. Pockets of resistance are still strong, however, at Omaha Beach.

"The Columbia Broadcasting System's news service has also learned that . . ."

For the past two days the radio news had talked of nothing but the landings at Normandy, the biggest invasion, it was being described, in the history of warfare. Michelle watched the woman stare vaguely into the appliance store. She had not once turned around to look at her little boy. He had his rain hat off now and was filling it with water.

"Michelle! Earth to Michelle! Hey, get with it! The rain has stopped! Remember? The wet stuff? Let's go while we can!" Julie finally reached across the table and shook her friend's arm.

"I wonder if her husband's a soldier?" Michelle said, without looking at Julie. "The little boy's father. I'll bet he is."

"What *are* you talking about?" Julie shook Michelle's arm one more time. "C'mon! The rain's let up. We've got to leave now or we'll have to order another Cherry Coke. Either that or rent the booth."

Michelle and Julie said goodbye to their friends at the doorway to Kline's and headed up the street. For a few seconds, they, too, paused at Whippany Appliances and listened to the radio talk about Normandy. The woman and the little boy were gone. Somehow they had disappeared as the girls were getting out of the booth. The street began to fill with activity again, almost as if it had been waiting, pent up and hidden under shelter until the weather improved.

The two pedestrians from Vex's Pharmacy had crossed the street and were moving on ahead of the girls. Farther up they could see Mister Lum at Lum's Groceteria pushing carts of fruit and vegetables back into the sidewalk. Next to the appliance store two men got out of a truck belonging to Bitnik's Delivery Service and began to wrestle a soaking wet tarpaulin off a stack of cardboard boxes. Cars began to move up the street more quickly now, as though relieved by the prospect of drier progress.

Two minutes later, at the corner of Vine Street, Julie said goodbye, peeling off down Vine, leaving Michelle to continue on two more blocks to her home on Sanders Avenue. Michelle didn't expect to speak to Julie again until school the next day. For one thing, there was too much homework. More important, her parents had made one of those suggestions that parents tend to make about too much use of the phone on school nights.

The telephone rang anyway, about an hour after dinner, and it was Julie.

"Did you *hear* what happened? At Kline's?"

Michelle wanted to point out that obviously she had not, or why would Julie be calling, but she didn't get a chance.

"There was an accident! You know that truck? Bitnik's truck?" Julie was very wound up.

"It was right there when we passed. Remember? Those two guys unloading . . . uh . . . whatever it was? Anyway, *it rolled right into Kline's!* Right through the *window!* My dad says the brakes, no, no, the *emergency* brake probably failed."

"Julie . . ."

"I mean, right where we were sitting!"

"Julie . . ."

"Can you imagine? Like . . . if it hadn't stopped raining? We'd have been sitting right there! We could have been killed! Or really injured or something!"

"Not just us, Julie. But listen . . ."

"Don't tell your parents we were sitting right there in the window booth. I mean, I didn't tell *my* parents. You know what it's like. They'll get all worried and then they'll start thinking Kline's is dangerous and then . . . well . . . anyway. You know what parents are like. But isn't it *exciting?*"

"Julie!"

There was a pause followed by a soft and very tentative "What?"

"Julie, that was no accident."

Why is Michelle Link sure that what Julie Varughese has described was not an accident?

12

A Routine Check
in the Parking Lot

LOCAL LEGEND HAD IT THAT DINKS got its name in the 1920s when it sported one of the first neon signs in the county and the "R" in "DRINKS" refused to work. It didn't take a great deal of entrepreneurial flash for the then owner to realize that this fortuitous ellipsis had far more appeal to the passing public than his own four-syllable name, so DINKS the bar became, and DINKS it remained.

The name held up through a number of metamorphoses as the bar changed from a jazz cocktail lounge with upscale pretensions in its early days, to a dance hall catering to the army base nearby, to a juke box *cum* hamburger joint, to its present phase: a cocktail bar again. It had a live trio on weekends, deep, ruby-red decor, cheap drinks, and a reputation that struggled hard to stay just this side of sleaze.

The other constant in the history of the place was trouble with the police. Over the decades, the local force had learned to factor in DINKS as a normal part of their planning and projections. Situated on the edge of town, DINKS was where locals came to howl. So there were fights. Lots of fights. Most were the cracked-head, broken-tooth variety typical of a confrontation between drunks, but occasionally the brawls were serious.

DINKS was held up, too, with tedious regularity, almost always by strangers passing through who never knew where the real cash was kept. In the fifties, the huge parking lot had served for civil-rights sit-ins. Not long after the Vietnam War, it became known as a drug-exchange campus.

However, until this morning, there had never been a murder at DINKS. But now, even that marker had finally been achieved. In typical DINKS style as well. There was not just one body, but two. As it was, had Ron Forrester not been a veteran of some considerable experience on the police force, he might easily have bought into the murderer's ploy, for the bodies had been set up to look like the victims of accidental death.

It had been cleverly done. DINKS, quite naturally, was a choice rendezvous for illicit affairs. The bar was big, it was dark, it was on the highway, nobody asked questions, and no one would ever, ever, dare to bring a camera into the place. Therefore, when Ron cruised into the parking lot at 4:55 A.M., he was not particularly surprised to note that the large sedan, backed into the far corner of the parking lot, under the protective branches of an old elm tree, was occupied. There were two people in the front seat. For all he knew, there could have been two in the back as well. Not likely though.

Out of habit and not a little curiosity, Ron drove slowly toward the car for a look, leaving his high beams on to warn the two he was coming. After all, it was really no concern of his what two consenting adults were doing in a car at 4:55 A.M., even in the parking lot at DINKS. He just wanted to make sure they were consenting and that the consent was mutual.

The veteran policeman's first suspicion that something was wrong came when he saw no reaction to his high beams. Usually in situations like this, the guilty parties tried to hide, or at the very least, turned around out of curiosity or annoyance. Then as he got closer and saw both heads lolling on the back of the front seat, he knew immediately that something was seriously amiss.

Ron accelerated the last hundred feet, then stopped. In a hurry now, he got out, ran to the car and pulled open the driver's door.

It was too late. Without even taking a pulse, Ron Forrester knew from experience that both bodies had been dead for some time. He left the door open and went back to the patrol car, moving it perpendicular to the sedan so that the headlights would shine directly into the front seat.

On the other side of the man behind the steering wheel, a woman lay against the back of the seat, turned to one side, with her knees drawn up. Her shoes were off and her blouse unbuttoned. Her right hand dangled into the garbage carrier that straddled the center hump, and two fingers of her left were hooked into the man's belt. Ron couldn't see her face; it was tilted downward.

He could see the man's face, however. He'd been trying to ignore it all along, for the man sat leaning against the seat, his head turned to the left, eyes wide and lifeless, staring right at Ron, the whites gleaming in the lights of the patrol car. The pupils were tiny dots and the irises a washed out blue. The man's mouth was open, his tongue sticking out through lips that formed a perfect "O" as though he'd died in mild surprise. Like his companion in death, his shoes were off and his shirt unbuttoned. One hand lay on the seat beside him, the other, for what reason Ron could not figure, was stuck through the steering wheel, dangling at the wrist.

Ron turned on his flashlight and shone it around the interior of the car, even though the act seemed redundant in view of the powerful headlights behind him. The motor was still running, and there was about a quarter tank of gas left. The heater was on, too, set to "medium" with the fan set to "low." The radio played softly, an all-night station that Ron didn't recognize. In the back seat lay both headrests, a box of tissues, and a blue purse. Probably the woman's for it matched the blue shoes on the floor beside her lifeless feet.

The veteran policeman reached across the dead man's body with great care to turn off the motor, then stopped, hardly believing what he'd almost done. Fingerprints! On the keys! This wasn't a case of two lovers forgetting about the potential danger of carbon monoxide. This was murder!

Slowly, and with even more care than he had used when reaching in, Ron withdrew his arm. The action brought his arm against the dead man's cheek, and in the morning silence he could hear the stubble rasp against his uniform. It made him shiver.

He shivered again just outside the patrol car and blew in his hands to warm them, as much because of the shock of what he had just seen as from the December cold. He looked up at the sky. No sunrise for an hour or more yet, he calculated, but then for the two in the car, no sunrise ever again.

How does Ron Forrester know that at least one and probably both of the victims have been murdered?

13

An Answer for Kirby's Important New Client

"HERE'S THAT GUY AGAIN! THAT Smythe-Boliver!" Mara Silverberg was excited enough by her discovery to be shouting. "Listen!" She held up one of the faxed pages and read:

"'Major-General G. Smythe-Boliver, Royal Fusilliers: born 1708, at Ross-on-Wye; died 1779, at Chipping Sodbury; battles of Fort William Henry, 1757; Fort Carillon, 1758; Plains of Abraham, 1759. Fluent French and Spanish; signing delegate, Treaty of Paris, 1763.'"

"Yes, but," the voice belonged to her sister Krista, "the diary here is written by a *Major* Gerard Smythe-Boliver."

"So?" Mara was sure of her ground. "That doesn't have to mean he was a major forever, does it? Besides, how many officers in one war could possibly be named *Smythe-Boliver?*"

"You're probably right," Krista acknowledged. "In a war he'd get promoted faster. And he's upper class, so that means he gets to be a general, too, I guess."

Kirby Silverberg had been waiting patiently and finally broke in. This was, after all, her show. "Read that diary passage one more time, Krista," she said. "Remember it's *Fitzwall* we're interested in. More so than this Smythe-Boliver character."

Krista responded by lifting a page slightly and pushing her glasses to the bridge of her nose. "'Tuesday, 21 October,'" she read aloud, then put the paper down. "See?" she said. "Just like all the others. No year given." She shrugged and picked up the paper again. "Anyway." She cleared her throat. "'Only two months since the beginning of hostilities and I have just lost my batman, Fitzwall.'"

"What's a batman again?" Mara wanted to know.

"Personal servant. Sort of a valet," Kirby said. "Officers all had one then."

Krista started again "'. . . just lost my batman Fitzwall. Poor chap; exactly half my age. Cannonball took his leg just below the knee, and three fingers. Not likely he'll survive. His wife died last year. One child. A girl born when the wife was but fourteen and he only four years her senior! One finds it difficult to understand the lower classes.'"

Krista looked up at her sisters. "There's a bunch of blather next about the need for more trained troops, and a piece about the amount of drinking going on. Stuff like that. Most of the rest is about the problem of having to train another batman. Nice guy this Smythe-Boliver! No more about Fitzwall."

She turned to Kirby. "I've gone back twenty entries and ahead twenty. There's not one other mention of Fitzwall. You want me to keep going?"

Kirby put her elbow on the huge volume of case-law summaries she had been wading through to keep the pages from fanning out.

"Please?" she said, pointing to the stack of photocopies in front of Krista and then to the pile in front of Mara. "There's so little time. You have everything there that the Imperial War Museum was willing to send from their Seven Years War collection. Mom's got the stuff from Halifax and Dad's got the memoirs. The answer's got to be somewhere here in all this stuff, and I need it by eight o'clock tomorrow morning or I lose the commission. Worse, I could lose the first big client I've ever had."

Kirby was referring to the Boston law firm of Tory, Wigan, and

Best. She had been hired by the firm to uncover the year of birth of one Simon Fitzwall, first born of Ethan Fitzwall who had come to Boston with his father from England via Halifax, some time before the American Revolution. What was crucial was whether Simon had been born before or after 1788, the year the state of Massachusetts signed the U.S. Constitution. The date was important in a dispute over public versus private ownership of some land in the Boston area.

In their own search, the lawyers had been able to follow a straight track backward in time for almost two hundred years. Then the string broke. They had all kinds of data: personal histories, memoirs, diaries, photocopies of eighteenth-century newspapers, but the writers of the material, as was fairly customary for the time, seemed to have either a cavalier disregard for dates or simply felt they were unnecessary. Kirby Silverberg, P.I., had been hired to complete the paper chase. She had been given less than twenty-four hours to do it and had turned to her family for help.

As her sisters dug back into the material from the Imperial War Museum, Kirby turned to her mother. "Anything from Halifax yet, Mom?"

"I've been waiting for my chance!" the girls' mother replied. She had been poring over documents from the provincial archives of Nova Scotia.

"Listen to this." She took up the huge magnifying glass she had been using to decipher the barely legible print and held it with both hands. "It's from the harbormaster's report. 'Ship arrivals for the week.'" She looked up. "I guess I don't need to say it doesn't tell us what week. Or month or year either. In any case. 'Ship arrivals for the week: the *Endurance* and the *Titan* out of Portsmouth.' There's a long list like that. Must have been a real busy place! But get this." She shifted her chair and rotated the magnifying glass. "The *Earl of Shannon* out of Southhampton. Now . . ."

She flipped over several pages to one with the corner pulled down. "Here. 'Harbormaster's report to the Governor General.' It says:

'To Your Excellency's attention: with regard to the loss of the *Earl of Shannon* in Halifax Harbor on Sunday last, this ship until five years ago was the *Arquemada* out of Madrid. She was ceded to His Majesty's Navy under terms of the Treaty of Paris, along with . . .' Then there's a list of other ships and stuff like that."

"But Mom," Kirby tried to keep the exasperation out of her voice. "That doesn't . . ."

"I'm not finished. Listen. The report goes on to list the passengers from the *Earl of Shannon* who require passage on to Boston and who now await His Excellency's pleasure—he must have had to give them clearance or something, or maybe it was his responsibility after the ship sank. Anyway. Guess who's on the list? Fitzwall, Ambrose Esq., and three children, Abigail, Rachel, and Ethan!" She looked up triumphantly, blinking to clear the fuzz left by the magnifying glass.

"*All right Mom!*" This time it was Kirby doing the shouting. "Now all we need is . . . Dad's got Ambrose's personal history thing. That's got to have the rest of what we need. Where is he? Where's Dad?"

"He's asleep," Krista said. "You know what happens. Soon as you mention lawyers he either goes to the bathroom or falls asleep."

"Take it easy. I'm here!" A male voice came from the corner of the room. "What do you need to know about Ambrose Fitzwall? I've become an expert interpreter of his memoirs."

"Memoirs, Dad?" It was Mara. "There's only three pages."

"Not quite that simple," Laurie Silverberg replied. He got out of the big easy chair and joined his family at the table. "The man was self-taught. Had to be. It takes some figuring to get past his spelling. And the sentence structure!" Laurie shook his head. "Listen to this. 'This here is the story of my family after my first wife Etta died and I lost the leg and my fingers with the major and I married Solomon Lesham's second daughter Nattie what was already a widow with one child Rachel we had Ethan right away and come to America with my Abigail.' Now that's all one sentence. You should try . . ."

"Keep going!"

"Yeah, don't stop now!"

Laurie peered over his glasses and smoothed the curling edges of the photocopies with deliberate care before beginning again.

"'Nattie she died of the flux I never married again. We come to America on the *Earl of Shannon* a wormy tub she sank off Halifax good riddance.'"

"You should see—he spells that R-I-D-N-E-S."

"Dad, c'mon!"

"Yeah, don't tell us the spelling. What happened!"

"All right, all right, all right. Let's see. Okay, yeah, '. . . good riddance. Abigail she had a hard crossing young Ethan being only half the age of her when I lost the leg and Rachel only twice that but it don't rain forever four years later Abigail married and two years after comes a baby girl then three more all girls. Then Rachel she got married and Ethan too at the same age Abigail was and all had the first babies two years after. Simon the only boy though . . .'"

"Chauvinist!" Mara was indignant.

"Why doesn't he tell the girls' names?" Krista asked her mother who, in turn, raised her eyebrows at her husband.

"He doesn't," Laurie acknowledged almost sheepishly.

At first, none of them noticed Kirby waving her arms.

"It doesn't matter! It doesn't matter! I don't care if he's a chauvinist pig, we've got the answer! We know when Simon was born!"

How has the Silverberg family found the answer for Kirby's client? In what year was Simon Fitzwall born?

14

Two Shots Were Fired

THE YOUNG POLICEMAN AT THE gate stiffened when he recognized the senior officer getting out of the car that had just pulled up. Instinctively, a hand went to his throat where his tie hung loosely around an open top button. Inspector Vince Pogor was a stickler for proper dress no matter what the weather, and the young constable knew it was too late now to rebutton his collar.

"You look like that when the media was here?" Vince was also known for getting right to the point.

"No. No, sir!" The young man's face, already soaking from the heat of the sun, began sweating even harder.

Vince lifted his hands to his hips. The gesture reminded him that he himself wasn't in uniform at all, that in fact he was in a T-shirt and shorts—kind of ratty ones to boot.

"Okay. Okay." he said. "Just . . . Look, you know the regulation. Tie on or tie off. Not that half-way stuff. Now. Where's the shooting site? That it up there?"

"Yes sir!" The officer was so relieved he absently brought out a none-too-clean handkerchief to wipe his face. "Just around the corner of the building there. You'll see the yellow tape."

For a second or two, Vince toyed with the idea of going back to division headquarters to change clothes. The incident with the constable's tie had made him self-conscious about his own dress.

In the end he decided not to. The media had been and gone, especially the TV cameras. Besides—he looked at his watch—the incident was already six hours old.

Vince was calling it an incident, not a *crime,* for the time being anyway. The evidence so far pointed in that direction. It was an accidental shooting, but a dicey one because of the victim. The dead man, Big Dino, was well-known to Vince, in fact to just about everyone on the police force, especially the anti-racket squad which Vince headed up. Big Dino had roots deep in organized crime. Until this morning. This morning Big Dino had gone down with two bullets in the middle of his chest just outside the rear entrance to Galahad Storage. He'd been shot from inside the building by a security guard.

"Ah . . . sir?" It was the constable. He'd taken his tie off. "Up there? Around the corner? Sergeant King . . . ah . . . he's waiting for you."

Vince grunted, just a wee bit embarrassed, then began to walk toward the rear of the building. He was glad to stretch his legs for he'd had a long drive. Officially, Vince was on vacation. The first two weeks of August were always his. That morning before anyone else in the family was awake, he'd taken a giant plate of bacon and perogies out to the deck of his cottage, despite the threat of rain, and had just snapped on the portable to listen to *The World at Eight* when the telephone rang, summoning him away from his beloved Lake Muskoka.

He'd headed down to the city right away, but changing out of the shorts and T-shirt did not even cross his mind. The heat wave that stretched from the American Midwest right up to the Arctic was so fierce that even the thought of full-length trousers made him sweat. And the heat was getting worse, too. On his way south, the dull sky that had covered most of Eastern North America that morning reneged on its promise of rain and cooler weather, completely contradicting the weather forecasters. By the time Vince could see Toronto in the distance, the sky had turned blue and cloudless and the day was flatiron hot.

Not a day to spend walking on confounded asphalt, he

thought, turning the corner where the yellow boundary tape squared off a section of empty lot. He hardly noticed the tape at first, or even how much hotter it was on this side of the building. What caught his attention instead was the overwhelming, relentless noise from the traffic on the Queen Elizabeth Way. Ten lanes of speeding, bumper-to-bumper racket so loud he didn't hear Jack King until the third yell.

"Vinny! Vince! In here! Outa the sun!"

Vince ducked under the tape, stepped carefully over the chalk outline of a body, and walked through the only open door. It had a small sign that said "EMPLOYEES ONLY." Jack King was standing inside. His tie was pulled down and he had two buttons undone. Jack began to speak immediately.

"It was like this," he said. Vince realized that Jack had been waiting in the heat for some time and had no intention of dawdling through his report. He wanted to get back to headquarters and air conditioning.

"The guard sat here, his back to the door you just came through." He pointed to a battered metal chair and an old wooden table with a deck of greasy playing cards on top. "Says he was watching the front. That makes sense 'cause that's where all the break-ins have been coming through. Especially the one two days ago where one a' the other guards got beat up so bad."

Vince raised his eyebrows but said nothing. Jack went on. "Then all of a sudden, he says there's this dark shadow over him. From behind. From the doorway. He whips around. The sun's in his face. There's an awful big guy there so . . . *Boom! Boom!* Two in the chest."

"Sounds a bit trigger happy, don't you think?" Vince spoke for the first time.

"Yeah. But don't forget the guy was scared," Jack answered. "I mean, there's been so much trouble here. All the break-ins. They had that fire where the guy was trapped in a room. Then there's that guard who was beat up. Word is he'll never walk again. Can't say I really blame the guard for shooting. And Dino. He's a big guy. 'Sides, he had no business back here. We think he's a renter here. Least he had a key in his pocket. We're checkin' that right now. Anyway, how's the guard supposed to know? As it is, the place doesn't open to customers till nine o'clock. And not through this door." Jack was pointing out the door to the east. Through the opening Vince could see the skyline of the city in the distance and the surface of Lake Ontario shimmering in the brightness of midday.

"I don't know, Jack," he said. "It's still too neat. This door was open then?"

"Propped open," Jack answered. "Just like it is now. Haven't you noticed how hot it is in here? I can believe the guard when he says the door had to be open. And that means he couldn't hear anything either. With the highway traffic at that time of the morning."

Vince nodded. "Yeah, I guess so. Sounds like accidental shooting all right. There's only one thing that's not right."

"Yeah? What's that?" Jack King wanted to know.

What is the flaw in the security guard's story that Vince Pogor is referring to?

15

Northern Farms Ltd. Versus Dominion Spraying Company

TRANSCRIPT: Docket #432

COURT IS NOW IN SESSION, the Honorable Mary-Joan Westlake presiding. First case is Docket Number 432: Northern Farms Limited, plaintiff, versus Dominion Spraying Company, respondent.

WESTLAKE: Thank you bailiff. Who is acting for the plaintiff?

DOYLE: I am, Your Honor. Douglas Doyle.

WESTLAKE: Ah yes, Mr. Doyle. We've met before. The Palgrave Poker case wasn't it? Well, never mind that. Would you summarize your claim, please?

DOYLE: Thank you, Your Honor. My client owns a farm bordering on the Bolton Canal and Regional Road 7. On the morning of 27 June last year, Dominion Spraying Company conducted an aerial spraying, in error, of a field in that farm. There were fifteen registered Holstein dairy cows in the field, nine of which subsequently died of the effects of the spray. My client is claiming damages of $147,000, plus costs.

WESTLAKE: I have your statement of claim here, Counselor. You have one of the dead animals valued at $122,000?

DOYLE: Yes, Your Honor; that's Molly's Arch Dream III. I will be introducing evidence showing that figure as representative of an offer made for her on 16 May last year.

WESTLAKE: All right, Mr. Doyle. Mr. T.A. Jones, you're appearing for the respondent?

JONES: Indeed, Your Honor. In the interest of saving time, may I state that Dominion Spraying Company acknowledges that spraying took place over the field in question instead of over Bolton Canal on June 27, and that some cattle in the field died subsequent to that event. My client does not acknowledge that the deaths of the animals are connected in a direct way to the effects of the spraying. For the record, my client has offered Northern Farms damages of $25,000 for inconvenience. The offer has been declined.

WESTLAKE: Unless my mathematics is suspect, $25,000 is precisely the amount of the total claim, less the value of—what's her name—Molly's Arch Dream III?

JONES: That's correct, Your Honor.

WESTLAKE: Very well. Okay, is the plaintiff ready to proceed?

DOYLE: Yes. Plaintiff calls Mr. Fenton Purge. (*Purge sworn.*) Mr. Purge, you are the manager of Northern Farms Limited?

PURGE: That's right. We have a total of seven operating farms specializing in Holstein cattle and Landrace swine.

DOYLE: The property where the spraying took place on 27 June: would you describe it for the court?

PURGE: It's . . . well, a one-hundred-acre parcel bordered by a conservation area on two sides and by Bolton Canal and Regional Road 7 on the other two. We refer to it as Farm Number 3.

DOYLE: Specifically, I meant the field that was sprayed.

PURGE: Oh. Well, that's a . . . a . . . well, a square field about twenty-five acres in the southwest corner of the farm. It's about . . .

WESTLAKE: Mr. Doyle, what's this for? The respondent isn't denying that the spraying took place. Or where.

DOYLE: Background, Your Honor; I'll be brief. Mr. Purge, tell us what happened at this field on the morning of 27 June.

JONES: Your Honor, it hasn't been established that this witness was present at the field on the morning of June 27!

WESTLAKE: Mr. Doyle?

DOYLE: Very well . . . uh . . . Mr. Purge, what happ . . . rather, were you summoned to the, to Farm 3 on 27 June?

PURGE: Yes, in the early afternoon, when it was discovered that cattle were down in the field—collapsed. I moved fast 'cause that's where we'd pastured Molly's Arch.

DOYLE: Surely you called a veterinarian?

PURGE: Indeed. Doctor Logan confirmed the cause of the collapse as reaction to a chemical used in insect control.

JONES: Objection!

WESTLAKE: Oh, really? On what grounds, Mr. Jones?

JONES: I think the court would prefer to hear expert testimony from the expert, not secondhand.

DOYLE: We'll be calling Dr. Logan, Your Honor. No more questions.

WESTLAKE: Any cross, Mr. Jones?

JONES: Yes, thank you. Mr. Purge, is it customary to let an animal that is supposedly worth $122,000 wander around a pasture field?

PURGE: Entirely. Happens all the time when the rest of its herd is pastured. Cows are very social animals. It's not unusual for them to go into decline if they're isolated. You just need good fences, and we have that. Well, not from above though!

WESTLAKE: Confine yourself to the questions, Mr. Purge.

JONES: No more for this witness.

(*No re-examination; plaintiff calls Eulalia Bean; sworn.*)

DOYLE: Ms. Bean, you are an employee of Northern Farms Limited?

BEAN: Summer help. I'm a university student, but I work summers at the Canal Farm . . . we call it Canal Farm.

DOYLE: And you were responsible for the care of the cattle in the field in question?

BEAN: I put them in there on June 21. Fifteen black and whites. Including Molly.

DOYLE: Molly's Arch Dream III?

BEAN: Yes. We call her Molly.

DOYLE: What do you normally do to care for the cattle?

BEAN: When they're pastured like that it's mostly supplement feeding and water checks. And of course you keep an eye on them.

DOYLE: Supplement feeding and water checks?

BEAN: Pasture's not good this year so I take hay out with the tractor twice a day. To a feeding trough. And there's no water in that field so we pipe it out from the barn. Water trough's right beside the feed trough at the fence. I always check that the float valve's working right.

DOYLE: And did you take out hay and do a water check on the morning of 27 June of last year?

BEAN: Yes, about 5:30. Sun was just coming up.

DOYLE: Did you check on Molly's Arch . . . uh, Molly?

BEAN: That's even more automatic than checking the water!

DOYLE: And she was well and healthy?

BEAN: Standing orders are that if she's not, we call the vet, then the manager, in that order.

DOYLE. Thank you. That's all I have. Mr. Jones?

JONES: Ms. Bean. On the morning of June 27, did you actually see the airplane spray the field and the cattle?

BEAN: Actually, no. I was just turning back into the barn when I heard a plane in the distance, but there's nothing unusual about that. Besides, I had machinery running in the barn.

JONES: Well then, just when did you become aware that there might be a problem with the cattle in your care?

BEAN: When Mrs. Organ phoned about two o'clock to tell me.

JONES: That's all I have of this witness, Your Honor.

(*No re-examination; plaintiff calls Parthenon Andreikos; sworn.*)

DOYLE: Mr. Andreikos. Where were you at approximately 5:30 A.M. on 27 June of last year?

ANDREIKOS: In my truck on Road 7. Goin' south toward the canal to . . . uh, you want me to say what I saw?

DOYLE: Go ahead.

ANDREIKOS: So. I waved at Eulie . . . uh, Eulalia. Miss Bean. She'd just come out of the barn with the tractor. Then I drove past the herd. So. You want to know where I was going?

DOYLE: It won't be necessary. Are you familiar with a Holstein dairy cow called Molly's Arch Dream III?

ANDREIKOS: Oh sure.

DOYLE: And you saw her in the herd there?

ANDREIKOS: She's awfully hard to miss. Really big. And she has—well, *had* anyway—this most unusual mark on her right side. A perfect triangle. Takes up her whole side. Never saw anything like that, ever. Mostly on Holsteins, it's blotches.

DOYLE: for you to see that, the animal had to be broadside to you.

ANDREIKOS: So. They were lined up at the feed trough. You see, soon as they hear the tractor they know Eulie's coming and they get ready. Cows aren't as stupid as people think.

DOYLE: Molly's Arch Dream was at the end of the line then?

ANDREIKOS: Cattle always feed at the same spot. Same way they always go to the same stall in the barn. Every time. So. The end of the trough pointing to the road must have been her spot.

DOYLE: Mr. Jones?

JONES: Mr. Andreikos, are you usually driving around in your truck at 5:30 in the morning?

ANDREIKOS: In the summer. I'm in the feed business. My customers are up even before then. So.

JONES: I gather Northern Farms is a customer of yours.

ANDREIKOS: Oh, yes.

JONES: Seven farms. They must be quite a customer!

DOYLE: Objection! Your Honor, my friend here is very close to making allegations!

WESTLAKE: You know better, Mr. Jones!

JONES: No more questions.

(*Plaintiff calls Daphne Organ; sworn.*)

DOYLE: Mrs. Organ, you are a neighbor of Northern Farms Limited Number 3?

ORGAN: Right across the road. Born in that house. Lived there seventy-eight years now.

DOYLE: Where were you at approximately 5:30 A.M. on 27 June?

ORGAN: On my front porch. That's where I have my tea.

DOYLE: Could you tell the court what you saw that morning?

ORGAN: I saw young Eulie take hay to those cattle.

DOYLE: What else?

ORGAN: Then I saw her go back to the barn.

DOYLE: After that.

ORGAN: I saw the airplane come. It flew—it was almost touching the ground! Spraying this terrible-smelling stuff. All over the cattle, too! It's a disgrace!

DOYLE: You saw the spray hitting the cattle?

ORGAN: Of course! And all over the field too.

DOYLE: Then what did you do?

ORGAN: I went inside. I told you, it smelled!

DOYLE: We have heard from other witnesses that it was you who first noticed the cattle in trouble, and that you then telephoned Ms. Bean. Is that right?

ORGAN: Don't know if I was first. I only know what I saw. Those poor cattle staggered like drunks! When two o' them fell I got on the phone.

DOYLE: What time was that?

ORGAN: After my lunch. I have my lunch on the porch at one o'clock. Nice and shady then on hot days.

DOYLE: Your witness.

JONES: Are you familiar with a dairy cow called Molly's . . .

ORGAN: Of course I am. Who wouldn't know about a cow worth more than a hundred thousand dollars? Then she's got that funny triangle. Never heard of anything like that on a Holstein before.

JONES: Did you see this particular cow that morning?

ORGAN: I can't say for sure I saw her specifically. There's more to my life than watching cows, you know. I go out on my porch to have tea and watch the sunrise.

JONES: I understand. No more questions. Well, yes, one more. Mrs. Organ, didn't the terrible smell keep you from having your lunch on the porch?

ORGAN: The wind. Nice breeze blowing the other way. I wouldn't have gone out otherwise. I may be old but I'm not a fool, you know.

DOYLE: I have some re-examination, Your Honor. Mrs. Organ, could you pick out Molly's Arch Dream in a herd?

ORGAN: I already said I could.

DOYLE: Did you see her in the field from time to time prior to 27 June?

ORGAN: I surely did.

(*Plaintiff calls Dr. Robert Logan; sworn.*)

DOYLE: Would you describe your professional work, Dr. Logan?

LOGAN: I am a veterinarian in private practice.

DOYLE: Your Honor, I have here an autopsy report on the nine cattle in question, dated 28 June and signed by Dr. Logan. Mr. Jones has a copy. I would like to enter it as an exhibit.

WESTLAKE: Very well.

DOYLE: Dr. Logan, you describe the cause of death for the nine cattle as respiratory failure in reaction to a chemical substance. Does this apply to Molly's Arch Dream as well?

LOGAN: It does.

DOYLE: All yours.

JONES: Dr. Logan, would you explain the phenomenon "hardware disease" to the court?

WESTLAKE: Hardware disease? This better be relevant, Mr. Jones.

JONES: With respect, Your Honor, it's crucial to our response.

WESTLAKE: Very well. Let's hear about hardware disease then.

LOGAN: Indeed. Now, mammals of the suborder *Ruminantia*, which includes the *Tyloda* . . . uh, camels, and the *Pecoran:*

deer, giraffe and so on, and of course the *Bovidae,* your cows—
all these have multi-chambered stomachs. Now . . .

WESTLAKE: Maybe a briefer approach is in order, Dr. Logan;
I'm not sure we need a whole anatomy course.

LOGAN: Yes, I see. All right then. Now . . . now . . . a cow's stomach has four chambers. Most of what a cow eats is swallowed
whole, goes to one of the chambers, comes back up again to be
chewed as cud, and is reswallowed to another chamber. You
see, when they graze they tend to scoop and tear, often picking
up stones and bits of metal and garbage from the ground. It
collects in one of the chambers. Usually stays there for life.
Sometimes a beast will swallow something that just can't be
stored and it can cause problems.

JONES: Are the symptoms obvious? Of hardware disease, I mean?

LOGAN: It's not all that common a thing. When it happens
though, the problems can develop very fast.

JONES: Your autopsy report states that Molly's Arch Dream III
had hardware disease at the time of her death. Is that right?

LOGAN: Yes, but that's not unusual. You notice in the report
that several of the other cows had it, too.

JONES: But Molly's case was advanced.

LOGAN: It was serious.

JONES: Quite possibly fatal? In fairness, by the way, I should tell
you that I will be calling an expert in animal anatomy to comment on your report.

LOGAN: It might have been fatal.

JONES: In fact, is it not possible that Molly's Arch Dream III was
already dead when the airplane sprayed the field on June 27?

DOYLE: Objection! The witness has already testified as to the
cause of the death!

WESTLAKE: I think I'd like to hear his answer, Mr. Doyle. It
might clear up some of the fuzziness we've been listening to
from previous witnesses.

What is the "fuzziness" Judge Mary-Joan Westlake is referring to?

16

An Unlikely Place to Die

BECAUSE OF THE TRAFFIC, MOSTLY the snarl at the underpass on Wolfe Road, Brad Matchett got to the scene an hour later than he'd said he would. A late afternoon thunderstorm yesterday, with high winds and heavy rain, had caused so many power outages that some traffic lights were still out, making the morning rush hour worse than usual. Normally, Brad would have slapped the red flasher on the roof and driven around the line of cars, but because of the underpass, he couldn't do that. To make matters worse, he'd then made a wrong turn. The big estates in Cedar Springs were set in a maze of crescents and cul-de-sacs and one-way streets designed to discourage all but the most committed drivers. He'd become so lost he was forced to call the dispatcher to find out where he was.

The only upside in this case so far, it occurred to Brad, if indeed there can be upsides for the head of a homicide division, was that being late wasn't really a disaster because an accidental death, even if drugs are involved, is not usually a light-flashing, siren-blaring matter. Unless of course the victim happens to be a *somebody*.

In this case, it was close. The victim was almost a somebody. Not quite, but almost. Mme. Marie-Claude de Bouvère appeared from time to time on the social pages of *The Enterprise*. Not so much because she was the wife of the former Haitian ambassador;

more because she was a one-time tennis star. Good enough for two cracks at Wimbledon in her teens. That made her status too close to call, so Brad had gone out himself just to be on the safe side.

Mme. de Bouvère had been discovered shortly after sunrise by her gardener. The body lay in a gazebo set between the de Bouvères' huge house and their tennis court. On a table in the gazebo, along with her tennis racket, were all the appropriate paraphernalia for preparing and injecting a substance. Her tennis bag held three small bags of white powder. Brad knew all this from Sergeant Willy Peeverdale who, until Brad managed to get there, was the investigating officer in charge. For now, that was the extent of his information because the underpass on Wolfe Road had cut off radio communication. Now, almost an hour later, Brad was finally turning into a circular drive that looped the huge property at 23 Serene Crescent.

The property was very private. So were all the estates in Cedar Springs. A screen of sycamores and magnolias lined Serene Crescent so that even the most intrepidly curious driver would never see the house. Just to be sure, another screen, Colorado blue spruce this time, duplicated the effort about fifty paces behind the other trees. Interesting, Brad noted. Not one cedar.

Had it not been for the yellow crime-scene tape on the south side of the house, he would have spent yet more time looking for the gazebo, but the tape led him through a grove of honey locust and along a path of brick chips to the back of the house. The property here was even larger than the front. The gazebo, big as it was—to Brad it looked more like the band shell in Misty Meadows Park—appeared almost lonely and curiously out of place. It sat precisely midway between the house and the tennis court, completely surrounded by a perfectly manicured lawn.

"Nothing's touched, but we gotta move fast 'cordin' to the coroner." The voice behind him made Brad jump. He would never get used to Peeverdale's habits. The sergeant made no small talk, ever. He never said "hello"; he never said "excuse me." And if he was aware that he made people nervous by suddenly appearing behind them, he'd never made any effort to change.

Peeverdale pressed on. "Says she can confirm the drug thing better the sooner she gets into the postmortem. Figures death occurred between ten and eleven last night. Sure looks like they OD'd. The guy died first she thinks, but only by a bit."

"The guy? They?" Brad realized he was sounding excited.

"Yeah." Peeverdale was never flapped either. "Guess that didn't come through on your radio. Y'see, the gardener, he saw Maa-daam de . . . de . . . whatever . . . lyin' there in that thing, that gay-zee-bo, and he split for the phone. Waited for us in the drive-way. We found the guy. Figure it's Mister . . . Mon-*soor* de Boov . . . Boo . . . I can't get the doggone name right! Anyway we found him on the ground on the other side. Looks like he was sittin' on the rail and went over. For sure it's the missus on the floor, 'cordin' to the gardener. The guy's got no ID on him."

Sergeant Peeverdale dropped a pace behind Brad as they approached the gazebo, but continued talking. "Looks like the two of them were gonna play a little tennis last night. Or maybe they already played, it's hard to tell. And then they figured they'd get a little buzz on. My guess is they got some hot stuff they weren't expectin' and it did them in."

There were two steps up into the gazebo, and Brad stopped on the first one to study the body of Mme. de Bouvère lying flat on the floor. Well, not really flat. Reclining was more like it. The woman appeared so composed, so much an elegant study in white. Not a mark or a smudge or a speck on the white blouse or the white tennis skirt or the white sneakers. Except for the slight pinch to her eyes, it looked as though she had known she would be seen like this and had prepared for it.

Peeverdale, meanwhile, had not interrupted his monologue. "Gardener found her there at about 7 A.M. Comes every other day to mow the lawn. S'pose that's why it looks like a billiard table. Mine sure don't look like this. Anyway, he came to get some equip-ment he left yesterday and noticed the lights on over the tennis court. That's when he saw Maa . . . her. He didn't see the guy. You gotta look over the rail to see him. Uh . . . the coroner, she wants us to hustle, Captain. It's the drug thing. Says the sooner the better."

"Tell you what, Peev," Brad said. "You give her a call. Tell her we'll be a while. We've got to figure out first where this lady died. And maybe the guy, too."

"You mean," Sergeant Peeverdale reached inside his tunic and scratched absently, "you don't think she died right here?"

"No," Brad replied. "I don't."

Why does Brad Matchett think that Mme. de Bouvère did not die at the gazebo?

17

To Catch a Mannerly Thief

AS SHE STEPPED OVER THE potholes in the street and leaned hard into a fierce east wind, Agnes Skeehan made a promise to herself: never again was she going to attend a conference in November unless it was within walking distance of the equator. Actually, for Agnes, anywhere warmer than Liverpool would do. Liverpool may have produced the Beatles, and it could point with pride at its importance to the Industrial Revolution, but to Agnes that was hardly enough to make up for the miserable weather.

She mounted the curb, trotted across the sidewalk, and pulled hard at the entrance door of her hotel. Three days at the Birkenhead Arms had taught Agnes to yank with both hands at the ancient portal.

"Ah, young missy!" It was the hotel porter. He made a contribution all his own to Agnes's opinion of Liverpool. "You've got a telephone message here, young missy. All the way from Canada! A Deputy Commissioner Mowat. Sounds important, missy. Talked to him myself, I did. Told him you were out, I did."

Agnes mumbled a thank you as she grabbed the message and ran for the creaky old elevator. As things stood at the moment, she was only three hours away from her flight home, but she had a feeling this call was going to change her schedule.

It did.

"I want you to stay over there in Liverpool and help them with this case." Deputy Commissioner Mowat's voice crackled and sputtered across the Atlantic only minutes later. "As a favor from us, you know, international police cooperation and all that." He paused, but then jumped in again as though to head off the objection he was expecting. "You're simply the best there is on handwriting. They don't have anybody that comes close to you. Now what I want you to do right away is go to their headquarters—it's right by your hotel there—and report to Superintendent Anthony Opilis. He's the head of their CID: their Criminal Investigation Department. Now what I want you to do is consider yourself on temporary assignment there. Indefinite. As long as it takes."

Agnes struggled so hard to keep from telling Deputy Commissioner Mowat where he could stuff the international cooperation and the temporary assignment that she barely heard the rest. She didn't really need to though. The tabloids were full of the case that prompted his call. "The Friendly Filcher" one daily called it. "The Case of the Courteous Cat Burglar" another dubbed it. Whatever he—or she—deserved to be called, the case involved an amazingly successful thief who was breaking into homes and stealing jewelry. He seemed to have a peculiar respect for his victims, and this, in addition to the size of the take, was what the papers found so interesting. At each theft—there had been seven now—the thief left behind a neatly handwritten note of apology and an assurance that the stolen pieces would find their way only into the hands of people who would appreciate their beauty and value.

These notes, Agnes knew, were the reason she was being loaned to the Liverpool CID. Mowat was right when he called her the best. Agnes Skeehan, *Corporal* Agnes Skeehan, fourteen-year veteran of the Royal Canadian Mounted Police, had a special interest and an even more special knack in handwriting analysis. At graduation from the police training college in Regina, circumstances had presented her with a choice of more study, or assignment to a mounted patrol at the Parliament Buildings in Ottawa. Since race-track betting windows were as close to horses as Agnes ever cared to be, she picked the study and had never looked back.

Eight months ago, her article in the *Journal of Forensic Science* had led to an invitation to address a conference in Liverpool. Little did she realize when she came down from the podium there, to a huge round of applause, that the next move would be, not the airport, but into the superintendent's office at the Liverpool CID.

Superintendent Opilis, a long-time acquaintance of Deputy Commissioner Mowat as it turned out, was a plodder. His explanation of the jewelry thefts to Agnes was so detailed and so slow that she had to fight to pay attention. She kept turning her head toward the grimy office window to yawn, covering the move with a phony cough.

The superintendent must have sensed her mood for suddenly Agnes became aware of annoyance in his voice.

"Withenshawe?" he said, or rather, asked. "I say, Corporal Skeehan. You heard me? Withenshawe Purveyors?"

Agnes blushed. She had indeed been drifting. The problem was, she just didn't want to be in Liverpool.

"Yes, Superintendent, I'm sorry." She got up and walked to the window, trying to appear alert by focusing on a weathervane pointing at her from atop a pub across the street.

"Withenshawe Purveyors of Speke Street." She cleared her throat. "Every one of the notes was written on Withenshawe's letterhead. I'm aware of that. And your people have definitely established that they were all written by the same left-handed person. I'm aware of that, too. But don't you think the Withenshawe Purveyors stationery is a most clumsy red herring? After all, who . . ."

"Indeed, indeed Corporal Skeehan." Opilis got up and joined Agnes at the window. "But you see, there are other serious reasons why Alistair Withenshawe is a right handy suspect." He paused awkwardly. "We . . . er . . . we've summoned him. His office is just a short walk south of here. What we want you to do is . . . Why! That's him! Right there. Across the street."

"Him?" Agnes pointed at a tall, very nattily dressed gentleman holding down a bowler hat. "The dude with the hat? And the cane? Look at him!" Agnes was fully awake now. "Does he always walk like that in public?"

"Yes, well," Superintendent Opilis was almost apologetic. "Ah, we have dealt with him before. I'm afraid he's a bit of a showman."

To prove the policeman's point, Alistair Withenshawe, who had been bouncing his cane off the edge of the curb and catching it, now began to twirl it high in the air like a drum major, spinning it first over one parked car, then the next, and then a third, before he brought it down and made a crisp military turn off the walk and into the street toward the police station.

Opilis let a touch of admiration creep into his voice. "Snappy, what?"

Agnes looked at him. "Yes, I agree. Snappy. But I'll give you any odds you want he didn't write those notes."

Why is Agnes Skeehan so sure of that?

18

Tracing the Couriers from Departure to Arrival

"SEAMUS? DID I GET THAT right? *Seamus?*" Mary Clare McInerney realized she was shouting the instant she saw heads in the outer office turn in unison toward her. She didn't have a lot of choice, however. The connection was very poor.

"Is that a first name or a last name? A code name more likely. Which?" she wanted to know.

She waited for the unnerving pause so typical of trans-global telephone calls, particularly from places like Northern Africa, the delay that always made callers think they'd lost their call. But the answer came through. Struan Ritchie was at the other end of the conversation. He was in Addis Ababa and he was shouting even louder than Mary Clare.

"Yes, Seamus!" Struan's voice was buried in crackle and hiss. "It's the only name I have, so it's likely a code name. The other one I have is a single name, too: Rothsay."

"Rothsay!" This time Mary Clare really turned the heads in the outer office. To make it worse she had forgotten the transmission delay and had almost spoken over the rest of Struan's sentence. It was important information.

". . . say," Struan was saying, "is the one who is flying out of Dorval in Montreal. It's confirmed. But I don't know where she's going."

Mary Clare waited and then, as quietly as she could in her excitement, said, "She?" and waited again.

"Yes, *she*," was the reply. "Two of the four couriers, it would seem, are women. Rothsay is one of them."

"And 'Saint' is the other then." Mary Clare didn't wait this time. "We got that yesterday. So that means 'Seamus,' and the other one we got yesterday, 'Felipe,' are males. Well, that helps. Not much though if they are good at disguises. What we really need to know is where each of the four is going and what airport they're flying out of. The only way we can coordinate this bust is if each of the couriers is tailed from departure to destination and nailed when they arrive. That way we scoop the parties at both ends, too."

Struan's voice came in over top of Mary Clare's. "I've got to get off. There's a lineup behind me and there's something going on down the street. Listen. I've got two more pieces. Seamus is going to Brazil, to Rio. Got that? But I don't know where he is now or what airport he's going to use. The other is . . ."

At that point there was a fierce crackling on the line, followed by an electronic whirr, and finally a dial tone. This time, Mary Clare's shout of frustration brought the entire outer office to its feet. She chose the moment to wave Harvey Bottrell and Cecile King into her office.

Mary Clare McInerney was a member of the Drug Enforcement Administration working out of "E" Division in Seattle. For the past six months she had been coordinating a team investigation into an illegal narcotics ring. Over the last three days, things had come together at a rapid pace; the team was about to close in on the four key couriers and, through them, the leaders of the ring.

What her team had been able to put together was that each of the four couriers, within the next forty-eight hours (using GMT-9 as the reference point, because she was working out of Seattle), would be flying to separate destinations with major deliveries. Mary Clare was certain her team could break the ring if the four could be identified and followed from airport to airport. They now knew who the four were. At least their code names—that was enough.

"That was Struan Ritchie in Addis Ababa," she said to her two assistants after they had seated themselves at the coffee table in her office.

Harvey nodded. "We know."

"The whole office knows," Cecile King added.

Mary Clare reddened slightly. "It was an incredibly dirty line," she explained, "with all kinds of ambient noise from where he was phoning, too. Sounded like he was out in the street. Come to think of it, he could even have been on an off-shore phone. The real problem is I think he had more to give us before the line broke down."

"Maybe what we've got will make you feel better," Harvey said. "Just some little pieces, but we're definitely getting closer."

Mary Clare got up from her desk and joined the two at the coffee table. "Lay it out," she said.

"We have three of the destinations," Harvey took three pens from his jacket pocket and set them on the table. "At the very least we can put a blanket surveillance on the airports." He held up both hands, palms out, before Mary Clare could say the obvious. "I know that's not what we want, but . . . anyway, one of the couriers is going to Hong Kong. That information is just five minutes old. It came in while you were talking to Struan. Another is going to Hawaii, to Oahu."

Cecile leaned forward. "And one is going to Bermuda. Better than that, we also know this one will be flying out of Orly, in Paris, to get there." She leaned back again. "What we don't have is who any of them are. We only know that three couriers are going to these three places."

Mary Clare picked up one of Harvey's pens from the table and began to play with it, bending it with both hands into a bow shape. "What did you come up with in the call to Chicago?"

Harvey made a face. "According to our contact there, uh . . . uh . . . do you think I could have my pen back?"

Cecile finished for him. "One of the couriers is definitely leaving from O'Hare there. But we had the destination wrong before. Originally, we thought it was Hawaii, but it's not, and we don't know what it is, either."

Mary Clare was sufficiently distracted by this information for Harvey to surreptitiously retrieve his pens, all three, and stuff them back into the safety of his jacket pocket.

"So." Mary Clare was speaking to no one in particular. "So. We are this close." She made a tiny space with her thumb and forefinger. "If only the time wasn't so short. If . . ."

"Mary Clare!" Cecile King was pointing at the winking light on her desk. "Your telephone. Wonder if that's . . ."

It was Struan Ritchie again.

"Sorry about that cutoff before." The line was very clear this time. "Just down the street, these two guys on a camel . . . Why am I telling you this? You'd have to be here. Listen. This is what I didn't give you. You know that Felipe, the one you said you got yesterday?"

Mary nodded as though he were sitting in the office.

"Well, I've had that one for a little while but couldn't confirm it. Guess if you got it from a different source, it must be right. Anyway, Felipe is at Heathrow right now, according to my information. In the departures lounge. Where he's going, I don't know. It's not Hong Kong, if that helps. Wish I could tell you, but I can't."

"No need." Mary Clare McInerney had a huge smile on her face. "That's the last piece of the puzzle." She held back the receiver so her grin could include the two assistants. "Let's call out the dogs," she said, "the chase is on!"

How has Mary Clare McInerney figured out where each courier is going and where each is flying from?

19

Not All Lottery Winners
Are Lucky

FOR AT LEAST THE TENTH time that day, Captain Frank Ricketts pulled his head down turtle-like into his coat and wondered how on earth his parents could possibly have left Jamaica for a climate like this.

He pulled his hat down, too, so it would fit tighter over his head. The business of headgear was another issue. Just inside the back door of his home there was an array of hats and caps and toques of every possible weight and design, and never once did he seem to pick the right one as he left in the morning.

Chinooks. That's what everyone called the extreme, almost instant changes in weather here in Calgary. Abrupt rises in temperature of up to twenty degrees, sometimes in less than an hour. "It's what you get for building a city on the east side of the Rocky Mountains," everyone in Calgary said, as though the first pioneers had planned it that way. "You just have to get used to it," was always the next comment. Frank had never gotten used to it.

He took a step toward the body, trying to put chinooks out of his mind and being careful to put his feet down flat in the snow. He also had the wrong shoes on for these conditions and didn't want to slip and fall.

It had been a typical Calgary winter so far. Two days ago, right in the morning rush hour, a sudden chinook had turned the snow into slush. Then before noon, the temperature had plunged to Arctic levels and stayed that way until earlier this morning when it warmed up just enough for snow to fall for an hour. Frank knew that one careless step on a layer of snow over ice would put him on his backside. That was an indignity he didn't need in front of the whole crime-scene crew, so he was very cautious as he approached the body and squatted down beside it.

"His name is Archie Deschamps-Lebeau, Captain. Or was anyway." Frank looked up to see Nick Andropolous, the oldest member of the homicide unit. Nick secretly fascinated Frank, for even though he had been born and raised in Crete, he always dressed like a typical urban Canadian, with no hat, no gloves, boots undone, and coat open.

"Seventy-three years old. Widower," Nick went on, reading from a ragged spiral-bound notebook pinched between his thumb and index finger. "Lived alone in the house over there. Stinking rich."

Nick closed the notebook and hunkered down across from Frank. "This is the guy, Captain," he said in almost a whisper, "the guy that won that giant lottery. It was—how many millions?—eighteen or something? Lotta good it does him now! You remember that don't you? He fired a shotgun at some reporters not long after to chase 'em away."

Frank remembered all right. Everyone did. Archie Deschamps-Lebeau had won the biggest lottery prize in history and had spent the time since trying to avoid the limelight that went with it.

"Yeah, I remember, Nick." Frank spoke softly, staring at the outline in the ice and snow where the body had lain face down. Two paramedics had carefully pried it up and rolled it over so that the lifeless eyes of Archie Deschamps-Lebeau were now staring at the gray afternoon sky.

"And I don't have to ask, do I, if you got all the pictures, since you decided to roll him over before I got here?" The annoyance in Frank's voice was clear. "And the measurements? What's the distance there between those indentations where his feet were in the ice? And what about that button over there? Is it his?"

"Hey, hey, Captain! Wait a minute!" Nick squatted down beside Frank, self-consciously waving his notebook. "We got everything. Anyway, we don't even know this is a homicide. There's no marks on the body. No signs of violence. Anybody else but this guy, we probably wouldn't even be here! The coroner's been and gone—by the way she says there's no way she can do time of death for sure 'cause the old guy's been frozen." Nick lowered his voice. "And some of the guys here are freezing, Captain. Er . . . you know what it's like. Some of them can't take the weather. They want to get going."

Frank looked up at the detective and grinned. "How come you never wear a hat, Nick? No! Don't answer that! I don't want to know!" He stood up and pulled down his own hat again. "Okay, let's get out of here. Incidentally," he nodded at the body, "who found him here?"

"His two daughters." Nick relaxed a bit and opened his notebook again as they walked toward their cars. "They dropped in on him every second day to see that he was Okay. He had a bad heart. But that's as much company as he put up with. Apparently they came and made him lunch and then cooked things for him and put it in a freezer. Cleaned the place a bit. Stuff like that. They're the only ones he ever let into the house. The neighbors confirm that. The daughters were here last time and everything was all right. Today they show up and he's nowhere around. They go looking, figuring he's caught the big one. Sure enough, here he was out at the end of the backyard."

The two policemen had reached their cars as Nick finished talking. Frank got into his, started it, and turned the heater on full blast before getting out again. "Nick," he said, "these two daughters. They in pretty good shape?"

"What do you mean?" Nick wanted to know.

"Like, husky," Frank said, "strong. Do you think they could have carried the old guy out here by themselves and dumped him, say if he were dead, or maybe if he had a heart attack but wasn't quite dead and they wanted the weather to finish him off?"

Nick looked surprised. "Well, yeah, one of them in fact probably could do it all by herself. Why? You think they did it?"

Frank nodded. "Sure looks that way," he said.

What has led Captain Frank Ricketts to suspect the two daughters of Archie Deschamps-Lebeau of murder?

20

Spy Versus Spy

"IN COUNTERESPIONAGE, HAUPTMANN AUGUST, we are not interested in spies as much as we are in spy *networks.*"

"I understand, Herr Oberst, but . . ." Ernst August tried to break in, but it was Oberst Dietrich Staat's favorite lecture, and he was not about to have its delivery interrupted by an officer of inferior rank.

"So if we act upon your suggestion, Hauptmann," he continued, "we will succeed in doing what? We will arrest this . . . this Kopenick of yours, and what will we have? Nothing but another foot soldier, another pair of eyes and ears that can be replaced just like that!" Oberst Staat snapped his fingers. It was a constant habit of his, one he indulged in almost as frequently as asking himself rhetorical questions.

Hauptmann Ernst August yielded to the defeat that crept from the back of his brain, ran over his skull, and fixed his face in an immobile, neutral expression. There was no other way but to endure it. He had been through this lecture before: the same words, the same intonations, the same gestures. The same stinking cloud of cigarette smoke. It made him wonder yet again what devious gremlin of fate had conspired to have him transferred from the Abwehr, the military intelligence service led by his hero, Admiral Canaris, to the Sicherheitdienst, the infamous SD. It was bad enough that he had to admit to his fellow career officers in the Wermacht that he was now working for that madman, Heydrich. Worse was that his superior officer was Dietrich Staat, the most short-sighted drone in the service.

Staat's lecture went on, "Stuttgart is full of little traitors like your Kopenick, full of closet communists. I understand your enthusiasm and I commend it. Your skill, too, in identifying Kopenick. But what does he mean to us?" The colonel paused to squash out his Gauloise and insert another into the end of his ivory cigarette holder. He did not offer one to August. "It may mean one less instrument in the network for a very short while. But before long, he will be replaced. No, in counterespionage we must ask ourselves . . ."

Staat made an elaborate show of lighting the fresh cigarette with a table lighter on his desk. "You realize of course, Hauptmann, what would be of interest, what would be most useful . . ." Staat had forgotten the question he was going to ask and inadvertently, almost got right to the point, ". . . what would be most useful would be to find out who Kopenick's *cutout* is. Now. What would that do for us?"

Ernst August swallowed noisily. He was struggling to keep his mouth shut. The last time he'd endured this lecture, which was during the second time he had reported Kopenick's activities, Staat had laboriously explained "cutout" to him, as though both did not already know well that a cutout's role was to act as a protective connection between an agent and various subagents. The practice preserved security for the agent since, most of the time, a subagent never even learned the identity of his or her agent.

"If we knew who the cutout is, we could follow him. And then! And *then!*" Staat was reaching a plateau in his monologue. Ernst knew that either he would end it here, or God forbid, branch out in another direction. Before either could happen, Hauptmann Ernst August jumped in.

"Most astute as usual, Herr Oberst. You see, I know who the cutout is. Also, I know how they communicate. If you want to see them together and see how Kopenick passes the messages, we will have to go now while it is raining. If their pattern remains as consistent as it has been, they will rendezvous shortly near the Stiftskirche. At 1730 hours."

Luckily for Ernst August, his outburst coincided with one of Staat's elaborate inhalings. The officer corps had been very much influenced in its smoking habits of late by French movies. But what Staat had just heard stopped all the mannerisms. And the lecture.

"You have his cutout?" The Oberst did not realize his mouth was agape.

"Yes, Oberst Staat. His name is Traugott Waechter. Swiss. At least he has a Swiss passport."

"Aha, a Swiss passport! Now what does that mean? It means . . ."

"Yes, Herr Oberst. He travels back and forth once a week. Stuttgart to Bern. I suspect that it is because of this Waechter that you—that *we* have not been successful with the radio location equipment. I believe that in Stuttgart, at least, *Rote Kapelle* makes very little use of radios. With Waechter available as a courier, there is no need."

For the very first time, Oberst Dietrich Staat was silent. His mouth stayed open, but there were no words. His cigarette burned away unnoticed at the end of the holder. The mention of *Rote Kapelle* often had that effect on German intelligence.

To the SD and the Abwehr, and the Gestapo, too, the *Rote Kapelle* or "Red Orchestra" was a cause of profound embarrassment. It was a highly successful Soviet operation, a network that especially in the first years of the war, sent amazingly accurate, thorough, and extensive reports to Moscow on German war production, military maneuvers, and even some of the long-range planning of the general staff. Many of the agents at the bottom of the chain—subagents—were ideological communists, a great number of them German, some Swiss, and some, like Kopenick, Czechs from the Sudetenland.

On two previous occasions, Ernst August's reports about Kopenick to Staat had stirred no response, a result he attributed to the continuing jealousy between the Abwehr and the SD. This time, what he offered Staat stimulated commitment to the common cause.

The commitment, or else the irresistible pleasure of wounding the Red network, boosted August over another hurdle with Staat, too. The two men were now sitting outside the Stiftskirche in August's somewhat battered, three-year-old Volkswagen. Staat had wanted to use his chauffeured Mercedes-Benz, but the captain had convinced him of the need for a small car, because to score their coup with Waechter and Kopenick they would likely have to maneuver through the medieval section of the city with its narrow streets and alleys.

They had arrived in the square in front of the Stiftskirche at 1728 hours and were lucky enough to be able to back into a parking space that concealed them from the street. Kopenick appeared at 1729 hours, making August look very good indeed. He stopped in front of the main entrance to the church for about thirty seconds, then drove off.

"Good! Where's the cutout? Why aren't we following?" Staat said through a thick cloud of cigarette smoke.

"He will be back." It occurred to Ernst for only the first time that Staat probably had no street experience at all. He was just an administrator. "They communicate with their cars," he added.

"Their cars?" Staat was asking questions to which he did not have a ready answer planned. Real questions. Ernst liked that.

"Do you see the little truck across the square? The plumber?" Ernst deliberately pressed on before Staat could answer. He knew the colonel had not noticed the truck. "That's Waechter. He uses different vehicles, but I've seen this one twice before. He also uses a . . . ah, here's Kopenick again!"

Both men watched as the *Rote Kapelle* subagent drove into the square in his tiny, black Renault. This time he did not even stop but drove straight through.

"He's waiting for the traffic to pick up just a bit more," Ernst explained. "The more traffic, the more vehicles, the better for them. But they're running out of time, I think. Waechter can't sit there much longer without attracting attention."

Almost on top of his words, Kopenick reappeared. This time, Waechter pulled out into traffic ahead of him. August accelerated out of the parking space and over the next block slipped the Volkswagen in behind Waechter's truck. Within a few seconds, in what to anyone else would appear to have been natural traffic flow and interchange, the Renault was directly in front of Waechter. The three vehicles moved in single file that way for the next block.

"At the stop ahead," Ernst said. "That's where it'll start." Staat said nothing but smoked furiously as the line of cars slowed.

"Now! See!" Ernst August could not suppress his excitement. Or his righteousness. "See the message being sent? In Morse! Clumsy, but right in front of our noses! There!"

He translated excitedly.

"Bomb site—No!—*sight*. . . man . . . man . . . must be manufacture—Yes! *manufacture*—moved to Ess . . . Ess . . . *Esslingen!* What did I tell you! 'Bombsight manufacture moved to Esslingen.' They get . . ."

"Hauptmann! They're moving!"

In his excitement, Ernst had almost forgotten he was driving.

"Now wait till we stop again, Herr Oberst, and you'll see more! At this one, perhaps you will read the message for us. I can't stay right behind Waechter too long. He's a careful one!"

Dietrich Staat was exuding extreme discomfort and Hauptmann Ernst August basked in it. He knew the colonel had no idea what was going on.

"What's the matter, Oberst, is it the Morse?"

"Of course not!" the commanding officer snapped. "I know Morse! It's . . . I don't . . . I'm not . . . *How do you know it's Morse?*"

The Abwehr captain rolled his window down slightly to let some of the smoke out, then took even more time in an elaborate assessment of whether the ensuing draft caused any discomfort for his superior. Only after he'd stretched the situation to the fringes of bad manners did he reply.

"Under the truck, Oberst Staat. Look under the truck."

What has Hauptmann Ernst August discovered? How are Kopenick and Traugott Waechter communicating in Morse code?

21

The Search for Olie Jorgensson

THE INSTANT DETECTIVE-SERGEANT CONNIE MOUNT signaled the little team behind her to halt and take a short break, they all turned to a patch of wild raspberries that grew in profusion at the edge of the trail and began to eat greedily. It was just one more thing that upset her about this search and rescue mission. The searchers were supposed to lie flat and relax totally to conserve their strength; there might be many miles to cover yet and there was plenty of daylight left.

Connie's uneasiness had been growing steadily from the very second this whole affair had started. That was at 7:03 A.M. this morning, when she walked into the Healey Lake detachment office where she was commanding officer. The night dispatcher, "Lefty" Shaw, still had a half hour left on his shift. He was standing at his desk with his finger on the PLAY button of the answering machine. Connie heard only the very last part of the tape, but she recognized the voice in spite of the panic in it.

". . . don't know how long ago but he isn't anywhere on the campsite! We've looked everywhere! Won't you please hurry! He's so little!"

"That was Svena Jorgensson, wasn't it Norman?" Connie said.

She was the only one in the detachment—in the entire community—who didn't call him "Lefty"; she felt it kept him on his toes.
Police work—his job—became secondary in Lefty's life whenever
he was able to lay his hands on a new, or rather, new *old* car. Lefty
was a collector of classics and two days ago a 1912 Reo had made
him completely forget why he was being paid a salary.

"Before you tell me all about it, *Norman,* why is her call on the
answering machine instead of on your backup tape? This means
you weren't at your desk, were you?"

Lefty's normally ruddy countenance glowed a notch brighter at
Connie's challenge. "I had to go to the can!" he said indignantly.
"It happens from time to time, you know!"

Connie nodded. "I suppose so. Nature, right?" She took a step
forward and pressed REWIND on the answering machine. "You
know, that reminds me. It's certainly time those washrooms were
cleaned. Especially if we've got to get rid of that Number 90
gear grease you managed to get all over yourself when you were
in there."

Lefty turned full red this time but Connie didn't notice. By
now she'd punched PLAY and was listening to Svena Jorgensson
tell the detachment that her little Olie was missing from their
campsite at the lake. As far as she, Svena, knew, he'd gotten up
while she was still asleep and wandered off and out into the bush.
Olie was only four years old.

That had happened six hours ago, and although Connie had
put together a full search and rescue response within forty-five
minutes, she still felt that the whole thing might be just a wild
goose chase; there were so many things that weren't right to
begin with, and so many things that turned out wrong as they
went along.

For one, the armed forces helicopter she'd called in to fly over
the area with a heat sensor turned out to be a waste of time. There
were simply too many wild animals in the area and their body
heat made the sensor work like a popcorn machine. The system
worked better as the helicopter flew some miles farther from the
lake, but there was no point to that because it would have been

impossible for a child Olie's age to get that far away in six hours.

The tracking dogs caused another problem. One was a Shepherd, the other a Blue Tick hound that Connie had worked with once before. Both dogs led their handlers directly to an abandoned railway line several hundred yards from the Jorgensson's campsite. At that point, the animals disagreed. The Shepherd circled and circled and then simply sat down as if to say, "That's it. End of Trail." The Blue Tick bounded down the former railway line in complete confidence, enthusiastically dragging the handler and the search team after him. But then he stopped, too, and like the Shepherd, circled a few times and sat down.

By this time, it was eleven A.M., and the August sun was heating up everyone's nerves, not least Connie's. It was at that point that, against her better judgment, certainly against her best instincts, she let Willy Stefan take over. Not that Willy was incompetent. On the contrary, he was regarded—and rightly so—as the best tracker the area had ever seen. Local wags loved to explain to tourists how Willy could track a mosquito through a swamp. But Willy was not exactly a neutral party in this case. He was Olie's uncle, Svena's brother-in-law, and in the Jorgensson family, that meant complications. Svena and her former husband were involved in a frightfully bitter and ongoing custody dispute over little Olie. That's why Connie had immediately recognized the voice on the answering machine. Olie's father regularly failed to bring him back after "visit" times. Once, the father, with the help of his sister and her husband, Willy, had snatched Olie out of the backyard of the Jorgensson home and had taken him away for two weeks.

These contradictions and complications had been rumbling away in the back of Connie's mind as the search team followed Willy Stefan at a respectable distance down the railway line. Now he stood, after she had called a halt, waiting for her to catch up.

Willy wiped the back of his neck with a peach-colored cloth that said Dunn & Dunn Service. "Slow going," he commented, giving expression to yet another burr that Connie was feeling. They had been moving at a snail's pace all along.

"Tourist season," Willy added as though that explained every-thing. He held the cloth at the corners and made it flap before wiping his face with it. "There's just so many people hiking along here this time of year," he said through the cloth. "Makes it so hard to read the signs. No wonder the dogs got mixed up."

Connie's reaction was instant. "That does it!"

She turned and yelled back to the others. "You people! I want you to go back a bit. Back up. Go around the curve and wait there till I call."

"Now, Willy," she lowered her voice. "You and I are going to talk. No. Strike that! *You* are going to talk. Talk a lot and talk fast! I want to know where that little boy is!"

Why does Connie Mount believe that Willy Stefan has something to tell her?

22

Murder at the David Winkler House

CHRIS BEADLE PAUSED IN THE narrow hallway and looked back at the doorway she'd just come through. Her height was average; yet she'd still had to duck.

"Atmosphere," she said out loud to no one in particular. "Anything for pioneer effect. But then . . . why not?"

There was more pioneer effect right in front of her, for the door into the inn's only public washroom was just as small and would be sure to make a patron stoop. In fact, everything about the David Winkler House was small: the rooms, the halls, the doorways, the windows. But with clever restorations, the place seemed far more dainty than cramped. The David Winkler House had been built in the late eighteenth century by David Winkler—no surprise there—to accommodate his large family at a time when people were smaller than they are today. The present owners, the four innkeepers who had turned it into an extremely successful country dining room and inn, had been careful to preserve everything they could to make the place as authentic as possible.

From the moment Chris had left the graveled parking lot which was quite carefully and deliberately separated from the building by a row of lilac bushes and a profusion of hollyhocks in full bloom, she had felt herself slide backward in time. The owners had done such a good job. From the squeaky gate in the stockade fence to the milk paint on the shutters to the weathered cedar shingles on the roof, the David Winkler House spoke "authentic." And it spoke "charm."

They had succeeded inside, too. Only someone who looked carefully for them would ever find electrical outlets or switches or wires. There was no evidence of a telephone anywhere, not even when the hostess greeted the guests. Even the washroom, where Chris now stood, was hidden away from the dining area. It couldn't be found without asking. Not easily, anyway.

Chris ducked and stepped inside, remembering why she'd come back here in the first place. There wasn't much room. Not only was it a unisex facility, it barely accommodated one person at a time. She pushed the door open right to the wall. It just cleared a sink styled in antique porcelain that stood on a thin pedestal in the corner ahead of her and to the left. On the wall opposite the door hung a framed mirror, surrounded by dried roses, dried fern, and Queen Anne's Lace. To her right, the unavoidable stark modernity of the toilet was softened by an identical mirror on the wall above it, this one holding up a tangle of green foxtail. In a deliberate sequence, Chris flushed the toilet, turned each tap on, then off, and gently pushed the door closed.

"Not bad," she said, again out loud but to no one in particular. It was impossible to make a washroom look eighteenth century, certainly in what had been a pioneer home. But everything was designed for silence. The door did not squeak, and the plumbing was absolutely hushed. No modern noises to intrude on the atmosphere.

On the remaining wall hung the sampler that Kate Mistoe said she was nailing up when Menelaus Atko was shot. It was a delicately embroidered piece of work, set in a frame similar to that used for the mirrors. It didn't have the familiar proverb or Biblical quotation, however. This sampler held another oblique intrusion from the twentieth century. What it said, in very fine needlework, was:

O, Winkler patrons, please take heed,
These things our septic does not need.

A most unpoetic list of the jetsam of modern living followed: matches, cigarette butts, napkins, hairpins, aluminum foil. Chris counted nineteen items that Winkler patrons were not to throw into the toilet!

Kate Mistoe had been here in the washroom when Menelaus Atko was shot in the dining room earlier this morning. Or so she said. Her story was supported, though, by Sandy Sanchez. Sandy's account was that he was going past the washroom on his way to the propane tanks out back at the time the shots were fired. He and Kate had stared at each other for what seemed like forever, frozen in shock and fear. Then they wasted more precious time colliding with each other in the narrow hallway in their effort to get to the dining room where they found the body of Menelaus, bleeding but not breathing. Through the window, both swore they'd seen a blue car roar onto the road from the parking lot in a plume of gravel and exhaust.

That part of the story was verified in turn by Karl Schloss who had been driving up the road to the David Winkler House from the opposite direction. He'd seen the blue car turn to the right in a skid at the intersection a short distance away, and then disappear. The dust from the gravel, according to Schloss, along with the exhaust, hung like a trail over the parking lot and down the road. Schloss had run into the dining room to find Sanchez and Mistoe clinging to each other, as far from the late Menelaus Atko as they could get.

All three, Mistoe, Sanchez, and Schloss, were now sitting in the kitchen waiting for Chris to finish her walkabout. To her, they were still prime suspects, in spite of the story of the blue car and the fact that their alibis all dovetailed so neatly.

Chris had questioned them separately an hour before. Schloss's story would be the easiest to check. He said he'd been in town at a service station getting the oil changed in his car. Normally that would make his alibi entirely solid, but there was a hitch. He had not come directly back to the Winkler House but had detoured via one of the farms where the inn bought fresh produce each day. When he saw that there was no one home there, he'd left and arrived back at the David Winkler House just in time to see the blue car speed away.

Sandy Sanchez, during his interview, had been exceptionally animated. As he spoke, his hands were constantly on the move in sweeping, dramatic gestures. The fittings on the propane tanks needed tightening, he'd said, making big round clockwise circles at Chris with his fist, as though they were holding a wrench. It was while he was on his way to do that, when he and Kate heard the shots.

Chris felt the man's animated style was natural; he probably talked that way all the time. In any case it would be easy enough to verify. So would his knowledge of propane systems. What bothered her most was that his story supported Kate Mistoe's, and it meant then that both were lying. So then what about Schloss? Was there a three-way conspiracy here at Winkler House?

One thing she had to do right away was talk to Atko's lawyer. The three prime suspects each owned ten percent of the inn. Atko held the rest. What she wanted to know was what kind of in-the-event-of-death clause there was in their partnership agreement. If Mistoe, Schloss, and Sanchez stood to gain substantially from their late partner's death, then . . .

Why does Chris Beadle believe that Kate Mistoe and Sandy Sanchez are lying? Why does she want to find out what Sandy Sanchez knows about propane systems? And how can she check out Karl Schloss's story?

23

Incident on
the Picket Line

12 October
Memorandum

To: Yvonne Hawkins,
     Manager of Claims,
     Belwood Insurance Company

From: Eileen Cook,
       Claims Investigator

THIS IS MY PRELIMINARY REPORT on the claim by Mr. Roger Monk
of Roger Monk Transport Limited, for damage to his tractor-
trailer.*

Mr. Monk is the owner-driver of the following vehicle: a diesel-
powered, cab-over-engine style Freightliner tractor with a rear
tandem axle. The cab has a sleeper compartment attached. The
trailer is a flatbed type, with a single rear axle. Complete specifications for the vehicle will be in the appendix to my final report.

---

* Please note that Mr. Monk is British, and describes the vehicle in his own claim as an
  "articulated lorry." The police refer to it as a "semi."

The police report states that ten days ago, on October 2, Mr. Monk drove his tractor-trailer to the entrance gate of the Agromax Farm Machinery Company. He acknowledges that he was aware of a strike at Agromax, and that there had been several incidents of violence on the picket line. However, he contends that because his trailer was empty, he felt that the picketers would let him through unchallenged.

As Mr. Monk drove to the gate, members of the picket line set upon his equipment, presumably causing the damage listed in his claim. The police report confirms that during the incident both exhaust stacks were damaged beyond repair, along with the windshield and both headlamps. It also confirms that every single tire was slashed, so that both tractor and trailer had to be towed away after order was restored. Also, a striker entered the sleeper compartment and had to be forcibly removed. A complete copy of the police report is being sent to your attention.

Roger Monk has listed the following in his claim:

—towing charges
—complete repainting of the tractor
—replacement of the windshield and two headlamps
—replacement of two exhaust stacks
—replacement of sixteen tires
—replacement of one set of bagpipes.

My recommendations are as follows:

One: that the towing charges be paid immediately.

Two: that the repainting of the tractor be negotiated. This tractor is four years old, and the need for painting is at least partly the result of normal wear and tear.

Three: that damaged parts be replaced only if confirmed in the police report.

Four: the bagpipes are a special problem. According to police, a striker did indeed enter the sleeping compartment during the incident, but there is no independent confirmation that it was the striker who damaged the bagpipes, or that the bagpipes were even in the sleeper.

My recommendation is that the company decline to pay for

them in view of the fact that there is already an attempt at fraud in this claim.

My full report will follow in two days.

Respectfully,
Eileen Cook

What is the attempt at fraud that Eileen Cook refers to?

24

Footprints on the Trail

TORREY MAZER HAD MADE IT to the top of the Criminal Investigation Branch for one very simple reason. She was a darn good cop. She knew it, too, as did the people in her department, which explained why there was never a hint of resentment from inside the force. Even when she encountered the inevitable smart remarks from people on the outside, her self-confidence always helped her to ignore it. However, what Torrey did not deal with very well was the fact that she was short. So short that her personnel file carried the minutes of an appeal meeting on the matter of her height held when she was a cadet-in-training fifteen years before. A physical education instructor had made the mistake of refusing to graduate her from his course, claiming she was too tiny to meet his standards.

In fact, Torrey topped the height requirements with even a bit to spare. But her legs were abnormally short and made her appear small. This was one point on which the male officers in her department showed no mercy. Though she could never prove it, Torrey knew that none of them ever *walked* with her. They took strides. Big ones, stretched to the limit so that she had to almost canter to keep up. Yet she could never bring herself to say anything, so that "almost cantering" became her on-duty style.

At the moment, just behind and to the right of Constable Wally Harris, Torrey Mazer was cantering as usual—and she was more than a little embarrassed about it, too. She wasn't helped at all by the terrain. The rough, frozen field they were crossing was covered with flattened weeds and scrub brush that snagged at her feet and at the edges of her bulky overcoat. It had been a cold but snowless winter, bleak and ugly. Everything in the field was gray and dirty brown.

"We're coming right up to it now, Inspector," Wally Harris said over his right shoulder. "You can see there's some smoke still rising on the other side of the hill just ahead. If the wind was in our faces, the smell would gag you. We're lucky today."

The smell Wally referred to came from the charred bodies of thousands of turkeys that had died in a barn fire two days before. The Criminal Investigation Branch was involved because it had been a clear case of arson. Clumsy arson, too, but successful because of a terrible coincidence. Just before the fire, in a first promise of spring, a day and night of mild thaw had prompted the turkey-farm owners to move extra stock into the barn from other buildings. Thus the number of turkeys burned was much larger than it might have been. By the time the alarm was called in just before dawn, Mother Nature had suddenly reversed herself. The temperature plunged so fast that when the fire trucks arrived, the hose connections at the farm had to be loosened with torches. The delay had been costly.

Torrey doubled her cantering speed and caught up to Wally Harris just as they crested the hill. Then both of them stopped abruptly. It wasn't so much the sight of the smoldering ruin below them as it was the odor. Vile, pungent, and penetrating. Neither officer made any pretense about covering their faces.

"Normally we could go down right here, Inspector," Wally said. "But the footprints we came to see are over there." He pointed to a very steep hill on their left that ran straight down to the edge of what had been the barn. "The path is on that hill," Wally continued. "It goes from the barn up over the hill to an equipment shed. The path is so steep, they only use it in summer.

It's a shortcut. Anyway, the footprints are there. It's pretty obvious that whoever torched the barn came down that path and set up with a slow-burning fuse, but, uh, Inspector, I think you're gonna see it can't really be Tibor Nish who made those footprints."

Torrey had come to the site to see for herself a set of footprints that may or may not have belonged to Tibor Nish who, for the present, was the only suspect. On the path down the hill, investigators had found a set of footprints made by a pair of size twelve Kodiak work boots. Tibor Nish not only wore size twelve Kodiaks, he had been dismissed by the turkey farm for drunkenness only a week before the fire. Nor did Nish deny that his footprints might be on the trail. He said he had returned to pick up a pair of coveralls four days ago. When he couldn't find them in the equipment shed, he went to look in the barn. He had used the path down to the barn because he was in a hurry, knowing he was not welcome on the farm. He'd found the coveralls, then hurried out the front gate. Another farm worker had seen Tibor Nish at the barn. She did not think it was four days ago, but rather, on the day *before* the fire, in the late afternoon. When pressed, however, she admitted she couldn't be absolutely sure.

Torrey could see the footprints in question easily, even before she and Wally came up the path. A single set of tracks leading down the hill. They were from big shoes all right, stamped into the middle of the path. The indentations were clear, especially deep at the heel. Kodiaks without question.

"Well," Torrey began, straightening up after a close look at the prints, "it's going to be pretty hard for Tibor Nish to explain these. My guess is if we lean on him a little he'll admit his guilt. Lucky for him nobody died in that fire."

Wally's face reddened. His lips shaped a number of words before he finally spoke. "But, Inspector." He put his own feet beside the footprints and took a step down the hill. "Nish has got . . . Nish has got. . . ." Wally found this hard to say. "Nish has got long legs," he finally blurted. "Longer than me even. He's taller than me. These footprints. They're so close together. Watch." He took a step that easily covered two of the paces showing in the frozen ground. "Whoever made these prints must have, well, *really short legs!*"

By now, Wally's face was far redder than a cold winter's day could make it.

"Wally," Torrey was being very patient. "Trust me. I'll give you any odds you want, that it was Nish. Let's walk down to the barn, *slowly*, and I'll explain."

Why is Inspector Torrey Mazer so certain that the footprints have been made by the suspect, Tibor Nish?

25

A Very Brief
Non-Interview

THE OFFICE WAS ULTRA MODERN, a place of hums. A hum came through the air-conditioning grate above the door. A double bank of fluorescent lighting hummed in the ceiling. Over in one corner, a 386 AT desktop hummed in droning, flat counterpoint to the spectacular, silent flowerbursts that looped in random delight on the screen.

Sheila Lacroix stood quietly in the midst of the hums. She could hear them, but paid no attention. There were too many other things to take in. The desk, just a few steps in front of her, was bulky, silent, imposing, and impeccably neat. Bookshelves on the wall to her left were filled with leatherbound volumes standing in silent, parade-ground readiness against the time when a user might have need of them. Below the shelves, a selection of newspapers was arranged carefully across a table. Sheila made a quick estimate; there were twenty different issues at least.

Across from her, and beyond the desk, the wall was glass from floor to ceiling, the panes set in almost invisibly narrow frames. She might have been on the 22nd floor of any office building in New York, London, Geneva, or Toronto. . . . Except for the newspapers. The New York and London *Times* were in the lineup all right, and out of the corner of her eye Sheila could see *Zeitung* on one of the mastheads. But the majority of the headlines were in Arabic. The view through the window told her where she was, too. Without moving her head, Sheila could count five of the mosques in central Amman.

But most especially, what told her—what would tell anyone— she was not in a western country was the very tall man bending over a tiny table near the remaining wall. He was turned away from Sheila, and except for the hand resting on the back of his hip, an incredibly long index finger pointing at the windows, she could not see any part of him as he was entirely covered by his pristine white, flowing *thobe,* and over that a shorter *aba* in desert brown. The tall man, whose other hand was furiously signing documents, was Ibrahim Jamaa, leader of the Brotherhood of the Eternal Light of Allah. It was he whom Sheila Lacroix had come to see.

"Now don't stare at him, whatever you do!" Sheila could re- member every one of the attaché's instructions clearly. "As a matter of fact, don't make eye contact at all, or for more than a second or two. He knows you're western so he'll forgive you a glance, but . . . ," he shrugged, "you're a woman. Hey, I don't make the rules! This is Jordan, not Saskatchewan."

It had struck Sheila at the time that the attaché was exception- ally world-weary for one so young. "I have no idea how you did this," the young man had said, shaking his head. "No one—like, literally *nobody*—from any of the embassies has ever seen this guy close up; his organization is fanatical about secrecy—probably about a few other things, too! We've tried to get in here for months with no success, and here he gives you an appointment just like that!" He lifted his hand to snap his fingers for emphasis but then decided such behavior would be undiplomatic.

Sheila wanted to point out quite firmly that a year of traveling and beating on doors and shouting and bribing and threatening was hardly "just like that." Fourteen months ago, her husband had been kidnapped, presumably for political reasons, somewhere in Haseke province in Syria, where the border meets Iraq and

Turkey. Bill Lacroix was a doctor working there with Kurdish refugees. From the time of his disappearance until now, not a single one of the Middle Eastern groups known to use kidnapping for political purposes would acknowledge they held him.

Sheila had let the Canadian Department of External Affairs prove itself useless before striking out on her own. Since then, although she was only vaguely aware of it, she was probably the only western non-diplomat and non-journalist to speak personally to the leadership of Black September, Hamas, the PLO, even the PPK. All of them had denied any knowledge of Bill Lacroix. Now Sheila was about to score the most significant coup of all, in the eyes of the diplomats anyway; she was about to speak directly to Ibrahim Jamaa of the Eternal Light of Allah.

"Don't speak first under any circumstances." The attaché had been full of advice. "You let him initiate the conversation. Somehow you've got to make it seem like you're answering *his* questions rather than the other way around."

"And . . . and . . ." The flow stopped suddenly. ". . . Uh . . . there's one more thing, Mrs. Lacroix, if you would?" For a few seconds, the attaché's diplomatic mask came off. "We . . . we know nothing about this Ibrahim Jamaa. We're not even absolutely sure what he looks like. One thing we know is that he's very tall. Unusually so, like, really basketball-tall! He wears a patch over his right eye; we know that. Speaks perfect English, Italian and German, too."

"So I'm supposed to bring you his birth certificate and his wedding album?" Sheila had long ago lost patience with External Affairs.

"No, no, no!" The attaché reddened. "You see—and I'm being very frank with you here—what we have about him comes from the CIA and Mossad." He looked over Sheila's shoulder. "We really don't have a lot of faith in them anymore. So if there's anything that you see that is, well, *interesting*, we would like to know. Please?"

Sheila had taken one step into the elevator when he rushed to her and pulled her back gently. "One more thing we know. I don't really believe it would have anything to do with the whereabouts of Dr. Lacroix, but . . . Jamaa professes to be *mujtahid*. Means he's sort of a freethinker, especially about religion. Now the Shiites generally go along with that, but the Sunnis don't, and since Jordan is about eighty percent Sunni, that could make him a bit unwelcome here."

Standing in the office only a few minutes later, while Ibrahim Jamaa continued to write, helped Sheila understand all too well what it felt like to be unwelcome. However, when the man finally turned to face her, she forgot the feeling altogether. It was replaced by a sense of overwhelming menace that she knew would stay with her for a long time.

He was tall, all right, possibly seven feet, but that could be, Sheila later reflected, because of his power, his presence. Ibrahim Jamaa would have been a tower of malevolence at only six feet. He turned to her in what seemed like slow motion. First the patch appeared. Black, set in deep creases on the cheekbone. It was so striking that the rest of his face, Sheila was convinced, followed with abnormal slowness.

Despite herself, she stared. First at the patch, then at the single dark eye that appraised her without a flicker of response. Only when he brought his fingertips together in front of his chest—the incredibly long index finger had a matching partner—in what was just barely a gesture of greeting, did Sheila take her eyes away.

Jamaa took a step, then another. It brought him to the edge of the desk.

"Mrs. Lacroix," he said. Then there was silence. Sheila was suddenly aware of the hums again. She dared to glance up at the face and then looked down. The single eye still revealed nothing.

"Mrs. Lacroix," he said again. The attaché was correct about the English. Not a trace of an accent.

Sheila watched a long index finger as it tapped, first the edge of the desk, then the shoulder cradle attached to the telephone. He appeared to be searching for the right words. The finger traced the slim, arching neck of a desk lamp. The man was clearly used to commanding long silences while others waited for him to speak.

"Your husband . . ."

Finally! The reason she was there! She was surprised the subject was broached so quickly.

". . . Your husband," he repeated. "The doctor. We have no interest in him. Our organization does not interfere with the work of medical relief. We seek only justice for true believers, the people who are thwarted in their search by the Zionist aggressors. I do not know where your husband is. The Brotherhood does not know where your husband is." Jamaa brought his fingertips together again in front of his chest and inclined his head ever so slightly. The interview—the *non*-interview—was over. He turned, slowly, and went back to the table where he had stood before.

Sheila had to pull her feet off the floor in order to turn and go out the door and across the hall to the elevators. She wasn't in the least surprised that the attaché got to his feet far more eagerly when the elevator doors opened than he had when they first met.

"What did you find out? What's he like?" He pressed in most undiplomatic style.

Sheila shook her head. "Nothing you'd be interested in. But it's a step ahead for me. The Brotherhood of the Eternal Light of Allah knows about my husband. They must."

"What makes you say that?" The young attaché was subdued, but curious.

"Because that was not Ibrahim Jamaa. Or if it was—which I doubt—that was not his office."

What has led Sheila Lacroix to this conclusion?

26

Murder at 12 Carnavon

HONEY SPEHR WAS UPSET. And whenever she became upset, the color would rise in her face. It would start beneath the formal collars she always wore in court, and then flush up her neck until her cheeks fairly beamed with a crimson hue. Right now she could feel them burning.

"Mrs. Spehr?" Judge Ellesmere was speaking to her. "Mrs. Spehr? Do you wish to cross-examine?"

"Your Honor." Honey cleared her throat and willed her cheeks to dim.

The judge spoke again, "Would you like a few minutes first, Mrs. Spehr?"

"Thank you, your Honor." Honey was relieved. Now at least she didn't have to *ask* for a recess. "That would be helpful. Unless my friend here objects."

She forced herself to look at Gilbey Barnett's attorney, for she knew that Todd Roland could see her cheeks, too.

Gary Ellesmere peered over his half-glasses. "Mr. Roland has no objection, I'm sure. Do you, counselor?"

It wasn't a question. His Honor was rather unsubtly re-clarifying the pecking order. Todd Roland had been occupying center stage very successfully all day, and Ellesmere didn't care for the performance. Still, because Roland knew he was winning, the judge's arbitrariness didn't bother him in the least. Why would it? The jury had been nodding in unison with him all morning.

"Of course not, Your Honor. I'd be happy to let Mrs. Spehr have as much time as she needs to . . . ah . . . as she needs."

"Very well." The judge jumped to his feet, causing all the court officers to scramble to theirs. "Fifteen minutes," he pronounced over his shoulder as he headed for his chambers.

From where she sat at the prosecuting attorney's table, Honey's law clerk, Marion Kent, wondered whether the real reason for the judge's unaccustomed sensitivity was that he had to go to the bathroom. She didn't have a chance to comment, however, for no sooner did she and Honey get to their own ready room when Honey let go.

"He's lying, that slime, and he's getting away with it! He killed that woman! I know it. You know it. Anybody who bothers to think knows it. But he and Roland have got that jury thinking he's Francis of Assisi!"

She began to pace, tapping the index and third fingers of one hand into the palm of the other with each step. The effect was calming.

"Somehow I've got to make that jury realize that Gilbey Barnett may be smooth all right, but underneath the enamel is a liar! The thing is . . ." Honey's voice grew quieter, more deliberate. The rosy color was gone altogether now. ". . . The thing is . . . *how?* We'll never swing that jury back to rational thinking now. Not with what we've got to offer!"

Marion wished Honey wouldn't use the first person plural. Like the jury, she had been quite impressed with Barnett's defense; she wasn't at all as convinced as Honey of the man's guilt. But then—she had often admitted this to herself—no one had Honey's, "nose for phonies." Was Gilbey Barnett a phony? Was he lying? Did he kill his wife? If anybody was ever going to find out, it would be Honey Spehr.

Her case had begun with a building superintendent whose testimony showed that Barnett kept a mistress. Then there was the late Mrs. Barnett's sister, who described the fighting between her brother-in-law and his wife. This was reluctantly corroborated by a member of the Barnetts' cleaning service.

Mrs. Barnett had been shot in the back of the head at close range with a .22 caliber pistol. No weapon had ever been found, but a smug little clerk from Records and Registrations had stood in the box long enough to hold up a registration card for a Smith and Wesson of that caliber. The name on the card was W. Gilbey Barnett.

A combination of testimonies from a forensic pathologist and a neighbor, who had seen Mrs. Barnett pick up the morning paper on the porch, established the time of death at between 10:20 A.M. and 11:40 A.M.

Honey's ace was Constable First Class Jeff Baldwin. She had called him last. ("Responded to a dispatch at 11:44 A.M.; a shooting at the rear of 12 Carnavon Boulevard.") Baldwin's notes were always impeccably precise. He had entered the sunporch at 12 Carnavon to find "the defendant standing over the deceased."

Despite the fact that no weapon was found, the smoking-gun impression that Baldwin left with the jury was very powerful. It was Honey's intent to show in final summation that the time frames, no matter what Barnett's alibis, were such that given all the other evidence, Gilbey Barnett was a guilty man.

Todd Roland, however, had a few surprises and they were very effective. To begin with he didn't cross-examine a single prosecution witness. A very chancy strategy, but if it works, one that creates the impression that these witnesses and their testimony are not really very important. It can also make the prosecution case seem short. Roland's second surprise was to call Barnett first, not last, as everyone expected, and his third was to ask Judge Ellesmere to clear the courtroom of all the subsequent witnesses. By then Honey knew what he was going to do but was powerless to stop it. Any objection would have strengthened his ploy.

Roland's strategy was to draw out Gilbey Barnett's own account first, replete with detail upon detail, then corroborate it piece by piece, bit by bit, inexorably, with a parade of witnesses, until it became concrete in the collective psyche of the jurors that the defendant simply had to be telling the truth.

Barnett acknowledged that, yes, he had a mistress and that, yes, his marriage had been in difficulty ("You see, I suspected my late wife of being a drug user and we argued a lot about that.")

Honey had leapt in with an objection because there was absolutely no proof of that, and Ellesmere sustained but it was too late. The idea was already planted in the jury. Roland managed to slip it in again as a reason for having a license for a gun ("I was sure she'd been consorting with some very shady people: drug people and that like").

On the day of the murder, Barnett testified, he left for his office at 7:40 A.M. and left there in turn at 9:20 A.M. to have some breakfast at First Came the Egg ("You understand, she just wouldn't make breakfast anymore, so to avoid conflict I simply ate out"). He left the restaurant at precisely 10:30 A.M. ("How do I know that, Mr. Roland? Well, the waitress—poor thing, I felt so sorry for her—she was so busy that she tripped right by my table and spilled ketchup on me!") As he said that he turned and held his left leg out of the witness box as though to show the jury the stain was still there. That was when Honey's color began to rise fast for the jurors turned as one to look at the pant leg. *And they were nodding!*

Barnett finally got around to explaining his precise 10:30 departure by saying that this particular waitress had left the restaurant at the same time he did, and she had told him she only worked the early morning shift and was now going home to change clothes for her other job.

Then he went to Harry's Men's Shop for a final fitting on a suit. And that call was memorable because the tailor, who was normally so adept, stuck him with a pin ("right in the ketchup on my sock!").

After the fitting he left. ("I left at 11:10 A.M. How do I know? Oh, because I was late now. I wanted to go home to change clothes before my luncheon meeting and I looked at my watch. I had to get from Harry's to home and then to Le Coq d'Or by noon. It was going to be very tight.")

Barnett went on to testify he'd arrived at 12 Carnavon at about

11:40 ("I looked at my watch again at the top of the street") and that while going up the walk, he heard a shot at the back of the house. By the time he ran through the house, whoever had fired it was gone ("and I was just frozen there until Constable Baldwin found me just like he described").

The rest of Barnett's testimony went just like that: precise, unhesitating, completely forthcoming. Every time Roland backed him up to fill in a blank, the response came through as though it was scripted. Which in Honey's opinion, it was. She knew that by this time there was not a single juror who wasn't thinking dismissal. All they needed was some reinforcement to tip them into absolute certainty. And with the next witnesses, Roland gave them that in a flood of verifying details. That the main point was left essentially untreated—namely, that Roland had not shown at all that Barnett was elsewhere when the shot was fired—didn't matter. All the jury heard was how exact Barnett's testimony had been.

It began with the security guard at his office. ("Certainly I know Mr. Barnett. Everyone does. He's so generous to all of us especially at Christmas. He . . .")

"*Objection!*" Honey's objection had been so vigorous that it didn't even seem necessary for Ellesmere to sustain.

The guard went on to say that he signed Barnett in at 8:16 A.M. The secretary, who was up next, verified that he left at 9:20. ("No. Mr. Barnett didn't use to go out for breakfast, but for the past year he did all the time.") The waitress followed the secretary then, with testimony that Honey knew she'd never poke through. ("Oh, it was so embarrassing when I fell, but he's such a nice man . . .")

Ellesmere looked at Honey. His face said: "Go ahead. Object. I'm getting sick of this, too!" But Honey knew it would turn the jury away from her even further.

The waitress went on to say that Barnett left with her at 10:30 ("I always leave at 10:30. I have another job at Ruskin's department store. It's hard when you're raising two kids all on your own with no help. Anyway he . . .").

Roland shut her down quickly then and called the tailor. That's when Honey's hope sank altogether. The little tailor was right out of Central Casting! Short, bald, pudgy, the most benign face she had ever seen. The guy was a fairy godfather!

And he had an accent. No, not just an accent. A *cute* accent! ("I haf been thoaty yeeahs tailor. Harry's-a ma brother.) By now, Honey knew the jury was watching a movie. This was entertainment! That was when the color started to creep up her neck. The tailor pointed at Barnett. ("Yes. He's-a come . . . oh . . . ten-toaty, maybe ten-foaty.") Then he smiled. ("That's-a my suit! Foaty-two tall. You like . . . eh, Mistah Bahnett?") *Now the jury was laughing!* ("Dat morning. I'm-a rememba de ketchup. On da floor I kneel. Mesha da cuff, and-a there's-a ketchup on da sock.")

Wisely, Roland stopped him there. Although the jury was enjoying every minute, he could see that Judge Ellesmere's sense of humor had reached its limit. It wouldn't do to have the jury's mood blown away by a tirade.

Honey, on the other hand, was nearly apoplectic. That's when Ellesmere, instead of getting angry as well, called the recess. Now, in the ready room, Honey was trying to prepare herself to go back out. But to what? She knew that the jury was entirely in Barnett's camp. She knew that without doubt, in their room right now, they were regaling themselves trying to imitate the little tailor or clucking in sympathy with the waitress.

She knew that logic would not win them back. No matter how relentlessly she focused on the time frame and showed that Barnett *could* have made it from Harry's Men's Shop to his home in time to shoot his wife, nothing was going to penetrate the web of certainty that Roland had woven.

"The only way," she said to Marion, "the only possible way to make them listen to me is to break up that perfect story. I've got to show them they're being misled. The story's a layer cake; it's *manufactured.* If I can only show them one single contradiction then they'll listen, and we can go to work on the *real* evidence. Now we . . . Oh! Marion! I almost missed it!"

The color began to rise again in Honey Spehr's cheeks, but this time there was a glint in her eye.

Honey has found the contradiction, she thinks, the crack in the carefully crafted defense that she needs to return the jury to rationality. What is it?

27

The Case of Queen
Isabella's Gift

TWO MONOLOGUES WERE FIGHTING FOR attention in Geoff Dilley's brain. One was by Vicar Titteridge. He was talking about keys.

"Tourists would be entirely disappointed in these," he was saying as he took a pair of shiny brass keys from his pants pocket and inserted one into the padlock hanging from a hasp on the old church door.

"They much prefer this kind of thing, of course." He held up a worn leather thong in front of Geoff's face, dangling a huge, black iron key larger than his hand. "Interesting, what? Can't blame them, really, the tourists. A blacksmith made this quite some time before locksmiths and that sort of profession were ever heard of, you see."

Geoff wanted to point out that the Romans had padlocks, that the Chinese had used combination locks for centuries, and that in the Middle Ages locks were made that could count the number of times a key was inserted. But the vicar struck him as the type that was unaccustomed to contradiction.

"The key is almost two hundred years old, we think. Can't be proven, of course, but church records indicate the door here was replaced in the same year George IV became Prince Regent. You know, when his poor father went bonkers once and for all. At any rate, it's only logical to assume the key was made at the same time."

He rapped on the door firmly. "Solid oak this. From the New Forest. Very unusual that. Needed royal permission to cut the tree. Still, the door's a relative junior compared to the church itself: 1320 it was dedicated. Legend has it Edward II himself was here for the ceremony. Doesn't seem likely though, for it's sure that Queen Isabella was here. And you know about those two."

Geoff wanted to say that yes, he did know all about those two, but he didn't for the vicar had finally inserted the big key and turned it. The door opened easily and noiselessly, exposing the cool darkness inside. It occurred to Geoff that tourists would prefer some nice, authentic creaking, but he said nothing and waited in the doorway while the vicar stepped inside and turned on the lights.

"You'll have to come up to the altar," the vicar said. "The candelabra were up there."

"Candelabra" triggered the other monologue, the one Geoff Dilley had been trying to suppress. It came back again, though. Verbatim.

"*Candelabra!*" It was Chief Inspector Peddelley-Spens and he was shouting. "Bleedin' *candelabra?* We've got seven—count 'em, seven—homicide investigations going on at this precise moment. There's mad Irishman bombin' the country to bleedin' bits. I've got a bunch o' bleedin' fox-kissers chained t' the fence at Marlborough Hunt. The bleedin' prime minister o' bleedin' Portugal is comin' this afternoon. And *you!* You want to investigate the theft of a bleedin' pair o' candelabra?" Peddelley-Spens stopped to take in a huge breath. "I suppose that next you'll want the weekend off, too, so you can join hands with those frog-kissers that want a bleedin' tunnel under the bleedin' M5?"

Suddenly, the Chief Inspector had softened to half volume. "One!" he said. "You can make one call!" And then to normal volume altogether. "Look, Geoffrey. I know how much you like bleedin' old things. But you're a good investigator. I need you

here! Now you can trot off to—where is it?—St. Dunstan's-by-
the-Water? But I want you back today before tea. Somebody's got
to mind the crime rate while the rest of us are guardin' his Por-
tuguese worship!"

Geoff's love of "bleedin' old things"—he had long ago despaired
of instructing Peddelley-Spens in the use of "antiquarian"—made
him more than anxious to visit St. Dunstan's-by-the-Water. He
knew the ancient church but had never been in it. St. Dunstan's
was a tiny but most unusual structure. A chapel really, rather than
a church, but it was Norman and that made it special. Since it was
built in the early fourteenth century, when Gothic architecture
had wholly supplanted all other forms, St. Dunstan's lay claim to
being the last piece of Norman architecture built in England.

In the hour it had taken him to drive there, Geoff came to realize he would never be able to make Peddelly-Spens appreciate just
how valuable, how utterly priceless and irreplaceable the stolen
candelabra really were.

"A gift of Queen Isabella," the vicar had said on the telephone.
"You can still see her seal. Gold, of course. Each piece has some
quite lovely stones, too."

Geoff knew that if the candelabra were not found right away,
their fate would go one of two ways: they would either be fenced
to a collector or, more likely, the stones would be pried out and
the gold melted down. Either way, no one would ever see the
ancient pieces again.

"Watch your step." The vicar's monologue returned just a
shade too late to save Geoff from stumbling as they walked up the
short aisle. "Original floors, you know. Even stone wears after six-
and-a-half centuries."

Geoff had been following the vicar as slowly as possible so he
could look around. He wanted to spend time in this church. It
was Norman, all right. Thick walls, round arches, windows that
looked more like arrow slits.

"Right there. Above the altar. They stood on those two
pedestals."

Geoff stared at the altar.

"No, no. Higher. Up there." The vicar directed Geoffrey's gaze to a point well above the altar where two small stone platforms jutted out from the columns leading from the ends of the altar to the room.

"I assume . . ." the vicar was still talking. Other than introducing himself, Geoffrey had yet to say a word. "I assume he, or she—maybe even *they*. There were several dozen strangers here last night. Isn't it curious how we automatically believe it is males who commit crime? I assume the perpetrator, or perpetrators, attended Evensong last night and then hid in the church until it was empty. The candelabra were definitely here, for they were lit. Everyone saw them. They're only lit for Evensong. Too much of a bother, even with a step stool and extended candlelighters. And I assume that since we lock the main door on the outside as you saw, that he or she or they went out here."

The vicar led Geoff to a door behind the altar. "It's the only other way in or out," he said. "A concession to the twentieth century. Fire regulations and all that, you see."

He leaned against the crash bar, covering the little red-and-silver sign that said "Emergency Exit Only" with his bottom, and opened the door. Geoff followed him outside and turned to watch the door close and lock automatically.

"When I'm alone, I normally enter this way." The vicar produced the pair of brass keys again and opened the door. "Less fuss. Did so this morning."

Geoff followed the vicar back inside.

"Really don't know what made me look up. At any rate they were gone, and straight away I rushed back out and telephoned you."

For the first time, Geoffrey opened his mouth and was actually going to speak, but the vicar anticipated his question and beat him to it. "You're going to ask me about the verger, aren't you? Well, we don't have one at St. Dunstan's. Poor old Albert died over a year ago, and we never arranged for a replacement. This is only a chapel, really. A Sunday morning service and then Evensong, so there's no need. One of the parishioners comes every second Tuesday. I let her in and we clean together."

Geoff took a breath and got out "How . . ." before the vicar said, "There were between forty and fifty last night. About fifteen regulars. No, no. This way."

Geoff had turned to go out behind the altar.

"So we can turn the lights out and double lock the main door again. Pity we have to do that. House of God and all that, but then I certainly don't have to tell you about it. The crime rate, I mean."

The vicar paused to straighten a hymn book, and Geoffrey blurted, "No, Vicar. I know all about it." The voice of Peddelley-Spens rumbled like distant thunder in the back of his mind. "But it's even worse when a man of the cloth adds to it. The crime rate, I mean."

Why has Geoff Dilley concluded that Vicar Tetteridge has stolen the pair of candelabra?

28

Quite Possibly, the
Annual Meeting of the
Ambiguity Society

NORMALLY, BEING ASSIGNED TO COVER a yearly dinner for *The Citizen's* society page would be an out-and-out drag for any reporter, let alone one whose passion was investigative journalism. Being sent to the annual May dinner meeting of the Ambiguity Society, however, was a bit of a coup for Bonnie Livingston, so she didn't mind the traffic she had to fight on Derry Road, or the downpour that hit while she was pulled up at a gas station.

The members of the Ambiguity Society were an incredibly strange bunch. The principle aim of the group was clearly stated in the motto that adorned its letterhead.

"Prevaricate! Obfuscate! Flummox!"

That the letterhead contained neither telephone number nor address, was, of course, entirely to be expected.

Although the abiding tenet of an Ambiguity Society member's existence was to live life without ever responding directly or communicating clearly, as individuals they were harmless enough, and they were certainly amusing to the few outsiders who had ever heard of them. But their relationship with the press, whose self-appointed guardianship of the truth was as passionate as the society's love of deception, had become a competition. To reporters, the members' evasive and misleading responses to their questions were such an irresistible red flag that they were invariably willing to wade through the most enigmatic conundrums to find even the tiniest kernel of factual information.

Bonnie's excitement stirred, therefore, as she pulled into the parking lot of the Mono Cliffs Inn. When she got out of her car, she walked right into Bruno Steubens, the society's outgoing president.

Bruno nodded without smiling. "You found us again this year, Mrs. Livingston." It was not a question, simply a greeting.

"This will be the third consecutive annual meeting of the Ambiguity Society for me, Mr. Steubens. Quite a feat you have to admit. Now, since nobody from the media has ever covered four . . . ah . . . you wouldn't care to tell me the date of next year's meeting, would you? So my record can continue intact?"

She hastened to add, "I've always been fair in my coverage, haven't I?"

Bruno Steubens stroked his chin slowly and nodded ever so slightly. "That you have, I suppose. Been fair, I mean."

"So," Bonnie pressed a bit harder. "It's not unreasonable to ask for next year's date is it?"

Bruno continued nodding. "I guess not. I guess not. All right, well. It's going to be like this year, in the middle of the month."

"Oh really, Bruno. You can do better than that. She's really such a nice young person. For a reporter." It was Sally Steubens. Bonnie had not seen her get out of the car. "It'll be after the thirteenth, dear," she said to Bonnie. "After the thirteenth."

"Just a minute there!" The incoming president, Karen Di Creche, suddenly appeared from the other side of the parking lot along with her husband Julio. "Are you discussing next year's meeting? That's my territory now! Look, we'll tell you this much.

Next year's meeting will be on an odd-numbered date. Now does that help you?"

"Not only on an odd-numbered date," Julio contributed, "but on a date that is not a perfect square."

"I think you're going to confuse her with that, Julio." Karen turned to Bonnie and smiled indulgently. "He does that, you know. Sometimes he's just so misleading. Now, you'll have to excuse us. The executives can't be late for dinner, can we?"

With that, the four brushed past Bonnie toward the inn. She was writing furiously, concentrating so intensely that she was unaware of Sally Steubens until she whispered in her ear.

"Before the thirteenth, okay? It's all so ambiguous, dear, isn't it? You know none of us is supposed to tell you the exact truth, but I just did, so now you should have the answer." With that, Sally hurried after the others.

When will the next annual meeting be held?

29

The Case of the Missing Body

FOR SOME REASON, EVEN BEFORE she picked up the telephone, Lesley Simpson knew she wasn't going to like this call. Then when the smarmy voice of Eddy Duane greeted her, she knew her instincts had been right on. Eddy Duane was a lawyer in the crown attorney's office. He was not on Lesley Simpson's list of favorite people.

"Hey Les! How are ya?" "Les" would have spoiled the day in any case. Lesley hated being called "Les." Her name was "Lesley," spelled with an E-Y. "The British way," her mother had explained.

"Better brace yourself, Les! We're finally gonna charge your favorite client with murder." That got Lesley's attention. "You see, Les, old kid, we found his wife's body. Well, her skeleton really. It's the late Mrs. Vincent Gene, all right. Absolutely no question. We'll need the dental records to confirm it, but there's no doubt it's her. The ring on the finger, the one earring, the clothes, the shoes. And you know where she was found? Right in the backyard! Your boy's not too bright, Les! Burying his wife in the backyard!"

Suddenly Eddy Duane's voice became more serious. "Look, Lesley," he said. "I'll meet you in, say, an hour or so out at Vincent Gene's house. Cops are there now. The coroner, too. We've agreed to leave everything till you get to see it. One hour. Okay?"

With that, Eddy Duane hung up. Lesley realized she hadn't said a single thing on the telephone other than answering with her own name. Still, conversation wasn't necessary. Not in this case. It was three years old, but Lesley knew every detail as though it had started only yesterday.

Three years ago, the wife of gentleman-farmer Vincent Gene had left her husband sitting at the breakfast table of their expensively renovated Caledon farmhouse and was never seen again. That there had been foul play was pretty certain. Her car was found only minutes away from the house on a barely passable, unmaintained sideroad. It was full of blood—the type matched hers; the front seat had been sliced, presumably with a knife; and a single earring was found on the floor of the passenger side. But her body, if indeed she was dead, had never been found.

Vincent Gene, the husband, was Lesley Simpson's longtime client, and although he insisted he was innocent, the police had focused on him from the beginning. Only the lack of a body, Lesley knew, kept them from laying a murder charge. Now, it seemed, the last hurdle may have been cleared.

It took Lesley only forty minutes to get to Vincent Gene's farm. She noted with relief that Eddy Duane wasn't there yet. Lots of activity though—several police cars, an ambulance, a growing knot of neighbors gathering around the forsythia bushes at the end of the laneway. Near the back of the property, standing beside a backhoe, Lesley recognized Sergeant Rodney Palmer. The recognition was mutual.

"Ah, Ms. Simpson. We've been expecting you," the sergeant said as Lesley approached. Rodney Palmer was as polite as Eddy Duane was pushy. "Over here, if you want to take a look." He took Lesley over to a narrow trench that began where the bucket of the backhoe rested on the ground and ran to a small barn some distance away. Two policemen in coveralls were standing in the trench, their heads just below the top edge.

"It's supposed to be for a water line running to the barn," Palmer said. "They've been digging here four or five days." He nodded at the backhoe. "Operator found the body—uh, the *skeleton*, rather—first thing this morning. Well, actually, he turned up a shoe first; then when he saw a bone, he stopped and called us. We've almost finished uncovering the whole skeleton now. Wasn't that difficult 'cause the clothes are still in good shape. You want to see?"

Lesley took a deep breath. Then another one. "Yes," she replied.

Rodney Palmer took a few steps and pointed down into the trench without speaking. When Lesley followed and looked down, she knew the sight would stay with her forever. Whatever she had expected, it certainly wasn't color, yet that's what she noticed most of all. Color. The green grass at the top of the trench. Trampled but still green. Then the neat, precise layer of dark brown top soil. And under that, almost as if someone had drawn a line, a band of yellow. Sand, Lesley figured. Then below that, right to the bottom, blue clay. Maybe it was the blue, she thought that made the clothing on the skeleton look so, well, so elegantly crimson, dirty as it was.

"See the one earring inside the skull, Les?" The sudden intrusion of Eddy Duane almost made Lesley stumble into the trench. "Quite a sight, huh? One your client never expected to see again, I'll bet. And you know what, it almost worked, too. You see the trench? It was supposed to go over there." He pointed to a spot several yards away. "But there's too much rock, so without even asking, the backhoe guy dug this way and *voilà!* The late Mrs. Vincent Gene. Right in her own backyard!"

Lesley Simpson looked straight at Eddy Duane. "Mrs. Gene," she said, "if indeed that is Mrs. Gene, was not buried here. Not when she died anyway." She shifted her gaze to Sergeant Rodney Palmer. "My guess is that if you can find out who dumped the skeleton into this trench last night and covered it up, you'll have the person who did the killing, too."

How does Lesley Simpson know that the skeleton was dumped into the trench last night?

30

The Case of the
Marigold Trophy

JANICE SANT BIT INTO A fresh wedge of orange and concluded that at least one of her five senses was working normally. The other four had slid into that never-never land the body finds when it has been doing the same thing in the same place for too long.

Since five o'clock, when the Palgrave Community Library opened for its Tuesday hours, Janice had been sitting in front of a microfilm viewer, slowly winding her way through back issues of *The Daily Enterprise.* Her sense of touch had long since disappeared into the hard wooden chair on which she sat. Only her right hand, which slowly cranked the microfilm across the screen, gave assurance that she could feel anything. She knew her eyes were still working for they continued to refocus after each movement of the old-fashioned type. But whether the focusing was a conscious act or simply a reflex after hours at the screen, she couldn't be sure.

Before she could assess the two remaining senses, Eugene Weller's cologne told her that at least one of them was still working.

"I'll be closing in about five minutes, Miss Sant." The gentle, elderly librarian beamed down at her. "It's actually five past nine already."

Janice looked over the viewer at the portly little man. He was compulsively arranging the little boxes of microfilm into three separate piles: 1903, 1904, and 1905.

"How have you done?" He walked around the table and put his face very close to the screen. The cologne was even stronger now. Janice knew he must be one of those types who dab it on all day long. "Goodness!" He straightened slightly, leaving a wave of scent behind. "March 3 already! You've done quite well, haven't you? Still think you should have taken a break though. Young people like you shouldn't skip meals." He walked around to the other side of the table again and tapped one of the piles of little boxes to make it absolutely symmetrical. "Just turn off the switch when we close. I'll put things away tomorrow. Sorry again about the missing October. No one knows why that month was never filmed. Don't forget now," he said as he walked away. "Five minutes."

Janice sighed and then sighed again when she tried unsuccessfully to wind the film along, for her hand had gone to sleep. What made her weariness and discomfort even worse was that this job was a freebie. Normally, she charged between $50 and $75 an hour plus expenses for an investigation, but this job she had volunteered for. On the surface it had seemed very simple. Ownership of the Palgrave Horticultural Society's proudest and by far most valuable—and most beautiful—possession was being challenged. It was a trophy, a marigold, about the size of a teacup, set in a cluster of natural Baffin Island graphite on a base of local black walnut. The flower itself was twenty-four carat solid gold. On a rectangular plate set into the walnut were etched the words:

M. TOOCH
Grand Champion Marigolds
Albion Agricultural Exhibition
10 July 1904

When Miss Maribeth Tooch died in 1960, well into her nineties, her will had bequeathed this most unusual trophy—work of art, really—to the society. Unfortunately, it was tainted with an unresolved controversy. Maribeth's twin sister, Maribel, until her death in 1959, had steadfastly claimed that she had been the rightful winner and not the runner-up as the records indicated, because Maribeth had broken the rules.

Undaunted, since 1960 the Palgrave Horticultural Society had proudly displayed the Tooch trophy until two weeks ago, when its ownership was challenged in court by Rachel Tooch-Rothman, a grand-niece of Maribel, and her late husband, Denison. Janice's task, if it could be done, was to find out the truth once and for all.

So far, from *The Daily Enterprise*, she had learned that Maribeth had indeed been awarded the grand championship with Maribel coming second and that this most valuable and unusual trophy was a one-time gift of an anonymous benefactor. She had also learned that there were indeed rules for the marigold contest: requirements governing the type of seed that could be used (Stratus or Givern); specifications regarding exactly when the seeds could be sown (on February 23); instructions that the flowers had to be cut on the day before the Exhibition (on July 9); and a rule that winners were ineligible the following year. Janice had also discovered that she could wind her way through about five months of newspaper every hour, and although she had worked through the issues of *The Daily Enterprise* carefully and in sequence, she had still not found anything to help her clear up the controversy itself.

Not until Eugene Weller and his cologne had intruded to tell her it was closing time. That had woken her up, and later, she acknowledged she'd have missed it otherwise. Really, there had been no logical reason to pay attention to the story on the screen at the time. The headline was at best curious, and the story itself similar to the stuff she had been skimming over with steadily decreasing attention as time wore on.

TWO TIME RUNAWAY

For the second time in only a very brief period, a horse owned by Mr. Curragh O'Malley has run away and injured a citizen. In yesterday afternoon's incident, the horse made contact with Mr. Ezra Templeton of Gibson Street while he was standing in his front-yard. Mr. Templeton has suffered a broken arm. Mr. O'Malley explained that the horse was tethered in front of the Dominion Hotel while he was conducting business inside, and it was frightened by some young boys playing hoop-and-stick. On the same day a week earlier, this horse broke its tether at the same hitching rack and struck down Miss Maribeth Tooch of Pine Street. Coincidence being what it is, Miss Tooch had only just stepped outside her solarium for a few seconds of fresh air after seeding marigolds for the annual exhibition in July. It was at this precise instant that the horse ran onto her property. Miss Tooch suffered bruises but no broken bones.

Her friends and acquaintances, and those of Mr. Templeton, will be pleased to know that both of these fine citizens are recovering nicely. Nevertheless *The Enterprise* believes that tethering by-laws in Palgrave must be more rigorously enforced if innocent people are to enjoy the simple privilege of standing in their own yards.

"I'm turning the lights out, Miss Sant. Oh, Miss Sant, I'm going to turn . . . Why Miss Sant! You look very upset! What's the matter?"

Eugene Weller rushed over to her in a cloud of concern and freshly applied cologne.

"Our beautiful trophy," Janice said. "We could lose it!"

Why does Janice Sant think the Palgrave Horticultural Society could lose its most prized possession?

31

The Coffee Break
That Wasn't

"RECEIVING AND DISPOSAL LOOK ALL right," Di Froggart said as she came back from what had started out as a simple trip to the washroom. "As a matter of fact, not bad at all for a place like this, since they've got to share space with the deli next door." Having once been a health inspector, Di couldn't resist an opportunity to check things out. "Bit messy at the loading door," she went on, "but nothing that would warrant a charge. Normal really, for a Friday morning."

As she sat down, her knee bumped the single leg in the center of the table causing Lennie Strachan's cup of coffee to sway danger-ously in its bright white plastic cup. Quickly Lennie put her spoon in the steaming brew to stop the swirling and without looking up said, "Don't apologize. I bumped it twice when you were out. There must be a special annex in hell for people who design fur-niture like this." She lay the spoon on the table and grinned at Di.

"Just try to sit up straight and be comfortable for more than three seconds. The seats are even worse!"

Lennie and Di were sitting—or at least were attempting to sit—in a small restaurant at the end of a shopping mall. The little restaurant was ultra modern. It's very name suggested what was expected of the clientele: *Eat 'n' Run* it was called. The place was exceptionally bright, almost painful to the eyes with its intense fluorescent glow, and in an antiseptic kind of way, it appeared to be squeaky clean.

To anyone who ate but failed to run immediately, it was soon obvious that the designer of the restaurant did not intend that customers should relax here. The tables were a study in flimsy molded plastic; so were the chairs. But it was their color that mounted the final assault: bright mauve with even brighter orange trim. As a result, most of the customers at *Eat 'n' Run* did exactly that, many of them without even realizing why. Except for, on this particular morning, Lennie Strachan and Di Froggart.

Di took a deep breath and sighed. "Well, it sure isn't Lum's Café, is it?"

Lennie nodded. Di was referring to a comfy old diner, now long gone, that had stood on the site of this same shopping mall. The two friends had met regularly at Lum's Café years before. They had both been inspectors then with the city's Department of Health. Now retired, they got together once in a while for coffee and a chat. But there was something about getting together like this that always turned them back into inspectors again. Somehow they couldn't help it.

"Y'know, these things," Lennie said, changing the subject as she held up a tiny plastic container with the cream sealed inside, "imagine how much easier our job would have been if these had been around?"

Di smiled. "Yeah, if we had a free cup of coffee for every jug of cream we poked our noses into, we'd go into permanent caffeine surge!"

"Yes," Lennie replied, "but in one way these things have a serious drawback. Look at this." With her index finger she pushed four of the little containers one after the other. "Both of us drink it black, yet the waitress gave us two each. Had them in the pocket of her apron. I wonder how many of these get thrown out. Years ago it was hygiene. Now it's pollution."

Lennie kept on talking, but Di Froggart wasn't listening. She was staring at Lennie's left hand as it came up to the edge of the cup of coffee. Clamped between her thumb and index finger was a fly. A *plastic* housefly!

Di was flabbergasted. "Have you still got some of those things?" Her tone indicated she didn't need an answer.

"Three more boxes at home." Lennie said without changing expression, and dumped the little black offender into her cup of coffee. It disappeared and then surfaced immediately, floating passively on top. "Never know when they'll come in handy. Ever want to get your grandchildren to leave the table? Oh Miss!" Lennie called the waitress. "Miss!"

The waitress appeared immediately.

"Miss. Look at this!" Lennie's indignation was quiet but unmistakable.

The waitress peered a little closer, saw the fly, then without a word took Lennie's cup away and disappeared with it behind the counter. She came right back and set the cup down in front of Lennie, mumbling, "Sorry," and then dug two more cream containers out of her apron pocket. "I'll tell the manager," she said.

"Yours okay?" the waitress said to Di.

Di just nodded her head. She was intent on Lennie's next move.

The waitress set down another two cream containers, this time in front of Di, and then moved away to another table.

"Well," Di said, "are you going to finish the test or not?"

Lennie's nostrils flared in mock indignation. "Watch me!" With a serviette she wiped the tip of her little finger and then touched the surface of the coffee twice. She licked the finger and looked at Di.

"I'll be darned," Lennie said.

Di leaned forward. "You mean you caught them?" she said.

This time Lennie Strachan's indignation was real. "Bet on it!" she replied.

What offence has Lennie detected at the Eat 'n' Run and how has she done it?"

32

Who Shot the Clerk at Honest Orville's?

MARY CREMER LEANED BACK OUT of the doorway at 26 Division to see who had called her name.

"Here! Mary! Over here!"

This time Mary recognized the voice of her sister Caroline, but in the busy pre-Christmas bustle on the sidewalk, it took a few more seconds to locate her.

"All *right!*" Mary's enthusiasm when she finally saw her was genuine. "What are *you* doing here?"

Caroline pointed to the 26 Division lobby and gave a smile of chagrin. "Kee Park," she said.

"*What!*" Mary blurted, loud enough for a few passersby to pause in the crush and stare at the two young women.

"That . . . that . . . *jerk!* He's done it again! What is it that makes him think we're a package just because we're sisters?"

Caroline shrugged her shoulders. She tended to be just a bit calmer than Mary.

"It's just Baxter," she said. "I don't think he can help himself. Don't sweat about it. You've only got a few more weeks. Besides, this one's really interesting! Kee Park, I mean."

"I suppose," Mary replied. At least . . . *Omigosh!*"

Both young women had forgotten they were blocking the doorway of the busiest police station in the downtown area, until two burly plainclothes types rapped on the inside of the glass simultaneously.

"Sorry," Mary said. She opened the door and slipped in quickly. Caroline came right after her.

"At least," she went back to her point, "it isn't support payments for a change, or crummy break-and-enter again."

"No!" Caroline was definitely excited. "Kee Park could be really big. They charged him this morning. Murder. I . . ."

"He's *charged?*" Mary grabbed her sister's coat sleeve. "I thought . . ."

"That's why I'm here." Caroline said. "Baxter got a call from Detective . . . Detective . . . let's see." She fished a piece of paper out of her coat pocket. "Blanchard! Yes, Blanchard. Didn't we deal with him once before? Kind of cute."

"*Charged?*" Mary was still absorbing the fact that her—*their* client had been charged with murder.

She and Caroline were law students completing their one year of practicum before being admitted to the bar. Mary's time was to end in a month. Caroline was only midway through. Their firm, Baxter, Baxter, Quisling, Keele, and Wilson—only one, the second Baxter, was still alive—regularly took on a small number of legal-aid cases, all of which were with equal regularity turned over to students. "Freebies," the surviving Baxter called them, although both Mary and Caroline had been shocked when they saw the number of hours the firm billed the government for services.

Most of the cases were single parents chasing delinquent support payments or juveniles on break-and-enter charges or shoplifting. The case of Kee Park was different. Dramatically so. He had been picked up last night at a shooting in front of Honest Orville's, the biggest discount emporium in the city, perhaps even the whole country.

At first, Park was held as a material witness only, then on suspicion of manslaughter. That's when Mary came onto the case.

Now things had spun ahead by one more step during the time she traveled to the police station.

She pulled Caroline over to a bench in the lobby. "You had better fill me in."

Caroline opened her coat as she sat down. "Things have moved pretty fast in the past couple of hours." She stood up with a look of discomfort on her face and took her coat off. "I thought the city was supposed to be on a tight budget. They could save some money on the heating bill in this place. Anyway. You know all about Park claiming he was out on the sidewalk, just standing there when it happened." Caroline stopped to take off her scarf and paused to concentrate on a recalcitrant knot.

"For heaven's sake, what's the rest of it?" Mary insisted.

"Okay. Sorry. And he claims he didn't even know there was a robbery going on until these two guys burst out the door, chased by the clerk."

"Dumb." Mary shook her head. "The clerk I mean. What did the guy think? Chasing two people with a gun!"

"Yeah, but dumb or smart, he's dead," Caroline replied. "And our client is charged with his murder, and it doesn't look good."

Now Mary stood up and took off her coat. "You're right about the heat. But then, right now I guess it's got to be a lot hotter for Kee Park." She pursed her lips. "I just can't buy the murder charge. There's too much circumstantial stuff."

She sat down again. "Let's review what we've got. Two guys rob Honest Orville's about 8:30 P.M."

"8:40," Caroline inserted. "There's a time fix from the patrolman across the street."

"The witness?" Mary asked. She held up her hand. "Don't answer. It had to be him. Right?"

Caroline nodded. "Confirmed, too. He was calling in at the time."

Mary continued. "And the two guys—the robbers—run out onto the street, presumably to get lost in the Christmas shopping crowds. They're chased by the clerk. When he gets to the doorway, he gets shot."

"Not quite," Caroline said. "The patrolman had modified that a bit in his report. The shooting took place well out on the sidewalk. Under that great big huge sign. You know, the one with the fifty thousand bulbs or something like that."

Mary shook her head reflectively. "Okay. On the sidewalk, then." She paused again. "Then one of the two gets away, probably with the gun because no gun is found. That hasn't changed, too, has it?"

"No. Still no gun."

"Well, that's got to help our guy, doesn't it? So at this point our patrolman's partner comes out of the doughnut shop, and the two of them stop all the traffic and run across the street and arrest Kee Park and one other guy. The other guy's Asian, too, right?"

"Yes," Mary replied. "But Kee Park's Korean. The other one is Chinese. Name's Sung something. I've got the full name in here." She tapped her briefcase.

Mary frowned. "I still don't see how they can come up with a murder charge if they don't have the gun."

"Agreed," Caroline said. "They've vacuumed out the catch basins and gone over the sewers and picked through every garbage can for blocks and there's definitely no gun, but here's what you don't know. This morning the other guy, Sung . . . whatever, after holding out all night, confessed to the robbery *and* fingered Kee Park as his partner and the trigger man. His story is that he didn't even know Kee Park had a gun."

Mary got to her feet. "And our guy's story is that he was just standing there on the sidewalk when two guys—he said they were Chinese, didn't he?—burst out of the store. One of them shoots the clerk and walks away. *Walks!* Into the crowd. The next thing he knows is he's been collared and taken here to 26."

"And now," Caroline added, "charged with murder."

Mary began to pace. "I can't believe there isn't another witness. Only that patrolman."

"In that part of town?" Caroline raised one eyebrow. "You know what it's like down there. Hear no evil, see no evil." She grinned. "Speak it though. And for sure, *do* it!"

"So what does Baxter want us to do?" Mary asked, as much to herself as to her sister.

Caroline reached for her briefcase and stood up. "He's confident that getting the murder charge reduced as a first step will be pretty easy. Everything's so messy. No gun for instance. But what he wants us to do is to slow things down until we can get more time to assess what really happened. Also, to see if we can find any holes that will either reduce the charge further or maybe even blow it away. He said that once Kee Park is charged, then it becomes a case of our having to *dis*prove. It's easier if the burden of proof is on the other side."

"So we have to find reasonable doubt," Mary said.

"And the faster the better," Caroline replied.

Of the several elements in the case that Mary and Caroline can present to make "reasonable doubt," there is one that stands out just a bit. What is that one?

33

Speed Checked by Radar

"WHO'S THAT?" FRAN SINGLETON POINTED at a young man who had come out a side door and was now walking at a measured pace through the parkette toward a little annex building nearby. "And what's that building he's going to?"

"Dunno," Aaron Gold answered. "The guy, I mean. The building—it's for duplicating. Serves the whole complex here." He leaned closer to the steering wheel to get a better look at the young man without being too obvious. "No, I dunno," he repeated. "Could be what we're lookin' for. Maybe. Bit young though, don't you think? He's probably a grunt. Sure doesn't look like a terrorist, anyway. But then neither did that little old granny who carried in the bombs at Woodbridge, did she?"

"Grunt?" Fran thought she knew, but the young constable with her loved to use words that he knew she was unsure of. Aaron Gold did everything he could to make Fran think the generation gap was a chasm.

"Yeah, *grunt.* One of those career minimum-wage types. Room temperature IQ. Does all the donkey work. Nothing that takes any cells." He tapped his forehead. "Can't tell time at 9 A.M., but scorches the mat when it's 5 P.M. Lots of those types in there."

Fran watched the grunt—or terrorist—pause at the bottom of the steps to the windowless little building and look around, first to the left, then to the right. She saw the young man shift what appeared to be a bundle of file folders from under his right arm to under his left as he went up the steps. Then from a huge ring chained to his belt, he selected a key, and in a single motion, unlocked the door, opened it, and walked in. The grey metal slab closed automatically behind him.

"You see him look around like that?" Aaron Gold asked. "Before he went in?" When Fran didn't answer he kept on talking. "Could be checking things out. There's always duplicating to be done at this time of day, and they may have sent him out so things would seem normal. And so he could take a look, too." He paused. "Then on the other hand he could just be planning to sneak a smoke when he's in there and was just checking for supervisors. These are all non-smoking buildings now. That's hard on the grunts."

Fran didn't respond out loud; she just nodded. She was looking back at the main building again, looking for signs of anything unusual. If the building was under some kind of threat, there was nothing obvious. It was a small building by government standards, only two stories, easy to take in at a single glance. All of the windows had standard-issue vertical blinds and all of these were open, presumably to take advantage of the late afternoon sun. After a long, uncomfortable winter, this was the third day in a row of balmy spring weather.

Fran peered even harder. There was nothing unusual at all. A single fresh graffito made a cynical comment on the brass door plate that proclaimed the building to be the property of the Internal Revenue Service, Investigations Branch, but that certainly was not unusual. No, Fran could not see anything wrong at all. There was the expected amount of movement behind the blinds. Except, come to think of it, the corner offices on both floors. And the blinds on those two weren't as wide open as the others! Or was she overdoing it? Nothing says there *has* to be movement in every office, does it?

Ever since the bombing incident in Woodbridge last month, which had flattened still another IRS building, everybody was jumpy; the slightest suspicion was treated very seriously. Still, Fran thought, there is a limit.

"The thing is, the guy appeared normal enough, didn't he?" Aaron Gold was still speaking, and Fran realized she hadn't been paying attention. "But then they're not stupid; they're not gonna send somebody out to make things look cool and then have him draw attention to himself are they? Y'know, maybe we should . . ." *Beep beep beep beep beep beep beep . . .*

On the dash, the radar monitor lit up and started the incessant beeping that every officer hated with a passion. At the same time, it shut down Aaron Gold's continuing assessment of the subject's likely purpose and Fran Singleton's analysis of what was happening in the Revenue building.

"A live one! Good!" Fran began to talk fast in spite of herself. "Get out and pull him over," she instructed Aaron, "but just chew him out and then get him out of here! This has got to look normal, but no citations! I don't want you bogged down and I don't want any bodies between us and the building, so get rid of him as fast as you can."

Before she even finished, Aaron was on the street pointing a silver-gray Mercury Sable to the curb.

"Okay," Fran said, grabbing the transmitter, "if this is cover, then now we're covered."

She tapped the SEND button twice. From outside it would surely appear like a normal call-in. Possibly a check of the Mercury with a central computer.

But what she said was, "This is Command. This is Command. Stay put! Everybody stay in place! This is just a speeder. Everybody stay put."

Fran Singleton was speaking to eight heavily armed personnel in combat uniforms. They were deployed, well out of sight, around the IRS building but ready to move on her signal.

About thirty minutes ago she had been sneaking a listen to the four o'clock news, waiting for the sports and the Stanley Cup commentary—the Flyers played the first of two weekend games tonight—when Sergeant Horowycz had interrupted.

148

"IRS building again, Inspector Singleton," he'd said. In their precinct that needed no elaboration.

"No response on the 4 P.M. check. Phone company says the line's okay, but we can't raise their switchboard. Probably we're all spooked by Woodbridge, but I don't like it. Thought I should tell you."

Horowycz was experienced. He didn't panic. And because he didn't like it, Fran took only about ten seconds to decide that the Emergency Response (E.R.) team was needed. She simply couldn't afford to fool around. The building was a regular for bomb threats. At income-tax time they cleared the place at least every second day on average; that's why her precinct made a telephone check every hour on the hour. After the Woodbridge incident last month—two fatalities in that one—everybody was understandably on edge.

What she didn't want to do, however, was turn on the crazies, and that was her dilemma. She knew that if the E.R. team rushed the building for a false alarm, the media would have a field day and every nutcase in the city would get the idea. That's why she and Constable Gold had set up a radar speed trap out front— a perfectly logical and, she hoped, unobtrusive way to case the place first.

In the few minutes they'd been out front, neither Fran nor Aaron Gold had seen cause for suspicion, except maybe those two quiet offices on the corners. The only activity they'd seen was the young man going to the annex.

He came out now—burst out actually—pushing the door open with his bottom, both arms loaded with paper, and sprinted down the steps.

As he hustled back to the main building, Fran tried to convince herself that he wasn't really moving a lot faster than he had when going the other way. The young man looked out at Aaron who still had the driver of the Mercury at the curb. Although Fran studied him closely, she couldn't be sure whether the young man had a smile or a sneer on his face. In any case, the tableau of Constable Gold and the speeder didn't appear to warrant more than a glance before he disappeared back into the IRS building.

She reached for the transmitter. For a few seconds she held it in front of her, evaluating her choices. Then she popped the SEND button twice.

"Command here. This is Command."

She paused again, just a bit longer than usual.

"Stand down. Repeat. The order is to stand down. Everyone stay in place, but I want nobody, I repeat, *nobody* visible." She looked at her watch. It said 4:28. "In about two minutes I expect a bunch of people to leave the building. . . ."

Fran slumped a bit behind the steering wheel, then adjusted the radio transmitter before tapping the SEND button several times. "This is Inspector Singleton for Sergeant Horowycz. Leshie, it's . . ." She looked at her watch again. "It's 4:29. At 4:35 I'm going into the IRS building with Constable Gold. No one else. I'm 99 percent sure things are normal. Just a check. If I don't get back to you by 4:40, assume there's trouble and send in the E.R. team."

What has made Fran Singleton 99 percent sure that things are normal in the Internal Revenue Service building?

34

Where to Send "This Stuff Here"

BEFORE LUNCH ON HER VERY first day on the job, Sue Hageman realized why she was the third assistant to equipment manager Jurgen Nodl in as many months. By the end of the first week, she was not in the least surprised to learn that hers had also been the only application for the job. For the moment, however, how she got the job, or why, was not at issue.

What was at issue was that:

1. She was in the LAME Room (lost, abandoned, and misplaced equipment) of Meadowbanks Stadium in Edinburgh, Scotland.

2. She was standing in the midst of a pile of items which, except for a set of skis to go to Turin, were like Iago Cassini's photography bag and had nothing whatever to do with sports, especially football.

3. She had been handed a ratty brown envelope labeled: *Dipersal—Names & Addresses* by Nodl, who had apparently taken off for parts unknown.

4. He had told her to arrange for the immediate shipment of "this stuff here," to the "names and addresses in there."

151

"This stuff here," she was able to figure out, with the help of the equipment manager of the Glasgow Rangers, the only other person in the LAME Room when Nodl disappeared, was the personal belongings of the Veneto Thunderbolts. Well, not quite. "This stuff here" was only *certain* personal belongings of the Veneto Thunderbolts left over after Jurgen Nodl, in a rare fit of efficient performance, had trundled the rest of it, in fact all except these four open cartons, off to the shipping dock. The four cartons, each with items belonging to four different players from four different cities, had found their way into the LAME Room and into Sue Hageman's charge.

The Thunderbolts had celebrated long and hard last night after taking a week to win a soccer tournament (Sue was still having trouble getting used to calling it "football" here at Meadowbanks). Then except for Sue, Nodl, and one assistant coach, the players had run for the airport, leaving the team administration to send on their belongings and equipment.

"You just have to get it to the right airport." The manager of the Glasgow team was very helpful, in part, because he was one of the many former employees of the Thunderbolts and felt sorry for Sue. "It's the players' responsibility from that point. Half these fellows never go straight home anyway. Now you take those chess sets there." He half-waved at a carton Sue was straddling. "Belong to that fellow from Capri, I forget his name. Now, he won't go right home. Never does. I'll bet he'll be off to play for one of the South American teams. Season starts there real soon. They're all like that. Except maybe for the center-half from Milan. He and his wife got a business there."

He pointed to the brown envelope in Sue's left hand. "Jurgen's awfully unorthodox, but strangely enough he gets the job done. They say you just have to get used to his ways. I never could though. Not very many can. Still, I'm sure the four names and locations you need'll be in there."

After that, Sue dared to look in the envelope for the first time. There was nothing that even approached a manifest or an inventory or a list of names and addresses. Instead there were scraps and bits of paper. There were personal letters, one from Tino Savi declining Nodl's invitation to go skiing. Savi said that he did not ski, and that in any case, he and Giovanni Moro would be visiting in Naples at the time. Interestingly, there was an invoice for skis and ski boots; it was marked paid but the name had been torn off. Another invoice was addressed to Mrs. Gino Bellissime in Milan, but that was it. Just name and address. What was being invoiced was not included.

Sue sighed. This was not going to be easy, but at the very least, now she knew where to send the guitar.

Where and to whom will Sue Hageman send the guitar?

35

A Witness in the Park

AT THE BOTTOM OF A little knoll, Mary Blair paused and looked back at her footprints in the frosty grass. She was grateful she'd decided to wear flats at the last minute. With high heels she would never have been able to walk on the lawn like this for the ground was not yet frozen.

Mary turned a complete 360 degrees. There was no sign of Alicia Bell yet, but that didn't surprise her. It was still too early. She shaded her eyes against the sun as it rose over the top of the knoll, shortening its shadow and shortening hers, too.

Both the public park just to her left, surrounded by an imposing if somewhat ancient iron fence, and the unfenced section of lawn where she was standing had been landscaped years ago into a series of mounds or knolls. None of them were any higher than the average adult, but they gave the impression of rolling terrain, especially from far away. In the park itself, a series of gravel paths and beds of exotic flowers wound their way around the little knolls. Someone had once explained to Mary that the park had been landscaped this way in order to force people to walk through it slowly.

Indeed there was no other park like it in the city. Even its name was impressive: Rousseau Place Botanical Observatory. And it was also unique because it didn't cost the city a cent. Rousseau Place

Botanical Observatory was maintained—and very well, too—by a pair of wealthy but extremely eccentric flower growers. One of them, Jack Atkin, was Mary Blair's biggest client. The other, Ron Minaker, couldn't be for he was Jack Atkin's arch rival. It was yet another incident in the long-running feud between the two that had brought Mary to the park at a time of day when she preferred to be in bed, or at the very least, dawdling over breakfast. Mary was not an early riser.

"Here I am!" A voice disturbed Mary's reverie. "I say, Ms. Blair, good morning!" A rather stout lady in a tweed suit and an odd Victorian-looking hat was covering the closest knoll at a half trot. "You *are* Ms. Blair, the lawyer, aren't you? I hope I'm not late, am I? You did say eight o'clock. I had to walk all the way around the park because the gates are locked. They're not opened till ten."

"It's okay. It's okay. You're not late," Mary assured the newcomer. "And yes, I'm Mary Blair. If you know who I am, then you must be Alicia Bell, the witness." She shook Alicia's hand. "Thank you for coming. It's important that we go over what you saw Ron Minaker do before I initiate any formal legal action. You see, you're the only witness, and I want to get a handle on things right here at the scene of the crime so to speak." What Mary Blair did not add was that she also wanted to get a handle on Alicia Bell.

"I understand," Alicia replied. "I've been involved in this kind of thing before. As a witness, I mean. For Mr. Atkin, too, about ten years ago. It was the time that Mr. Atkin and Mr. Minaker got into that dispute over who had developed a blue azalea."

Mary's eyebrows went up at that one. It had been before her time. She had become Jack Atkin's lawyer five years ago, and in the period since, Atkin had sued Minaker—or vice versa—no less than six times. Every single one of the cases had been thrown out by the trial judge, who then proceeded to scold the two adversaries. And their lawyers! Mary was trying to avoid a repeat embarrassment, which was one of the reasons she had asked Alicia Bell to meet here.

"Now tell me one more time," Mary said, "what it is you saw Mr. Minaker do."

Alicia Bell cleared her throat. "It's quite simple really. As you know, inside the park there are twenty-six flower beds. Mr. Atkin has thirteen. Mr. Minaker has thirteen. The bed over in the far southeast corner is Mr. Atkin's. Has been since they took over the park. Two days ago, in the morning, I saw Mr. Minaker on his knees in that bed. He had a little shovel and he was digging flower bulbs. Digging them *out,* and putting them in a garbage bag."

Mary Blair's voice dropped a few tones as she slid into her cross-examination mode. "You're absolutely sure which flower bed it was?"

"Oh indeed!" was Alicia's reply, "the one in the southeast corner for sure. No doubt about that."

Mary pushed a little harder. "But surely Mr. Minaker saw you, and he wouldn't dig the bulbs out if he knew you were watching."

"Ah, but he couldn't see me!" Alicia Bell's eyes lit up. "Well, he *could* have, I suppose, if he tried real hard. But he didn't. You see, he didn't know I was there. I was behind the knoll in back of the flower bed, something like you and I are right now."

Mary pounced on that one. "But if you're behind one of these knolls," she said, "you can't see what's on the other side!"

Alicia Bell was waiting for it. "Of course not. But I wasn't all the way down at the bottom. More like halfway." She pulled at Mary's elbow and led her up the knoll a few steps. "See? Look! Here we are, only halfway up and you can see *everything* on the other side. They're only little mounds, these things."

Mary nodded but didn't say anything. She had to admit that it was really quite easy to be concealed and still see everything on the other side.

"If you doubt me," Alicia went on, "just wait until we can get into the park, and I'll show you precisely where I was standing. It was a day just like this. Sunny, but a real nip in the air. Leaves falling." She pointed to the frosty grass. "And you could see your tracks in the lawn just like ours here."

Mary nodded again, and again she didn't say anything. But she had heard enough. She was glad she'd got up so early, for she was convinced now that Alicia Bell was a professional witness. A witness available to the highest bidder.

What has led Mary Blair to this conviction?

36

An Urgent Security Matter at the UN

IT HAD ALWAYS BEEN CHRIS FOGOLIN'S personal conviction that problems come in series of three. His brother Paul insisted that when you worked at the UN building, it was never quite that simple. Paul maintained that if diplomats were involved, there was always sure to be a fourth problem, which, given time, would turn out to be not the fourth, but the first of a new series of three. In the past half hour, the two brothers were already up to five problems and counting.

Chris and Paul Fogolin were members of the security branch at the UN building in New York. (Paul had once argued that just being in New York and working for the UN counted as problems one and two all by themselves!) At 8:45 A.M. their director had given them hands-on responsibility for a meeting to be held in the Singapore Room on the 22nd floor, at 10 o'clock. The security level was "Red AA." For the Fogolin brothers that meant problem number one, for Red Double A signified a situation involving antagonists. Usually, this meant diplomats from countries at war or about to go to war or just finished with a war. It was not at all unusual to have all three conditions at once.

The second and third problems were making the room entirely

secure and establishing an entrance/exit-pass system. Normally this would not be difficult, for there were laid-on procedures for both situations. But Chris and Paul had only an hour and fifteen minutes to activate them.

The fourth problem—or the first in a new series of three—was the seating arrangement. Diplomats sparring with each other over political issues often spent days, sometimes weeks, fighting furiously about protocol. One of the most intense, not to mention tedious and sustainable battles at a UN meeting was over just who would sit where. Fortunately for the Fogolin brothers, the chair of the meeting in this case was Ambassador Manamoto of Japan. Not only was he a neutral party in this conflict, he was a diplomat of long experience and a popular choice as chair because of his reputation for being utterly impartial. One of his unvarying conditions was that during face-to-face meetings between antagonistic parties, the delegations had to be intermingled.

He was also very astute. Manamoto had already sent Paul to replace the rectangular table in the Singapore Room with a large round table so there would be no dispute over who sat at the head or the foot. Then he sent both brothers to canvass the six participating diplomats in order to learn their seating preferences in advance.

"The vice-chair will be Mr. Bjarni Benediktsson, the attaché from Iceland," Manamoto had said to them just before they left. "Now I'm sure he will have no particular seating preference, but it would be an act of courtesy to consult him."

Even though the Fogolins thought there was no time for it, they knew all about the crucial importance of diplomatic courtesy, so they went immediately to the office of the attaché from Iceland. As it turned out, it was from him that they learned the problem count had gone up to five.

"I cannot verify this," Benediktsson intoned, "and I surely don't have to tell two such as you about the way rumors ricochet about this building. Nevertheless," he cleared his throat, "the information I have, the source of which, naturally, I cannot reveal, is of sufficient force and credibility that you should neither discard nor discount it."

Paul chanced a sidelong glance at his brother. The two of them never failed to be impressed by the fact that the quality of English they heard in this building, from people who had had to learn the language, was always so much better than what they ever heard on the streets of New York.

"My information is that there may be an assassin among the delegates at the table today. Of course I don't know who it is, or I would tell you. However, I can tell you that based on my involvement in, and knowledge of, the conflict being discussed here today, it is my . . . my . . . my *gut feeling*," Benediktsson cleared his throat and made a face, "that the intended victim is Bishop Leoni, if only because he is a most vociferous exponent of his cause and certainly, as a result, has the most visible profile of anyone on that negotiating team. Even more than General Nardone."

Chris raced back to Ambassador Manamoto with that information while Paul went off to Bishop Leoni's office. Manamoto expressed mild surprise, mostly at the thought that he had not heard the rumor by now, but agreed that if it were true, Bishop Leoni was certainly a likely target. Before Chris was able to suggest a postponement, however, the ambassador went on to say that if meetings at the UN were canceled every time such a rumor floated to the surface, absolutely nothing would get done in the place.

"Just get on with the task, young man," he said, ushering Chris into the hall. "Ten A.M. As planned and scheduled." He placed his right palm over the back of his left hand and held them in front of his chest. "This does indeed make the seating arrangements more important, as I'm sure you realize?"

With that, Chris double-timed it down the hall to the elevators. There were six diplomats to speak to in—he looked at his watch—fifty-five minutes! Luckily, his first stop was productive. Dr. Perez was not in her office, but her secretary, a frowsy gum chewer in a sweater that was way too tight, told him in classic in-your-face Bronx style that "If Dr. Perez has to sit beside that Gestido witch from the other side, she walks. Is that clear?"

Chris was almost out the door before she could shift the wad of gum around to add, "And she won't sit beside Leoni. Or her creep boss, Nardone, either. They're grabbers!"

Chris turned and ran, as much to get away from the gum as to find Paul, but first he had to stop at Ambassador Haruna's suite. Haruna was head of his delegation and had a reputation for arrogance that was fully sustained when Chris was ushered to his desk. Without even looking up, Haruna motioned "just stand there" with his index finger and then continued to read the front section of *The New York Times*.

He still hadn't even looked up or even acknowledged Chris's presence when he started to speak. "As head of the delegation I expect to be seated next to the chairperson, naturally. And I would like to arrange that . . ." A door in the wall to Chris's left opened, and the ambassador looked up for the first time, an expression of extreme annoyance on his face. It stayed that way while an aide tiptoed to the edge of the desk, turned the intercom to "Off" and then disappeared as quickly as possible through the same door. The silence continued for a few more long seconds.

"I understand the table will be a round one. Very well. I would like one of my delegation directly beside me—Ms. Gestido. That should be no problem for you? She's essential to me for translation. You know what happens to General Nardone's English when he gets excited. Now, of course she won't want to sit beside the bishop, so I expect you to take care of that, too."

The ambassador had looked up at Chris only briefly. He was concentrating now on preparing a large Cuban cigar. "I trust you have been told by my aides that I have a need for ample supplies of fresh water because of some medication I am taking." Chris hadn't been told, but he had no intention of getting an aide in trouble by saying so. "So I would appreciate it if you would see to that. Those are all our requirements. You may seat our new delegate, Mr. Cresawana, wherever you wish. One must cooperate in these affairs, after all." Haruna looked up again and delivered Chris an entirely insincere smile. "I imagine you have already had enough instructions from Dr. Perez to keep you busy, haven't you?"

With that, Haruna returned abruptly to *The Times,* and in seconds, Chris was moving down the hall as fast as decorum would permit. Paul was coming from the opposite direction at the same pace.

"I can't find the bishop anywhere," Paul said as soon as they were close enough to talk. "His staff says he'll be at the Singapore Room all right, but they don't know where he is. Nardone was in though."

"Anything unusual?" Chris asked.

"Strangely, no." Paul replied. "I really thought he'd want something awkward, maybe to take Leoni down a peg—you'd almost think Leoni and not Nardone was the head of the delegation—but no, he had nothing. So are we set?"

"Well, year," Chris said. "We're not only set, we're being set *up!*"

"What do you mean?"

"You know your theory about the fourth problem being the first of a new series of three? Well, it's right. We've got problem number six now!"

"I don't get it."

"Wait till I tell you about the seating arrangement that Haruna wants. It's manipulation, plain and simple. He's got everybody sitting exactly where he wants them. I don't know why or what for, but he's done it. Have we got time to check the security clearance of that Cresawana guy?"

Chris turned and watched as an aide bustled past them down the hall. "Who knows?" he went on. "Maybe Benediktsson's assassination rumor is true."

How has Ambassador Haruna manipulated the seating arrangement? And why does Chris want to check the security clearance for delegate Cresawana?

37

The Body on
Blanchard Beach

LIKE THE OTHERS SITTING ON THE SIDE facing the window, Sue
Cremer pulled her chair closer to the table as soon as K.D. Lapp
came in. Everyone did it automatically and almost at the same
time, a habit they'd developed because K.D. always whipped his
crutches forward one after the other in a wide half-circle, and he
needed extra room to get by.

As her boss settled in at the head of the long table, it occurred
to Sue that she might have lost her carefully planned advantage in
the pull forward. This afternoon's meeting was about the body
found on Blanchard Beach earlier in the day. There would be
slides projected at the wall across from K.D. Lapp, slides of the
site and—the reason Sue Cremer had got her usual early seat—
slides of the murdered body.

For two years as director of Information Services in the office
of the county coroner, she had successfully avoided ever looking
at a dead body, either the real thing or even a picture. It was a
secret she'd kept from her colleagues all this time by doing things
like sitting third chair from the end on Chief Coroner Lapp's
right. That strategy ensured she would always have the obsessive
Doctor Reuven Shallmar immediately beside her, blocking her

view of the screen. Shallmar was a brilliant pathologist whose forensic skills were almost as legendary as the tantrums he threw whenever his notions of order and sequence were disturbed. One of those notions was that he had the right, always and absolutely without exception, to sit in the same place at every staff meeting. No one opposed him.

The man's wishes and his peculiar behavior made no difference whatever to Sue. What mattered to her was Shallmar's abnormally large head, made even larger by a sunburst of crinkly red hair. She had learned through practice that by sitting just so, she could appear to be gazing intently at the screen when in fact her line of sight was entirely obscured by the pathologist's mighty skull.

When the call came down for today's meeting, she had, as usual, positioned herself with time to spare, for this was going to be a bad one. In the past six months two bodies had been found on Blanchard Beach, at different times but less than a kilometer apart. Both had been adult females and both had been mutilated after death. Whoever was responsible was a very sick person. The tabloid press was already ranting about a serial killer and the more responsible media was on the brink of joining the chorus. This morning's discovery of a third body was sure to tip them over the edge. That's why, in every office around the city that was even remotely connected to law enforcement, there had been meetings like this going on all day.

Chief Coroner Lapp rapped his knuckles for attention.

"All right, people. Let's get on task here. I'm leaving for the police commissioner's office in thirty minutes and I want to be able to take something with me from this meeting. Now the slides we have here are—Ah! Dexter. Thank you for coming."

The door had opened after a single knock. A short black man moved along the wall to an extra chair between Lapp and the window. He wore jeans and a faded T-shirt that loudly proclaimed "No Sweat, Mon!" over an oasis of sand and waving palms.

Lapp introduced him. "I'm not sure all of you know Dexter Treble. These are his photographs we're about to look at and I've asked him to narrate." He lowered his voice slightly. "Can we get going on this right away, Dexter? I'm due at the commissioner's task force and . . ." He let his sentence drift away while Dexter Treble beamed a smile in return.

Dexter acknowledged Lapp's request: "Of course!" Contrary to the initial impression his appearance may have created with some at the table, Dexter was efficient, articulate, and possessed of a crisp British accent.

"Of course," he repeated, and picked up the remote control, turning on the slide projector in the same fluid motion. "It would be helpful if someone could dim the, ah, thank you.

"The first photograph here,"—Dexter clicked a slide into position on the carousel—"is of the pertinent section of the area known as Blanchard Beach. It's not my work. This is from the county files. It was taken by the pollution control group about a year ago. No particular significance to our work here other than I thought it would be germane for you to be reminded of what Blanchard Beach looks like when it's not famous, or rather, infamous."

Sue edged forward slightly to see around Reuven Shallmar's bobbing mane. The photograph was a safe one and she had been in the beach area only once before. Blanchard was a lonely stretch about ten minutes' drive from the edge of the city. The beach itself, between the sand dunes and the water, was flat and sandy, but swimming was banned because of a fierce undertow. It was a lonely place most of the time. Even teenagers chose other spots to drag race and carry on. An ideal place to dump things. Sue was leaning forward intently when Dexter Treble clicked in the next slide without warning. Her stomach lurched but then calmed. The shot was innocuous enough. It was a body wrapped in something brown.

"This is taken from a dune looking down on the site. One of mine." Dexter carried on smoothly. "According to the couple that discovered the body, this is exactly what they saw when they came upon it. As you can see, there is the body, then a single set of tire tracks. A remarkably clean site actually. No footprints, unfortunately, but the tread marks from the tires are quite clear. The police lab is working on those right now."

Dexter Treble popped ahead to a close-up of the tire treads in the sand. They were a perfect set. Sue found herself leaning forward just a bit more as Dexter went back to the previous slide.

"Notice the symmetry too. The investigating officer believes that the vehicle was reversed in and driven out after disposing of the cargo. The body itself was wrapped in that beige tarpaulin just as you see. That's the right hand of the victim protruding ever so slightly. Without the hand it would have been difficult to distinguish the body from other flotsam on the beach, especially from a distance. Now, if there were any doubt about murder, this next slide . . ."

Just in time, Sue slid back to safety behind Doctor Shallmar as Dexter clicked in the slide she'd been dreading, but in that second the door opened without a warning knock. It was one of the young whitecoats from the morgue downstairs. He was excited.

"Cadaver's here, Doctor Lapp."

Reuven Shallmar jumped to his feet. "What I've been waiting for!" He turned to the door, then stopped heron-like on one leg and looked back to K.D. Lapp. "Kirk?"

K.D. Lapp waved him on. "Yes, by all means. Call me at the commissioner's office in one hour, no matter what."

Shallmar was released into flight before Lapp even finished speaking. Almost without warning, Sue Cremer's protective barrier had disappeared!

Later that evening she was unable to explain, even to herself, how she'd carried it off, but the instant Doctor Shallmar slammed the door she turned away from the screen to face her boss.

"Doctor Lapp," she said calmly, "could we return to the previous slide, please?"

He looked at her with mild curiosity. Sue almost never spoke at these meetings. Lapp nodded to Dexter, who immediately returned to the close-up of the tire tracks.

"No, sorry. The one before that," Sue insisted.

Dexter accommodated. By now everyone was staring at Sue instead of the screen. More dramatically than was her style, she swept her arm along the table and then pointed at the screen.

"Do you know, Dr. Lapp," she began to wave her finger at the screen in remonstrating fashion, "do you know whether the search for a vehicle has concentrated on a van, by any chance?"

K.D. Lapp peered at Sue and then looked back at the screen.

"By Jove," he said. Then louder. "By Jove!" He grabbed at his crutches. "I don't believe so, not to my knowledge! I don't believe so! By Jove!"

He caught his crutches on the edge of his chair and they clattered to the floor. "Drat!" he shouted at them.

Sue rose to her feet quickly. "I'll go do the telephoning, sir. You're needed here anyway."

Without waiting for an answer, Sue Cremer got to her feet and exited the room, being careful not to look at the screen just in case Dexter Treble decided to move ahead before she was ready.

Sue Cremer has successfully extricated herself from the meeting and at the same time provided what may be a valuable clue. Why does she believe the body was brought to Blanchard Beach in a van?

38

Esty Wills Prepares
for a Business Trip

THE ELEVATOR WAS AGONIZINGLY SLOW. It was overheated too, and smelly, filled with the odor of institutional cleanser and cooking smells, which provided an unwelcome and unasked-for accounting of who had what for dinner the previous night. Still, it gave Sean Hennigar a twinge of mildly vindictive pleasure. All things being equal, the apartment was a dump, a major comedown in lifestyle for Esty Wills—Mr. Flash, as he was called in the D.A.'s office.

Sean moved to lean against the back wall but then thought better of it. No point in having the graffiti come off on his overcoat. Certainly he wanted no souvenir of a visit to Esty Wills, even if the visit was part of his job. Sean was a parole officer, working out of the D.A.'s office in Market Square. Esty Wills was one of his "files." His least favorite: Wills was a notorious con man, well known in Chicago. Nightclubs knew him as a big spender. Mercedes-Benz and Lexus dealerships vied for his attention. Chi-Vegas Charters automatically bumped passengers to suit his demands, and everyone working for the Blackhawks, Cubs, or Bulls knew his seating preferences.

On the other side of the coin, insurance companies had tagged his name on all their software programs. So had practically every police department in northern Illinois. And although the Consumer Protection Agency had not used Wills's name in a recent flyer to seniors, it was clearly him the group had in mind. To Sean Hennigar, and everyone else in the D.A.'s office for that matter, Esty Wills was nothing but an unrepentant career crook who consumed an entirely disproportionate amount of their time and who, despite his convictions, still seemed to be able to wheedle privileges out of the department.

Take now, for example. Wills was about to leave Chicago for three days on a business trip to Asuncion, a clear violation of the conditions of his parole. He had served only four months of his three-year sentence before being paroled (to no one's surprise) and was already applying for special exemptions. In a classic Wills deal, he had managed to have himself retained by the International Monetary Fund, a partner with the Japanese government in an experimental project investigating the viability of growing mulberry bushes in Paraguay, the ultimate object being the raising of silkworms.

The Banco Nacional de Fomento had leaned on the Japanese representatives, who had leaned on the IMF, who had leaned on an assistant deputy secretary at Commerce in Washington, who had leaned on the Cook County D.A., who promptly signed the permission-to-travel form and then called Sean into his office. Wheels spinning wheels, and now Sean was bringing the form to Wills.

Sean reached out to knock on the door of 14B. He couldn't help noting that somehow Wills had snagged a corner apartment. The door opened immediately to reveal a loudly dressed middle-aged man in standard used-car salesman pose. He was holding a wool sock in one hand.

"Don't they come in pairs?" Sean asked without any preliminary. It took Wills aback, but only for a second.

"Ah!" He smiled beneficently. "My favorite mother hen is becoming a wit! What next? A song and dance?"

Sean stepped into the apartment without waiting for an invitation. He wasn't smiling. Nor did he take the bait. "Let's get this over with," he said. "Show me your ticket and visa, and I'll give you your passport."

Reading Sean's mood, Wills led the way across the small bachelor suite to where his suitcase sat open on a chesterfield, and extracted the two items requested. Sean looked at the airline ticket very closely. At first, he hardly noticed the discrepancy, distracted as he was by the scarf and gloves labeled L.L. Bean and by the other wool sock. Esty Wills was buying from mail order catalogues, it seemed. A far cry from the personal tailor he'd been used to. This gave Sean an inordinate amount of satisfaction, but only briefly, until the ticket upset him.

"Four days?" He frowned at Wills. "What are you trying to pull here!"

Wills spread his hands in another used-car salesman gesture. "Gimme a break! It's travel time! I got to go via Buenos Aires, and connect there to go back north to Asuncion. Takes almost a day. Same thing coming back. And I need two days there. Look, phone the IMF if you want. Or Washington!"

Sean tossed the ticket at the suitcase, and then very reluctantly followed it with Wills's passport. Without another word, he left the apartment and walked down the hall to where the slow elevator waited for him. All the way down he felt uneasy, bothered by something he couldn't put his finger on. The uneasiness stayed with him through the tiny lobby into the parking lot, where he took a minute to blow a skiff of snow off the windshield and peer into Esty Wills's car.

The used stub of a bus ticket on the front seat said Chicago-St. Louis Return. The thought of Esty Wills traveling by bus should have given Sean some satisfaction. The fact too that the car was a two-year-old Pontiac should have reinforced the feeling. But it didn't. Somehow, Sean couldn't shake the conviction that Esty Wills was not going to Asuncion, but for the life of him, Sean couldn't figure out what had triggered that thought.

The suspicion bothered him even more as he left the parking lot. It wasn't helped, either, when he noticed that the Pontiac was in the choicest parking spot in the lot. "Reserved: 14B" had been painted recently on the little sign on the curb.

What is nagging at Sean Hennigar? Other than the fact that Esty Wills is a known con man, which would make one suspect him in any case, what is it that has twigged Sean's subconscious?

39

The Case of
the Buckle File

BEAVER LIFE AND CASUALTY
INSURANCE COMPANY

1 October 1992

Mr. Ernie Buckle
104 West Fort William Road
Thunder Bay, ON
P8L V1X

Dear Mr. Buckle:

Re: <u>Joint Life Policy BV 297562</u>
<u>Ernie & Audrey Buckle</u>

I have received your letter of 25 September 1992 and the enclosed forms authorizing the addition to your policy of a double indemnity clause for accidental death.

Please note that Mrs. Buckle has not signed Form 22A. Since yours is a joint policy with you and your wife as each other's beneficiary, it is necessary that both of you sign. Accordingly, I am returning Form 22A for her signature.

Further, you have not designated a beneficiary to receive the indemnity should it occur that you and Mrs. Buckle encounter a terminal accidental event together. The funds, if such were to occur, would thus be paid to your respective estates on a 50/50 basis, and would therefore be subject to probate fees and taxation. If this is your wish, you and Mrs. Buckle must initial clause 12 on page 2 of Form 22A. However, should you wish to designate a beneficiary, please enter his/her/their name(s) and address(es) in the space below clause 13 on page 2.

I will hold your cheque until I receive the completed Form 22A, and other instructions on the above matters.

Sincerely,

Christine Cooper

Christine Cooper
Client Services

Oct. 12/92

Beaver Insurance Co

Dear Miss Cooper,

Here is the form with my signature that you asked for. Sorry I didn't do this before. Ernie usually is the one who looks after these things. Also, like you said, for ~~beneficiaris~~ beneficiary we picked my cousin Reenee Clubek in Gibralter.

Hope this is alright now.

Audie Buckle

BEAVER LIFE AND CASUALTY
INSURANCE COMPANY

12 November 1992

Mr. Ernie Buckle
Mrs. Audrey Buckle
104 West Fort William Road
Thunder Bay, ON
P8L V1X

Dear Mr. and Mrs. Buckle:

Re: Joint Policy BV 297562

Enclosed please find notice of confirmation regarding changes to
the above policy, with copies for your files.
 The changes are effective as of 15 October 1992.

Sincerely,

Jack Hal for Christine Cooper

Christine Cooper

July 29, 1993

Ms. Christine Cooper
Beaver Life and Casualty

BY FAX

Your telephone message of 27/07/93 handed to me this A.M.
 Body of Ernie Buckle recovered from Wabakimi Lake at 3:15
P.M., 25/07/93. Coroner has ruled accidental death by drowning.
No inquest scheduled.

Search for body of Audrey Buckle terminated this A.M. Overturned canoe located in Wabakimi established as belonging to the Buckles. No further search planned. Status of Audrey Buckle is "presumed dead."

We will have full reports available by 10/08/93. You can get these through usual channels from district headquarters in Thunder Bay.

Constable Allan Longboat
Ontario Provincial Police
Search and Rescue Unit
Sioux Lookout

March 18, '94

To Whom It May Concern,
Beaver Life and Casualty Insurance
7272 Barton Street
Hamilton Ontario
CANADA

VIA AIR MAIL

Dear Sir or Madam,
I am writing in regard to the deaths of Ernie and Audrey Buckle. As you know, I am the beneficiary named in the life insurance policy they held with your company.

Very shortly I will be moving from Gibralter to a project in east Africa. My new address, effective March 31, '94 will be

c/o Central Postal Station
Box 241
Haile Selassie Blvd.
Nairobi 17
KENYA

It would be helpful if you could tell me when the policy benefit will be issued.

I appreciate your help in this matter.

Sincerely,

Irene Clubek

Irene Clubek

On April 2, 1994, Christine Cooper wrote a memo to her immediate superior stating that one item in particular made her feel that Beaver Life and Casualty was being defrauded in this case, and that the case might also involve a felony. What made her feel that?

40

While Little Harvey Watched

THE STARLINGS CAME IN EARLY the night before Ollie Wicksteed was killed. Little Harvey had watched them from his bedroom window. Black, raucous, a seething, constantly shifting mass that filled the air with ugly croaking. Usually, they came in just before sunset but that night they were early, hundreds of them filling up the branches of the old beech tree behind the house.

Grandpa Bottrell said starlings were bad luck. Two years ago, in the fall, the first time Little Harvey remembered them coming in such numbers, Grandpa had taken the old twelve gauge and fired into the tree. It drove the starlings away, but not far and not for long. At the peak of the echoing bang they had risen in an elastic cloud that grew and shrank and shifted above the tree and then simply pulled itself down on the barn roof not far away. Five minutes later they were back in the beech tree and they stayed there, because Momma had taken the shotgun and hidden it. Momma didn't have much patience for behavior like that. It was another one of the things she called "nonsense" (a word she used a lot).

Little Harvey rather agreed with her. The shotgun scared him. As for the bad luck part, well, that was different. Grandpa Bottrell always seemed to know about that stuff, and even though Momma called it foolish old peoples' talk, the next day Poppa fell off the ladder out by the implement shed. He was laid up a long time and the neighbors had to finish the ploughing.

It was the next year that Grandpa Bottrell got sick. The same week the starlings showed up. Not as many as the year before—at least Momma said so—but still enough to fill up the old beech tree at sunset and make it impossible to hear anybody talk if you were outside unless they shouted right into your ear. What scared Little Harvey so much was that the day they went away for good that year was the day Grandpa died.

Now they were here again. And Harvey no longer had any doubts about the bad luck. He was in the second grade now and for the first time he was really beginning to like school. This year he didn't even mind the long ride every morning on the old yellow bus. Ms. Caswell was the reason. She was just the best teacher. Every day was fun, but now he couldn't go. The day the starlings arrived Little Harvey had got scarlet fever and he had to stay home. Nobody gets scarlet fever these days, Momma had said to Doctor Sannalchuk, and what about the vaccinations when he was a baby? And Doctor Sannalchuk said there were always a very few kids in whom the vaccines didn't "take." Little Harvey had to be one of those. Just bad luck. So he had spent most of a week in his room.

At first he didn't mind, because he was so sick. But by the time Ollie Wicksteed was killed, Little Harvey had felt more like doing things and the starlings at least gave him something to watch. That's why he was looking out the window when Ollie was crushed by the big beech tree. Harvey's room was the only one that faced the back yard.

At the funeral folks said it was an accident and maybe even a blessing seeing as how Ollie gave his brother such trouble all these years and wasn't really good for anything. Harvey listened to the talk outside the church and he wasn't exactly sure what they meant by "good for anything," but he had a feeling it was because Ollie was funny in the head. People called him retarded but there

was a girl in Ollie's class in school who everybody said was retarded and she didn't act the way Ollie did.

Ollie's brother, Carson, was always having to take things out of
Ollie's mouth. Once Little Harvey had overheard Poppa say that
Carson had had to pull Ollie out of the manure pile at the south
barn because he'd tried to burrow in like a groundhog.

"Shame what Carson's had to do for that man these years,"
Poppa had said. "Every minute he's got to watch. And what does
he get for it? His wife leaves him, and you can't blame her after
what Ollie done to her that time. Carson, he can't go nowhere.
Can't even do a decent day's work. Not much money in firewood
no more anyway but a man's got to work. No wonder Carson
drinks so heavy."

Momma's response was muffled but Little Harvey was sure he'd
heard her mention the special home where Ollie had lived for a
time and where he got kicked out and they wouldn't take him
back. It was something about a girl there but Harvey didn't know
for sure what it was because every time the grown-ups talked
about it, they changed the subject when he came near.

It was not only because of the scarlet fever that Harvey was
watching from the bedroom window when Carson came over to
cut up the beech tree. It was because he was afraid of Ollie. He
didn't used to be, but then Momma had said, "Now the Wicksteed's are neighbors and I don't like to tell you this but you stay
away from that Ollie. Don't you dare ever let me catch you makin'
fun of him but you stay away."

That's why Little Harvey watched from the safety of the second
floor. The night before, a big wind had toppled the old beech,
torn it out roots and all, so that it lay tipped on its side like a giant
that had fallen with its feet in the air. The hole left by the roots
was wide, but because of the way beech trees grow it was shallow,
and when Ollie stood upright in it his head was above the surface
of the ground. Harvey had watched him rest his chin on the rim
of the hole and lick the stones where one edge of the root system
still clung to the ground. Then he'd seen Carson turn off the
chain saw up at the other end of the tree and throw it down by

the branches he'd just cut off and come over and swear at Ollie and kick away the stones. Ollie just sat in the hole for a while after that, but before long he got up onto his knees and began scooping out a burrow with his hands, putting the sandy ground in the pockets of his overalls. That's what he was doing when the stump came down on top of him.

That night the starlings came back at sunset, but they were confused because the beech tree wasn't there. They hovered where the branches used to be as if waiting for them to return, shifting and floating and diving the way they always did. What Little Harvey noticed most of all was how quiet they were. It was as though they knew something. That bothered him a great deal. He knew something too, something about Ollie and the way he died. But who should he tell? And how should he explain it?

It would seem that Little Harvey doesn't accept the idea that Ollie Wicksteed's death was an accident. Why has he cause to be suspicious?

41

The Murder of
Mr. Norbert Gray

JIM LATIMER HUNG UP THE PHONE. "That was F.A.R.," he said.

From his desk across the overcrowded squad room, Mike Roslin nodded absently. He was staring at an open evidence bag.

"Thought so," he acknowledged finally. "And don't tell me. The Beretta's hers, right?"

"Uh huh." Jim Latimer nodded. "Registered in 1984, uh, let's see, on March fifteenth. No, the sixteenth. Firearm Registration's got data on disk back to 1986. Anything before that they gotta dig out by hand. That's what took 'em so long to call back."

Mike Roslin rubbed his elbow back and forth along the arm of his chair. "And the Luger?" he asked, picking a deadly looking weapon out of a holster that bore the double lightning bolts of the SS on the cover flap.

"His. Registered the same day. They bought both guns at Intutus Firearms Shop on Mount Pleasant. Luger's registered for range use. The Beretta can be carried."

"Humpf." Mike was clearly unimpressed. He began to invert the evidence bag over his desk.

"Wait!" His partner shouted so loud that the two other detectives in the room rose out of their chairs. "You know what happened the last time we used your desk!"

The others chuckled and went back to their work. Mike Roslin had a reputation as the best problem-solver on the homicide squad, but one whose desk, locker, car, and apartment were so covered in flotsam that even he no longer knew what he owned.

"Here," Jim directed. "Dump it on my desk. Then at least we'll know which murder we're trying to solve."

Without a word, Mike carried the bag around to his partner's desk and slowly eased the contents onto the surface. Except for the Luger and its holster, both nestled in the pile of incomplete reports, empty coffee cups, and Mr. Submarine wrappers on Mike's desk, the story of Norbert Gray's untimely demise now lay spread out on Detective Jim Latimer's desk blotter.

Just forty-eight hours ago, Norbert Gray had been shot in the back of the head while sitting at the solid oak rolltop in his den. After an acrimonious and very public divorce from his wife of seventeen years, Gray had been living alone in their custom-built log home in the exclusive Pines district. The ex-wife, Aleyna, was in custody, but not yet formally charged.

There had been one shot at close range from a 9 mm Beretta. Apparently, the shooter—the evidence pointed overwhelmingly at this being the former Mrs. Gray—had stood behind the victim, fired once, and then threw the gun out the balcony doors. It had skidded down the side of the ravine that backed onto the Gray home, and came to rest (lucky for the investigators) against a tree trunk at the edge of a bike path. The techs had quickly determined that the Beretta was indeed the murder weapon, and that it had a single fingerprint on it. At the end of the barrel, curiously, but a clear print nevertheless. More to the point, the print belonged to Aleyna Gray.

The Beretta lay in the center of the pile on Jim Latimer's desk. Mike stuck the eraser end of a pencil inside the trigger guard and absently spun the little gun in circles.

"Something really stinks about all this," he said.

"Yeah," Jim nodded. "You said that yesterday. And this morning too."

"Well, it does," came the reply. "I don't like these near-smoking-gun cases."

This time it was Jim who used a pencil to play with the evidence. "Yeah, but . . ." He stuck the point under an envelope and flipped it over so that Norbert Gray's name and address looked up at them. "There's two of these letters," he said. "Both from her. The one from two weeks ago tells him what a jerk he is, how inadequate he is, what a lousy father, worse as a husband. Sure glad I never had to tangle with this woman. The second one, it's what? Three days before the murder? Tells him what she'd like to do to him."

"Okay, but . . ." Mike took the pencil out of the Beretta's trigger guard and tapped the postal mark and then the stamp on first one letter, then the other. "Personal letters, sure. But everything's typed. WordPerfect, I'd say, and a laser printer. Lots of those around."

"Then what about the will?" Jim asked. Norbert Gray's will had been found on the surface of the rolltop. A line had been drawn through the clauses relating to Aleyna, but there was no signature or initialing near it.

"Sure, what about it? Watch this." Jim winced in disbelief as Mike drew a line across a report lying on Jim's typewriter. "Doesn't tell us a thing!" Mike continued.

"And the cigarettes?" Jim asked the question in almost a whisper. He was still staring at the report.

"Easy to set up. He didn't smoke. She does." Mike pointed a finger at a half-empty pack on the desk. "Yes, it's her brand. Yes, her prints are on the pack, but look, this is garbage. It's all circumstantial."

Jim finally took his eyes off the report. "Still, she sure had motive," he said. "Hated the guy, at least according to the transcript of the divorce. And she's got no alibi: 'I had a cold and took some aspirins and went to bed early.' Pretty weak."

"On the other hand," Mike replied, "we have no eyewitness,

and there's really nothing solid here. Look, I'm not on her side, but maybe somebody's setting her up. Maybe somebody's setting *us* up!" He picked up the evidence bag. "All a good lawyer has to do is show that one of these pieces of evidence is phony and the whole lot goes out the window!"

"Yeah." Jim picked up the destroyed report tenderly. "What we need is something like DNA."

Mike looked at his partner. He became so animated that Jim moved to protect his cup of coffee. "That's it!" Mike shouted. We can use DNA to prove one of these pieces of evidence is solid— or phony, for that matter! At least then we'll know if we have a real case or not."

The excitement affected Jim as he too caught the idea. "Yes! DNA!" He reached across the desk, and as he grabbed the evidence bag, a large, grayish-white wad fell out of it. "What's this?" He peered hard at his partner. "This wasn't in here before!"

Mike looked perplexed. "Looks like my sock."

"What's it doing in the evidence bag?" Jim asked.

"I dunno."

What, in the evidence the two detectives have, can be subjected to DNA testing?

42

A Holdup at the Adjala Building

IT WAS ONLY 4 P.M. ON A CLEAR MIDSUMMER DAY, but Jeff Ercul expected the street to be in shadows by now. That was yet another reason he had come to deeply regret the transfer from Loretto to the city: urban canyons—long, winding tubes of semi-darkness between rows of skyscrapers.

On this particular stretch of Richmond Street, however, the buildings on the other side were quite a bit shorter than the norm, a trubute to the days when an environmentally sensitive city council had put height restriction bylaws into effect. For that reason, the sun was still lighting up the south and west sides of the Adjala Building, its unique coppery sides and floating design making the kind of grand and lofty statement that prompted even bored frequent fliers to lean over from their aisle seats to get a look.

Jeff squinted as he stood in front of the Adjala Building's main doors. Unlike the outside walls of the building, which were paneled with metal, these were thick plate glass, although they had the same copper tint. It was a glorious building, no question. There was nothing like it in Loretto, where he had spent his first five years on the force. Loretto didn't have live theater either, or big league sports, or the incredible restaurants, or the astounding variety of shopping opportunities. But then, it didn't have crack either, or doors with multiple locks, or people with "subway-elbows," or slums, or beggars on the streets.

The transfer to the city had been offered to Jeff as an avenue to promotion.

"You want to make sergeant," the Human Resources weenie had pointed out to him. You can't sit up there in the boonies for another five years. You gotta get some time where the action is."

Actually, the decision had been easy; Jeff wanted to make sergeant. And the truth was, he really had believed the city would make him feel more like a cop. But the feeling didn't last long. It wasn't just the amount of crime here, and the nature of it. And it wasn't just his disappointment at Twelfth Precinct headquarters. (At first glance, and ever afterwards, it looked to Jeff like a Third World bus station.) Nor was it things like the downtown streets blocking out the sun. He wanted to go back home because, some-how, crime was different there. Not just that there was less of it, and indeed there was much less. Rather, it was more the fact that crime was harder to commit. People watched out for other peo-ple. They knew what was going on, and they cared. Here, nobody watched. It was an urban virtue to be isolated from what was going on around you.

Take the theft he was investigating right now, a holdup in broad daylight, just before lunch, right here where he was stand-ing. Not a single witness could be found. Even the victim had not seen the thief.

A courier carrying bearer bonds had felt a gun in her back—an iffy point in Jeff's view; she said it was a gun, but she hadn't seen it, only felt it. The thief had ordered her to stand still and not turn around. Then he'd pulled the strap off her shoulder and over her head, taking her delivery bag.

"Then he says . . . he says . . ." This had all been reported to Jeff through an enormous wad of bubble gum. "He says, 'Walk inside the building. Look straight ahead. You turn around, you're finished.' So, like, what'm I gonna do? Like, I mean, I'm not gonna take a chance. But I'm gonna play it smart, see? Like, I'm in this building all the time. An' I know there's this security guard by the elevators. So I go in like the guy says, an' I don't turn around. An' then I run for the guard."

At this point the gum began to pop with even greater ferocity.

"An', well, like you know the rest. Jerk's not there! Whatsa point of havin' security? Right?

"Anyways. That's all I know. 'Cept fer his voice. The holdup guy. Told you that b'fore. It's, like, really deep, the voice. Like that actor. You know, whaddayacallim . . . James Earl Jones. That guy."

Jeff sighed deeply. He found he was doing a lot of that lately. Sighing. This would not have happened in Loretto, he was sure. He sighed again, wondering whether, by putting pressure on the courier, maybe arresting her, or threatening her, he could get her to tell the truth.

Jeff Ercul has determined that there is a flaw in the account the courier has given him. What is that flaw?

43

Filming at L'Hôtel du Roi

*Barney, must—absolutely must—complete shoot before noon to be
sure of the lighting. Also, rushes from Monday show that early
1940s time frame is not clear enough. Suggest you take Charlotte*

LOBBY SCENE: To be Reshot Wednesday A.M.
Barney King's Copy. DO NOT TOUCH!

*through the lobby much slower. Have camera linger over the three
women extras in the obviously forties clothes. Maybe focus longer on
their gloves and hats. Also, I've now got a TIMES front page
with a head that says "ROOSEVELT SIGNS LEND LEASE BILL".
Might be overkill but we can always cut. S.*

VID—Establishing shot under opening credits. Medium close-up
of bottom one-third or so of elevator doors. Should pick up bottom of brass scroll ornamentation. Hold two seconds after credits.

AUD—Palm Court-style music. Not loud. Lots of violin. Bring
up volume when elevator doors open.

VID—At final credit, doors open to reveal two pairs of legs.
Approx. knees down. One is uniform of elevator operator. Be sure
shoes are lace-type. Highly polished but worn.

Barney, check this. That dumb kid wore loafers in Monday's shoot. S.

The second pair of legs is elegantly feminine. Skirt just over the knees. Shoes are pumps with satin bow over toes. These legs exit the elevator. Camera follows at MCU as the legs turn and go to end of hallway. Pause at entrance to main lobby beside large candia palm. Stay on MCU while one hand comes down and checks that seams are straight. Hand has a diamond ring but not on wedding finger. Diamond bracelet on the wrist.

AUD—Low buzz of conversation noise as legs enter lobby. Does <u>not</u> overwhelm the music. Footstep sounds should accompany the legs.

VID—After the stocking seam check, pull back from legs for wide angle to take in whole lobby and then come back in slowly to CHARLOTTE. Make clear the legs are hers. She starts moving into the lobby. Follow her at medium long as she turns left toward the set of elevator doors on the opposite side of the lobby. CHARLOTTE slows then stops at another candia palm between her and these elevators. Camera keeps on moving to the doors, closing in but keeping full-length shot as doors open. VAN SLOTIN exits elevator. Pull back for longer shot. VAN SLOTIN exits elevator. Pull back for longer shot. VAN SLOTIN walks straight toward camera. Hold camera until diamond stickpin in the tie is clearly visible. His silver-headed cane is <u>used</u>. Not just an ornament.

B. Get an ECU of his hair. (Guy can't act but he looks good.) Also, rushes show slight tear in left sleeve of suitjacket. S.

AUD—Hold music and conversation buzz. Add more lobby-type sounds here. Bring up bell sound as bellhop crosses in front of CHARLOTTE and VAN SLOTIN with message card. Fade right out when CHARLOTTE walks into VAN SLOTIN.

VID—From behind VAN SLOTIN.

CHARLOTTE emerges from candia palms, glancing over her shoulder. This should be the first shot of CHARLOTTE from the front. Her suitjacket is buttoned. The veil on her pillbox hat covers her forehead and comes down right to the eyes. Camera stays on her for the whole of the following exchange. Both she and VAN SLOTIN are apparently distracted by the bellhop. She walks into VAN SLOTIN.

CHARLOTTE: Oh, I'm so terribly sorry! Are you all right?

VAN SLOTIN: (more than a bit confused but recovers fast) Ah . . . ah . . . why, ah, yes I believe so. Perhaps I should pay more attention to where I'm going.

CHARLOTTE: Are you sure you're all right?

VAN SLOTIN: Indeed, miss; in fact, I think I'm going to remember our meeting with some pleasure!

CHARLOTTE: Oh . . .

VID—CHARLOTTE puts out a power smile and withdraws at a speed that's just inside good manners. Camera pulls back to medium long and rolls left, following CHARLOTTE in full length as she moves toward the revolving doors at the street exit.

AUD—Music is now very faint, covered by a much more intense melange of lobby sounds. These come right up for a second or two as RAUL steps out of the alcove and blocks her path and then fade right out. No FX or music during entire exchange that follows.

VID—After RAUL blocks her path, move in to MCU for entire exchange. Shoot speakers face on.

B. No need to reshoot the ECU of Charlotte's hand going inside Van Slotin's suitjacket. Perfect in the rushes. S.

Sy,

 Agree with your comments above. Rest of scene is basically OK in the script but I want you to take the piece above back to the writers. It's the same thing that bothered me before. They've made Charlotte just too obvious a dipper. Unless they can fix it, this scene isn't going to work.

Barney

Why does Barney King feel that Charlotte is too obvious as a pick-pocket?

44

Whether or Not to Continue
Up the Mountain

DETAILS WERE EMINENTLY CLEAR through the lenses of the big Zeiss field glasses. There were no fences to be seen that far up the mountain, but then, she didn't expect any. She could see the cattle clearly though. Could even see them placidly chewing their cud and see their ears twitching away as they clustered together in the weak autumn sun. Funny, she thought. She'd never really noticed before how they seemed to gather together like that from time to time during the day. Almost like a planned social event. Just above the cattle, behind a rock, a pair of ganz, timid little Alpine deer, grazed furtively. Most importantly, she could see the path, see where it wound cautiously around big rock formations then zigzagged where the terrain was unobstructed but steep. And finally, where it took a short, straight run up to and over the top.

It wasn't the first time Chris Beadle was glad she'd just happened to be the ranking officer present when the townspeople pulled that SS Oberleutnant out of the cave where he'd been hiding. That's how she got the glasses. The Oberleutnant was carrying a Luger, too, and the famous SS dagger, but the Zeiss was all Chris had taken. A minor bit of pilferage in light of what was going on all over Germany in the first few months following V-E

Day. Besides, they had served the Allied cause well for the past year. At the moment, they were offering information that might well preclude a trek up the mountainside.

Chris lowered the binoculars to her waist and scanned the mountainside without them. With the naked eye, she noted, the path simply couldn't be seen.

" 'E's not up there, m'um."

She did not turn around to acknowledge the man behind her. He was an informant whose name was Werner, or Horst, or Jeurgen—he answered to all three—who had learned English from cockney troops. Privately, Chris referred to him as "Fifty-Fifty." Four times she'd used him in her searches for accused war criminals. Twice his tips had paid off, and twice they had turned out to be not just transparent fabrications but quite possibly indications that he took money from the other side from time to time.

" 'E's not up there. Wastin' yer time, m'um."

This time Chris Beadle turned around. He stood a few steps below her, for the terrain was steep here; they'd ridden up from Feldkirk, the town beneath them in the valley, on a ski lift.

"What makes you so sure?" Chris peered directly into his eyes. That always made him look away. "Switzerland's just over the other side. Once he makes Switzerland . . ." She let the thought hang.

"Too cold, m'um. 'E'd never go up."

"Too cold? Then what are the cows doing up there?"

"Swiss Browns, m'um. Bred fer it. Likes the cold, they do. 'Im, 'e's got the asthma. Can't breathe in the cold."

Chris turned around again and raised the glasses. The Swiss Browns had begun to disperse a little. The ganz were gone. No surprise. They never stayed in one spot for more than a few minutes. It took her only a few seconds to work out the math: five tips, two good ones. That worked out to forty percent. So much for "Fifty-Fifty."

It seems Chris Beadle does not believe Werner, or Horst, or Jeurgen. What has led her to discount his advice?

45

Nothing Better than
a Clear Alibi

IT WAS NOT JUST THE OLD WOMAN'S EYES that warned Nik Hall to go easy; it was the whole package. At Your Peril! was written all over her.

Beginning with her clothes. The dress, made of satin (or something equally expensive) was buttoned very carefully from bottom to top, encasing her like a fortress against all assaults. The gate was protected by a brooch that was guaranteed to be worth more than a month of Nik's salary, and matched by earrings that, well, he didn't care to speculate.

Even the physical weaknesses that should have betrayed her years—Nik figured she'd be in her late eighties at least, but he certainly wasn't prepared to ask—even these weaknesses were subdued, some by subtle means, some by force of will. An example of the former was the scarf in her lap that attempted to conceal, ever so casually, hands that were ravaged irremediably by arthritis. The latter was evident in the osteoporosis that had clearly won the battle for her spine but not her spirit, for whatever effort and discomfort it cost her, Augusta Reinhold met Nik's gaze head on. She would not be the one to blink.

It was the eyes that made Nik wish someone else had picked up the telephone an hour ago at the Major Crimes section. So dark and piercing. If the eyes really were windows to the soul, then Augusta Reinhold's had one-way glass.

She spoke first.

"Are you going to stare, detective, or do you want to hear what I have to say?"

Normally, Nik would have blushed, but somehow her question fit the pattern he'd expected. He wanted her to do the talking, and that meant she would have to lead. This was not a lady accustomed to control from outside. The only way into the fortress would be through gates she unlocked herself.

Nik licked his upper lip slowly, then the bottom one, while bringing his fingers together into a steeple. Augusta Reinhold watched him intently, the powerful eyes boring in on his face. He looked back over his left shoulder.

"In the bedroom there," he said, "was your granddaughter—"

"Who raised you?!"

Nik turned back to the eyes immediately.

"Don't you know enough to look at people when you speak to them?!"

He bowed his head in apology. The gesture let him enjoy a small grin of triumph. He'd confirmed what he suspected: that she was hard of hearing. No hearing aids, though. That would betray weakness.

"Young man." Augusta grabbed the reins with authority. "Let us get on with this. What you need to know is that my granddaughter was with me when that fool was shot. I won't pretend I'm unhappy he's dead, the parasite, but it was not Siobhan who did the shooting. She is impetuous, I'll grant you. How else could one account for her marrying him so hastily? Marrying him at all! And he abused her terribly. You'll have no difficulty verifying that. But she was out in the hall with me when the shots were fired."

Nik sat expressionless. He already knew that three bullets had brought about the untimely end of Paisley Wendt, and that the noise of three shots had issued from Suite 5 within a minute before or after 11 A.M. Confirmation of the time had come from two different tenants and the building janitor.

"I was in my solarium having coffee with Esther. That's Esther Goldblum. She's in Suite 14 right across the hall from me. My only neighbor, and a widow like me. We have coffee together every morning when we're in town. Until quarter to eleven. That's when Esther leaves to do her trading. Currencies, mostly. Don't like them. Never have. Too much depends on strange little people thousands of miles away.

"No matter. When Esther left, I went and got dressed as you see me now. On Thursdays I have lunch at the League, you see, and I always take Siobhan. You can verify that easily, too.

"When I got off the elevator here on the third floor, Siobhan was waiting to get on. She was coming to get me, you see. And before you ask, there was no one else on the elevator. It was right then we heard the shots in her suite, and well, the rest is . . . is distasteful, to say the least."

"Mrs. Reinhold." Nik was careful to look straight at her this time. "Do you have a companion or a maid or housekeeper?"

A flicker of wariness crossed the dark eyes.

"Raythena comes in every day at one. She stays as long as is necessary and does what is necessary."

"And how many shots did you say you heard, Mrs. Reinhold?"

The flicker grew to a smolder.

"I didn't say."

"Yes, indeed. Excuse me." Nik spoke very softly. "Er, how many shots do you recall hearing?"

"You think I'm deaf, don't you?" The eyes were sparking now. "That's why you're almost whispering! Well, I'll tell you how many shots I heard. No! First, I'll tell you what you just said. You asked me how many shots I recall hearing, didn't you? I heard three, young man. Three!"

Nik bit down on his lower lip. He took a chance and looked back over his left shoulder again. What he had to decide, and fast, was whether to press harder on Augusta Reinhold to ferret out the truth, or instead to push on the granddaughter. In the end, it was the eyes that helped him decide to go after the younger one. Even if Siobhan was as tough as her grandmother, she had to have softer eyes.

What has led Nik Hall to believe that he is not getting the truth from Augusta Reinhold?

46

Guenther Hesch Didn't Call In!

SUSAN VINT STOPPED WITH ONE FOOT in the doorway of the little room, then leaned back and motioned to her partner to come take a look.

"Just what you'd expect," Bill Willson said, more to himself than for anyone else's benefit. "Probably hasn't been a surveillance base this neat on the entire planet. Ever."

Susan grinned and stepped into the room with Bill right behind. The two were careful about where they put their feet but it didn't take much effort. Instead of the usual flotsam that covered every available space in a room being used for a stakeout, this place looked more like someone had been preparing for surgery. A telescope stood poised and ready between a shuttered window and an adjustable stool, and except for a small table in one corner and an old-fashioned chrome and ersatz ivory ashtray stand beside the telescope, there was no other furniture.

There were no fast-food wrappers either, and no pizza boxes, no newspapers, and no electronic games—nothing to betray the tedium that accompanies surveillance.

On the table sat a camera with a telephoto lens, a cellular telephone, and a small bowl made of orange glass.

"Bet you the filters are in there," Susan said, and took a few steps to the table. She looked in the bowl and smiled grimly, first to herself, then at Bill Willson.

Bill nodded. "Nobody more predictable than Guenther Hesch." He took out his pen. "Go ahead and count 'em. Then we can tell how long—God, it stinks in here! I can't believe the way he smokes! He even rolls some of them. Every four butts he cranks into a roll-your-own. Him! For a neat freak, it doesn't add up."

Bill Willson and Susan Vint were in command of a four-site surveillance. Guenther Hesch, assigned to one of the four sites for the 8 A.M. to 4 P.M. shift, had failed to make the check-in call at 1:15 P.M. Normally a single missed call would not have triggered a quick visit like this from the two chief operatives, but this was Guenther, and Guenther was the most obsessive-compulsive person they knew.

Guenther Hesch wore a brown serge suit on Mondays and Wednesdays, a tan check on Tuesdays and Thursdays, and the jacket from one with the pants from the other on Fridays. He had three ties and wore them in rotation on consecutive days. He went to a movie matinee every Saturday afternoon, and every Sunday ate breakfast at 8:15 in a highway diner that served the same special week in, week out. Guenther always arrived at his assigned work sites at exactly three minutes before the beginning of a shift, and no one had ever known him to be late, even when impossible weather snarled traffic to a standstill. Even his dreaded chainsmoking habit was compulsively regularized. He never smoked in his car or in his apartment, and not at headquarters. He only smoked on surveillance, lighting a cigarette on the hour, and precisely every fifteen minutes thereafter.

Guenther was fanatically intolerant of any disruption of his routines and would go to any lengths to ensure this would not happen. Unfortunately he was so annoying to his colleagues that Bill and Susan constantly scrambled to find assignments like this one where he could work alone. One former partner, while pleading for reassignment, had described Guenther as so uptight that he could sit on a lump of coal and create a diamond in four days.

Another had come screaming into headquarters because he couldn't stand to watch Guenther's habit of snapping the filter off cigarettes and smoking them from the freshly defiltered end. A third had resigned rather than face a second pairing with him.

Still, in the words of the commissioner, Guenther Hesch was a "keeper." He was never late, never sick, and never asked for favors. Needless to say, he not only make every required check-in call while on surveillance duty, he made them to the scheduled second, and when the 1:15 P.M. call was not forthcoming, it took no time at all for Susan and Bill to agree they needed to see for themselves.

"Seventeen," Susan said. "And a butt. Something's wrong."

"I agree," Bill replied. He frowned at Susan Vint. "No sign of a struggle, no note anywhere. Phone works. I don't get it. He was here. Why didn't he call?"

How do Bill Willson and Susan Vint know that Guenther Hesch was still in the surveillance site at 1:15 P.M.?

47

Right Over the Edge
of Old Baldy

DIRECTLY AHEAD ABOUT TEN PACES OR SO, a double white blaze on the trunk of a large oak told Pam Hall the trail turned sharply to the right. She paused for a moment, putting out her hand to lean on another oak. The edge of Old Baldy was just ahead but Pam chose to stop anyway to enjoy the moment. It was her favorite time of year, every hiker's favorite: early fall.

Absently shifting her backpack to a more comfortable spot, she let her eyes drift across the multihued canopy above her. Then she looked back down the trail toward Kimberley Rock, where she'd stopped for a drink of water about ten minutes ago. From Kimberley on there was almost no underbrush on the Bruce Trail. Just huge, old-growth forest enclosing a deep silence that even the birds respected, a silence that went right into the soul. It was like being in an empty cathedral in the late afternoon, one of those moments that all hikers know they share with cloistered monks and nuns.

Perhaps it was the silence. Certainly it was the deep peacefulness, the precious sense of the moment, that made the scream leave such a ragged tear in Pam's consciousness. It began as a moan. Even though it lasted only a second or two, this was the part that would linger more intensely than any other in her nightmares. At first it sounded almost like pleasure, not unlike the aaahs one frequently heard from people who first encountered the vista from the lip of Old Baldy. But there was no pleasure in this moan. It turned from an "aaah" into an "iieee" and then into a long "nooo" that faded out and away like oil running down a funnel. Someone had gone over the cliff.

Later, when Pam was explaining her suspicions about Hadley Withrop to the officer from the Park Service, she realized that the entire event had taken place only a minute or so ahead of her on the trail. It had been two years since she'd hiked this part of the escarpment and she wasn't aware she was quite so close to Old Baldy when it happened. That became another part of her nightmare. Had she not stopped at the double blaze to drink in the quiet, would Sheena Withrop still be alive? Or would she, Pam, have been pushed over the edge too?

Either way, she'd gotten there too late. When the scream first pierced Pam's senses and the logic of what was happening finally tumbled through, she found herself gripping the oak tree in panic with both hands, wasting precious seconds in the process of absorbing the shock. In her nightmare the next sequence always came back in slow motion: the bending over to pick up her walking stick and then inadvertently kicking it away so she had to bend again; the slosh of her water bottle working its way loose in her backpack as she ran up the trail, affecting her balance; the spiderweb that grabbed the bridge of her nose and pushed into both eyes as though it was trying to capture and hold her right there in the middle of the trail; the sight of a pair of turkey vultures circling high out over Beaver Valley, obvious to the drama below them; and then, as she came up to the shaking Hadley Withrop at the edge of the cliff, the echo of Sheena's cry. An "aaah" and an "iieee" and a "nooo" all over again, in precisely that order.

She was sure she had heard an echo too. Positive. And her nightmare confirmed it. But it was also the part of her account that made the officer from the Park Service exchange quick glances with his partner. The doubt in their faces was plain.

"As I came up to Baldy," Pam told the officer, "he—Withrop— is standing there. Well, not quite standing. He's kinda bouncing around. You know, upset. Pacing.

"I think I really scared him. He obviously wasn't expecting any- one. Certainly didn't know I was on the trail. But he didn't say anything about that. He just said, 'She went over, she went over.' But not panicky, you know, not all cranked up like you'd expect. He talked to me like we'd just met on the trail. Casually, you know, as people do.

"We just came up from Kimberley,' he said to me. 'Ate our lunch at the rock there. And we weren't here two minutes when . . .' Now that's when he started to cry. Went down to his knees and put his face in his hands, and started to shake. Really sounds like shock, doesn't it?

"But here's why I don't like his story, Officer," Pam added emphatically. "And I don't think you should like it either."

What is Pam Hall about to tell the officer from the Park Service that will explain why she doesn't accept Hadley Withrop's account of what happened?

48

Sunstroke, and Who Knows What Else!

LYING PRONE ON HIS BACK with his wrists tied to stakes, Evan Strachan was keenly aware of his vulnerability, so he spoke to his sister with the least possible assertiveness. She was two years older than he, as well, something he could never get himself to discount.

"I still don't see why you can't get Pindaric to do this," he said. "It's his case."

Sara wouldn't have noticed his tone anyway. She was too preoccupied with a pair of stakes and with pieces of nylon rope that she had wound around her brother's ankles.

"Because you're about the right size," she replied. "Pindaric, on the other hand, is a fat slob. And a jerk," she added. "He's profane, obscene, and vulgar. He hates women. And he's got dog breath. Need more?

"Guess that about covers it," Evan mumbled.

"Besides,"—Sara's explanation wasn't finished—"he's head of the firm. And the head of the firm doesn't lie on his back on a rifle range and let a law student tie him to stakes!"

"Not at the glorious firm of Brutus, Judas, Machiavelli and Quisling anyway!" This time Evan's tone suggested more confidence in his opinion. "Lawyers!" He blew at a long blade of coarse grass that kept tickling his face in the early morning breeze.

"I told you to stop calling it that! It's Pindaric, Pindaric, Krafcywcz and Steinberg. They're creeps but they're going to hire me when I graduate. Now move up a bit so I can put these ankle stakes in the exact same holes too!"

"But then the sun'll be in my eyes," Evan protested. "This way I get some shadow from the stake. It's hot already, in case you didn't notice, and it's gonna be a scorcher. Or do you want me to get sunstroke too, like that kid?"

For the first time in several minutes, Sara Strachan drew her attention away from tying down her brother's ankles, to look back at the first stage of her handiwork. Evan's wrists were tied to stakes, angled into the ground. He was lying in precisely the spot where, forty-eight hours before, Cadet J.D. Elayna had submitted himself to the indignity that had allegedly put him into intensive care at Etobicoke General. According to reports, his chances of complete recovery were still slim at best.

Cadet Elayna had run seriously afoul of the rules at Nobleton Military Institute, and under the self-discipline policy followed by the school, his barrack-mates had decided to stake him to the ground below a target on the rifle range, where he lay during a morning practice with live ammunition. He'd survived that part (physically at least), but then he'd been left there on a day that turned out to be the peak of a week-long heat wave. By the time the school's administration found out and intervened, the cadet was dehydrated and totally delirious. Whatever emotional trauma he had suffered was still undetermined, but his parents hadn't waited to find out. They'd already formally notified the Nobleton Military Institute of their intent to sue, and the Institute had immediately retained Pindaric.

Sara's eyes narrowed. She was deep in thought and didn't notice that her brother was scratching his still untied ankles by crossing one over the other and drawing them back and forth like a carpenter with a handsaw. She was only vaguely aware that he was talking to her.

"Do you know how to tell if lawyers are lying, Sara?" he was saying.

"Evan," Sara said very softly.

"Their lips move."

"Evan," she repeated.

"How can you tell the difference between a dead skunk and a dead lawyer on a highway?"

"Evan!" Sara got to her feet. "That cadet. He could have got up and walked away if he wanted to! Well, not when the bullets were flying, of course, but right after!"

How has Sara Strachan come to this conclusion?

49

Should the Third
Secretary Sign?

HAD SHE BEEN MORE OF A FEMINIST, Ena Mellor would likely have raised Cain, or at least been resentful, over the fact that last spring's round of promotions had gone exclusively to men. But she wasn't particularly intense about her feminism; nor was she the type to hold a grudge. Besides, she'd gotten a bit of a prize in any case. Her rank may have continued to be Third Secretary, which she'd been for the past two years, but now she was Third Secretary at the embassy in Vienna instead of in Cairo.

For Ena the transfer meant an apartment in which the plumbing worked as a rule and not an exception. There was no baksheesh to pay every time she needed anything done. She could picnic in the grounds of the Schonbrunn Palace with no beggars playing on her guilt. There were concerts—oh, were there concerts! Mozart, Beethoven, Mahler . . . And museums. And churches. And history. Ena knew that if she had pushed hard last spring, she might have become a Second Secretary, but in Katmandu. Hard to get good schnitzel in Katmandu. No, Third Secretary in Vienna was definitely a better deal.

Admittedly, the Soviets had messed up her pleasure temporarily. When their tanks rolled into Prague last month and forced

Alexander Dubcek and the Czech government to accept "normalization," a flood of refugees had spilled into Austria. Most of them ended up in the Traiskirchen camp. Among other things, the location of the camp interrupted Ena's now thoroughly established habit of lunching at one of the street cafes in St. Stephen's Square. Still, Traiskirchen wasn't all that bad, for it was set in a vineyard near the city.

What bothered Ena a lot more was making decisions that deeply affected the lives of the refugees. Her signature at the bottom of a single document could mean freedom for a refugee. Without her signature, the applicant could well be sent back to the repression behind the Iron Curtain. It was a power that made Ena Mellor extremely uncomfortable.

Well over half the refugees had no papers, for they'd fled that night of August 21 with only the clothes on their backs. Ena often had to rule on the truth of an applicant's identity on the basis of a driver's license, or a photograph, or a work card. Yesterday, the only proof one refugee could offer was the few koruny in her purse.

The man who sat before her now offered her a first, however. He had no passport—nothing unusual about that for someone from behind the Iron Curtain—no driver's license, no work card, in fact, nothing but a very worn and creased photograph. Nevertheless, it was a photograph that certainly suggested his life would be in danger if he were returned to Czechoslovakia, and police officials there knew he was coming.

The picture had been taken in Moscow. Even without Ena's experience in foreign affairs, she would have recognized Red Square and the Lenin Mausoleum. It took a magnifying glass, however, to see that the man in front of the Mausoleum was also the man sitting nervously on the other side of her desk. The same glass showed, very clearly, that he was vandalizing one of the USSR's most important monuments by painting over Lenin's name. Most noticeable was that the "L" had been changed to a box, and the "I" had been altered to resemble a Byzantine cross. How he had accomplished this in the middle of Red Square, with all the guards about, was incomprehensible to Ena, but it was a crime that, if he'd been caught, would have meant a long stretch in a gulag. Still, how he'd done it was not Ena's problem. Her problem was whether or not to sign his application.

Should Ena Mellor sign the application? Why, or why not?

50

A Successful Bust
at 51 Rosehill

WHEN WORD GOT AROUND THE SQUAD that geraniums had figured in the high-profile drug bust Jack Atkin made at 51 Rosehill,
no one was the least bit surprised. As the rumor went, Jack had
bolted upright out of a sound sleep at 4 A.M., shouted "Geraniums!" into the darkness, and within less than two hours there
were narcs all over the illicit lab on Rosehill.

Jack's partner explained it all to the others in the squad that
afternoon, down in the coffee room. She and Jack had entered 51
Rosehill late the previous day—with a warrant, of course—and
found absolutely nothing. At least, nothing illegal.

That was contrary to expectations. The stakeouts were convinced that the townhouse at that address held a tiny but very
efficient lab where cocaine was being diluted and bagged for street
sale. Yet, as Mandy Leamington had said, "When me 'n' Jack did
the search, there wasn't a thing that'd say drugs.

"It's like somebody made them with a cookie cutter, those
townhouses," Mandy had explained. "They all look exactly the
same. Same size, same shape, same everything top to bottom. And
they're all the same size and shape inside too. Like somebody
made a bunch of boxes and set them one on top a' the other.

Thirty a' them. Fifteen each side a' the street. Woodington Manor, it's called.

"Anyway, you go in from the back, from the parking area. Like, the back door is really the front door. Weird, eh? OK, so you step in, and you're on a landing that's halfway between the basement and the first floor, and there's a staircase on the left, six steps down, and beside it, one that goes six steps up. To the first floor. We went down first, and on the wall across, facing west, there's this shelf under the window well, with a two-seater sofa under that, same length as the window. And there's geraniums on the shelf. Five of them. Really gorgeous. Big blooms and red as can be.

" 'Course, you know Jack. Place could be on fire but he's got to check the geraniums first. You know how he always sticks his middle finger into the pots?

"Me, I head right for one of these massage chairs they got in there. You know, the big easy chairs that vibrate? They got rollers to go up and down your back? Really pricy. Coupla grand, right? And they got two a' them! Jammed in on each side 'tween the sofa and the wall. So I sit in one a' them, but it's not plugged in. Jack, he sits in the other, when he finally gets his finger outa the geraniums, that is. Now, that one works, we find out eventually, but he doesn't find the switch at first 'cause there's no lamps and it's kinda dark, and we didn't turn the overhead light on 'cause, well, you 'member that Lake Rosseau bust when the light switch was booby-trapped?

"Now here's the real deal. Upstairs on the first floor, they got two more a' these chairs! Can ya believe it? Set up just like the basement! Sofa in the center, below the window, just the same. Shelf full a' geraniums. Gorgeous geraniums again. And these chairs on either side! Only thing different is these got nice lamps beside 'em this time, on end tables. Oh yeah, and six geraniums instead a' five. Jack says there's more light so they can put more on the shelf. Squeeze 'em together a bit. Lotsa books upstairs too. We figured this is where they do their reading 'cause there's no TV up here. But these chairs! Y'ever sat in one a' them? We gotta get one in here. Yuh can be asleep in five seconds!

"Anyway, I says to Jack they may not be into drugs but into stolen massage chairs, but he doesn't even hear me. Got his finger in the geraniums again, and lookin' out the window, checkin' the sunset and mumblin'.

"Got to hand it to him, though. It was him that figured out they were hidin' a lab."

How has Jack Atkin figured out that a lab has been hidden?

51

The Case of the Body
in Cubicle 12

"SUICIDE, BUT I DON'T BUY IT."

Aaron Penfold spoke without looking at his partner, who was also named Aaron—Aaron Walmsley. Back on the third floor at District 18 headquarters they were known as A-1 (Penfold) and A-2 (Walmsley) or, more frequently, as "Double-A."

A-2 was standing just inside a main entrance door, in an office cubicle. It was one of thirty such cubicles, each precisely the same size and configuration, all squeezed into a large, windowless, rectangular room. Each cubicle had half-walls with tiny quasi-doorways opening into a quasi-hallway that ran around the inside circumference. The only departure from this cookie-cutter design was a raised dais in the center of the room. Five steps led up to a platform where a circular desk with a hole in the center commanded an aerial view. A chair stood inside the doughnut-shaped desk. The supervisor's chair.

"Yeah, but . . ." A-2 had arrived some time after his partner and was still getting a feel for the scene. "Sure seems like the kind of place that would drive someone to suicide."

He took a single step, managing to cross the hallway by doing so, and stood at the entrance to Work Area 12. From there, he could see the note in the printer.

"Sorry," it said. "But there's just no point."

It wasn't signed.

"What do they do in here, anyway?" A-2 continued. "Place looks like a bunch of fattening pens."

A-1 pulled his gaze away from the body of a woman slumped over the counter in the cubicle. At first glance she was of indeterminate age, but the neatly coiffed hair covering the upturned side of her face appeared to be naturally black, suggesting she was likely younger than older. She sat in a standard-issue, armless office chair, with castors designed to roll her efficiently across the Plexiglas platform that covered the standard-issue gray broadloom. Her torso lay across a desk blotter that took up the only flat space on the counter.

As for the rest of Work Area 12, it was obvious that computer equipment had priority. There was a gooseneck lamp with a strangely incongruous Tiffany-style shade, but it had to fight for its spot behind a hard drive. Beside one of three keyboards sat an inkwell and an ornate fountain pen that, whatever the woman's age, was certainly older than she had been. Everything else was plastic and high-tech metal alloy—hard drives, a scanner, three screens, three keyboards, and a printer. Work Area 12, like the rest of Work Areas 1 to 30, was geared to output.

"They're programmers," A-1 replied finally. "The sweatshop of the twenty-first century. They spend their miserable working lives in these boxes, grinding out software for their masters until the next technical revolution, and then they're tossed because they're as outdated as the equipment they work with. Friend of mine— he's a real techie—says these people last about five years."

Aaron Walmsley grimaced and stepped forward to look more closely at the bottle that lay open beside the woman's right hand. He used a tweezers to lift it so that he could read the pharmacist's label and verify his prediction that it had contained barbiturates.

"One on the floor too." A-1 pointed at another prescription bottle under the counter. It too was empty, and had rolled under a Gordian knot of wires and connectors and surge protectors to stop against a pair of patent leather, high-heeled pumps.

"Downers?" A-2 asked.

"Uh-huh. More of the same. If both bottles were full, she got at least eighty pills down. Enough to do the job."

"Yeah, but I agree. I don't think it's a suicide either."

Why are both Aarons convinced that the situation they are investigating is not a suicide?

52

The Case of the
Broken Lawnmower

NEITHER WOMAN WORE A UNIFORM, so that standing on the sidewalk that paralleled the quiet street, both looked more like suburban housewives having a morning chat than detectives (first grade) from Homicide Division. Mary Blair stood with one hand in her pocket, the other on her hip. She was frowning at a small rectangle that Kristy Bailey had just spray-painted onto the lawn that edged the sidewalk. For her own part, Kristy was looking with some distaste at the yellow paint that, despite great care, she'd managed to get on her fingers.

They were the first ever mother-daughter team on the force and for that reason attracted a degree of media attention which made the commissioner extremely uneasy. Fortunately for his peace of mind, the commissioner had no idea that dialogue like the following was a regular occurrence between these two high-profile officers.

MARY BLAIR: (*wrinkling her nose at the painted rectangle*) The only spot on his front lawn where you can see between the houses across the street there, into the alley.

KRISTY BAILEY: (*rubbing thumb and forefinger*) Darn stuff is so sticky.

MARY BLAIR: Everywhere else the view is blocked by something. Houses, trees, the victim's garage with that purple door. Guy probably deserves to die for painting it that color.

KRISTY BAILEY: Took almost a week to get it off last time.

MARY BLAIR: (*stepping into the rectangle*) And it's precisely this spot where his lawnmower handle comes apart.

KRISTY BAILEY: Makes my fingers look like I smoke roll-your-owns! Such an ugly yellow.

MARY BLAIR: So our witness turns off the mower and then hears a shot. Looks up to see his neighbor getting it in the chest. Very coincidental!

KRISTY BAILEY: Yeah, but this is where we found the nut.

MARY BLAIR: The what?

KRISTY BAILEY: The nut. It came off the bolt right here, and then the lawnmower handle came apart. You know, for want of a nail the shoe was lost, for want of a shoe . . . Like that.

MARY BLAIR: I've got yellow paint on my toe!

KRISTY BAILEY: (*taking Mary's elbow*) And there's the bolt! Over there, about five or six steps away. Almost on the sidewalk. I wonder how we missed it earlier?

MARY BLAIR: Should be able to get it off with kerosene, don't you think, or cleaning fluid?

KRISTY BAILEY: Just goes to prove again, you can't check too many times.

MARY BLAIR: We got kerosene back at the station?

KRISTY BAILEY: Janitor probably does.

MARY BLAIR: Right! Never thought of that! Wonder why the witness lied.

KRISTY BAILEY: Well, that's our next step, isn't it?

MARY BLAIR: Let's go back right now. We've got to do the paper on this anyway. (*Steps very carefully out of the rectangle.*) Imagine! Painting your garage door purple!

KRISTY BAILEY: Actually, it's puce.

MARY BLAIR: That's even worse.

Why do Mary Blair and Kristy Bailey conclude that the man mowing the lawn was lying?

53

A Quiet Night with
Danielle Steel?

"COULD BE WE'VE CAUGHT A BIT of a break, Steve. According to the list of emergency telephone numbers at the kitchen phone, her regular physician lives two doors east of here. That'd be the odd-looking house with the cupola over the front portico? No lawn? Pushed right out to the street almost? There's a patrolman on the way over there right now. Maybe we can wrap this up without needing to do an autopsy. Almost for sure, no inquest, right?

To anyone unacquainted with Steve Lanark, it would have looked like he was paying no attention whatever to his partner. Chantal Breton was used to these stone-faced responses, though. They had worked together for several years in a one-two ranking in the coroner's office. In fact it was widely expected that Chantal would take over as chief when Steve retired in three months, and widely held that she deserved to do so.

Chantal kept talking. "What we've got isn't all that dramatic, except maybe for the Jacuzzi." She wrinkled her nose and stared with dispassionate professional interest at the body lying in the now-cold water of the large bathtub.

"Woman in her late forties. Executive. Married and divorced twice. Lives alone. Sunday night she pours a Scotch, fills the

Jacuzzi, picks up the paperback she's got going, and gets into the tub. There's no marks or bruises, no signs of violence, no bumps on her head or back of her neck. She's even wearing her glasses.

"Tell you what." Chantal Breton looked around to be sure none of the police officers in the next room could hear. "I'll give you two to one the physician tells us she had a bad heart. Or very high BP.

"No, I'll go you one better! I'll give you *three* to one that if we have to do an autopsy, we don't find water in the lungs. Like, she died before going under the water. OK?"

Steve Lanark still behaved as if he did not even hear his partner. Instead he was hunched over a small ersatz marble slab on one side of the bathtub. It was about the size of an end table and, indeed, was designed to serve that purpose. At one corner of the slab, farthest from the tap end of the tub, a facecloth in a deep burgundy lay folded neatly with a bar of soap sitting on top. Neither had been used. At the diagonal corner, within easier reach, was a cocktail glass, its bottom still covered with the remains of a drink. Scotch, the two doctors concluded earlier.

Steve appeared to be using the platform as a mirror to examine a shaving cut on his chin. The marble was ivory, with subtle streaks of gray and an occasional hint of ocher. Its surface was pristine, like the rest of the place, and gleamed in the high light.

"Really neat, this woman, wasn't she?" Chief Coroner Lanark spoke for the first time. He lifted his face from the side platform, but still didn't look at Chantal. "I mean, look at her robe there on the floor. She folded it before getting into the tub. How many people do you know do that?"

He got to his feet, arched his back, and then tapped first one foot on the floor then the other. "New shoes," he said. "I hate new shoes." He twisted his right foot like someone extinguishing a cigarette butt. "This whole place . . . Why don't you give one of those cops out front there a three to one that they can't find a toothpaste spatter on that mirror there above the sink?"

"Or a dust bunny under her bed?" Chantal added. "Yeah, she's neat all right. Or else her cleaning lady comes in every day. I know what you mean about the shoes, by the way. You should try it from my end. Men have no idea at all what shoe designers do to women's feet. I mean, they expect that—"

"Help me lift the book out of the water." Steve interrupted what he knew would otherwise become an extended commentary on women's podiatric tribulations. "I think if we use that long-handled shoehorn over there, we won't have to get ourselves wet."

Silently Chantal went over to the back of the bathroom door and lifted the necessary implement off a hook and brought it over to the tub. It slid easily under the sodden paperback.

"Danielle Steel." Steve made no effort to control the distaste in his voice when he saw the cover. "Now tell me, is a woman like this going to read this kind of stuff? I mean, she's CEO of her firm, a big success. Appears to be a totally no-nonsense type. I mean, Danielle Steel?"

Chantal sighed with the patience of one long inured to male obtuseness. "Hey, it's her own private bathroom. It's the end of the day. She's got a Jacuzzi. She's having a drink. You want her to read Kierkegaard or something? Give me a break!"

Steve pursed his lips and nodded. "Yeah, I guess not," he agreed finally with a sigh, although his tone suggested he was not entirely convinced. Then he added somewhat grumpily, "And before you offer, I'm not taking any bets on whether we find more novels like this in the rest of the house. Whoever was in here after this woman died wouldn't be that stupid."

On what basis does Chief Coroner Steve Lanark conclude that someone was in the bathroom after the victim died?

54

Vandalism at the
Bel Monte Gallery

ROBBIE DEXEL PACED BACK AND FORTH on the sidewalk, forcing himself to go slowly and deliberately, at a measured pace, but his distress was obvious. Every few seconds he would stop, put his hand to his mouth, and cough hard. Then the pacing would resume. Alongside him, in the street, cars passed by in a regular rhythm. On the other side, just a few feet away, under a chestnut tree that towered over the building behind her, a uniformed police officer watched with interest. Eventually she grinned and spoke.

"Stomping back and forth like that isn't going to get them here any faster, you know. I mean, they're late. The roads are icy. Nothing we haven't encountered before."

Robbie stopped and glared hard at her. "Hey, it makes me feel better, OK? You got a problem with that? I prefer to walk and cough instead of stand and cough. Now if that bothers you then, then . . . Look, I'm sorry. It's this lousy cold. Makes me so cranky. Happens this time of year without fail. Ever since I can remember, just before Christmas I get a cold."

Officer Dale Dunn grinned again and nodded. She moved a few steps closer.

"No problem. I'm not much good at waiting either, really. And

I don't have a cold! Quite frankly I don't see why we can't wait inside in the gallery instead of out here in the cold."

She waved at the building behind her. It was a two-story, turn-of-the-century brick structure, very tastefully renovated. The whole street was like that: restored buildings that housed boutiques, all of them upscale shops with limited hours and one-of-a-kind inventory. The facing immediately behind Dale framed a large wooden door, which in turn held a brass plaque announcing in delicate letters that the Bel Monte Gallery awaited its very special clientele on the other side.

"At least if we were inside," Dale went on "we could look at the paintings. A lot more interesting than staring at the traffic out here."

Robbie took a deep breath, slowly, so that he wouldn't make himself cough. He spoke slowly too, trying to get a whole sentence out without having to clear his throat.

"We have to wait out here," he said, "because here is where the new witness says he was standing when he saw the job being done."

Robbie was referring to an incident at the Bel Monte Gallery that had taken place several months previously. During the night, someone had broken into the gallery through the roof, thereby defeating the security system, and had damaged a number of very valuable oil paintings by slashing them with a knife. The police had made an arrest within days, however, and at that very moment in the county jail one of the city's best known art collectors, Marc-Jean DiBeau, was being held without bail for his upcoming trial.

Dale had been the arresting officer and Robbie was the investigator from the agency that had insured the paintings. The two of them had returned to the Bel Monte site together because of a somewhat startling development. A witness had surfaced the day before, telling a story that put an entirely new twist on the case. It was their job now to question him, and they wanted to do it at the scene.

Dale pointed up the street to where a police patrol car had

pulled over to the curb. "Here we are," she said. "Our witness." She lifted her eyebrows at Robbie. "Don't be shocked."

Robbie pivoted slowly and focused on the two people getting out of the car. One was a police officer, an older man, and the other, well, in spite of Dale's warning, Robbie couldn't quite restrain himself.

"Him? That's the witness? He's a streetperson, a . . . a bum!"

Dale shrugged her shoulders. "Think about it. Who else is going to be out here at two o'clock in the morning? This is a commercial district. There's nobody living here. By the way, his name is Patchy Lomax."

"Patchy?"

"Look at the clothes. What would you call him?"

As Patchy and his escort came closer, Robbie swore he was looking at a circus clown. There was barely a spot on Patchy's clothes that was not covered by squares and rectangles of every imaginable texture and hue. Perched on top of this kaleidoscope was a mass of crinkly gray hair that grew up and down and out, covering every facial feature except for a very red, round nose that moved like some kind of battery-powered toy.

Patchy wasted no time. "Up there. Up there at the window, 'at's where I seen her." A skinny, nicotine-stained finger appeared out of a rainbow sleeve and pointed at a window on the second floor of the Bel Monte Gallery. " 'At's where I seen her do it. Slash them pictures. Big woman. Tall. Lotsa hair. Long. An' I seen her. No question."

Robbie frowned. One of the partners who owned the gallery was a tall woman with long hair. He started to talk but the coughing took over, so Dale asked the obvious questions.

"OK, so you saw a woman at the window, but you're going to have to do a lot better than that. What were you doing here at two o'clock in the morning? And it's dark then. You can see in the dark maybe?"

Patchy raised his red nose in the air. Another skinny, yellow-brown finger appeared, this time pointed accusingly at Dale. Before Patchy could speak, Robbie interjected.

"What we want to know more than anything is why you didn't tell us all this four months ago when it happened. Why now?"

The finger was joined by its colleagues, the grimy hand now held out like a traffic cop, first at Robbie, then at Dale. Patchy lifted his red nose even further. With great dignity, he turned to the bus shelter a few feet from where they were standing. "In here, lady cop." He took a step and turned to Robbie. "You too. It's answers you want? Then one at a time. We start in here."

Both Robbie and Dale followed obediently; neither of them caught the smile on the face of the older officer.

"I was in here," Patchy announced once he was fully satisfied he had everyone in place and fully attentive. "'Cause you could tell it was gonna rain hard."

Robbie stole a quick glance at Dale. Patchy was right about that. It had rained the night of the break-in, a harsh downpour that, according to the weather office, had begun at 2:15 A.M. and lasted about ten minutes.

"Now yuz look up there." The finger came out again, leading them back to the second floor. "That winda'. Right b'tween them branches there. Ya see? 'At's where I seen 'er, 'cause the lights is on all the time in that buildin'. Leastways all night they are. Ya knew that too, didn't ya, lady cop? Tryin' t' fool old Patchy, weren't ya?"

Through the labyrinth of hair, Robbie could see a pair of dark eyes gleaming triumphantly. He took a long breath very slowly and said, "But this doesn't explain why you waited all this time to tell anybody what you saw."

The gleaming eyes bored into the young investigator's. "Well, young fella, it just happens that I don't read the art news every day. How'm I supposed to know that somebody has ruined a painting? So far's I know, she mighta been doin' that 'cause she was supposed to. Ya know, cuttin' it up and then callin' it art.

"Anyways, I didn't know nothin' about this until I met yer Mark John Dee Bo fella down at th'county. Some right interestin' people in that jail from time t' time. Anyways, ya got the wrong guy. It was a woman done it. I seen her."

Without waiting for a response, Patchy Lomax turned and left the shelter, heading back to the police car that had brought him. Dale Dunn, meanwhile, continued to stare at the window, as did Robbie Dexel, each waiting for the other to speak.

It was Robbie who finally broke the silence. "Pretty solid, you agree?"

Dale nodded.

"I almost bought it," Robbie continued. "You too?"

Dale nodded again.

Apparently, neither Robbie Dexel nor Dale Dunn have been convinced by Patchy Lomax's story. Why not? What's wrong with Patchy's version?

55

Laying Charges
Too Quickly?

HOPE ROGERS STARED ABSENTLY at the empty chair opposite her, letting the back of her mind speculate on the truth of the old adage that bad things come in threes. If it was true, she felt, then she and her team were due for a turn of luck. Three times in the past several months, the empty chair had been filled for meetings like this by DeWitt Thompson-Cruze, the most inept—in Hope's opinion—prosecuting attorney she'd ever had the misfortune to deal with since she'd become Senior Investigator. Three times Thompson-Cruze had bungled the cases she and her colleagues had so carefully worked out together. This afternoon's meeting would launch their fourth together. If the wheel of fortune had any grease on its axle, as Hope fervently prayed for, her success rate just had to roll into better times.

"Should I start anyway?" Don Reilly's voice startled Hope. Don was the team's case analyst. "I've got that presentation at four, you know. To the Safety Commission?"

Hope replied without releasing her gaze at the empty chair. "Give it another minute. The traffic out there doesn't make distinctions between lawyers and idiots, so maybe he—"

A loud crash in the hall and a sudden opening of the door announced the arrival of DeWitt Thompson-Cruze.

"Elevator," he said, making circular gestures with his left hand, more or less in the direction of the hallway. No one was sure what he meant, but no one really wanted to know either.

Don Reilly cleared his throat and, when he had Hope's attention, asked "Now?" with his eyebrows. Hope held up her hand just slightly.

"DeWitt, are you quite ready now?" she asked.

"Elevator was jammed," he replied. "Couldn't reach the button for the seventh and I had to ride up to ten, and then it expressed . . ."

"DeWitt!" Wayne Brogan spoke for the first time. He made everybody jump. "DeWitt, shut up. Okay? This is about the Scalabianca murder. The rest of us want to get on with it. Now if you feel you can concentrate . . ."

Hope indulged herself in the putdown for just a few seconds, and then quickly turned the team to business.

"Go ahead, Don," she directed.

"The videotapes are being sequenced and numbered as we sit here," Don began. "Should be ready later this afternoon. Maybe we . . ." He paused to let Hope fill in.

"We can see them individually," Hope said. "I want everyone to do that, by the way. But tomorrow afternoon, same time, we view together. Everybody clear on that?" She looked pointedly at DeWitt Thompson-Cruze. "At 2 P.M.?"

There were nods all round.

"Just give us the summary for now," Hope said to Don, who immediately began reading from his notes.

"Loredana Angelica Scalabianca. Aged fifty-four. Wife of Nunzio Gregorio Scalabianca for thirty-six years. 241 Lambeth Gardens, that's over in the Albion Park district. Found yesterday morning by her daughter, at . . . at . . ." He shuffled his notes several times. "Eleven, no—ah, here it is! At somewhere between ten to and ten after eleven. Daughter's not absolutely sure."

"We're onto that, Hope," Andy Biemiller broke in. "The

daughter's, uh, name's Theresa Manno. She's pretty sure now it was before eleven. I'm seeing her later today. She's kind of shook up, needless to say."

Don waited for Andy to add more. When it didn't happen he went back to his notes. "M.E. puts time of death at about 4 A.M. yesterday morning. Body was found in the kitchen. Severe blow to the back of the head, but her head, neck and shoulders were wet. Water on the floor too." Don looked up from his notes. "What it looks like, I mean, you can judge for yourself from the videotape, what it looks like is that she was surprised. Well, I don't know about surprised. Anyway, it appears the murderer came at her from behind, bonked her and either she fell into the sink or he held her in to finish the job. You know, drown her?"

"Why 'he'?" Wayne Brogan wanted to know.

Hope looked over her glasses at Don, who replied without animosity. One of the purposes of these meetings was to challenge assumptions.

"Granted," Don replied with a nod. "But the victim was a big woman. At the very least, the perp would have to be good and strong."

"The daughter's no will-o-the-wisp, for what it's worth," Andy chimed in. "She's got to go 145 pounds or more. And that's power big, too. She's not fat."

"OK," Don conceded. "He or she—the perp—it seems, hit the Scalabianca woman and then—this is appearances again— drowned her."

Wayne Brogan held up one hand. "Before we go down that road any farther. My examination shows she was killed by the blow. No water in the lungs, not even in the mouth or trachea."

Hope pressed a little. "But her hair and neck and shoulders were wet?"

"Well, not soaking," Don clarified. "I guess, more on the damp side, but definitely not from perspiration. Somehow her head and shoulders were in water."

"What on earth was she doing at the sink at four o'clock in the morning?" Hope asked.

"I've got that," Andy said. "You want it now?"

"You got any more?" Hope asked of Don.

"Just the videotape," Don replied. "You said you only wanted summaries for this meeting."

Hope nodded. "OK, Andy, let's have yours."

Andy didn't use notes. "Nunzio Scalabianca, the husband." He cleared his throat and began again. "Nunzio Scalabianca does ornamental metalwork. Apparently he's really an old-world-type craftsman. An artist. One of the uniforms at the scene is into that stuff. Said Nunzio is the one they all want to be like. Anyway, he's freelance. Works in a shop out the back. His story is that because of the heat wave, he'd reversed his schedule. Was working nights."

Andy shifted in his chair and looked briefly at DeWitt Thompson-Cruze, who'd been writing busily. "That's credible, I'd say. He's got all that hot welding equipment. There's a forge in the shop too. Anyway, he says that Angie—he calls her Angie—has been having real problems sleeping for the past year. According to him, her behavior's been totally weird for a couple of years now, and getting worse. Gets up and goes to the kitchen at all hours. The daughter verifies that. Stubborn woman too, according to the daughter. Wouldn't wear her hearing aid any more, for example."

"The way I have it," Hope broke in, "Nunzio was supposedly off at a job site a mile or two away. Is that right?" She looked at Andy for confirmation.

Andy nodded.

"So his hours are just as offbeat as hers," Hope added.

Andy nodded again. "No witness for this," he said. "No night security at the job site. I've got some uniforms canvassing the neighbors right now. Maybe one of them went to the can at 4 A.M. and happened to look out."

"Anyway." He shifted in his chair. "Here's the damning piece. We found a ball peen hammer at the bottom of the toolbox he carries in his car. Cheap thing you can get at any department store. Stood out 'cause it's new. No marks on the head or dirt on the handle."

"Prints?" Hope asked.

Andy shook his head. "Wiped. But not carefully enough. We got some blood off it. Ninety-five percent certainty it's hers. We'll get to 99.9 with DNA. That's by tomorrow, I hope."

Wayne broke in. "Ball peen hammer's consistent with the cause of death. Three blows. Likely died immediately from the first one. Dead center in the back of the head."

"Right- or left-handed?" Hope asked.

"Right," Wayne answered and then looked at Andy. "Nunzio right-handed?" he asked.

DeWitt Thompson-Cruze waited for Andy to nod "yes" and then jumped in. "Sounds like enough to me," he said to Hope. "I'd say we stop wasting time and charge this Nunzio."

Each of the others watched Hope carefully. Hope had trouble suppressing a grin.

"DeWitt," Hope spoke slowly. She was looking out the window. "You ever heard of the old saying that bad things come in threes?"

Thompson-Cruze shook his head, frowning. He had no idea where Hope was going with this.

"What I want to know is, when there's a fourth," she continued, "is it really the fourth, or is it in fact the first in a brand-new series of three?"

Thompson-Cruze's frown deepened, but Hope didn't wait to let him articulate his confusion. "Because if you've missed the obvious hole here," she said pointedly, "Nunzio's counsel is going to bury you in it."

Hope Rogers is aware of a weakness in the cast that, in her opinion, would preclude laying any charges against Nunzio at this stage. What is it?

56

Taking Down the
Yellow Tape

SERGEANT SAGER'S VOICE CARRIED right through into the washroom, adding to Geoff Dilley's agony. He was sure it was Fate, some powerful, enduring curse that had been visited on a misbehaving ancestor and had now passed down to him. There was certainly no other reason, at least not a logical one, to explain why, of the six sergeants in 42 Division, he had to land in Sager's section. She was career-driven, demanding, unreasonable, and impossible to please. In Geoffrey's opinion anyway. Sager was even to blame for the stomach cramps that had driven him to the washroom for over half his shift. Had he gone to his regular Friday poker game the night before, as both his instinct and his inclination told him to do, instead of to Menna Corracci's retirement party just to please Sager, then he wouldn't have eaten egg salad sandwiches. It had to be Fate, for he never missed poker. And worse, he never ate egg salad sandwiches. It was the egg salad—he knew this for sure—that gave him the cramps that had kept him in the station for his entire shift, instead of out in a patrol car where he much preferred to be.

"Constable Dilley!" For the second time Sergeant Sager's voice pierced through three sets of concrete block walls. Geoffrey hunched down in the cubicle and braced himself for another wave of cramps.

"I say! Constable Dilley!"

Why couldn't the woman say "Geoff" or "Dilley" like every other section leader in 42 Division? And the accent. Did she always have to sound like a docent at the Tate Gallery?

"He's in the washroom, Sergeant Sager." This time Geoff heard Frank Paul's voice. Frank had shared the reception desk over the shift. Did most of the work too, Geoff had to admit. He'd lost track of how many times he'd run to the washroom over the past eight hours.

"Well, tell him to attend at my desk before he leaves."

Geoffrey gritted his teeth and fought off another impending cramp as he exited the cubicle. He had to get out there and "attend at Sager's desk." He owed it to Frank.

"You wanted me, Sergeant Sager?" It occurred to Geoff as he walked in that he might not have buttoned his uniform properly; her fixation on proper attire was legendary. But if that was the case, she didn't notice.

"The Lindenmacher site, Constable Dilley. It's on your way home, isn't it?"

It wasn't a question. The site of this recent murder was a good twenty minutes out of his way and Sager knew it, but Geoff made no reply.

"I've just been notified by 'D' Court that the suspect has been denied bail, and charges will be laid tomorrow morning." Camilla Sager, thus far, had not taken her eyes from the papers on her desk. She was making small tick marks in the margin of a document. "Now, the site. I cleared it yesterday. Signed it off personally. But just in case, I left the yellow tape in place." For the first time she looked up at Geoffrey. "One is wise to be patient in situations like these."

Geoffrey neither spoke nor nodded. He knew that annoyed her.

"Since it's on your way, would you mind awfully . . ."—she leaned hard on the "awfully"—"going round and removing the tape. The real-estate people have been allowed in to begin cleaning up. I gave them permission. But I don't want those people taking the tape down. Even touching it." She made "those people" sound like bacteria.

Geoffrey held off responding as long as he could without being blatantly insolent, and then nodded. The truth was, he didn't really mind. Especially if the cramps left him alone. The Lindenmacher murder was 42 Division's first big case in a long time and offered more excitement than most of his colleagues were used to.

Dietrich Lindenmacher lived alone in a country home, where his mutilated body had been found by the rural mail deliveryman. It appeared he'd been killed in his own bed, first struck on the head and then had his throat cut. A suspect was arrested in less than six hours and right now was two floors below in 42 Division's holding cells. He'd been there a week. The local media had buzzed with praise of the division's quick work in apprehending the murderer.

As Geoff approached the site a few minutes later, glad to be finally out of the station, he could see that the real-estate people had come and gone already. Their For Sale sign leaned against the open gate, ready to be tamped into the ground as soon as the yellow tape came down. They'd been cleaning too, just as Camilla Sager said. The raccoons had already been at the garbage bags set out at the road for pickup. He stepped carefully through a litter of empty soup and dog-food cans, and kicked aside a completely shredded box that, despite the damage, still proclaimed its point of origin as Deedee's Doughnuts.

"This would have to have been last night. Or near dawn today," he said aloud, musing on the thoroughness of the raccoons. In a sardonic way, it pleased him that they hadn't waited for permission from Sergeant Sager.

He walked on, curious. Although Geoff had not been on the investigating team, he, like everyone else in the division, was familiar with the details. Robbery appeared to have been the motive. Lindenmacher's VCR was missing, as was the TV, as well as several small appliances. Lindenmacher must have had a laptop too; Sager had found a manual for one. Interestingly, not one of the items missing from the house had turned up anywhere. Not in the suspect's van, and not in the hands of any of the known fences in the area.

The suspect had vigorously denied everything about the case. He was a vagrant, with no fixed address except for his van, which apparently had been his home for some time. The van had been seen by three different witnesses on Lindenmacher's side road on the day before his body was found, and given that the road was one that went from nowhere to nowhere, there was really no good reason for a stranger to be on it. The kicker, however, was that the suspect had a record. He was on probation for two B&Es.

Geoffrey peered through the picture window at the front of the house, into Lindenmacher's sitting room. Ordinary enough, but the big easy chair had a great view of the valley across the road. Moving to his left toward a second window, Geoff's foot caught on a small coil of electric wire. A small piece of yellow tape hung from it and fluttered in the breeze. This must be where the guy jumped the burglar alarm circuit, he thought. That conjecture was confirmed when he saw the cut wires under the sill of the second window. He shook his head. Pretty clever, he thought. But maybe not quite clever enough.

The wind was coming up a bit stronger as Geoff Dilley walked back to his car. He still hadn't taken down the yellow tape, and he wasn't going to. It suddenly occurred to him that he hadn't had a single stomach cramp since turning into Lindenmacher's driveway.

"Could it be?" He was musing aloud again. "Could it be my stomach is feeling better because Sergeant Sager has quite possibly missed something?"

As he opened the car door he concluded with more than a little pleasure that this was likely the case.

What clue, or clues, has Geoffrey noticed that Sergeant Sager apparently may have missed?

57

Problem-Solving
in Accident
Reconstruction 101

BY THE END OF THEIR SECOND DAY at the police academy, students taking Accident Reconstruction 101 from Chief Instructor Barry Stranks invariably learned that once he settled back in a chair and lit his pipe, they had been given all the information they were going to get in order to solve an assigned problem. That's why the class had immediately dispersed into two almost equal groups as soon as Lieutenant Stranks sat down. One group had wandered down the hill, checking both sides of the road for evidence. They were now measuring the distances between the shoulders of Humber Trail Road and the respective edges of the large, swampy pond that the road bisected. Most of them were already slapping at mosquitoes.

The members of the other group were only a few steps away from their teacher, studying the chalk marks on the road.

"Your first driver," Barry Stranks had told them, "the one approaching from the west, her story is she was simply coming down the road, minding her own business, when the other driver, the one coming up from the east, swerves to miss a big turtle and crosses the yellow line. So the driver from the east is now in the wrong lane. The first driver responds by swerving to the south side, but her right front wheel gets pulled down in the soft shoulder."

He had paused then and looked at them all. "Everybody with me so far?

"Now, you're going to have to use your imagination here," he continued, "as well as your logic. Obviously this accident is hypothetical. We can't afford to be wrecking cars every time I teach this course. However, I've chalked the spot on the road right there, where she says the turtle was. In fact, two of you are standing on it!"

Immediately two of the students shifted over, with sheepish grins on their faces.

Chief Instructor Stranks continued. "Just down there a bit, on the other side, I've also marked the spot where she hit the shoulder."

He paused to be sure everyone was listening for the next piece of information. By this time he had taken out his pipe and held it, unlit.

"Now here's the rest of the scenario. This driver tries to pull back onto the road but overcompensates and crosses to the north side, onto the shoulder further down there." He pointed with his pipe. "I've chalked it; you can see. But now the angle of entry is too obtuse and she goes right off the road and into the swamp. Car's a write-off."

He took out a lighter and held it over his pipe. "Any questions?"

"The other driver, sir?" one student ventured hesitantly.

"Indeed." Barry Stranks put the lighter back in his pocket. "The other driver carried on. Took off. Unless you can find a witness—and in a case like this you should assume you're not going to; country road, midsummer afternoon, light traffic, no houses nearby—all you have is the account by the driver going west."

The students parted as Barry made his way toward the lawn chair he'd unfolded a few minutes before. "The issue is insurance," he said as he sat down, taking out his lighter again. "It's a matter of assessing fault. If our eastbound driver was making legitimate and sensible avoidance moves because somebody pulled into her lane, then there's no fault on her part. On the other hand, without a witness . . ." He held up both hands and shrugged. "Could it be she wants a new car and set this whole thing up?

"What you have to do is reconstruct this event as best you can and then analyze it. Is it a straight story, or is there a hole in it?"

With a motion born of long practice, Barry put the lighter to the pipe and settled deeper into the chair.

"Most of the time," he said between puffs, "a class can solve this in one pipeload."

In the accident scenario Chief Instructor Stranks has constructed, is the driver's account plausible, or is there a "hole" in it?

58

Before the First
Commercial Break

DIRECTOR'S NOTE: Edit this piece to three minutes ten seconds. Insert between credit and first commercial break.

SCENE ONE

Camera Notes for Storyboard, Scene One:
#1. Pull back so that entire prison building can be seen. Gilhooley appears from behind wall in distance and walks into camera toward gate. Hold until Gilhooley reaches gate.

#2. Track him to motorcycle west of gate where rider is already astride. Move in as Gilhooley boards motorcycle behind rider. Hold close for a view of back and side of rider. Pick up rider's leather vest, cutoff T-shirt, long hair, and snake tattoo down length of left arm.

#3. Track left to follow motorcycle as it drives away and out of shot.

#4. Fade to black.

FX, Scene One:
Sound of Gilhooley's footsteps builds as he walks toward camera. Voice-over of Assistant Warden Brackish starts after footsteps are established. Sound of idling motorcycle comes in over Brackish's last words. Motorcycle sound follows Gilhooley and rider out of scene and fades.

Script, Scene One:
ASSISTANT WARDEN LEONARD BRACKISH: (in voice-over) Getting to be a habit, Mr. Gilhooley, isn't it? What's this, our third goodbye? No. Let's call it an au revoir. Men like you, Gilhooley . . . it's not a case of if but when. You'll be back, and I'll be waiting. You're bad, Gilhooley. Just bad seed. Like a snake. You can't help yourself. You're poison.

SCENE TWO

Camera Notes for Storyboard, Scene Two:
#1. Establishing shot of seedy storefront from across street.

#2. Move in and pan slowly left to right over gold lettering on door: RARE COINS AND ESTATE JEWELRY

#3. Continue panning right, pulling back until shot encompasses Gilhooley talking to another man on sidewalk. Arms are moving to emphasize what he is saying. Man has snake tattoo on arm. Might be biker from Scene One but dressed better. Listens and nods. No face.

#4. Continue pan past two men and fade to black.

FX, Scene Two:
City traffic noises.
No Voices in Scene Two

SCENE THREE

Camera Notes for Storyboard, Scene Three:
#1. Inside store at rear. Full shot. Gilhooley stands on one side of rear door and police officer on other side. Gilhooley wears slacks and shirt with long sleeves rolled to just above wrist. He is cowering. Officer is in uniform. Her stance is confrontational. One hand on door handle as though to keep Gilhooley from running. On the floor between them is a revolver. Back of butt is against the door so that muzzle points at camera. To her left and in front, Katzmann sits in a wooden chair.

#2. When Katzmann begins talking, move back to pick up array of shelves above him and scatter of diamond and ruby rings on working surface behind him. Katzmann wears loupe like a monocle, raised to his forehead. All his dialogue is emphasized by a rigidly pointed index finger at Gilhooley, the officer, and the door.

#3. Gilhooley gives impression he'd like to be sucked into the wall. Throughout scene fingers the barrel of the middle hinge on the door. While talking, retreats back along the wall a few inches but continues to hold the hinge as if for security. With right hand gropes behind him feeling for a small table just inches away, but never makes contact until the final shot.

#4. Gilhooley's hand bumps the small table, nearly upsetting a cup of coffee in a Styrofoam cup. He turns to rescue it and for a split second reveals a snake tattoo on his arm.

#5. Fade to black.

No FX in Scene Three

Script, Scene Three:
KATZMANN: . . . and two minutes after I see Gilhooley talking to this guy—another bum—the guy's in here with his gun out.

He's been tipped off, no question. 'Cause he comes right to the back here. This is where all the good stuff is, the really valuable pieces. I mean, how does the guy know to do that unless he's been told? Right, Gilhooley?

GILHOOLEY: I didn't say nothin' t' him 'bout that.

KATZMANN: And there's no way the guy's going to know I've got the safe open this morning to work on the new stuff unless he's been told. And, AND, who leaves the security screen wide open? The one separating this area from the rest of my store? You see what I get, officer, for hiring parolees? If it wasn't for my alarm system . . . I dunno. As it was, I thought he was going to shoot me anyway. When the alarm went off, I mean. But he panicked. Dropped his gun and run out the back door. That's when his partner here came back.

GILHOOLEY: Look, it just ain't like that! He—like, Katzmann—sends me across the street for coffee. That's every morning this time. The guy on the street? I never seen him before. He was just askin' directions. Alls I know is I come back here with the coffee and the alarm's ringin' and then you cops come in. I don't know nothin' what he's talkin' about!

If it is the director's intent to have viewers wonder whether Gilhooley is guilty or is being set up, then the director is going to have to correct a serious mistake before these scenes are shot. What is that mistake?

59

More than One
St. Plouffe?

"THIS IS LUDICROUS. You've got a written confession, written and *signed* confession, but you've also got two different suspects claiming it's theirs?"

"Yup."

"Two different suspects with exactly the same name?"

"Unnh."

"Alfred-Louis St. Plouffe—*Junior?*"

"Yup."

"And they are father and son?"

"'S right. Father and son."

Struan Ritchie looked up from the confession. "Careful, Kamsack, you almost spoke a whole sentence!"

Effam Kamsack raised both eyebrows in the general direction of his boss and took a deep breath. "Yup," he said again.

Struan waited a second or two just in case there might be more, but he knew from experience that it was more expedient just to forge ahead.

"Now, just to add to the astounding clarity we are all enjoying in this case, it seems there are actually *three* living Alfred-Louis St. Plouffes," he continued. "Senior, the original; then his son,

243

Junior, and then Junior's son, Alfred-Louis St. Plouffe the Third?"

Kamsack leaned forward again and with his right index finger tapped the report lying in front of Struan. "Yup," he said for the fourth time, and then folded back into a slouch.

"Except that the Third has always called himself Junior also, so in effect there are two Juniors?"

"Unnh."

"So the confession I'm reading here, signed Alfred-Louis St. Plouffe Junior, is claimed by both the Juniors?"

The toothpick in Kamsack's mouth elevated ever so slightly. Struan took that as a "yup." The fifth.

"Well, thank you, Detective Kamsack," he said. "I couldn't have laid it out more clearly myself!"

Kamsack took a while before responding with a grunt, but Struan by then had turned to the source of their mutual interest. The confession was typed on plain white bond paper and signed in a clear, unelaborate script, one that would be simple to forge. The information itself was but three short paragraphs.

On 1 May last, I administered poison in the form of arsenate of lead, to Her Ladyship Teresa Elana Giurgiu, formerly the Countess Covasna of Romania.

Her Ladyship attended Mass at St. Sofia's on 1 May, as has been her uninterrupted custom on each of Romania's national holidays since the abdication of King Michael in 1947. During her absence, I added the aforementioned substance to the medicine she consumed three times a day. The effects of the substance, along with all other pertinent details relating to her demise, are known to the police, and I do not dispute their findings or conclusions.

I hereby stipulate that what I have written here is offered of my own free will and without coercion.

Alfred-Louis St. Plouffe Jr.

"You know, Kamsack," Struan began, but then stopped abruptly. Kamsack was shifting the toothpick from one side to the other, a sure sign that he was about to volunteer something.

"Got 'em both here for yuh," the detective said very softly. "Think you'll wanna talk to 'em. One a' them's spinnin' yuh 'bout the confession." He slowly undulated to his feet. "Here." He tossed a sheet of paper on Struan's desk. "Ask 'em both these three questions."

Before Struan could react to the longest discourse from Kamsack he could recall in some time, he found himself facing the elder St. Plouffe Junior and, after a few preliminary probes of his own to which the suspect was entirely forthcoming, asked the first of Kamsack's three questions.

"What intrigues us, Monsieur St. Plouffe, is your motive. According to our findings, Lady Giurgiu had very little money. . ."

Alfred-Louis cleared his throat. "Your findings are correct. She had very little money. Indeed, she was nearly destitute, excepting for some ornate jewelry, which I'm convinced she purloined from the royal treasury in 1947."

Struan nodded, using the movement to glance surreptitiously at the second question. "But then, why?" he asked. "She was just a harmless old lady."

"Not harmless when she was younger. Previous to King Michael's abdication, she fabricated a web of intrigue that effectively dissolved our family's fortune. In fact, my family as well. It killed my mother. I can give you the details if—"

"Not just yet," Struan interrupted. "Before we go any further, I have to ask if you are fully aware of the possible consequences of your confession? We have the death penalty in this jurisdiction, you know."

"Yes, I know. But I am not adverse to the idea of death. Not now that I have satisfied the family's honor. And incidentally,"— St. Plouffe moved to the edge of his chair—"I'm also fully aware that you have to decide between my son and myself as to who is guilty. He foolishly advanced the premise to one of your investigators that it was he who poisoned the Countess. A noble act, but one you should ignore. I did it. The confession is mine."

Struan avoided eye contact with Kamsack while ushering the elder St. Plouffe Junior out of his office and the younger one in. The father and son were remarkably similar in appearance and behavior. In manner of speech too, for to the first of Kamsack's three questions, the one about Lady Giurgiu's financial state, the younger St. Plouffe replied, "Indeed. Unless I have been misled— a distinct possibility, by the way; she was remarkably devious —the Countess Covasna was, how shall I put it, er, impecunious."

"But then, Monsieur St. Plouffe, it's only natural that I ask you *why.*" By now Struan had allowed himself to become fascinated with the whole process. "What did you have to gain from poisoning an old lady?"

St. Plouffe's lips curled but didn't quite lift into a smile. "Because of that *old lady's* activities when I was a young child. My health—" He stopped abruptly. "Look, this is superfluous to the matter at hand. I poisoned her. And I am fully cognizant of the potential consequences. Those are the only points about which you need concern yourself. As to my father's attempt to divert you from the truth by claiming authorship of my confession, I can only say that while his gesture is a noble one, it is futile."

Struan stole a quick glance at Kamsack, who was basking in a huge grin. The grin continued long after both St. Plouffes were deposited in the outer office. And it stretched to the limit when Struan said, "My hat's off to you, Effam. Pretty clever. We've got a lot more digging to do on this thing, that's for sure. But at least we know who wrote the confession."

Which Alfred-Louis St. Plouffe has written the confession?

60

When the Oxygen
Ran Out

THE ROOM WAS SPARSELY FURNISHED and, as a result, uninviting.
There was only one place to sit; a single, straight-backed chair, a
refugee from an uncomfortable dining room suite, that sat disap-
provingly in one corner, just to the left of the window. Under the
window itself, an old-fashioned hot-water radiator hissed softly.
More or less in the center stood a burnished walnut end table. It
was highly polished but had no gleam, and it didn't match the
chair. Behind the little table, there was a floor lamp with a shade
that may once have been ivory-colored but had aged now to a rus-
set orange. Altogether, though, there was enough furniture for the
room. More would have made the place seem crowded. With or
without the dead man in the wheelchair.

As it was, the dark wooden bookshelves, and the deep brown-
ish-red rug, and the heavy, flocked wallpaper made the room
appear even smaller than it was. The first thing she would do if it
were her place, Fran Singleton decided, would be to lighten it up.
Get rid of the wallpaper first. Maybe even paint the shelves,
although that would take some courage, for they were genuine
oak. Solid too, no veneer. And the rug. To her, the color choice,
especially in a room like this, was almost a criminal act.

Fran always redecorated her surroundings when she found herself in an unpleasant situation. It took her mind off grim details that she didn't want to deal with. In this case, it was the not-unexpected demise of the late Humbert Latham.

She was not here by choice.

"All you've got to do is sign the death certificate," Lenny Stracwyz had pleaded over the telephone. Lenny was the county coroner and a classmate of Fran's from med school. He was in the Bahamas on vacation and had asked Fran to do him this favor, for he had no intention of leaving the beach to return to the cold of Toronto in January.

"Just sign the death certificate for me," he had repeated when Fran hesitated. "There's no question he's dead, from what I gather. Natural causes. Simple as can be. It just needs a signature. You don't have to do anything else—except, uh, uh, well, maybe you'd better make a few notes just in case I have to call an inquest."

Fran had tried to say something at that point but Lenny Stracwyz cut her off.

"Just sign," he said. "Please? Make it official? So I don't have to come home? You don't even have to do time of death; that's done already. OK?

The mention of a possible inquest had made Fran more hesitant than ever, but the plaintiveness of Lenny's voice had pushed away her natural reluctance. She had wanted to remind him that she was a pediatrician and didn't "do death," but in spite of that she found herself, less than an hour later, holding the cold wrist of Humbert Latham, confirming the nonexistent pulse.

The body of the old man still sat, bent slightly forward, in the wheelchair where he had died. His silver hair, always so perfectly groomed, reflected the lamp's wan glow, lending an impressive dignity to his death pose. Except for the slightly odd position, and the bit of drool that had dried along his chin and on the lapel of his blazer, Humbert Latham looked much as he must have when he'd been wheeled into the room yesterday afternoon, but somehow, more peaceful. There was less pain in his face than Fran remembered from the last time she had seen him. That was after the stroke. And the hands with their clawlike gnarl—she particularly remembered the hands because her own patient, Latham's great-grandson, was terrified of them—their once frightening, crippled grip seemed to be quite relaxed now. In a sense, Humbert Latham almost looked relieved that the oxygen had run out and he could finally let go.

Fran checked the oxygen bottle under the seat of the wheelchair and then followed all the tubes and checked each connection. They were all properly in place and intact.

"Sergeant Hong from homicide says it ran out between three and four this morning and the forensic specialist says he stopped breathing about fifteen minutes after that." It was the voluble rookie cop assigned to guard the scene. Sergeant Hong had not spent much time in the room. He'd simply ordered that everything remain untouched and had headed off to headquarters to coordinate the search for Latham's night nurse.

"Too bad, really. The poor old guy." The young policeman was still talking. "Lousy way to go even if it looks like he wasn't going to be around much longer anyway. I mean, you're totally helpless and you depend on someone to change your oxygen, and she doesn't show up. I mean, Jeez. Then the day nurse—I mean, like, she's the one who started all this—she's the one that finds him dead this morning!"

Fran knew the details and tried to ignore the prattle.

The day nurse regularly wheeled Humbert Latham into this room in the late afternoon so that he could enjoy the winter sunset through the west-facing window. At least everyone speculated that he enjoyed the sunset. The stroke had taken away Latham's ability to communicate. The nurse had left him alone there as she did every day at this time, and then had left the house five minutes early. Latham's valet, a man with a reputation for ironfisted control, had given her permission to do so, and had also arranged for the night nurse to come in early. It was the night nurse's job to take the old man down the hall to his bedroom, connect a fresh bottle of oxygen, and prepare him for sleep. But the night nurse had never shown up, and as yet had not been located.

"And that valet, Mr. Latham's 'gentleman'?" The policeman was leaning closer to Fran now, trying without realizing it to capture her full attention by hovering over her. "I mean, he's always here, right? Anyway he's supposed to be. But what does he do? He has a car accident! With that big Rolls. Just goes to show you, a patch of ice don't respect the make of your car. Anyway, so he gets taken to the hospital, all woozy and can't talk. So poor old Mr. Latham's got nobody. No nurse, no valet . . ."

Fran turned and leaned into the young policeman's face. He had been saying "val-ette," and that bothered her almost as much as his interference.

"It's 'val-AY.' Like the letter 'A.' French. And I know all this."

She turned to the window and took a breath, surprised by her vehemence. The morning sun was now reflecting off the windows on the building across the street, and the beauty and promise of it calmed her. Slowly, and just slightly self-conscious, she turned back to the officer.

"There's a security guard on the grounds at night, isn't there?" The more the thought took hold of her the more she forgot her annoyance. "There is if I remember correctly. Seems to me he gave me a hard time once when I came on a house call."

The policeman looked at her uncomprehendingly.

"Because," she went on, excited now, "unless he too was missing last night—seems like everybody else was—I'd bet Sergeant Hong will want to know if he's the same one that's on every night."

Why is Fran Singleton interested in this information about the security guard?

250

61

The Terrorist
in Fountain Square

SPECIAL AGENT CONNIE MOUNT took a sheet of cleansing tissue out of her shirt pocket and carefully wiped the eyepiece of the telescope. There was no need. The lens was spotless. But she cleaned it anyway, without paying the least attention to the task. It was a way of keeping her hands busy until she had to make the final decision.

Connie looked at her watch: 8:57. Three minutes left before she had to send in the team. Three minutes in which to be sure she was making the right choice.

One more time, she bent to the eyepiece and sharpened the focus on Fountain Square. The big instrument didn't need focusing any more than the lenses needed cleaning, but she was working on automatic. The only information her mind would process now was what she saw before her in the square.

A few years ago the telescope would have picked up spruce branches and not much more. This had been a spruce forest then, a piece of open country in its third life. The first had been its natural state, also a forest, mostly spruce, ironically enough, all of which the settlers had cleared. The work, though, had been in vain, for they had only managed to turn it into a wasteland. Reforestation then brought the spruce back, but this third phase lasted only twenty years. The spruce were taken off again to prepare for stage four, its present one: a shopping center, a structure so ultra-modern that, except for a few embarrassed birch trees clinging to life in big concrete pots, there was no wood to be seen at all. Just shiny aluminum, red brick, and clear glass, shaped into stores that surrounded a square made of still more aluminum and brick and glass.

At the center of the square sat the elaborate fountains that gave the place its name. With the precision that only a computerized drive system could muster, these fountains came to life every four minutes, and for exactly thirty-seven seconds, twelve jets of water shot toward the roof, while on the surface of the pool, large, viscous drops looped in mesmerizing, continuous arcs around the edge. It was this simple but attractive feature that, far more than the fountain jets, brought the patrons to stare.

Connie was watching five of them right now. Actually, four patrons and a terrorist. One of the five people staring at the water loops was carrying a switch for a bomb. The bomb was already in place, somewhere in the shopping center. That much she knew. She also knew, or at least was convinced, that the bomb was not yet armed. Someone was going to remedy that deficiency with a switch, and Connie's task was to put her team on that person—by 9 A.M.

She looked at her watch again. Just two minutes now. If only there were a bigger team, or time to bring in more people. Then she'd simply scoop up all five. That was one way to be sure. But there wasn't a bigger team and there wasn't more time. She had three agents concealed in three different stores around the fountain. Connie herself would be a fourth, but participating in the scoop would blow her cover. Even then, the best she could hope for would be to get four of the five people in the square. No, a mass grab was no good. The team had to get the right person, and there would be only one chance to do it. In two minutes—less than that now—the stores would open and people would start filling Fountain Square. All five down there could scatter in seconds if they chose to.

Connie resisted the urge to adjust the eyepiece yet again as she concentrated on the man dressed in blue overalls and yellow hard hat. He was wearing yellow work gloves. On the back of his blue shirt, yellow letters declared him to be an employee of "Your Friendly Telephone Company." Connie called this one Number Three. He had come into the square ten minutes ago, carrying a coil of rope over his left shoulder. He'd walked directly to a big steel grate in the floor, just a step or two from the edge of the pool, and he'd been standing there ever since.

Number Four in Connie's inventory was a painter. He'd only come in a few minutes ago in his white cap, white T-shirt, and paint-spattered white overalls. Number Four had come in with a paint tray and roller under one arm. In the other hand he carried a can of paint which he'd pried open and was now stirring as he sat on the floor, leaning against the wall of the pool. Four was the only one not looking at the water.

More than once in the past few minutes, Connie had felt a surge of admiration for the manufacturers of her telescope. With only a small twist of the knob, she'd been able to zoom in on the painter's hands to see that the paint under his fingernails was real. The same twist had shown calluses on the palms of Number Two, the street cleaner.

Number Two had appeared at almost the same time Connie had set up her equipment fifteen minutes ago. He carried a canvas bag over his shoulder, and in his hands a short broom and hinged shovel. There had been only a few pieces of litter to gather up, and now, like Number Three and Number Four, he had parked himself by the fountain.

In front of the Wells Fargo office, farther from the fountain than the others but staring at the looping water drops, was Number One. She was a short, painfully thin woman dressed in a severe gray business suit. On the pavement beside her, the polished finish on her briefcase reflected the halogen lighting panels that beamed from the top of each storefront. Connie had checked the briefcase carefully. It was not new, just well cared for.

Unlike Number One, who had been as still as a mannequin the

entire time, Number Five, the last one to enter the square was steadily on the move. And no wonder. She was a professional dog walker, or certainly seemed to be. Three dogs were leashed on her left hand, a pair of overweight cocker spaniels and a somewhat perplexed shelty. Two entirely unruly Afghans pulled constantly at her right hand. In the past minute or two, the walker had settled into a pattern which took her and the dogs around the perimeter of the square in a counterclockwise fashion.

For the last time, Special Agent Connie Mount looked at her watch. "Fifteen seconds," she muttered to herself. "This better be right." She turned to the tiny microphone pinned to her lapel. "Twenty-one, do you read?"

Immediately a double click sounded in her receiver.

"Twenty-two?"

The same pair of clicks followed.

"Twenty-three?"

This time there was a gap of a second or two but then the clicks came through.

"OK. I'm giving the count. Break out on five. Here's the one you go for . . ."

Which of the five people in the square has Connie selected as the most likely terrorist?

62

A Matter of Balance

NOT UNTIL THE FOLLOWING MORNING, a Monday, did Tom Jones conclude, yet again, that life is a series of balancings. Maybe not quite Newtonian, he felt, in that every reaction is equal and opposite to the initiating action; more in the sense that the events of life roll back and forth over a fulcrum of fate, so that things even out inexorably over time.

This notion had been exemplified twice the evening before, the first time in the elevator of the Federal Building on Danforth Avenue. Tom had been first to board the elevator and, as was his wont, he'd stepped politely to the back. Although only two more people got on, Tom got the unmistakable impression that one of them, the marine lieutenant, had deliberately and rudely jammed him against the back wall, keeping him there until the operator let the officer off at the fourteenth floor. Lording it, Tom understood. Big people often did that, especially the younger ones. But what the marine obviously didn't know was that what he confidently believed to be his commanding, uniformed presence was undermined by dandruff. A bad case too, trailing so far down his back that Tom held his breath each time the sway of the elevator rocked him closer to the man's protruding shoulder blade.

Balance, Tom realized. Nature equaling things out. It was almost pleasant, if just a touch malicious, to contemplate the officer's embarrassment when he discovered that his image of himself had been betrayed.

A second reinforcement of Tom's reflections on balance he owed to a radio program that night. Well, perhaps not entirely; his own listening skills deserved some of the credit too. When the FBI had telephoned him just after dinner, Tom had been preparing for a quiet evening, looking forward to an unhurried scan of the as yet unread sections of the Sunday paper, interrupted by a few chuckles from the *Chase and Sanborn Hour* on NBC at eight o'clock. Tom Jones, like most of the country, was a devoted follower of Edgar Bergen and Charlie McCarthy and rarely failed to have his radio on, on a Sunday night.

But then the call had come.

"Just a few moments of your time, ah, tonight, Doctor Jones," Agent Bronowski had purred into the telephone. "A matter of national security. The Bureau is appealing to your sense of duty. That's why the timing is, well, rather unusual, I admit. However, I'm sure you'll understand the importance when I explain."

It had taken almost an hour to get to the Federal Building, and when he entered through the revolving doors, Tom had realized, for perhaps the very first time, that not everyone listened to Edgar Bergen on Sunday nights. The doorman, obviously not functioning in the role his uniform dictated, was standing under the wall directory, totally absorbed by his radio, tuned (rather loudly) to a CBS station, which was pouring forth a paroxysm of anxiety about some alien-looking cylinder that had landed in New Jersey and had just incinerated some state troopers who tried to approach it.

Tom waited for the elevator just long enough to hear a station break remind listeners that they were listening to a drama. The doorman didn't hear that, however; he'd been racing for the bank of telephones at the other end of the lobby. Many others didn't hear it either, apparently. The next day the morning news described a major panic in the streets that night as a result of the radio show.

Once again, Tom realized, balance had asserted itself. He had been dragged out of his home on a Sunday evening and into what could have been very serious danger. On Danforth Avenue alone there had been several dozen injuries. Yet he'd missed the entire imbroglio, sitting in the FBI's fifteenth floor office.

The meeting itself lasted far longer than Agent Bronowski had promised, almost the first hour alone taken up with the agent's sycophancy.

("We realize, Doctor Jones, what an imposition this is on your time. After all, Sunday evenings are precious to us all, heh, heh, heh. But I'm sure you understand why we have to be circumspect, heh, heh, heh.")

("For someone of your stature, Doctor Jones, it must be an unaccustomed phenomenon for you to be asked to attend elsewhere. Surely you are more accustomed to be the summoner than the summonee, but then you see . . .")

Tom had tuned out quickly. But he was kept from nodding off—another habit of his—by the discomfort of the government-issue chairs on which he and the G-man faced each other across a table, and by his fascination with a birthmark on Agent Bronowski's scalp. Clearly visible through the man's thinning hair, it looked so strikingly like the outline of a tiny barbershop quartet that it was all Tom could do to resist tracing over it with his fountain pen.

Agent Bronowski did eventually get to the point in the second hour, although he was just as circumlocutory as he'd been while gushing over Tom in the first.

("I'm confident you spontaneously analyzed the nature of the investigations that originate in this office . . .") Tom had indeed made a note of the sign on the door: Federal Bureau of Investigation—National Security.

("It's your work, Doctor Jones, in, in—this is terribly awkward—I believe the word is polyesters? Our interest is in that. Well, it's not quite that simple.") Tom had remained entirely expressionless, letting Bronowski lead.

("As you know, with war almost certain in Europe, and, well, with your company's rather close relationship with the industrialists of the Third Reich, I, ah, well in a nutshell, what we need from you, ah, what your country needs from you is, well, what you are doing with this, this new polyester formula.")

The interview ended not long after that, with Tom agreeing to meet Agent Bronowski again in two days after thinking over what he'd been asked. When he'd prepared for bed that night, setting out his blue uniform as he always did, the one with the Janitorial Services tag over the pocket, the issue of balance did not occur to him immediately. He was more preoccupied with how the FBI could have confused him with the other Tom Jones, one of the company's research chemists. It was only when he realized that the whole thing was a set-up—that particular insight came the next morning—that the idea of balance came to him as well. What he would do, he decided, was speak to the real FBI. The agency would be quite interested, he was sure, in doing a little balancing of its own.

Why does Tom Jones know that his interview was a set-up?

63

Paying Attention
to Esme Quartz

IT WAS NOT UNTIL AFTER THE JURY had returned a guilty verdict
without even retiring to deliberate, that detectives at the 17th
Precinct acknowledged MaryPat St. Martin's role on the day of
the shooting. She had been the only one in the station on that
extremely busy day to pay any attention to the woman who
turned out to be the prosecution's star witness.

Not that a reasonable person would point a finger of blame at
the others for this. The witness, Esme Quartz, was well known to
the 17th, and everyone in the station, MaryPat included, did
what they could to avoid her. With her chin pulled back and her
mouth fixed in a pucker of disgust, Esme conveyed the impression that at a very early age she had stepped in a dog turd and
decided then and there that life was never going to get any better
and, if it was going to be that way, then others were going to share
her misery.

At least once a month, the 17th had to deal with a complaint
either by or about Esme. She warred with her fellow tenants in the
old brownstone just blocks from the station. She seemed unable
to complete even the simplest transaction in the little stores that
lined her street without getting into shouting matches with the

owners. Even her dog (and only friend), along with her several cats, shared her sour disposition and was yet another source of agony for the beleaguered cops. Perhaps worst of all was Esme's paranoia. Her conviction that everyone around her—neighbors, strangers, service people, even the police—was out to cheat, maim, and steal was unshakable. It was no surprise, therefore, when she appeared at the duty sergeant's desk on that rainy day, before the shooting scene had even been secured. And when she announced in her clipped tones that she knew not only who the shooter was but where to find him, only MaryPat had bothered to look up.

The shooting had been one of those big-city crimes that make police and civilians alike shudder in the awareness of how helpless both can be in the face of random violence. It came at the end of a day and a half of steady rain that seemed to push the city into a frenzy of aggressive crime, taxing the 17th to its limits. A male in his thirties had walked out of a movie theater into the middle of the street, taken out a gun, and begun to fire into the crowd sheltering under the theater's marquee. He then escaped the carnage he'd created by running over the roofs of cars and disappearing into a subway tunnel.

As though to reinforce the kind of day the 17th was having, no fewer than eleven 9-1-1 calls reported the incident within five minutes of the shooting, despite the fact that the streets were empty because of the rain. Yet not one witness had been found who could provide a reliable and credible description of the gunman. Except, as it turned out, for Esme.

Less than an hour after the first 9-1-1 call, Esme planted herself in front of the duty sergeant's desk and bleated for attention. Her physical appearance that day, while typical seemed to symbolize the chaos in the station. One shoe had no heel. Her coat was misbuttoned and ringed at the bottom with dog hair. It was also soaking wet, and dripped a steady stream onto the tile, making it slippery and dangerous. Sheets of the newspaper she'd held over her head gradually parted company with one another as she made tentative grabs at the detectives who ventured near her.

Only MaryPat had stopped. What she learned by stopping to listen led to an arrest, charge, conviction, and sentence. Still, Esme's reputation had jeopardized the outcome even after Mary-Pat had the name and address of the shooter, for when she took the information to the precinct commander, his immediate response was to dismiss it, pointing out to MaryPat that no one, not even a nutcase like Esme Quartz, would have been out on the street in that heavy rain. Esme, he said pointedly, had walked down to the station because she smelled disaster and wanted to enjoy it, and that was how she'd gotten wet.

Only after MaryPat insisted did the commander realize that Esme just might be a genuine witness.

How did MaryPat St. Martin know that Esme Quartz had a reason to be on the street in the rain, and therefore just might have seen the shooting?

64

Investigating the Failed Drug Bust

THERE WAS STILL A BIT OF SNOW on the ground, small piles of it wrapped around the base of the trees that lined both sides of the path. There was even more of it just a few feet off the path where, years before, the Department of Parks and Recreation had made yet another attempt to create the illusion of a natural environment in the middle of the city. Betty Stadler rather enjoyed the irony of it all. The trees grew and the snow fell, and every winter weekend enthusiastic urbanites, dressed better than Scott's polar expedition, pretended they were confronting the forces of nature—without ever straying off the path.

Still, phony as it was, Gallenkirk Park was better than no park at all. A lot better. And Betty Stadler, Lieutenant Elizabeth Stadler, recently appointed to Internal Affairs, had to admit she preferred to be out here, especially if the alternative was another smoke-filled committee room back at headquarters. Years before, more years than she cared to acknowledge, when she was the force's first female officer, Gallenkirk Park had been in her precinct. She had been part of an experimental bicycle patrol group that covered the park, along with an adjacent public housing project that had been put together during the Eisenhower administration with a lot less planning than Parks and Rec had put into trees.

She'd loved the park then, and did even more so now. The trees were mature now, and had attracted some wildlife. There was irony in that too. Nature, "red in tooth and claw," as Tennyson had put it, had returned to the middle of the city. But the fauna was far less dangerous than the wildlife that dominated the drug trade in the high-rise projects next door, a trade that contaminated everyone and everything that came into even the remotest contact with it.

Betty was acutely aware of the ultimate irony in her situation this morning. She was here in one of her favorite places in the whole city, but only because it might provide a setting for one of her least favorite responsibilities: investigating whether a cop might be dirty.

Not a rookie this time, not like the last time when her investigation turned up a scandalous mess that traced back to the police academy. The one this time was an officer with some fifteen years' tenure. He has spent the last three years undercover on the "old clothes" detail, living in shelters and on the street, soaking up information and cheap wine. In a way she felt sorry for the cops on "old clothes." They volunteered for it all right; no one forced them, even though it could be a real career boost because it was one of those ugly but very important police jobs that few wanted. But so many of the personnel on this detail eventually developed a real problem staying level. Either they became fanatics, crusaders, so that Betty and her team ended up investigating them for unnecessary force or illegal entrapment, or else they became so soiled by the world they dealt with that they became part of it.

Betty had met Officer Dana only once before. He'd been a member of the mounted patrol then, a coveted assignment, and she couldn't understand why he'd volunteered to transfer out. It could have been the divorce, she thought when reading his file. The break-up had been messy, and for Dana, excruciating. His two kids now lived with their mother over a thousand miles away. Yet the shift to "old clothes" seemed to be the right thing to do, at least in the beginning. In his first year he'd turned over enough good stuff to earn three citations. But his markers slowed after that, and in the third year his file showed such a sharp decline that Internal Affairs had flagged it. A few hours ago that attention had made Betty notice something in the morning reports that, most times, would have slid through without even a raised eyebrow.

The night before, the narcotics squad had pulled off a major bust that was coordinated across several points in the city. It had taken months of preparation, and although the squad had proceeded with its customary secrecy and, in Betty's opinion, utter lack of cooperation from the rest of the force, it was impossible to hide the fact that something big was going down. By the time of the bust, the where and when, and even the who, were common knowledge. Even so, the squad went ahead with every expectation of success and everything went as planned, except for one small and, on the surface, entirely peripheral part: a failed arrest in Gallenkirk Park. The only collar the squad made there was a wino who so far had refused to talk.

According to the detective from narcotics—he was the only one who saw it firsthand, other than Dana and the drug dealers who had gotten away—the potential collars had been approaching from three different directions for their meet. When they were almost within speaking distance of one another, the sound of someone walking through the leaves just off the path tipped them off. Although it was too dark to see much, the dealers were taking no chances and scattered. The approaching person, the one who scared them off, turned out to be just a wino, but by then the operation was dead. The wino, who Betty knew to be Officer Dana, had been charged with obstructing police business. It was a sour-grapes charge at best and, if the stories all checked out, one that would be dropped quickly to save everyone embarrassment.

Had Betty not come out here this morning to confirm her suspicions, it all might have ended there, but now she knew there was dirt. More than she'd originally suspected, because now there were two cops to investigate.

She took a deep breath, and turned completely around for a

last long look. She was sure she'd seen a robin at the top of an oak tree just ahead. An early returner, but a good sign. Further ahead she saw the sun trying to push its way through the clouds. Another good sign. After a week of almost steady drizzle and gloom, some sunshine would be welcome.

Why has Lieutenant Betty Stadler determined that there are now two cops to investigate?

65

A Surprise Witness for
the Highland Press Case

NORMALLY, JANE FORRESTER DIDN'T WASTE her time even thinking about buying a lottery ticket. The logic of such a move, given
the odds of winning, had always eluded her. It was only after she
left The Toby Jug, the day before Christmas, that Jane gave the
idea serious consideration for the very first time. Standing there
in the parking lot, digging in her purse for her car keys, it occurred to her that she might well be on a streak of good luck.

First, there was the matter of bumping into Wally Birks. Well,
not just bumping; she'd walked right into him. Almost knocked
him over. She'd been heading for the one empty stool at the bar
in The Toby Jug, then suddenly changed her mind and walked to
the back to use the washroom. With her thoughts on trying to
identify just which one of the patrons was Wally Birks, she
crashed into the back of a man in a blue parka who'd stopped suddenly at the entrance to the little alcove. Directly ahead a bright
red door said "Private." On the left wall was the "Ladies" door,
and opposite it the "Gents." Both in bright red.

Funny how she remembered the colors: the red doors and his
blue parka, and the truly ugly carpeting. Ocher. Who on earth
picks ocher?

Probably the colors stuck because of the phone call just before noon.

"You're Forrester, they tell me, Jane Forrester?" a gravelly and very pedantic voice had asked. "Well, I'm Birks, Wally Birks. That's Walter of course, but the only one ever called me Walter was my mother, and actually, she's been dead now, oh, some twenty years. Even my teachers never called me Walter—"

"Sir!" Jane broke in before she got a life history complete with favorite foods. "You wanted to speak to me about something, sir?"

"Well, actually . . . yes. You see, I've been sitting here thinking. Got lots of time to do that now. Actually, I'm retired, you see, and—"

"Sir! Could you tell me what it is you wanted to speak about?" Jane tried to keep the edge out of her voice.

"OK. Yes. Right. Sure. The Highland Press thing. Outside The Toby Jug? That's my favorite pub. And I saw something . . . Well, actually, I should have called you before this, but you see, a person doesn't always want to get involved, now, does he? And I was thinking . . . Matter of fact, I was just saying to my brother-in-law the other day . . ."

Despite herself, Jane held off interrupting. The Highland Press case was one of the open files on her desk, and every lead had been exhausted. Only a plum like a surprise witness was going to give her a break.

". . . so I was thinking, actually, I should meet you there. At the pub?"

Jane took a deep breath. "Yes, sir. That sounds like a good idea. Could we meet this afternoon?"

"Actually, I was just going to suggest that. I'll be there wearing a grey parka so you'll know who I am. It's got a nice black fur trim on the hood. My daughter and son-in-law gave it to me for Christmas two years ago. They live—"

"Mr. Birks, can you be there at three o'clock?"

"Well, now, I suppose I could. You see, the pub's right on the way to—"

"That's great, Mr. Birks. See you then. Bye for now."

Between the time of that call and her visit to The Toby Jug, Jane Forrester tried without success to put Wally Birks out of her mind. It was obvious he was the kind of person who could make the Charge of the Light Brigade sound like instructions for repotting azaleas, but the Highland Press case was a stickler, and if he could help, then . . .

As it turned out, Jane's time at the pub was mercifully brief. When she apologized to the man in the blue parka, he turned around very slowly.

"Now, I recognize that voice, don't I, Jane Forrester? Actually, I was wondering how we'd meet. This is a pretty big place. And busy. I have to go in there, you see." With his thumb he pointed over his shoulder at the doors. "At my age, a person has to, well, I don't want to talk about that to a lady. But you see, the thing is, I don't have my grey parka on like I told you I would. You'd never guess what happened. I went out to the back porch to get it. You see, before my wife got sick we had the porch closed in. She always called it 'the sun room' after that. I could never get used to that. A porch is a porch, I always say."

At that very moment, another piece of good luck happened. Jane's beeper screamed at her, and even before she'd scanned for the number, she was saying, "Oh, Mr. Birks. I'm so dreadfully sorry. An emergency. Look, I have to go. Now, someone from my office will call you for your information. It won't be me. One of my colleagues."

With that, she'd spun on her heels and disappeared before Wally Birks could wind up again.

Three bits of luck, she thought to herself in the parking lot, each saving her from wasting time with Wally Birks on the Highland Press case. Definitely worth considering a lottery ticket.

Jane Forrester's accidental bump, and her beeper sounding, are two bits of good lick. The third is the clue that tells her Wally is likely not a reliable informant, for he's already lied to her once. What is that lie?

66

The Last Will
and Testament of
Albion Mulmur

"IT TAKES ALL KINDS, MS. MACDUFFEE. Forgive me for using such a worn cliché, but there are times when a platitude can be surprisingly appropriate."

The words of the chief interviewer still resonated in Kay Mac-Duffee's memory.

"According to these aptitude tests, you're really a poet at heart," he'd said, "and I'm sure you'll agree that poets don't make terribly good trial lawyers. Here at Finnerty, Coolihan and Gore, that's what we specialize in: trials."

He'd paused—another image clearly etched in Kay's memory —and puffed on an enormous cigar.

"But somehow," he went on, "I have a sense that you could be very valuable in our investigation branch. Poets feel things, and they can see better. I'm sure you know what I mean . . ."

That was eighteen years ago, and over that time, Kay MacDuffee's poetic insights had turned her into Finnerty, Coolihan and Gore's star investigator. Those skills were serving her at this very moment, in the case of Albion Mulmur's last will and testament, skills which had now convinced her that old Mulmur's granddaughter, Regina, was attempting a neat piece of fraud.

Kay was sitting in what had been the old man's harness shop, relishing the soft smells of old leather, neat's-foot oil, and pipe tobacco which had worked their way into the wooden floors and walls, and into the naked pine beams supporting a loft where no one had climbed in years. She twisted in her seat, her eyes working in the gloom to pick up every nuance, imagining the stories that might emerge through the dust covering every one of the harness-making tools. She thought of what it must have been like to be a child in here, to lie in the loft and look down to watch Albion Mulmur turn rolls of leather into bridles and traces and cruppers.

It was a poet's room all right, one that appealed to the soul far more than the body. A dark place where, in winter, you chose between baking and freezing, depending on how close you pulled one of the old buggy seats to the potbellied stove; a place where the door hinges were so worn with use that unless it was given a shove to force the latch into place, the door would open ever so slowly, gathering momentum as it responded to the slant in the floor. It was the kind of place where the dirt, well, the dirt just belonged. To sweep or dust would have been almost an act of violence.

By itself the harness shop did little to support the notion that the old man's will could possibly require anything remotely resembling an investigation. But in 1938 Albion Mulmur, in an act regarded by those around him as one of sheer insanity, had purchased a thousand shares of IBM stock. Right now the original certificates and Mulmur's signed and duly witnessed will were safely stowed at the offices of Finnerty, Coolihan and Gore, along with letters, not yet mailed, from a senior partner advising various charities that they were the beneficiaries of several million dollars.

The letters had been held up because another will with a later date had been found in the harness shop by one of the firm's law clerks. This will left all but ten percent of Albion Mulmur's estate to his only grandchild, Regina.

Kay's meeting with Regina—the granddaughter had left about half an hour before—had almost ruined her experience of the harness shop. She had arrived early and was only just beginning to bask in the place when Regina came—intruded, as far as Kay was concerned. The shop seemed to demand quiet and patience, and measured, deliberate movements. Regina, however, literally blew in.

"Gawd! I haven't been here since I was a little kid!" she said, a look of self-conscious disbelief on her face. "Almost used to live in here then! Can you imagine?" She pushed the door closed with one shoulder. "Still stinks of those pipes, doesn't it? And the dirt. Gawd, my mother hated the dirt. And the cobwebs. They're thicker than ever!"

With a gloved hand she repositioned a pair of designer frames to the bridge of a very long nose, then assessed Kay in an unabashed stare.

"Sorry I'm late. How long you been here? Aren't you cold?" Without waiting for an answer, Regina looked away from Kay and grimaced as she looked up at the loft.

"Hasn't changed in twenty years. You don't mind if I stand, do you? Those buggy seats—you sure you want to sit there? There's probably something living in them, you know!"

The interview wasn't really an interview, Kay reflected later; Regina Mulmur had delivered a monologue that had lasted about fifteen minutes, and then departed in the same style she'd entered. Still, for Kay it was long enough. She was more than happy when Regina left, for it meant Kay would be able to return to her enjoyment of the place. Besides, she was convinced now that the recently discovered will was definitely a phony one.

What has convinced Kay MacDuffee that the newly discovered will is likely fraudulent?

67

What Happens in
Scene Three?

SCENE ONE

(Dark stage except for a small area lit by a single spot upper right. The edges of the spot vaguely pick up the sitting room of a gentlemen's club. Center of the spot, in a leather easy chair, facing stage right is a man with elegant silver hair. There is no reason to conclude he is old: just dignified, and apparently wealthy. The light, in any case, is not strong enough to reveal other than hazy details. What is clear, however, is the white, business-size envelope in his left hand, stuffed to the maximum and secured with cellulose tape. The man holds what may be a glass of wine, or more likely sherry, in the other hand. His legs are crossed at the ankles, underneath a small, rectangular coffee table.

The man on the other side of this table is standing, so that his face is above the light. He is wearing a three-piece suit, gray pinstripe. Over a slight but visible paunch, a gold watch chain loops across his vest.

No dialogue is heard in this scene, but over its twenty or so seconds' duration, it is apparent that the man in the chair is talking, for his hands move in a gesticulatory fashion. In the final seconds, he places the envelope on the coffee table. The other man picks it up slowly. His right hand lingers at the table long enough for his ring to be obvious. The principal stone is a large ruby set in a circle of diamonds.

Start chamber music just before he picks up the envelope. Bring up music; fade to black, and hold music into Scene Two.

SCENE TWO

Almost immediately, a spot comes up downstage from Scene One, and somewhat stage left. The lit-up area is larger this time, but still does not pick up walls or anything that might suggest the confines of the stage.

The gray-suited man from Scene One is now standing in front of a small bar in a luxuriously appointed private library. He's facing slightly stage left, because the bar runs upstage-downstage. The watch chain and ruby ring clearly identify him, but again his face is above the light. This time, he is holding a gun with a silencer on the barrel.

The weapon is casually pointed at GEORGE FEWSTER, standing behind the bar. He's shorter than the gunman [*Note: If necessary, use altered stage floor levels to show height differential.*] and unlike the gunman, his face can be seen. FEWSTER's mustache and hair are streaked with gray. He's wearing a smoking jacket, and has just poured a drink which he places on the bar. Fade music but hold softly throughout.)

GUNMAN: You're not joining me?

FEWSTER: Hardly a celebratory occasion, wouldn't you say?

GUNMAN: Depends on your point of view, Mr. Fewster. Now, your partner, I'm sure, is quite likely enjoying a libation or two, in anticipation of the outcome of this, ah, how shall I say, event?

FEWSTER: What I don't understand is, why didn't you just

shoot me when I came into the library? That's what you've been paid to do. Why prolong the matter? Or is this some sort of perverse pleasure you have arranged for yourself?

GUNMAN: Perverse, Mr. Fewster? Surely not perverse. No, I see it as an exploration—how shall I call it?—a probing into the human spirit.

FEWSTER: You want to see how I conduct myself, knowing that I'm about to be, er . . .

GUNMAN: Precisely!

FEWSTER: . . . perhaps to see what steps I'll take to thwart you.

GUNMAN: Oh really, Mr. Fewster! A man of your perspicacity! Thwart me? I really do know how to use this weapon. It has served me well. And you must have deduced by now, that inasmuch as I knew the balcony doors were not locked, I also know you are alone tonight. The silencer is merely a precaution. And the drink here? Now that was just a trifle amateur, Mr. Fewster. When I leave, I'll take it with me. DNA and all that. It is good Scotch, nevertheless. A single malt, I assume. A bit peaty for my taste, but elegant.

FEWSTER: So the conclusion here is foregone, in your opinion.

GUNMAN: Oh, without question. It's only an issue now of assessing how you approach the inevitability of it.

FEWSTER: I see.
(In a very natural move, and without looking up to note the gunman's quick flinch, Fewster reaches under the bar for the Scotch and pours himself a drink. Then he looks up.)
Changed my mind. A legitimate, last-minute prerogative, I'm sure you'll agree. By the way, have you ever given thought to examining your own motivations, Mr. . . .

GUNMAN: Smith will do.

FEWSTER: It usually does.

GUNMAN: When you say "motivations," surely you're not thinking of some trite concept like morality or ethics?

FEWSTER: Actually, I was thinking of something a touch more fundamental. Like greed.
(*Other than the reaction seconds before, the gunman has not moved until this point. Now he rotates slowly left then right, but only a few degrees.*)

GUNMAN: A reasonable ploy, sir. You were thinking of offering me a better proposition than your partner has, perhaps one of the paintings in here? I did recognize a Corot in the hallway, and a Monet.

FEWSTER: There's a Picasso in the foyer.

GUNMAN: Indeed! A Picasso! Tempting! But, you see, I lead such a peripatetic lifestyle that, well, portability is essential. Liquidity even more so. I'm sure you understand. It's a disadvantage in my calling. Now, your partner. He would be the one to listen to such an offer, wouldn't he? A most greedy man, as you have apparently discovered. It's why he can't afford to let you live.

FEWSTER: No doubt he's given you cash.

GUNMAN: A commodity for which there is no substitute.

FEWSTER: Not even my Fabergé eggs? Look at "The Peacock" here. Made for the Dowager Empress Maria in 1908.
(*This time the gunman does not move as Fewster reaches unhesitatingly toward a glass case at the end of the bar and removes one of several very ornate eggs. Whether it is genuine, or a replica of one of*)

the famous bejeweled eggs made for the Russian royal family by Peter Carl Fabergé, it is incredibly beautiful.)

GUNMAN: I must admit, sir, I did allow myself to examine them before you came in. Jewelry is one of my very few . . . They are especially exquisite, aren't they? I, er, I've always wanted to hold one of them. I—goodness!

(Fewster tosses the egg to the gunman, who catches it instinctively with his free hand. He raises the gun at Fewster slightly and, for what seems like an inordinately long time, examines the egg from every angle before handing it back.)

A sore temptation, I admit. And I do confess to an extraordinary fondness for precious stones. But then, surely you realize I could just avail myself in any case, after we conclude here?

(As Fewster delivers his next line, he turns to a wall safe behind him and opens it. The gun rises only slightly.)

FEWSTER: The truly beautiful ones in my collection are in the safe here.

GUNMAN: Indeed? Perhaps there's time—WHAT ARE YOU DOING?

(Continuing the fluid motion that opened the door to the safe, George Fewster sets the Peacock inside, closes the door, and twirls the dial.)

That was regrettable, Mr. Fewster! Almost juvenile! I'm surprised. Now open the safe, or I'm afraid I will have to fulfill my contract immediately!

FEWSTER: Come, come, Mr. Smith. Such impulsivity in a student of human behavior! If you shoot now, you'll be missing a potentially inspiring opportunity.

GUNMAN: To what?

(Fewster holds his drink to the light, and examines it.)

FEWSTER: To analyze your behavior over the next hour. After all, the outcome of this, er, event, is foregone, isn't it? At the very least, you might try to examine your motivations as it proceeds. It's just short of ten. I believe my partner's club is open till eleven.
    (*Immediate fade to black.*)

SCENE THREE

From the gunman's perspective, and George Fewster's too, there is only one way now that Scene Three can play out and bring this issue to a final close. What is that?

68

Almost an Ideal Spot
for Breakfast

HE WAS RESPONDING TO A BURGLAR ALARM RELAY, but the first thing to cross Laurie Silverberg's mind as he led the way through the front door of the house and into the solarium on the left was what a wonderful place this would be to have breakfast each morning. The east wall faced the lake and, although all he could see on it now was ice, the view was still awe inspiring. The wall was completely windowed except for a sliding door at the extreme right end. Right now, the door was open ever so slightly—jimmied—which was almost for sure what had made the alarm go off.

Laurie lingered in the entrance so he could get a full perspective of the room. This was a legitimate move from an investigative point of view, especially given that the three officers who had arrived with him were now doing a room-by-room in the rest of the house. But what he really wanted to do was enjoy the solarium. The east view was certainly the choice one, for the north faced the road and was draped, and the south was shaded by a thick stand of spruce. The west wall, where he was standing, the wall that connected to the house, was bookshelved from top to bottom. He liked that. But the books were very much outnumbered by expensive-looking objets d'art, mostly soapstone carvings. Laurie pressed one of the three wall switches beside him and instantly spot lighting illuminated the pieces and held them in flattering circles of soft glow.

"Thought so," he muttered, and then added, "Let's see . . ." and pressed another. From hidden speakers Vivaldi's *Four Seasons* filled the solarium. This time Laurie nodded, as though he'd just won a bet with himself. When the third switch didn't produce any result he was curious, but soon forgot about it. There was so much more to look at.

Across the room there were more books, all leather-bound these, and filling a shelf that ran the length of the wall beneath an impressive array of foliage. Variegated pothos, dieffenbachia, anthuriums, peace lilies, a most luxurious Princess philodendron, and several nephthytis stood side by side on the window shelf, their broad leaves open toward him like hands offering a blessing. Someone here really cared about plants.

"More than reading if I'm any judge," Laurie said to himself. He glanced quickly over his shoulder and crossed to the books where, beneath the trailing fronds of a Boston fern, gold lettering proudly announced a copy of Dante's *Divina Commedia*. He pulled it out and opened it, smiling with more than a little satisfaction at the sound of the crack. Two more books on the same shelf, *Selections from the Romantic Poets* and Voltaire's *Candide,* made the same sound. It made Laurie's grin widen.

"Hey! Can I come in now or what? It's my house!"

Laurie jumped to his feet. He'd forgotten Eugenia Melch, forgotten that in life all good things have compensations, for in this house she would come with breakfast.

"Your men are out front already! They say there's nobody in the house!" Eugenia spoke at parade ground level. It made Laurie retreat. "Didn't think there would be! Probably miles away by now! Oh, my babies!" She ran to the plants. "It's OK, darlings! Momma's home now to look after you."

Eugenia's composure softened as she visited each plant along the windows, stroking some, putting her face into others, here and there adjusting the position of a pot just a tiny bit. Until she reached the sliding door.

"Aha! Right there, eh? The door! Got in that way, did they? Well, least the alarm still works! That's something. OK, what now? Don't you have to get fingerprints or something like that? Or take pictures? Hardly the time for reading, is it?"

Laurie had forgotten he was holding *Candide* in one hand and the Romantic poets in the other. His voice, naturally soft, invariably got softer when confronted by a barrage like the one Eugenia had just laid down, so he almost whispered a response.

"I think the first thing we should do is go through the house together to see what's missing, if anything. Certainly this room seems to be intact."

"Is that so? Well, you could be right!"

Eugenia Melch accelerated around the room, examining the carvings. Her massive earrings flashed each time she came to a lighted spot and geared down for a second or two before passing to the next.

"All Sully's soap stuff is here, looks like!"

She talked as she went. Laurie watched her, fascinated by the earrings, wondering if they could be used to locate hidden radio transmitters.

"What he pays for this stuff! You can't imagine! And he can't even say their names, the people that do it! They're Eskimos, you know!" She shook her head. "Anyway, I can't see anything missing. Sully might, though, when he gets here."

Laurie did whisper this time. "Where is he, Mrs. Melch?"

"At his office. I dropped him off. We've been at the condo for the past week, and we—"

She noticed Laurie's slight frown. "In Nassau! The condo. The condo's in Nassau! That's what you're frowning about, isn't it? Anyway, we just got back a couple hours ago. Tickets are here in my purse if you want to see 'em. Or maybe Sully's got 'em. Anyway, he wanted to go to the office first so I dropped him and came home. I could hear the alarm when I came up the drive so I stayed in the car till you guys came. We had one a' these once before and the cop that time said nobody should ever go in, so I didn't! So now what? You want to go over the rest of the house?"

"If you think this room is accounted for, yes."

Laurie Silverberg and Eugenia Melch went through the entire house and found no other points of forced entry, and as well, found nothing missing as they went. It was not until they reached the master bedroom that Eugenia discovered that her diamond tiara, with matching necklace, brooch, rings, and bracelet, had been taken. By then, though, Laurie had determined that if anything were to turn up missing, it would be a case of fraud, not theft. Why?

69

Investigating
the Explosion

"THERE." MARNI RAINTZ POINTED to the markings inked onto a large piece of plate glass, being careful not to touch them. "Right there," she said. "Now that's a swastika, isn't it? Or most of one anyway. I bet we'll find the one little piece of missing line when we find the rest of the door."

Doug Doyle nudged the glass ever so slightly with the toe of one of his gleaming Oxfords. He was the only member of the bomb squad who never wore sneakers or construction boots, and he was famous for being able to crawl around an explosion site for days without ever having to rehabilitate a shoeshine. Doug looked at the markings and wrinkled his nose slightly. He didn't appear convinced.

"And here." Marni pointed at some more marks a few inches above the swastika. "This looks like it was probably another one, but it got smeared by the sprinkler system."

She bent at the knees and squatted closer to the wreckage lying between her and Doug. There were three pieces of glass from the shattered front door, each about the size of a large dinner plate. Two of them still clung, one beside the other, to one side of the wooden door frame, directly above the door knob. The third one was very slightly larger, and attached to a different piece of frame. This third one had the swastika. The blast had been a fairly small one, taking out the ornate front door of a large private home, and much of the outside living room wall on one side, along with a piece of the garage on the other side. "Looks very professional," the fire chief had said to Doug Doyle when he arrived a few minutes ago. "As if it's a message, sort of. Most of the force appears to have been horizontal. Very controlled. Could have been a lot worse."

Marni stood up and drew her shoulders back to stretch them, waiting for Doug to comment. He was staring at the glass. The swastika, if indeed it was one, was about the size of an adult's hand, and had been drawn with magic marker or some kind of felt-tip pen. Freehand and hastily too. Doug took a sharp breath as though he was about to say something, but instead held his breath and then exhaled slowly. Marni spoke instead.

"What I want to know is if you're thinking what I'm thinking. I mean, this was a real professional pop here. Whoever did this knew what he was doing with plastic. It was plastic, by the way, as if you couldn't tell first thing. And then the swastika . . . I mean, on first impression it's hard to get around the idea that some Nazi types were busy here."

Marni squatted down again and motioned Doug to do like-wise. "But now look at what doesn't make any sense." She took out a ballpoint pen and with the blunt end drew a circle on the glass, around the swastika, as though to confine the symbol per-manently to that one spot. "What doesn't seem to make sense," she went on, "is that the arms bend the wrong way on this thing. Isn't a swastika supposed to go clockwise? The ends of the arms, I mean? These are counterclockwise."

Doug spoke for the first time. "Is all the photography fin-ished?" he said.

Marni nodded, just a bit perplexed.

"Then try this perspective," Doug Doyle said gently as he picked up the piece of glass and turned it over. "Now it's clock-wise, right? The way it's supposed to be?"

Marni reddened, but before she could say anything, Doug set

the glass down and touched her elbow so that both of them would stand up.

"The fact is," he said, "swastikas can go either way, clockwise or counterclockwise. When Hitler adopted the symbol, he picked the former direction." Doug looked at his young colleague. Her interest appeared genuine, so he continued. "It's a very ancient symbol, really, and quite widespread. The Hindu and Buddhist traditions have it. You would have found it in Mexico too, long before the Europeans came. Ever heard of Heinrich Schliemann, the guy that found Troy in the 1870s? He also found swastikas there. I believe he was the first to refer to them as an Aryan religious symbol, although there's no evidence that Schliemann himself was a racist."

Marni was listening intently, but by now Doug was on a roll and her interest no longer made much difference.

"Actually, it's generally believed that swastikas were intended to have a benign purpose. To represent the motion of the sun, most archeologists think. It's only after Hitler that the swastika became tainted, culturally."

Doug squatted down and, just as Marni had done, traced a circle around the swastika on the glass with the blunt end of his ball-point pen. He continued, without changing his tone even a little.

"There's an interesting legend about the Crusaders and the swastika. The story has it that they were laying siege to a fortress—somewhere in the Middle East, I don't know where—and as a ploy the inhabitants had their women place their bare butts over the edge of the fortress wall, just to show the brave knights how much they cared about the siege. And all the bottoms had swastikas painted on them."

For the first time, Marni's expression changed. Doug's didn't. He kept on staring at the swastika.

"I'm not making that up," he added. "There really is such a story. But anybody who believes that would also believe that some Nazi types are responsible for this bomb blast here."

Why does Doug Doyle suspect that this explosion was not set by what he and Marni call "Nazi types"?

70

Some Uncertainty About the Call at 291 Bristol

THERE WERE AT LEAST THREE GOOD REASONS why Shaun Hawkes was not prepared to accept the incident at 291 Bristol as a break and enter. Not as a robbery either, or an assault, even though all that had to be put aside for the moment while she looked after the young woman who'd called 9-1-1. Paige Kress was her name, eighteen years old and by all indications genuinely traumatized. In Shaun's mind it was a heck of a thing to happen to a young college kid on her Christmas break, so she was now puttering about the huge kitchen at 291 Bristol, looking for the wherewithal to brew a pot of tea, Shaun's standard response to trauma, illness, and global crisis.

"He was gonna, I was so scared he was gonna . . ." Paige's first words to Shaun degenerated into moans as she wrapped her arms around herself tightly and rocked back and forth.

"He was here before, the guy. Like, in the house . . ." had come through the tears. "See, we're gonna move . . . Daddy's company's got some kind of trouble . . . and he needs to . . . to. . . ." Paige had begun to hyperventilate. That's when Shaun had left for the kitchen. She wanted to make some space for herself, and tea for all hands.

Two of the uniforms on her squad were sitting with Paige right now, one of them the only other female member of the squad, a veteran of all of six months who had been the first officer on the scene. This same rookie, a month before, had investigated a report of three girls being stalked on the campus of the junior college nearby. One of the three had been Paige Kress.

The third cupboard door to the left of the triple sink yielded an electric tea kettle. Progress.

"Add that to the milk," Shaun said aloud, "and the dubious contents of that sugar bowl, and we're getting somewhere. Now, what's needed is a nice Darjeeling or maybe a pekoe."

The search went on. A second bank of cupboard doors presented an impressive array of serving dishes and baking tools but no tea, so she moved to the third. Actually, this was taking about as much time as she had hoped it would. Paige, in Shaun's opinion, needed some time before telling her story again. The first time, between the sobs and fits of quivering, and even a near-faint, Paige had told the officers how she had just stepped out of the shower when she heard—she was certain about this—she heard a sound in the hall. Wrapped in only a towel, Paige had peeked out the door, but saw nothing. It was when she had turned back inside that she saw the intruder in the mirror: a man, a short man, dressed all in black, carrying a painting. She'd screamed, locked the door, and called 9-1-1.

"Ah, gotcha!" Shaun's delight at finally finding some tea was short-lived. It was a herbal tea. Mint. In her opinion, that was as close to barbaric as one could get without resorting to coffee. This search for tea was becoming as bothersome as the case! Even the man in black had been easier to find.

Paige had identified him as the real-estate estimator who had been through the house the week before. He was now sitting in handcuffs in the back seat of a blue and white parked in the driveway. Shaun herself had picked him up only a block away.

She had to admit she disliked him immediately, probably because his black shirt was opened to mid-chest, revealing a cross on a gold chain, a St. Jude medal and, also in gold, a fist with middle finger raised in a rude gesture. He was short, dressed in black, and swaggery. Not Shaun's kind of person. Still, there had been no painting anywhere near; not that she'd expected to find one, even though the black Trans-Am where she'd picked him up was his. As well, his story that he'd returned to the neighborhood to re-evaluate his original estimate made sense enough. Paige's parents were selling their huge home and he'd been called in on the same day they were leaving for a week of skiing. His first go-round, he claimed, had been too rushed. The place needed a closer look, he went on. Too many things were not working: the garage-door opener, the burglar alarm, the carburetor. The house needed a thorough examination.

"Well," Shaun exclaimed as she opened and closed the very last cupboard door. "This is uncivilized! One cannot have a kitchen and not have tea! What do these people do for—"

With a look of chagrin on her face, she stopped and peeked over her shoulder to see if anyone had seen her search.

"Some detective!" she said, and walked to the sink. The set of canisters on the kitchen counter had labels clear enough to read from anywhere in the room: FLOUR, SUGAR, COFFEE, TEA. She peered out the kitchen door just to be doubly sure none of her squad had been nearby. Shaking her head in self-admonishment, she began to fill the kettle with water.

Shaun Hawkes almost overlooked the obvious in her search for tea, but she hasn't been fooled by this case. What are "at least three good reasons" why she is not prepared to accept this incident as break and enter, robbery, or assault?

71

The Case of the
Missing Child

THE TENSION BETWEEN THE COUPLE was like static electricity,
ready to crackle at the first sign of movement. But from where
Audrey Greenwood stood in the doorway, it didn't appear there
was going to be any movement unless she initiated it. Downstairs,
when she'd first come in, the couple had taken great care to avoid
any contact with each other, like a pair of magnets carrying the
same charge. Now it continued in the bedroom.

The father stood with his back to one of the windows, arms
folded tightly across his chest, the old-fashioned venetian blinds
framing his rigid vertical stance. Audrey felt that this corner room
was ideal for the tableau inside, for the mother stood equally erect
at the window on the south wall. She, however, held her arms
akimbo and was staring resolutely out the window into the apartments across the street.

As it turned out, the tension had an ultimate benefit in the
case, for its force made Audrey pause longer in the doorway than
she otherwise might have. Normally, in cases like this, when she
was first to arrive, she would assert herself quickly so that no
matter which way headquarters decided to play it, the victims involved would see her as the principal investigator. Audrey worked

out of Juvenile Branch, a more effective group, in her opinion, than the stumblebums from Felonious Crimes, one of whom would arrive shortly. On the surface, the issue was either a kidnapping with, quite possibly, murder involved, or a simple runaway.

The room where the two parents stood braced for combat was a child's bedroom in metamorphosis from nursery to little-girl sanctuary. There was a diaper-changing table along the wall the father was facing, but, covered in Barbie Doll paraphernalia, it seemed to have outgrown its original purpose. The bed on the fourth wall had only recently been a crib, but the sides were gone now. Only the wallpaper, a rigorously gender-balanced mix of pink and blue cherubs, obviously chosen before the child's birth, had survived the change so far.

The crayon marks on the wallpaper were the first indication to Audrey that there might be something different about this child. There were just too many of them. They were too random, too thick. Then there was the tiny shelf near the ceiling. Way too high and out of reach to be normally functional, it was clearly purpose-built. An empty pharmacy bottle suggested what it had once been used for. Other things begged to be explained too, especially the nails in the window frames. Like the blinds, the windows were old, this being one of three late-Depression-era buildings holding out against a growing forest of new high-rise apartments. But the windows were nailed shut. Behind the father, Audrey could easily see the nails protruding from both frames.

"Lexie has a behavior disorder." Was the mother reading her mind? The voice continued through lips that barely moved. "The doctors don't know what it is. We've—No! *I've* taken her to, oh God, it seems like a hundred of them. She's got drugs, but they don't work. Sometimes I think they make her worse. She's a head-banger, she runs, she screams . . . I, oh God . . ."

For the first time, the mother's defenses seemed to weaken. Her shoulders drooped and brought her head down.

Out of experience, Audrey resisted any feelings of sympathy as she turned to the father. "This morning, when you first noticed she was missing . . ."

"It's happened a couple of times," he sighed. "Once we found her under the laundry tub, the other time in a broom closet. That's why we didn't call you right away. We searched the house first. When we couldn't find her—"

"Your call was logged at 7:44 A.M.," Audrey interrupted him. "When did you see her bed was empty?"

This time the woman spoke up. "My clock radio's set for 7:20. See, sometimes she sleeps in. It's rare but it happens, so just in case . . . She's got to have medication before eight or the day's pure hell. Anyway, Buzz got up when the radio went off, and he . . . well, when he couldn't find her he woke me up and we called 9-1-1."

Audrey nodded. "When did you last see her, then?"

"When she was put to bed last night," the father answered. "Just after eight. We both did it."

"The second time you've helped this month!" Her rigid stance had returned. "Don't tell me this is a trend!"

Audrey ignored the sarcasm and put her next question before the father could lay out the response she saw was coming. "Didn't either of you, er, before you went to bed yourselves . . ."

"Go in to check? Tuck her in?" The mother's posture had stiffened even more. "Lexie is not very tuckable. Once she's asleep, you don't take a chance on waking her up. Sometimes her day starts at midnight. Anything can set her off—light, unfamiliar noise, even the wrong cooking smell." She slumped noticeably. "Besides, I fell asleep in front of the TV." The slump got lower and her voice became a pleading whisper. "Look. You don't know how exhausting it is to have a child like Lexie. It never stops! I . . . I just fell asleep."

By now she could barely be heard. Audrey could see tears.

"That's right." It was the father. "I was out last night. My poker night. Once a month. It's the only night I ever have for myself. I got back—oh, it had to be about 1:30—and she, er, Jean, she was asleep in the living room. The TV was on, so I turned it off and covered her with a blanket.

"Before you ask—No, I didn't go in to Lexie's room either.

You soon learn around here that when it's quiet you leave well enough alone."

The doorbell rang, making all of them jump. Audrey's partner had arrived.

"What have you touched in here this morning?" Audrey asked hastily. "You know, what have—"

"When I came in with you just now," the mother interrupted, "that's the first time since last night when I—oh goodness—when *we* put her to bed."

"And you, sir?" Audrey looked at the father.

"Just opened the door," he said. "Came in a few steps, I guess. Looked under the bed, of course." He paused. "Well, you can see the covers are peeled right down. It was obvious Lexie wasn't in the bed."

Audrey nodded and stepped back down the hall a bit. "Up here!" she called. "But we're coming down." She motioned to the mother and father to follow her and then called downstairs again. "This one is yours!"

Audrey Greenwood has decided that this is not a juvenile crime, such as a runaway or a missing child, but a felony. What has led her to that decision?

72

A Clever Solution
at the County Fair

IT TOOK ONLY A COUPLE OF SECONDS for Chris Fogolin to realize that the change in his luck was holding. On the other side of the gently flapping canvas wall, the executive director of the Quail County Fair Board was shouting into the telephone. Chris could hear it as plainly as if J. Loudon Glint was talking to him directly.

"Who is this? Pincher? I thought so. Are you right there at the exhibit?" Glint was getting louder. The answer must have been affirmative for the next question was, "Well, can they hear you— Stipple and Two Feathers, I mean? Are they right there beside you, or . . .?" There was the briefest of pauses and then a groan.

"Well, get private, for heaven sakes!" Glint was shouting now. "Why do you think we give you people cell phones! Honestly! . . . Yeah, yeah, yeah. Never mind that now! Look. Check your watch. Call me back in exactly one minute. On the inside line."

There was a slight thump and then a loud honk as J. Loudon Glint cleared his nasal tracks before shouting once more. "Ellie! Bring me the entry forms on that homing pigeon exhibit! Right away!"

Ellie, who was also on the other side of the canvas wall, must have hesitated or looked perplexed because Glint came back immediately with, "Yes, all of them! There's only half a dozen entries in that class. I was down there this morning before the judging. Do I have to do everything myself?!"

Glint honked again. Twice. Chris was sympathetic. He too had a cold and wondered if that was what made the fair's executive director so cranky. Earlier that morning, Chris Fogolin had given serious thought to using his cold as an excuse to skip the county fair and stay in bed. His assignment was, all things considered, hardly the cutting edge of journalism. Chris was a crime reporter. Well, more accurately, that's what he wanted to be, but when one worked for the Quail County *Gleaner*, crime was limited to the police report on the second page, and most of that dealt with nothing more dramatic than stolen sheep. What would make the front page of *The Gleaner* tomorrow, and the day after, and the day after that, was news about the county fair. That more than anything else had gotten Chris out of bed. Better to have a by-line on the front page than no by-line at all.

Still, he'd spent the morning muttering under his breath about bad luck. Rain had begun to fall as soon as he entered the fair grounds. Bad for his cold and even worse for his shoes. Now there were not only cow patties to watch out for but mud too. And the rain had thinned the crowd, reducing the opportunity for a story. Even on *The Gleaner*, you had to have an angle to get on the front page.

But then the rain had brought good luck. A sudden downpour had driven Chris into the swine and fowl tent—he'd been walking past it, having decided well in advance to pretend it wasn't even there—and the first person he spotted was Madonna Two Feathers. She was always good for news. Madonna Two Feathers was an advocate for Native American rights, and known well beyond the borders of Quail County for her less than discreet methods. If Madonna Two Feathers was here, Chris knew, there had to be a story somewhere. Even if it was only a picture of her with her beloved pigeons. That, in fact, was something he did immediately: photograph Madonna Two Feathers sitting in her wheelchair holding a pair of pigeons in a cage on her lap. He then took a close-up of the identifying tag on the cage. "Cream Rollers," it said, obviously referring to the breed. Underneath the tag, a blue rosette with a pair of trailing blue ribbons proclaimed "FIRST PRIZE."

Chris Fogolin had been working in Quail County long enough to be aware that this was not some simple pet-raising venture. Madonna Two Feathers and her family were internationally famous among pigeon fanciers. A prize-winning pair of Cream Rollers could fetch thousands from the right buyer.

That knowledge had made Chris hang around after the pictures were taken to peer at some of the other Cream Rollers. After all, the rain was still coming down. There were five other pairs of pigeons in the exhibit. To Chris, they all looked exactly the same, making him wonder how the judges went about making a decision. Despite himself, he had leaned closer to the line of metal cages, and it was then that he found his story. The exhibitor right beside Madonna Two Feathers was Maxwell Stipple. Stipple was almost as well known as his neighboring exhibitor, but not for the kind of news *The Gleaner* liked to print. Stipple was a self-proclaimed white supremacist who, only three weeks before, had paid a huge fine for distributing anti-Native American slogans in front of the courthouse.

For Chris, the opportunity was a golden one. Even *The Gleaner* would like his angle: pigeons as the great leveler, the reason to set aside ill will and racist ideas in the clean spirit of competition. He'd immediately finished a roll of film on the spot, and then, forgetting entirely about the rain, dashed off to find Madonna Two Feathers again. Stipple too, if he could. That had been an hour ago. In his excitement he'd almost forgotten his editor's principal instruction: to photograph and interview the 4-H Grand Champion. A feature for that was already half written for today's edition. With that obligation to see to, he'd lost track of both Stipple and Two Feathers, and as a last resort he had decided to turn to J. Loudon Glint, who, if he was certain to be part of the story, would be sure to help.

The sound of Glint's telephone brought Chris back to the present.

"Pincher? Yeah. OK. Yeah, yeah . . . Oh, no! Oh my God, what next?" Glint wasn't shouting anymore, but he could still be heard very easily. An office in a tent just didn't make for privacy.

"Well, who spoke to you first, Stipple or Two Feathers? Yeah, yeah. And Stipple says they're his Cream Rollers, and she says they're hers? Yeah, I know. They all look the same to me too. And he's claiming that the first-prize ribbon was for his birds and she switched the name tags? Or maybe the ribbons? Oh, great! I think—just a minute."

Glint stopped to put out a tremendous honk.

"Now, look. I can't leave here right now. Hey, there's no press there, is there? Good. Now here's what you do. Here's the solution. What you do is take the . . ."

"Sir!" It was Ellie, her large nose pushing right into Chris's face. "You can't be here, sir! This is a restricted area. It's for employees of the fair board only. Now if you need shelter from the rain, we're more than happy to . . ."

Chris didn't stick around for the rest of it. It would take at least five minutes to get across the fair grounds to the exhibit where Pincher was about to follow Glint's instructions, and Chris wanted to get some shots of it.

Chris knows what Glint told Pincher to do, even though Ellie interrupted at the time, and he's going to photograph it for his paper. What has Glint told Pincher to do?

73

Even Birdwatchers
Need to Watch
Their Backs

RON MINAKER COULDN'T HELP BUT MARVEL at the trickle of water down the rock face at the other end of the bog. Hardly the Devil's Torrent, as it was described in brochures for the birdwatchers who traveled great distances to hike through the park and add to their lists.

"More like the Devil's Piddle," Ron said out loud to himself. "And this," he added, gesturing with his chin at the utterly still surface of the water, "this will soon be the Devil's Puddle if we don't get some rain."

He squatted down where the path forked, wincing at the cracking sound his knees made. At a slight angle to his left, the trail bent gracefully but precisely around the edge of the bog, bulged somewhat at the base of the waterfall where shifting feet had widened out a viewing space, and then disappeared into a stand of hardwoods. Above the hardwoods, a grove of cedars covered the face of the cliff from which the Devil's Torrent issued. The grove continued on over the rock face to the other side and petered out into hardwoods again. Ron couldn't see that latter part from where he was standing, but he had hiked it often enough to see it in his mind's eye.

The body of water was called McCarston's Lake on the map. A flattering description as far as Ron was concerned, even though there had always been water in it as far back as he could remember. Locals called it McCarston's Banana. That described its shape far more accurately. Still, government geologists had declared it a lake, and who was he to argue? Besides, he had more important things to consider this morning. Like the death of Jos Poot.

A birdwatcher, Jos Poot had been. At least, he'd been decked out in all the appropriate gear with all the appropriate paraphernalia in his many pockets when his body had been discovered fifteen days ago. Another birdwatcher had found it face down in the grove of white birches that filled the loop between the path that followed the edge of the bog and the one that forked to Ron's right. The body had escaped notice by birdwatcher traffic, concealed by the dense thicket of underbrush that lined both sides of the right path.

Homicide, the medical examiner had decreed. Dead at least two weeks and definitely not an accidental drowning. Not even a drowning. The body had certainly been soaked at some point; in fact a waterlogged *Petersen's Field Guide*, a jackknife, and a buckle from a binocular strap had been found in the lake in ankle-deep water, but death had been caused by trauma, namely a blow to the back of the head.

In Ron's opinion, the blow had been delivered by Jos Poot's wife, Orma, but it was an opinion his colleagues did not share. True, they acknowledged, Poot had been a cruel man. No less than three convictions of abuse, so the lady had motive. And true, Mrs. Poot was seen going into the park with her husband about a month ago—the same time he was reported missing—so she had opportunity. But how, Ron's colleagues argued, could such a tiny lady, a mere wisp really, dispatch her 250-pound husband on the head, admittedly from behind, while they were standing in the lake, and then lug him all the way to where the body was found?

A sharp ratatat-tat made Ron look up sharply. He leaned back a bit. From the end of the birch grove, where the looping path rejoined the bogside one at the base of the Torrent, the sound came again. "Woodpecker," he declared, blinking rapidly against the low sun. "A Downy? No. Ah, it's a sapsucker!" he said, pleased with his identification.

"Enough birding." He squatted down one more time, this time bracing in advance for the cracking from his knees. "Better get more pictures," he said, fishing in his shirt pocket for fresh film. "Short of bringing them all out here, it's the only way I'll convince the doubters that the missus definitely bonked him. They'd only scare the birds away."

What argument will Ron Minaker use to explain to his colleagues how Mrs. Poot got the body to its point of discovery?

74

Two Embassy Cars
Are Missing

IT NEVER JUST RAINS. Not on this job. I got half a county of empty back roads, two cars to look for, and one helicopter.

"Captain? Captain Surette? I think I see his, like, cell phone? Down in the ditch? It's like really smashed?"

And the only officer around to help me is a rookie who speaks in the comparative interrogative.

"Should I, like, go down and get it?"

Why me? First day this spring we've had a west wind hold all day. I could have gone sailing. Well, I'm not going to rush. When cops rush, they screw up. One thing. They're embassy cars. Got to be the only two stretch Cadillacs in Dufferin County. Unless they're ditched by now. That sun feels so good on the back of my neck I hate to move. God, it's been a long winter.

"Might be a clue to what happened to them? Like, the auxiliary troopers, I mean."

Almost forgot the troopers. Why did this have to happen on my watch? The only witnesses and they're both missing. So much for auxiliaries.

"Captain Surette! The phone? Like, the cell phone?"

"Yes, Constable, er, Oldchurch. Go down and get it."

If nothing else, it'll keep you busy so I can think. Let me see. According to our man here—our missing man—we got two embassy cars down the road there approaching Checkpoint One like they're supposed to. They stop before the intersection. Let's see, that's a good half mile away. And our man calls in 'cause he thinks something's not kosher.

"Captain! The phone's like really in pieces down here!"

Then people get out of the car with the Sudanese flags. Carrying Uzis. They get into the car with the Egyptian flags. That's when the call ends. Probably the smashed phone explains—

"Do you want me to pick them up? The pieces? Like, in an evidence bag? I should get a picture first, shouldn't I?"

What I don't like is behind us, up the hill, Checkpoint Two calls to say the cars split off in opposite directions, but then her phone goes dead too! This really smells.

"I'm gonna get the camera outa the car. OK, Captain? Oh, look! Over there? Like, the helicopter? Here it comes! Which way yuh gonna send it? There can't be more than an hour of daylight left."

Yes, which way? Well, I'm sure both cars have something to offer, but since at least one of the auxiliaries had to be in cahoots, the car I'd most like to find is the one with the Sudanese flags on the front fenders.

"You wouldn't be able, by any chance, er, Constable Oldchurch, to describe the flag of Sudan, would you?"

"Sudan. That's in, like, Africa, isn't it? Or is it Asia?"

Aside from the fact that the auxiliaries are missing, what has convinced Captain Surette that at least one of them is cooperating with the people in the missing embassy cars?

75

A Most
Confusing Robbery

ALTHOUGH SHE WAS PERFECTLY AWARE how important the trails of spattered blood were to the case, Detective-Inspector Mary-Joan Westlake had difficulty paying attention to the earnest explanations of the FOS.

"This spot here," the First Officer on the Scene was saying, pointing to dried droplets of blood on the concrete, "it's the start of the track for one of the suspects. Now see? Four, five yards down the alley here is the next one. Pretty consistent like this until you get to the dumpster around the corner. Now if . . ."

Some time later, before she could sign off, Mary-Joan had to ask the officer to go through it all again, just to be sure. The problem the first time was that the words of the store owner kept intruding on her consciousness.

"He wuz 'cross th' street 'afore I got off m' first shot," the old man had cackled with undisguised glee. "Y'see, she's allus cocked kinda slow till yuh get off the first round. That seems t' loosen 'er up." He held up a .45 Navy Colt that in all likelihood was as advanced in age as he was. "Too bad he wuz 'cross the street b' then. Took off runnin' down th' alley. Mighta caught 'im otherwise 'n' finished the job!"

The words, the attitude, even the man's satisfaction at foiling the robbery attempt and successfully plunking the robber—these were things she'd heard all too often before. But this time it was special. Mary-Joan Westlake had grown up on this street when it was a place where people sat on porch stoops after supper to watch their kids play catch, where young couples strolled on the sidewalk holding hands while old men leaned on the store fronts and watched them with knowing expressions. It was a place where she would run to Mr. Evers's grocery store at seconds before six to buy a quarter pound of butter, and where Mr. Evers would hold off locking up because he saw her coming.

That neighborhood was gone now, along with Mr. Evers and his way of doing business. Replaced by things like the city-sponsored clinic that handed out hypodermic needles, and X-rated video stores where the owner kept a loaded .45 Colt under the cash drawer. Mary-Joan knew all about that of course, better than most quite likely, but she was never able to come here now without experiencing profound culture shock.

"The other suspect's trail starts in the same spot but across the alley." The FOS was still talking. "This is probably where the bullet hit. See the blood right there. Then . . ." He took a step. "Second one." A few more steps. "Third one here, and so on down to where you see those oil barrels. Suspect was in behind them."

Mary-Joan finally dragged her consciousness into the present.

"And you found them both on your first sweep?" she asked. "One by the dumpster, the other by those barrels? That's only about a hundred feet apart."

"It wasn't hard, Inspector," the officer replied. "When we got the 9-1-1 call, we were parked only a block away. Heck, in the summertime with the windows open, we'd have probably heard the shots. Besides, with those wounds they really weren't going to go far. The big problem is which one of them is the robber. The old guy at the video store sure isn't much help. All he can say is that the robber was average height and weight and wore a blue parka and a dark ski mask. Dark eyes, he's sure of that. Voice? Well, the robber didn't say anything. Really, all that old guy cares about is that whoever it was is carrying a .45 caliber slug. I don't think he even knows he winged two people."

Mary-Joan looked down the alley and then back at the video store. The waning evening light was reflecting off the windows, and were it not for the steel security bars behind them, she realized, it would have been easy to start thinking about Mr. Evers again. Instead, she grimaced and said to the FOS, "I've seen enough. You've done a good job here. I'm going to write you a positive for your file. Now . . ." She motioned to the officer to follow her. "Let's go back to the hospital and arrest the one you got at the dumpster."

"To the hospital," the policeman echoed. He started to ask a question but then thought better of it. Maybe at the hospital he'd have the answer, for at this very moment the two suspects were lying there in some discomfort on emergency ward gurneys. Both had bullet wounds estimated by the medical staff to be at best a couple of hours old, wounds that were made by a large caliber bullet.

Suspect One lay on a gurney in one of the examination rooms, his leg wrapped at the fleshy part of the calf. Suspect Two moaned about her shoulder wound from a gurney out in the hall of the overcrowded ward. Both were street people, their dark eyes red-rimmed from poor diet, lack of sleep, and, in all likelihood, drugs.

Suspect Two's story was that she was standing in the alleyway across the street from the video store when she heard a shout and looked up to see someone coming across the street toward her. She didn't see anyone shoot. Just heard a shot and then, from behind her, the sound of a ricochet. That's when she felt the hit in the back of her shoulder. After the second shot, she said, she wasn't about to wait around. She vaguely remembered running down the alley before she passed out.

Suspect One's account had no details at all. According to his version he had just stepped into the alley when he heard two shots. One of them hit him, he didn't know which. He didn't remember much of anything after that. Just wanting to get out of there as fast as possible and then waking up in the hospital.

Both suspects—somehow Mary-Joan knew this would be the case even before she asked—had blue parkas: standard issue from the neighborhood hostel.

Which of the two suspects is Mary-Joan Westlake going to arrest?

76

Transcript
(Copy #1 of 4)

PORT CREDIT, 28 MAY 1941
Inquiry into the Collision of the O.M.S. *Oliver Mowat* and private vessel, *Gadabout* *

MAE APPLETON-NAIRN, CHAIR

APPLETON-NAIRN: Good morning. This inquiry is now on the record. We are here to investigate the collision of the O.M.S. *Oliver Mowat* and a private vessel, the, the (unintelligible), yes, the *Gadabout*, on 30 September 1940. My name is Mae Appleton-Nairn and I head the Investigative Branch of the Department of Transport. Is there anyone who wishes to be identified for the record?

ST. CLAIR: Oakwood St. Clair, Madam Chair, representing the Port Authority.

*For specifications re both vehicles see Marine Registry File 498761HC. See also Appendix to Report 12-A, 1940, of the Port Authority.

HAGEMAN: Callan Hageman, Madam Chair, representing Captain Ralph Ransom.

FLECK: Stephen Fleck, Madam Chair, representing Brewster and Zonka.

APPLETON-NAIRN: Who's . . . ? Oh yes, that's the owner of the private vessel. Is that a company?

FLECK: An incorporated entity, Madam Chair. I have copies of all the appropriate registrations.

APPLETON-NAIRN: Very well, thanks. Anyone else? Fine. Now, before we begin, may I remind everyone that this is an inquiry only, not a trial. My recommendations will go forward as to whether or not there is fault to be assessed in this collision, and whether or not charges will be laid. Are there any questions? Very good. Miss Clarke is an officer with the Port Credit Marine Unit. Excuse me, Miss Clarke. This may be an appropriate moment to remind everyone that brevity and succinctness will be very much appreciated throughout this hearing. Have I made that clear? Good. Very well, Miss Clarke, you may proceed. Everyone has received a copy of your report, so I believe that all you need do is provide us with a very brief oral summary.

CLARKE: The *Gadabout* ran into the stern of the *Oliver Mowat*.

APPLETON-NAIRN: Actually, Miss Clarke, I didn't mean quite that brief. Perhaps, for the record, you could establish the situation, the time frame, and sequence of events? Maybe tell us about the ships? Flesh it out a wee bit.

CLARKE: The O.M.S. *Oliver Mowat* is a 32-meter double-ended R-O-R-O ferry—

APPLETON-NAIRN: R-O-R-O?

CLARKE: Roll-On-Roll-Off. Cars. They drive in one end and out the other.

APPLETON-NAIRN: I see.

CLARKE: Anyway, she's an R-O-R-O with three decks, bottom for cars, middle for passengers. Top deck is crew-only with duplicate wheelhouses bow and stern. The "*Ollie*"—that's her running name—makes 18 round trips a day across the Port Credit harbor to Mississauga Island. Leaves the city on the hour and the island on the half. Sailing time one way is 17 minutes. The *Gadabout* is a 9.7-meter pleasure yacht converted to a single covered deck, with a one-man control cab forward. Licensed for harbor cruises and private parties. On September 30th last year . . . Should I go on?

APPLETON-NAIRN: Please.

CLARKE: Eight minutes out on the return leg, the *Mowat's* entire lighting system failed. While she was dark the *Gadabout* ran into her stern. No damage to the ferry or injuries to passengers or crew. One death and seven injuries on the private boat. She sank.

APPLETON-NAIRN: The ferry can transport several hundred passengers, according to your report, Miss Clarke, and the group on the . . . the . . . *Gadabout* that night numbered fifteen. But your report stipulates there are no witnesses. Any chance your subsequent investigations have—

CLARKE: No.

APPLETON-NAIRN: That seems so unlikely—

CLARKE: Week night. Middle of the harbor. Heavy rain. Private vessel was totally enclosed except for the skipper forward. He's the fatality.
FLECK: I have a question, Madam Chair.

APPLETON-NAIRN: Go ahead, Mr. Fleck.

FLECK: Miss Clarke, your report does not give us the number of passengers on the *Oliver Mowat.* Why is that?

CLARKE: It wasn't available.

FLECK: Not available? That doesn't make—

CLARKE: Passengers board through a turnstile counter, but it wasn't operative on that crossing.

FLECK: Can you tell us why?

APPLETON-NAIRN: I think we'll wait for Captain Ransom on that one, Mr. Fleck. Do you have any more questions?

FLECK: Well, yes, one more. I have information—it does not appear in your report—that exactly two weeks before this collision, the same lighting blackout occurred on another Port Authority ferry, the *James Whitney.* Are you aware of this incident?

CLARKE: Yes.

FLECK: In your experience, Miss Clarke, is it normal for ships like the *James Whitney* and the *Oliver Mowat* to suddenly lose their lighting systems and go dark?

APPLETON-NAIRN: Mr. Fleck, you know better! This is an inquiry. Not the place for cross-examination. Now if you have no more questions, does anyone else . . . OK, Mr. St. Clair.

ST. CLAIR: The *Oliver Mowat,* Miss Clarke, and the *James Whitney*—these incidents with their lighting failures, could you tell us what steps the Port Authority took after the first occurrence?

CLARKE: The *Whitney* was found to have a faulty circuit breaker. This breaker was immediately replaced with another type of breaker in the *Whitney* and all the other ferries too.

ST. CLAIR: That would include the *Oliver Mowat*?

CLARKE: Yes.

ST. CLAIR: According to your report, no reason has yet been found to account for the *Oliver Mowat's* sudden blackout on September 30, is that correct?

CLARKE: Yes.

ST. CLAIR: But certainly one could not accuse the Port Authority of faulty maintenance practices, could one?

APPLETON-NAIRN: Mr. St. Clair! You're way over the line!

ST. CLAIR: I apologize, Madam Chair. Let me approach factually here, please. Miss Clarke, the two ferries in question, they are not the only ones run by the Port Authority, are they?

CLARKE: There are five altogether. All run out of the same dock as the *Mowat*, between the city and the islands. All in service daily except for November to March.

ST. CLAIR: And it's my understanding that these ships are inspected regularly, including their electrical systems, by the Port Credit Marine Unit?

CLARKE: Twice a week in high season. Before the first outbound at 6 A.M. Once a week otherwise.

ST. CLAIR: High season begins . . . ?

CLARKE: First of May. Runs five months.

ST. CLAIR: Oh, one more thing. There are red and green—how can I describe them—clearance lights, or warning lights, on the wheelhouses?

CLARKE: Yes. Red on the starboard and green to port. Oh, sorry! The other way around.

ST. CLAIR: And these are on a separate circuit, aren't they? That is, their power source is independent of the interior lighting system, isn't it? By that I mean, if the main system fails, these lights don't necessarily go out.

CLARKE: That's right. And they're supposed to be checked too, every time a ship leaves the dock.

ST. CLAIR: For the record, Miss Clarke, the Port Credit Marine Unit, is it associated in any way with the Port Authority?

CLARKE: The Unit is independent. Federal. The Authority is city.

APPLETON-NAIRN: Finished, Mr. St. Clair? Thank you, Miss Clarke. We are probably done, but please don't leave, just in case. Captain Ransom, would you come forward please? According to Miss Clarke's report, you were in command of the *Oliver Mowat* at the time of the collision?

RANSOM: That's right.

APPLETON-NAIRN: And you were in the wheelhouse at the time of the collision?

RANSOM: With the helmsman. That's regulation.

APPLETON-NAIRN: And according to what you told the Marine Unit, the collision occurred entirely without warning?

RANSOM: Like you said, I was in the wheelhouse. The *Gadabout* rammed our stern.

FLECK: Madam Chair!

APPLETON-NAIRN: No need, Mr. Fleck. Captain Ransom, I think it would be better if you avoided terms like "rammed" until it's established as appropriate, assuming it will be. I have one more question. On the 30th, were you in command all day?

RANSOM: No. See, the way it works is there's three watches, divided evenly. I was third watch that day.

APPLETON-NAIRN: Very well. No, don't step down. I'm sure there are more questions. All right, go ahead, Mr. Fleck.

FLECK: Thank you, Madam Chair. Now Captain Ransom, this inquiry has already heard about the lighting failures on Port Authority ferries, especially the crucial one on your ship on September 30. You acknowledge that these occurred, don't you?

RANSOM: Yes.

FLECK: And we have already heard from Miss Clarke about the red-green lighting system. Do you have anything to add to what she said?

RANSOM: No.

FLECK: Madam Chair, for the record, when—I'm sorry, if—if this case goes to trial, my client, Brewster and Zonka, will be contending that the *Oliver Mowat*'s green-red system had failed along with the main system just prior to the collision.

APPLETON-NAIRN: It's on the record, Mr. Fleck. Continue.

RANSOM: Look, before you ask, I inspect those marker lights personally, outbound and inbound, before we cast off. They've never failed on any ship, ever, no matter what else has happened. Not in the 23 years I've been with the Authority.

FLECK: I see, Captain. Perhaps we can look at something else just for a minute then. The turnstile that counts the number of passengers, it wasn't working. Do you inspect that too?

RANSOM: Look, it was raining. Started to rain on my third trip and, you know, it rained steady into the next day. Anyway, there was only a handful of passengers and that Mississauga dock's got no cover. Now if they have to line up to go through the turnstile, it takes a while and they get soaked. So I disconnected it. The turnstile.

FLECK: Is there a chance, Captain Ransom, that because of the rain you might have skipped the light check too?

APPLETON-NAIRN: Mr. Fleck, I can appreciate your need to argue on behalf of your client, but once again, this is an inquiry. It's not an occasion for cross-examination.

FLECK: That's all my questions in any case, Madam Chair.

APPLETON-NAIRN: It's not my intent to call more witnesses at this time. Are there any other questions of Captain Ransom? Mr. St. Clair? No? What about you, Mr. Hageman? We haven't heard from you at all.

HAGEMAN: Normally, Madam Chair, I might have questions, but I believe that in an inquiry established to ascertain fault, I think we have heard enough to conclude that the *Gadabout* should certainly have been able to avoid colliding with this ferry.

APPLETON-NAIRN: I'm inclined to agree, Mr. Hageman, and my assessment of fault will reflect that.

Why should the Gadabout *have been able to avoid running into the stern of the* Oliver Mowat?

SOLUTIONS

1

A Decision at Rattlesnake Point

Without doubt, Perry Provato will examine the body at the morgue, looking for possible causes of death other than trauma from the two-hundred-foot drop. Trevor, however, has drawn some preliminary conclusions because of the size of the dead person and the position of the steering column.

From Perry, and from Trevor's observation, it is clear that the dead person is big. Most particularly, he has a very big belly. If he had driven the Lincoln Town Car to the edge of Rattlesnake Point, parked it, and then jumped over in an apparent suicide, he would surely have tilted up the steering column and wheel in order to get out of the car. This is automatic behavior in large people whose cars have this feature (as all newer model luxury cars do). The fact that Trevor had to tilt up the steering column in order to get his own large frame in to peer under the seat suggests to him that someone else drove the car to Rattlesnake Point. That can only mean the victim was already dead when the car was parked there, or that he was thrown over the cliff.

This conclusion may or may not be strengthened when Ashlynne checks the pre-set radio stations. The owner surely prefers country music. If when she turns the radio on, it is not tuned to a country station, that would reinforce the contention that the driver was someone other than the owner. If the pre-set stations do not include country music stations, this may suggest further discrepancy.

Why the car was parked so carefully and locked is an issue. However, the open trunk revealed the neatness with which the vehicle was kept, likely a characteristic of the victim. It is probable that Trevor's investigation of "A." will reveal that he was an orderly person. The murderer, no doubt aware of that, must have deliberately parked and locked the car in the way that A. would have done.

2

Something Suspicious
in the Harbor

On this second trip to the big freighter, Sue was able to see from her rowboat the paint scrape, where that morning the police boat had bumped into the side. Yet *The Christopher Thomas* had been receiving heavy cargo for several hours before the first visit, it was being loaded all day, and it was still being loaded when she made her unofficial visit. A freighter receiving cargo like this settles into the water as it is being loaded. Therefore, Sue should not have been able to see the paint scrape from the morning visit. By now, it should have been under water. Tomorrow morning she is going to have a careful look at the cargo, probably to see whether it is really automobile engines, or maybe to see if there is any cargo at all.

3

In Search of Answers

It is understandable that Celeste would be suspicious of Virgil Powys. After all, he has been having difficulties with his freelance business, so a cleverly arranged theft might make it possible for him to garner two or even more fees for Hygiolic's medical discovery. But Celeste needs more than suspicion; she needs good grounds for suspecting that Powys intended to be out of the studio longer than the ten or eleven minutes he claims.

Her suspicions arise out of what she observed on the reproduction Chippendale table. The weather has been very hot so all the windows are wide open. Even though Powys's studio has windows on three walls and is on the second floor (or is, at least, elevated), there is still no movement of air for there is no breeze.

Why, then, would someone who intends to be out for only about five or six minutes (he didn't know he was going to get a phone call—or did he?) place a heavy metal stapler on his working papers unless he expected that they might be blown around? And they would be blown around only if a wind were to rise. Given the conditions at the time Powys left the studio, this was not going to be an immediate possibility, or at least not a possibility in five or six minutes. Powys apparently intended to be out of the studio for longer than he claimed, which, in Celeste's opinion, is worth probing further.

4

A Single Shot in the Chest

Brian Breton turned down an opportunity to use what were supposedly Manotik's binoculars to have a look at the ten o'clock aerobics class. His probable reason was that he did not share Roly Coyne's idea of what constitutes a good time. But what he told Roly was that he couldn't really use the binoculars because they did not have the little rubber cups on the eyepieces that are needed for people who wear glasses.

Even though there are no eyeglasses in the collection of evidence and personal effects on the table up in Roly's office, Brian realizes that Xavier Manotik wore glasses, and had for a long time, because of the calloused indentations on either side of the bridge of his nose.

These two facts indicate that Manotik was not looking through binoculars at the Nucleonics executive suites. At least not *those* binoculars. Obviously Brian wonders what else in the guard's account does not hang together.

5

The Case of the
Stolen Stamp Collection

Miles Bender described one of the "police officers" as having blue eyes and a reddish moustache. He also said the officers had real uniforms and genuinely appeared to be motorcycle police personnel, complete with the sunglasses they typically wear. But if they had sunglasses on, how would Miles Bender have known the eye color of the one who got close to him?

6

Not Your Average
Hardware Store

In a hardware store where customers can buy "real" hardware from bins and barrels and shelves, where things are not prepackaged in a cosmetic sort of way, the clerks get dirty hands, for obvious reasons. Over time, the hands naturally become somewhat marked by years of digging into barrels of oil-covered nails and shelves of greasy bolts. This victim had a soft white hand showing in the small of his back. Therefore, it surely is not Wilfrid Norman, a long-time hardware store owner.

7

Murder at
249 Hanover Street

The butler is the only one with a careless alibi. He said he went to his sister's in Kennebunkport on the 30th for two days. Even though his sister may prevaricate on his behalf, he has still made the mistake of saying the "30th." The day is October 1 (as the radio announcer said), so if he was in Kennebunkport for two days, he could not have gone there on September 30. There are only thirty days in September.

8

Head-on in the
Middle of the Road

Dust. Road dust from what must be an unpaved surface (or else why would a grader be used, and why would the rutting and potholing recur just about every year?). The accident happened at midday on August 9. In August, at midday, after the weather has been so nice and dry (according to Peter Hesch's testimony), and after a road has been repaired and graded, any car going along it will throw billows of dust into the air. The two plaintiffs would have had to be extremely inattentive—and therefore dangerous drivers—not to have noticed each other's dust, blind hill or not, and so to have been unaware of oncoming traffic.

9

A 911 Call from
Whitby Towers

Sandford Verity said that he looked up when he arrived at Whitby Towers to see if Mr. Seneca was watching the incident out on the street. That's when Verity allegedly saw him on the chair, which implies he was about to attempt to hang himself with a nylon rope. However, when Bev Ashby noticed the end of a piece of nylon rope and followed the rope to where it was clamped between the balcony doors, she had to part the drapes with her pen to do so. From the street, Verity could not have seen through the drapes.

10

The Case of the
Kramer Collection

Issue number one of *Reader's Digest* is dated February 1922, so that part of the Kramer Collection may be authentic. The *Times* was begun in 1785, so the collection could quite easily have an 1890 edition. The 1728 edition of the *Saturday Evening Post* may indeed be a "genuine fraud." The magazine began publishing in 1821. In 1899, the publishers fabricated the claim that it had actually been started in 1728 by Ben Franklin. Even after the claim was proved patently false, it was never fully abandoned.

The Arctic items are quite possibly genuine for the explorers mentioned did sally forth in the years given. (And the practice of storing food in cans was developed in England for the Royal Navy in 1810, so the can of beans is okay.) The Canadian—later American—explorer Stefansson stirred up an international controversy after his "discovery" in 1910 of a group of native people on Victoria Island with fair, European features by theorizing that they had intermingled with Scandinavian colonizers years before. Stefansson called them "blond Eskimos." Thus it could be that the material in the Kramer Collection is authentic. However, it is for the coins that George is needed, and if one of them is clearly fraudulent, it's quite possible that everything else is, too.

The George Washington coins are surely legitimate. Coins were still being issued with the label *Upper Canada* well after Upper Canada became the Province of Ontario in 1867, so a halfpenny dated 1883 and designated "Upper Canada" is real enough. In World War II nickels without nickel were issued so that the valuable mineral could be used in the war effort. Coins from Hadrian's reign are common enough. But no coin produced in the B.C. era was ever labeled *B.C.* The notion of B.C did not come into being until well after Christ was born.

11

Waiting Out
the Rain

While Michelle sat at Kline's Soda Shoppe with her friends from Memorial Junior School, she watched a little boy standing in the gutter, enjoying the rainfall. He had boots on and the runoff was rushing up against the toes of the boots. This is confirmed by the candy wrapper which flowed up to his toes and then floated between the boots. The flow of the water therefore defines the slope of the street.

Behind the little boy (and downstream) is a woman, quite likely, his mother. She is standing at Whippany Appliances, next door to Kline's, listening to the news about the D-Day landing in France.

When Michelle and Julie leave Kline's, they walk past Whippany Appliances and see the two men unloading a truck belonging to Bitnik's Delivery Service. The truck is still further "downstream" from Kline's. If its emergency brake failed, it would not have rolled toward Kline's Soda Shoppe, but the other way. To cause the damage it did, the truck would have had to smash into Kline's window while under power. It was obviously not an accident.

12

A Routine Check
in the Parking Lot

The victims have been arranged in the car as though they were lovers in a tryst. Because it is December, the motor is running to make the heater operative, and to a casual investigator that would suggest that they were overcome by carbon monoxide gas.

However, Ron notes the face of the male victim. The eyes are wide open, and most important, the pupils are very small. If the male victim had been sitting in the dark car with the lady for long enough for carbon monoxide to do its deadly work, his eyes would have adjusted to the darkness and his pupils would have been large.

Ron Forrester concludes, probably correctly, that the man was murdered elsewhere (in bright light) and then put in the car afterward. He concludes that if the man died that way, the lady probably did, too. It would have been easy to attribute their deaths to accidental carbon-monoxide poisoning if he had not noticed this detail.

13

An Answer for Kirby's Important New Client

Simon Fitzwall was born in 1789.

Ambrose Fitzwall lost his leg and three fingers two months after the Seven Years War began. Since the war ended with the Treaty of Paris in 1763, he therefore lost the leg in 1756. Smythe-Boliver was 48 then (born 1708) and Fitzwall was half his age, or 24. Fitzwall had a daughter (Abigail, according to his personal history) who, Smythe-Boliver says, was born when Fitzwall was 18, making her 6 years old in 1756.

Fitzwall came to Halifax, and then Boston, with Abigail and Ethan and Nattie's child Rachel in 1768. (The *Earl of Shannon,* on which they sailed, sank in Halifax five years after the Treaty of Paris in 1763, under the terms of which she became a British ship.)

At the time of the crossing, Abigail would have been 18 years old. She married four years later (at the age of 22) and had a first child two years after that.

At the time of the crossing in 1768, Ethan was 3 years old (half the age Abigail was when Ambrose lost the leg) and Rachel was twice that, or 6 years old. Both Rachel and Ethan married at the same age Abigail married (22). Thus Rachel married in 1784 and Ethan in 1787. And both, like Abigail, had their first-born two years after that. Simon was Ethan's first born in 1789.

14
Two Shots Were Fired

Because of the heat wave, it is reasonable to believe that the door was indeed propped open as the guard said. And it may well be that the guard faced the front if that's where previous break-ins occurred. Therefore, his back would have been to the open door. However, even though the open door faced east, and what would therefore have been the rising sun, the fact is there was no rising sun at the time of the shooting. The area was covered with gray cloud when the shooting took place, between six A.M. and seven A.M. (When Vince Pogor arrived, it was noon and the crime was already six hours old.) The sun did not come out until Vince was driving to Toronto, some time after he was about to listen to the eight o'clock news while eating his breakfast.

Given these conditions, the security guard's statement that he was startled by a dark *shadow* from the doorway behind him is highly suspect.

15
Northern Farms Ltd.
Versus
Dominion Spraying Company

Quite possibly Judge Westlake is bothered by the fact that not one of the witnesses has said, specifically and unequivocally, that he or she saw Molly's Arch Dream III in the field in question around the time that the spraying took place. Fenton Purge was not there at the time. Daphne Organ, although she is specific about having seen Molly *prior* to June 27 from time to time, says she did not pay particular attention on that morning. Eulalia Bean and Parthenon Andreikos are evasive. Their answers only imply that the cow was there at the time.

In combination, the answers become even fuzzier. Fenton Purge tells us the field is in the southwest corner of the farm. Daphne Organ, who lives right across the road from the farm, watches the sunrise from her porch while having tea (and then has lunch there because it is in the shade). Thus Daphne must face east. Regional Road 7, then, one of the borders of Farm Number 3, runs north-south. Since Parthenon Andreikos first waved to Eulalia Bean then, a few seconds later, saw the herd as he went toward the canal (south), the barn from which Eulie exits with hay is north of the field.

Eulie takes hay to a feed trough at the fence. Beside it is a water trough to which water is piped. Logically, the troughs are going to be at the fence nearest the barn.

Andreikos says the ends of the troughs pointed to the road. Therefore, the troughs were set up at the north end of this square field, perpendicular to the road. If he saw Molly broadside at her spot at the end of the trough, as he implies (having noted the triangle), then Molly would have to be facing north. The problem with his testimony is that he says the triangle was on her right side. If she was facing north, waiting for Eulie to arrive with the hay, Molly's right side would have been facing away from Road 7. Andreikos may have been able to see her broadside all right, but not the side that has the triangle. Judge Westlake has figured this out and probably wants to find out if this valuable animal might have died of hardware disease prior to or around the same time that the spraying took place. It could be that Northern Farms is simply taking advantage of a coincidence.

16

An Unlikely Place
to Die

The time of day is early morning because Brad got trapped in rush-hour traffic. The gardener discovered Mme. de Bouvère's body just after sunrise and turned on the alarm. The coroner estimates the time of death at between ten and eleven the night before. Therefore, if Mme. de Bouvère and the man lying outside the gazebo had gone out to play tennis and indulge in some drugs the evening before, they would have walked over the lawn that surrounded the gazebo while it was still wet or at least damp from the rain that accompanied the late afternoon thunderstorm the day before. Because the gardener cuts the lawn every second day, and because he cut it yesterday, *before* they walked to the gazebo, Mme. de Bouvère would surely have picked up a blade of grass (likely several) on her white sneakers. Yet Brad noticed that her sneakers, like the rest of her clothing, were pristine: entirely free of any specks. It appears to him that she somehow got to the gazebo without making contact with the lawn. Whether or not she died of a drug overdose, it is likely that someone carried her there after she was already dead.

17

To Catch a
Mannerly Thief

Agnes Skeehan walks into her hotel leaning into a strong east wind. She responds to Deputy Commissioner Mowat's phone call and he tells her to go right to the office of the Liverpool CID, specifically to Superintendent Opilis. Through the window of the superintendent's office, Agnes notices a weathervane on a pub across the street pointing right at her. Since the wind is from the east (blowing *toward* the west) the superintendent's office must therefore be on the east side of a street that runs north-south.

Both Agnes and the superintendent then see Alistair Withenshawe across the street, walking to the police station because he was summoned there. Opilis told Agnes that Withenshawe Purveyors has an office just a short walk to the south. Therefore, this "dude" as Agnes called him, is walking toward the north, on the west side of the street. His cane must be in his street-side hand, or *right* hand, for he first bounces it off the curb, then twirls it over parked cars.

Agnes concludes that to engage in such adept cane work, Alistair Withenshawe must be using his preferred hand, his right hand, the same hand he would use to write notes. Since the jewel thief's notes are written by a left-handed person, Agnes is willing to give odds that Withenshawe didn't write them.

18

Tracing the Couriers
from Departure to Arrival

Mary Clare McInerney and her investigating team need to find out from which airports the drug couriers code-named—or *possibly* code-named—Seamus, Rothsay, Saint, and Felipe are flying out, and their respective destinations as well.

The team has put together the facts that the couriers are leaving from Dorval airport in Montreal, Orly airport in Paris, O'Hare airport in Chicago, and Heathrow airport in London. The destinations that the team have discovered are Brazil (Rio), Bermuda, Hawaii (Oahu), and Hong Kong. The problem is to put the information together so that it can be determined who is flying where, and from where, so that they can be followed and the appropriate arrests made.

From Struan Ritchie, Mary Clare first learns that Rothsay is flying out of Dorval airport in Montreal, and that Seamus is going to Brazil.

Cecil King reveals that the one flying to Bermuda is flying out of Orly in Paris. That cannot be Seamus then, since he is going to Brazil. And Rothsay cannot be going to Bermuda, because she is flying out of Dorval.

When Struan Ritchie calls back he reveals that Felipe is flying out of Heathrow, which means he, too, is not going to Bermuda. When Struan says that Felipe is not going to Hong Kong, it is apparent that Felipe must be the one going to Hawaii. Rothsay, then, is going to Hong Kong. The courier code-named Saint must be the one going to Bermuda.

Once the team works out where the couriers are going, it is fairly easy to work out where they are flying from. They already know that Felipe is at Heathrow and Rothsay is leaving from Dorval. Saint (the one destined for Bermuda) is leaving from Orly, so Seamus must be going to Brazil from O'Hare.

19

Not All Lottery Winners Are lucky

Two days before Frank Ricketts visited the body of Archie Deschamps-Lebeau there had been a chinook. In the morning rush hour, the snow had melted to slush, and then before noon the temperature had dropped to way below freezing and stayed that way. On that day, the two daughters had supposedly visited Archie and made him lunch—this is *after* the quick thaw then freeze—and reported that he was okay. They say they found him today when they came on their regular call.

However, Archie's body had been impressed into the ice. Frank wanted to know whether Nick and the crew had measured the distance between the indentations made by his feet. He also noted that the paramedics had pried the body loose carefully and rolled him over onto his back. Frank has concluded that Archie's body was out there *before* the chinook of two days ago. (It had lain on the ice, then sank into it during the thaw, and then was frozen in when the temperature plunged.) Yet according to the daughters, the old man was all right during their visit two days ago.

20

Spy Versus Spy

Because the *Rote Kapelle* did not use radios in Stuttgart to any great extent (at least in our story) the counterespionage service of German intelligence did not have great success with the direction-finding equipment used to locate clandestine radios—and thereby spies—in World War II. It is reasonable to assume, therefore, that Kopenick is not sending Morse code messages to Traugott Waechter by means of special equipment they have had installed in their vehicles. (Besides, Waechter shows up in a variety of vehicles; that would have been too much of a technical challenge had they been using such equipment.)

For obvious reasons, they would not be communicating with written signs or hand signals, not in the midst of traffic in a German city in the middle of World War II.

Then there's the fact that Hauptmann August can read the code while he is *behind* Waechter's little truck and cannot see Kopenick at all. The only way that the Morse can be used, therefore, is through the brake lights. When the vehicle stops (Kopenick's) he taps out the code to Waechter right behind him. Ernst August told Oberst Staat they had to see the two spies rendezvous while it was still raining. Either by luck or persistence, August had no doubt learned that by driving behind Waechter when the pavement was wet, he could see the brake lights of the car in front (Kopenick's) reflected off the pavement beneath the following vehicle (Waechter's). By that means August could see and translate the Morse message.

This apparently naive method of communication (Ernst August called it "clumsy") was actually used from time to time, especially in World War II. It is highly likely that real spies would not have communicated in open Morse, however, but would have had a code developed for the purpose.

The use of Morse code had declined dramatically by World War II in favor of the far more economical Baudot Code devised by a French engineer (named Baudot, what else!) in 1874. Still, who has ever heard of Baudot Code?

The *Rote Kapelle* was exceptionally successful as a Soviet network in the early years of the war, but careless use of their radios, along with increasing sophistication in radio location techniques and technology on the part of German intelligence, reduced their effectiveness by 1943. Post-war analysis, incidentally, attributes the network's downfall largely to the fact that too many agents knew one another. They did not use "cutouts" sufficiently or effectively so that when one was caught, the domino effect was very damaging.

21

The Search for Olie Jorgensson

Willy Stefan, as Connie knew, is not a neutral party in this case, being Olie's uncle, Svena's brother-in-law, and perhaps most important, being married to the sister of Olie's father.

Willy has been leading the search team down the abandoned railway line at a very slow pace. He explained to Connie that the slowness was owing to the fact that signs along the trail were hard to read, there being so many tourists hiking down the line at this time of year. His mistake was in giving that as his excuse. If there were enough tourists walking along this line to disrupt the tracking process, those same hikers would have cleaned out the wild raspberries, too. Yet they grew in abundance at the edge of the trail. For reasons that Connie wants to uncover, Willy has lied to her.

22

Murder at the David Winkler House

Chris Beadle walked into the tiny washroom pushing the door open wide. The door barely cleared the sink in the corner ahead and to the left. The sampler is hanging on the wall behind this door. If Kate Mistoe had been nailing up this sampler when the shots were fired, she would have had to close the door. Otherwise she would not have been able to get at the wall.

The problem with her alibi arises out of the fact that Sandy Sanchez says he saw her as he passed, at the time the shots were fired. (They stared at each other in shock and fear.) If the door had been closed, he obviously would not have seen her.

When Sandy spoke to Chris and animatedly made clockwise motions with his fist to describe the tightening of the fitting on the propane system, he may have been inadvertently revealing ignorance about propane systems. Threaded fittings throughout the world are tightened clockwise and loosened counterclockwise. By international agreement, threaded fittings used in gas systems (e.g., propane) are tightened and loosened in the opposite way.

Karl Schloss had the oil changed in his car. The service station would have noted the odometer reading at the time of this oil change. By checking the odometer reading right now, Chris can calculate how far he drove after leaving the service station. By having him retrace the route he said he covered on the way back to Winkler House, Chris would be able to verify whether or not he actually did so.

23

Incident on the Picket Line

You don't need to be a trucking expert to know that Roger Monk is claiming an incorrect number of tires. The police confirm that all his tires were slashed, but no tractor-trailer combination has sixteen tires.

Casual observation as you drive along the highway confirms that on the very front axle of the tractor portion of a tractor-trailer, there are two tires, one at each end. On all other axles, whether they be tandem or single or center air-lift (the type you often see retracted up off the road surface), there are always four tires, two at each end.

A little bit of logic added to this observation tells you that the least number of tires possible on a tractor-trailer combination is ten. The next largest tractor-trailer has fourteen, then eighteen, twenty-two, twenty-six, and so on. Never sixteen.

In Roger's case, he is trying for two extra tires. His tractor has a tandem axle on the rear. "Tandem" means "one behind the other." That means a total of two axles at the rear then, each with four tires (making eight), which along with the two on the very front makes ten tires on the tractor. A single axle on the trailer adds four more tires, which makes a grand total of fourteen.

24

Footprints on the Trail

Tibor Nish does not deny using the path to get to the barn. And there is a witness who saw him there. But Nish said he came *four* days ago, which is two days before the fire. The witness thinks he came on the *day before* the fire but cannot be absolutely sure.

Then there is the matter of Tibor Nish's long legs versus the fact that the footprints are close together, implying a short-legged person. On the day before the fire, there was a thaw, a day and night of mild weather. Anyone walking down a steep hill on frozen ground, during a thaw, would necessarily take short steps, with special care to dig in the heel as much as possible to keep from falling. This is because the top few inches of earth in these conditions melts and becomes soft. This layer of soft mud on top of the frozen ground makes the surface impossibly slippery. Anyone walking on it has to be very careful and must take short deliberate steps, especially on a hill. Since the only tracks on the path are from size twelve Kodiak work boots, and since Tibor Nish does not deny using the path, the only day on which those tracks could have been imprinted was on the day before the fire; the day on which the witness thinks she saw him at the barn.

25

A Very Brief
Non-Interview

When Sheila Lacroix entered the office, the office door was behind her, and the wall to her left held books and newspapers. Ahead of her (the third wall) was glass through which she could see central Amman. On the remaining wall, Ibrahim Jamaa, or rather, his substitute, was signing documents.

He had his back to Sheila and he was covered with thobe and aba so that only one hand was exposed. Since the hand rested on the back of his hip and the index finger pointed to the windowed wall, the hand therefore must have been his right. He was signing documents with his left hand, and so he must be left-handed.

When Ibrahim Jamaa's substitute took two steps to the edge of his desk and spoke to Sheila, he ran one of his long index fingers over the shoulder cradle of the telephone and along the thin neck of a desk lamp. For a left-handed person, those items are on the wrong side of the desk.

If he prefers to speak on the telephone and write while doing so (hence the shoulder cradle), the telephone would be on the other side of the desk so that the receiver could rest on his right shoulder while he wrote with his left hand. If there is any doubt about this logic, it is dispelled by the position of the desk lamp. It's on the same, or wrong, side of the desk.

26

Murder at 12 Carnavon

As Honey states, to herself and to Marion, the task she has is to point out a discrepancy in the seemingly precise case that Roland has built, so that the jury will focus on the issue at hand. If she can show that at least one of these ever-so-carefully verified details is inconsistent, then perhaps the jurors will reconsider their position.

There's no compelling reason to suspect the waitress of collusion in spilling the ketchup to give Barnett a reason to go home at midday. After all, waitresses do spill things. Besides, if it were a contrived spill, it would more likely have been coffee. Still the weakness is in the spilled ketchup. During his testimony, Barnett held out his left leg to show where the ketchup had fallen. He then very carefully told the jury that he remembered being stuck with the pin by the tailor, right where the ketchup was still on his sock.

Anyone who has ever paid attention when pant cuffs are being measured and marked, especially by a professional tailor, would notice that the tailor always measures just one leg—the *right* leg. The little tailor, who would of course have been performing professionally, must have seen the ketchup on the right sock, whether or not he really stuck it with a pin.

This tiny point is precisely what Honey needs as a wedge.

27

The Case of
Queen Isabella's Gift

Even though the vicar is a clear suspect, his story that a visitor to Evensong hid in the church is entirely plausible. But the story breaks down over the electric lights. Geoffrey's visit to St. Dunstan's-by-the-Water takes place during the day. Chief Inspector Peddelley-Spens, during his tirade, said that the prime minister of Portugal was coming in "this afternoon" and that he wanted Geoff back "before tea." It took Geoff an hour to get to St. Dunstan's, so it is daylight when he and the vicar enter the church.

They unlock the main door and enter. The church is dark and the vicar turns on the lights, so lighting is necessary at all times, even daytime, to function in the church. Because the vicar asks Geoff to exit by the main door so they can turn the lights out and lock up, the only light switches must be at that door.

If the vicar entered that morning by the back emergency door (as usual) and looked up (which was unusual), would he have been able to see that the candelabra were missing without first going to the back of the church and turning on the lights? The candelabra, after all, were placed so high that even with a step stool and an extended candlelighter they were difficult to light. It is far more likely that the vicar already knew they were missing.

It is interesting to note that Geoffrey was also very much aware that the conflict between Edward II and his queen, Isabella, was so intense that by 1326, six years after the dedication of St. Dunstan's, it had degenerated into civil war or, depending on one's point of view, a legitimate revolution. It's quite possible that in 1320 they may not have attended a dedication together.

George IV became Prince Regent in 1810. His father, by this time, was reported to be having animated conversations with a tree in the Great Park at Windsor, thinking it was Frederick the Great.

28

Quite Possibly, the Annual Meeting
of the Ambiguity Society

Bonnie must assume that none of the members are telling her the exact truth; yet she must take their answers at face value for her calculations. If she does that, she will find that every date but one in the month of May appears at least two, sometimes three times, when all the answers are considered, thus representing the nature of the Ambiguity Society.

Sally's first answer specifies a date *after* the thirteenth of the month. Her second specifies a date *before* the thirteenth. Thus every day is accounted for at least once except the thirteenth.

Karen Di Cresce's answer adds the thirteenth along with every other odd-numbered date, and Julio's answer specifies every date of the month except May 4, 9, 16, and 25. Thus, every date in the month is mentioned at least two or three times (thereby establishing further ambiguity), except for May 4 and 16.

The very first response, the one from Bruno Steubens, specifies that the meeting will be held on the middle of the month just like this year. The middle of the month of May is the sixteenth, which means that date, too, has two answers. Therefore the only single, unambiguous choice of date is May 4.

29

The Case of the Missing Body

Lesley Simpson could see that at the point in the trench where the skeleton was found, the earth was being excavated for the very first time as the trench was being dug. Had someone buried the body of Mrs. Vincent Gene there three years ago, the earth would have been disturbed by that excavation. However, what Sergeant Palmer pointed out to Lesley was a skeleton lying in earth that was still in its natural layers. It is entirely likely that this earth hadn't been disturbed since the last glacier passed through.

Therefore, the skeleton of Mrs. Gene must have been brought to the trench from elsewhere, dropped in, and then covered with loose earth for the backhoe operator to find the next day. If Vincent Gene is charged, it will likely be Lesley Simpson's argument that he is being framed by someone who put the body in the trench in an attempt to make it appear as though she had been buried there some time before.

30

The Case of the Marigold Trophy

Janice has been reading back issues of *The Daily Enterprise* on microfilm. She has available issues from 1903, 1904, and 1905. When Eugene Weller tells her it is closing time she is looking at a date in March. Since she has been reading carefully and in sequence for four hours (from five to nine without taking a break) and since she can cover five months of issues in an hour, the

March she is looking at must be March 1904, the year the trophy was awarded to Maribeth Tooch. (She has covered twenty months; all of 1905 plus nine months of 1904 minus an October for either year. This would not work out if she had started with 1903 and worked forward in sequence.)

The date she is looking at is March 3. According to the article, Curragh O'Malley's horse ran down Ezra Templeton on March 2. On the same day a week earlier, it struck Maribeth Tooch just after she had seeded her marigolds. In three out of four years, the date of the same day a week earlier would have been February 23, the planting date for marigold seeds according to the contest rules, but 1904 is a leap year (any year divisible by four); therefore the date she was struck, *and* the date on which she seeded her marigolds for the contest, was February 24. The Grand Champion Marigold exhibitor of the 1904 Albion Agricultural Exhibition broke the rules!

31
The Coffee Break
That Wasn't

What Lennie is attempting to determine is whether she got a fresh cup of coffee or whether the waitress simply took out the plastic housefly and returned with the same cup of coffee. That's why she tasted the coffee with her little finger. She must have put sugar in the original cupful. When she tasted coffee from the "new" cup it must have been sweet, causing her to conclude the worst.

32

Who Shot the Clerk at Honest Orville's?

Certainly the missing weapon is one element on which Mary and Caroline will undoubtedly lean, but their strongest point is likely a simple matter of physics. The time is pre-Christmas, close enough to the day itself for the Christmas shopping rush. The two young ladies were wearing coats, and Caroline made note of the overheated police station. Therefore, this is Christmas time in the northern hemisphere, so that by 8:40 P.M. it will be fully dark outside. If Honest Orville's sign has around fifty thousand bulbs, as the discussion reveals, then the area where the shooting took place will have a great deal of bright artificial light. However, if the shooting took place well out on the sidewalk, under the big sign, Kee Park would have been *backlit*. It would have been extremely difficult, therefore, to make out his face, if not impossible. Given that the patrolman-witness had to run across a wide busy street to nab Kee Park and Mr. Sung, who were in a crowd, and had to stop traffic to do so (which would inevitably mean taking his eyes off the suspects), the two law students may well choose to press the witness on the issue of making a positive identification in, say, a lineup. He's not likely to succeed without reasonable doubt.

33

Speed Checked
by Radar

This was certainly not an easy decision for Fran to make. If there is something wrong, some threat in the building, then she will be held liable for failing to act. Yet to rush the building with the E.R. team could be disastrous for several reasons. Even for her to go in, with or without Constable Gold, could complicate things, too. And both choices attract lots of attention and would alert the crazies.

It behooved Fran to weigh the situation carefully, which is just what she did. Given what she learned from Constable Gold about the likely type of individual it was who was walking to and from the annex building, and given that it was very close to 4:30 P.M. on a Friday afternoon, she believes that in moving quickly, this possible "grunt" was behaving normally.

If it were likely that he was returning to a difficult situation, at least one that he couldn't leave by 4:30 P.M., he would probably have moved more slowly or deliberately. Quite likely the sight of a speeder being caught would have merited a longer look, too. He might even have tried to send a signal of some sort to the two police officers.

All this, however, is meaningless if the young man walking to the annex building is not a regular employee, but one of a group that has taken over the building, and who has been sent to the annex to further the appearance of normality. But one action of his signaled to Fran that he is a regular employee, and one familiar with the place. He not only anticipated the locked slab door while walking up the steps, he selected the right key from a large ring of keys and unlocked the door in a single motion. All his actions indicated that he has done this many times before. A "plant" would have been less automatic at some point in the procedure.

34

Where to Send
"This Stuff Here"

In the LAME Room, there are four cartons, each with items to go to four different players. Sue has to identify which item goes to which player and then arrange to send it to the airport of the appropriate city.

The former holder of Sue's job (now with the Glasgow Rangers) says that Nodl will have the names and addresses in the brown envelope she is carrying, however unorthodox they may seem. The names are Tino Savi, Giovanni Moro, and Gino Bellissime. Iago Cassini's name must be on one of the items already: the photography bag. The four cities are Turin (where the skis go), Naples, Milan, and Capri (where the chess sets go).

Iago Cassini gets the photography bag. Tino Savi does not ski, so he gets neither the skis nor the photography bag. Tino Savi does not live in Naples (he visited there) or Turin (where the skis are being sent). Since he does not live in Milan (where Gino Bellissime has a business with his wife), Tino Savi is from Capri and therefore gets the chess sets.

Giovanni Moro does not live in Naples or Milan (or Capri), so he must be from Turin, where the skis go. Since Gino lives in Milan, Iago Cassini must be from Naples. The remaining item of the four must be the guitar, which then goes to Gino Bellissime, or to his wife, in Milan.

35

A Witness
in the Park

The season must be autumn, for Mary Blair's shoes leave prints in the frosty grass. Alicia Bell says there are leaves falling. Yet it must still be early autumn, for Mary notes that the ground was still too soft to walk on in high heels.

Anyone who gets up early enough on crisp but sunny autumn days, when the temperature is close to freezing, has seen the frost on the grass sparkling in the sunlight. However, particularly in early fall, that sparkle disappears within two to three hours of sunrise at the latest as the earth warms.

Alicia Bell was doing fine with her story about Ron Minaker digging flower bulbs out of Jack Atkin's flower bed until she mentioned the footprints in the frosty grass. It's quite possible that two days ago when the alleged digging took place, the weather was identical to the weather on the day Mary and Alicia met. And it's quite possible that Alicia could have been concealed just over the brow of a knoll behind the flower bed in question. But she couldn't have stood there until at least ten o'clock for the park gates are locked until then. By that time, in early fall, the frost on the grass has long melted away in the sunlight.

It appears that Alicia Bell was enjoying her story so much that she went too far.

36

An Urgent Security Matter at the UN

There are to be eight people at the table in the Singapore Room: Ambassador Manamoto and Bjarni Benediktsson, who are chair and vice-chair; General Nardone, Bishop Leoni, and Dr. Perez from one delegation; Ambassador Haruna, Ms. Gestido, and Mr. Cresawana from the other. Chris and Paul Fogolin can begin the seating arrangements knowing that the delegations have to be intermingled, and knowing that the heads of delegations will sit beside the chair, Ambassador Manamoto.

However, Ambassador Haruna has manipulated the seating. He has accomplished this by requesting that Ms. Gestido, of his delegation, be immediately beside him. (It makes no difference whether she is on his right or his left; by extension, therefore, Haruna can be either on Manamoto's right or left; the manipulation works in either direction at this round table. For purposes of description here, assume that Haruna is on the left, with Ms. Gestido to the immediate left of him.) Because of Ambassador Manamoto's intermingling condition, Mr. Cresawana cannot sit to her left in turn, and she does not want to sit beside Bishop Leoni, so only Benediktsson or Dr. Perez can sit there.

Ambassador Haruna apparently knows that Dr. Perez will not sit beside Gestido, so Bjarni Benediktsson must then be the one next to Ms. Gestido. To Benediktsson's left will be Dr. Perez because Haruna knows she won't sit beside Leoni or Nardone. Then to her left, in order, will be Mr. Cresawana, then Bishop Leoni, then General Nardone, as the circle goes back to Ambassador Manamoto.

This is the only seating arrangement that is possible if all the diplomats' requests are to be honored. And it has been arranged principally by Ambassador Haruna. Whether or not he has help from others (like Dr. Perez) we cannot be sure. All we can be sure of is that he has manipulated the seating arrangement with only one simple request: that Ms. Gestido be seated beside him. And his reason for the request is entirely valid and reasonable, too.

What is achieved by the manipulation is getting Mr. Cresawana immediately beside Bishop Leoni. Since Leoni is the suspect target, and Cresawana is new, it is only natural for the Fogolin brothers to suspect him.

37

The Body on Blanchard Beach

Dexter Treble explained that although the tire tracks were clear and preserved, there were no footprints. Had the body been brought to Blanchard Beach in the trunk of a car, or the back of a pickup truck, the deliverer would have had to get out of the car and walk around to the back to remove the body.

38

Esty Wills Prepares for a Business Trip

Sean wears an overcoat and there is snow, so it's winter in Chicago. While Paraguay's climate may not be well known (it's generally tropical), what is well known is that the country is situated below the equator, and therefore it's summer there. That being the case, why is Wills packing a scarf, gloves, and wool socks?

Incidentally, Japan did undertake a mulberry bush experiment in the 1980s for silk production. It continues.

Flying time, Chicago to Buenos Aires via commercial airlines, is about sixteen hours. Flying to Asuncion adds two hours for time-zone changes.

39

The Case of the Buckle File

Gibraltar is spelled Gibralter in both the letter from Audrey and the one from Irene. The coincidence is too strong for Christine Cooper, who feels that Audrey, whose body, unlike that of Ernie, was never found, may be involved in a scheme to collect insurance. Irene's (Audrey's?) mistake is that she misspells Gibraltar even though, supposedly, she has been living there.

40

While Little Harvey Watched

Carson Wicksteed, according to Harvey's parents, has had a difficult time because of his brother. To some people, that would imply motive. Carson must also know what he's doing with a chain saw, especially if he's been making a living out of firewood as Little Harvey's father says.

The beech tree fell over intact during the storm, its roots still attached to the tree and, at one edge, still clinging to the ground. Unless a sawyer is deliberately trying to make the stump fall back into the hole, he will not cut away the upper part of the tree first, because it is the counterbalancing weight of the upper part that keeps the stump and root system from doing so. Since Carson is a professional, he would surely have known this.

41

The Murder of
Mr. Norbert Gray

The letters in the evidence bag are personal ones, mailed by someone. Mike Roslin tapped the stamps on both letters, so it is likely that whoever mailed the letters licked the stamps.

The saliva can be tested for DNA.

42

A Holdup at the
Adjala Building

The Adjala Building must function as an almost perfect mirror at almost any time of day, but especially before lunch on this bright day when there would be no direct sunlight on the copper-tinted plate glass doors. The courier quite certainly would have been able to see details about the thief in its reflection.

43

Filming at
L'Hôtel du Roi

Before the twentieth century's popularization of efficient, lobby-less—and characterless—hotels, the lobby of a grand hotel was designed to be part of the experience of a hotel stay, and it was usually quite a busy place. Therefore Charlotte's colliding with

Van Slotin can be entirely natural, especially if the acting brings it off effectively, because there would be more than enough distractions and activities to make a collision like this legitimate.

What bothers Barney King is that the writers have made Charlotte too obvious with her bare hands. In the forties, a lady, even one with questionable intent, would never have entered the lobby of a grand hotel without hat and gloves. (Sy's marginal note makes this clear.) Charlotte has a hat, but when she adjusts the seams of her stockings, it's clear she does not have gloves on. Perhaps she needs bare hands to make the dip, but Barney wants the writers to come up with a better approach.

44

Whether or Not to Continue Up the Mountain

When Chris looked through the binoculars the first time and saw the cattle calmly chewing their cud, she also saw their ears twitching. The only reason an animal does that is to shoo away insects. If there are insects bothering the Swiss Browns up the mountainside, then it cannot be very cold.

45

Nothing Better than a Clear Alibi

Only Augusta and Siobhan can support the contention that they were in the hallway when the three shots were fired that apparently killed Siobhan's husband, Paisley. Everything else can be attested to by other tenants, the janitor, and Esther Goldblum.

Where Augusta Reinhold's account breaks down, and what makes Nik Hall suspicious of Siobhan's alibi, is Augusta's statement that after Esther left, she got dressed "as you see me now" and came down the elevator to Siobhan's floor. Nik realizes that without the help of Raythena, who does not appear until one, Augusta would never have been able to button the dress she has on, in the space of time described, because her hands are ravaged by arthritis. She could never have made it to the elevator and be in it with her granddaughter within the time she claims.

46

Guenther Hesch
Didn't Call In!

If there are seventeen filters in the bowl, Guenther has lit twenty-two cigarettes, the first one according to habit at eight o'clock and the rest on the quarter hour thereafter. The first four, producing four filters and four butts, would have been lit at 8 A.M., 8:15, 8:30, and 8:45. The fifth cigarette, lit at 9 A.M., would have been rolled from the butts of the previous four. Continuing in this way, Guenther would have snapped three more filters and lit up at 9:15, 9:30, and 9:45. The three butts from these, along with the roll-your-own butt from 9 A.M., would have produced a roll-your-own cigarette for 10 A.M. In this fashion Guenther would have produced three more filters by 11 A.M., at which time he'd have four more butts for another roll-your-own, then three more filters by noon and three more by 1 P.M.

Since there are seventeen filters in the bowl, and one butt (from the 1 P.M. roll-your-own), Guenther must still have been in the room at 1:15, when he broke off the seventeenth filter and lit up.

47

Right Over the Edge
of Old Baldy

When Pam heard the scream, she was only a minute or so away from the edge of Old Baldy. She had been proceeding up the Bruce Trail from Kimberly Rock. Hadley Withrop said that he and Sheena had eaten lunch at Kimberly Rock and had been at the edge of Old Baldy for only two minutes when Sheena went over. If this account is true, then the Withrops had gone up the trail just ahead of Pam. By the same token, if that fact is true, the Withrops would have taken out the spiderweb that Pam ran into. There would not have been sufficient time for the spider to rebuild. If the Withrops had not come up the trail ahead of Pam, why does he say that?

48

Sunstroke, and
Who Knows What Else!

Evan is duplicating the position in which Cadet Elayna was tied to stakes, and is doing so in precisely the same place, with the stakes reinserted into the same holes. If Evan can use a shadow from the stake to keep the sun out of his eyes, the stakes must be angled toward him.

Basic laws of physics tell us that stakes angled away from him would be hard to pull out. Not so if the stakes are angled toward him. Cadet Elayna could have pulled out the stakes if he'd wished to.

49

Should the Third Secretary Sign?

Probably not, for the photograph is fraudulent. Russia uses the Cyrillic alphabet, in which the letters of Lenin's name, most particularly the "L" and "I," bear no resemblance at all to those letters as we know them in the modern Roman alphabet.

The Cyrillic alphabet, modified from Greek by St. Cyril (c. 827–869), is used for Slavonic languages like Russian and Bulgarian. As Third Secretary, Ena would surely have known that, and likely would have declined to sign.

When the USSR moved into Czechoslovakia on August 21, 1968, Austria became the first stop for most refugees.

Lenin died in 1924. In 1930 his tomb was built in Red Square, with his embalmed body visible behind glass. It became a type of shrine in Moscow but was removed after perestroika.

50

A Successful Bust at 51 Rosehill

The townhouses at Woodington Manor are all the same size and shape. And the interiors are also designed so that each story is the same size and shape. Jack Atkin has determined that Number 51 must have a false wall, because the basement window wall—the wall facing west—is not the same length as the west wall on the first floor. The first floor has the same furniture pieces as the basement, but with lamps on end tables. In the basement, as Mandy Leamington describes it, the two massage chairs are jammed in between the sofa and the wall.

How much he was influenced by the geraniums is moot, but as an aficionado of this flower, Jack certainly would not ignore the fact that there are six on the first floor and five in the basement. That discrepancy likely led to further analysis.

51

The Case of the Body in Cubicle 12

In a "sweatshop" environment, where everything is high-tech and geared to achieve maximum production, this woman's cubicle has a fountain pen in it. Given that there is also a bottle of ink (taking up valuable space along with a desk lamp), she must have been exercising at least some mild defiance of her sterile working conditions; i.e., she must have actually *used* the fountain pen. For something as personal and final as her own final note, this woman in particular would not have been likely to use the printer.

52

The Case of the
Broken Lawnmower

The rectangle Kristy painted marks the only spot on the mower's front lawn from where he can see across the street into the alley. It also marks the spot where the nut was found, and where the witness says his lawnmower handle came apart, causing him to turn off the mower and then look up to witness the shooting. However, the two investigators found the bolt five or six steps away. It is at this point where the lawnmower handle would have come apart. Even if the nut falls off a bolt, the structure will hold together, however loosely, until the bolt, no longer secured, comes out. Then the handle will come apart.

53

A Quiet Night with Danielle Steel?

The platform jutting out from the side of the Jacuzzi is completely clean. If the victim had taken a novel and a drink to the tub, and if the drink was almost entirely consumed, then the glass would have been lifted up and set down several times, leaving round marks on the surface of the platform. If she died of natural causes and then sank into the water, taking the novel in with her, those marks would still be there. Even an obsessively neat woman would not have wiped them after each sip. (Besides, the only cloth, the face cloth, was untouched.) Some one must have cleaned too thoroughly in an attempt to rid the place of evidence.

54

Vandalism at the Bel Monte Gallery

While Robbie paced on the sidewalk, waiting for Patchy, Dale stood between the sidewalk and the Bel Monte Gallery, under a mature chestnut tree. The time is just before Christmas, and there would not be any leaves on the tree. Four months ago, when the paintings were slashed, the tree would have been in full leaf. That it is a chestnut tree is not overly significant; however, the leaves of this type of tree are very large and the tree always leafs very fully.

From the bus shelter, Patchy draws the attention of the two investigators to the window "right b'tween them branches there." His ability to "witness" would almost certainly have been thwarted by the leaves at that time.

55

Laying Charges
Too Quickly?

Special Investigator Hope Rogers believes, at least at this stage, that someone is trying to set up Nunzio by planting the apparent murder weapon in his tool box. She suspects it is a plant because Nunzio Scalabianca is a craftsman, an artist in his ornamental metalwork trade. Until she can investigate further, it's far safer to assume that a true craftsman would never have a cheap tool in his own cache of equipment. A craftsman would use only quality equipment.

56

Taking Down
the Yellow Tape

When he came in the driveway and got out of his car, Geoffrey noted the garbage strewn about by the raccoons and saw dog-food cans. It's very unlikely that a stranger would be able to come in to Dietrich Lindenmacher's home at night and kill the victim in his bed, if the victim had a dog. The dog would surely have roused Lindenmacher to the point where he'd have gotten out of bed. And, if Lindenmacher had a burglar alarm system, it is equally unlikely that he would have been the type of person to treat the dog's barking casually.

Although the matter of the dog is itself enough to arouse second thoughts, the burglar alarm offers technical information too. All but the most primitive alarm systems are designed to go off if their circuit is cut. But it is possible to "jump" the circuit, rewire it so that the electricity bypasses the system. To do that, one needs to know where the alarm circuit is connected, and it's not likely that a stranger would know that.

At the very least, this suspect deserves a second look, either because he is innocent or because he is not a stranger.

57

Problem-Solving in Accident Reconstruction 101

Turtles do cross roads from one habitat to another, usually following some territorial imperative or breeding instinct. This happens particularly in the setting here, where the road has apparently created two separate swamps. And turtles do grow large enough to be a potential problem for car drivers.

In this case, the weakness of the driver's story is the place where she reports the turtle: at the top of the hill. Turtles—in fact all members of the order Chelonia—are not celebrated for either their logic or their adventurousness. Even so, for one to go up a hill, away from its natural habitat on either side, is unlikely in the extreme.

58

Before the First Commercial Break

It is too obvious that Katzmann is lying. The allegedly dropped-in-panic revolver is in front of, and against, a door that swings inward (Gilhooley fingers the barrel of the middle hinge). The alleged robber could not have left it like that and then opened the door to flee, because opening the door would have knocked the revolver away.

59

More than One St. Plouffe?

Alfred-Louis St. Plouffe Junior fils.

The confession is written in grammatically impeccable prose. The same quality applies to the speech of the younger St. Plouffe Junior. The speech of the elder St. Plouffe Junior, however, while grammatically elegant for the most part, has some awkward errors, suggesting he does not have quite the grammatical exactitude necessary to write the confession in the way it was offered.

The elder St. Plouffe says adverse when averse is the correct choice, and previous instead of prior. Further, he says *between my son and myself,* a very popular vulgarism, instead of *between my son and me.* The use of excepting over except is another grammatical sin.

60

When the Oxygen Ran Out

Either there is a series of genuine and unfortunate coincidences or there is a conspiracy that has led to the death of Humbert Latham.

The day nurse may have left innocently; after all, she had arranged to leave early. The valet's accident may have been real, along with the subsequent wooziness and inability to speak. As for the night nurse, we don't know why she failed to show up, but if the other two were legitimately absent, she could have been too. On the other hand, if there is a conspiracy by one or two or all three of the above, the security guard, if he was the regular patroller, would likely have been part of it.

Fran noted that the lamp was on in the room with Latham's body. If, as Sergeant Hong ordered, nothing was to be touched, then it must have been on all night. Since there was no blind or curtain over the window, the regular patroller would have noted the light and, unless he was in on a plot, would surely have investigated.

61

The Terrorist in Fountain Square

Number Four, the painter. With the information Connie has, it's a judgment call; all she knows is that one of them has the switch. With the exception of the painter, each has at least a legitimate claim to be in the square. Number Four, however, in this place of aluminum and brick and glass, has nothing to paint.

62

A Matter of Balance

Tom Jones knows his interview was a set-up because the man presenting himself as Agent Bronowski would not have made the height prerequisites to be an agent of the FBI. Although few police forces would dare to enforce height or gender or ethnic restrictions today, it was fairly common at the time Tom Jones had his meeting.

We know Tom is not tall because in the elevator he is careful not to let his face get too close to the marine lieutenant's dandruff-covered shoulder blade. Yet Tom, sitting on the same type of chair as Bronowski, is able to study a birthmark on the alleged agent's scalp, suggesting that Bronowski is even shorter than he.

That the story takes place at a time when height restrictions were enforced is confirmed by the fact that it is just prior to World War II. To be precise, the date is October 30, 1938, the Sunday night before Hallowe'en when Orson Welles's Mercury Theatre presented its adaptation of H.G. Wells's *The War of the Worlds*.

Polyesters were introduced to the world in 1940.

63

Paying Attention to Esme Quartz

Esme's one friend is her dog. This is a city neighborhood where dogs cannot roam free but must be walked. It had been raining for a day and a half and the dog, for biological cum hygienic reasons, had to be walked, rain or shine. The dog hair on Esme's coat told MaryPat that Esme had a genuine reason to be on the street in the rain, and since her walking-in-the-rain style would have been naturally different from the style of other pedestrians because of the dog, it is quite reasonable to believe that she had a good look at the shooter. That Esme actually knew the shooter was a bonus.

64

Investigating the Failed Drug Bust

Officer Dana is already under quiet investigation; that is a given. The second officer to be checked out now is the narcotics squad officer from Gallenkirk Park. He is the one who said that the approaching wino (Officer Dana) could be heard walking through the leaves.

Quite clearly, the time is early spring. There is some snow still remaining in shaded spots and in the lee of the tree trunks. Betty Stadler is sure she noticed a robin and remarks that it is an early returner. In early spring, the millions of leaves that fell from the many trees in Gallenkirk Park the pervious fall will be soggy and compressed and matted together. This would have been especially so at the time of the failed drug bust and during Betty's subsequent investigation because the effect of the melted snow has been compounded by several days of drizzle.

For Officer Dana to have made noise walking through the leaves, he would have had to stir up the surface very deliberately, implying some connection to the meeting of drug dealers about to take place. Another possibility is that the narcotics officer is not telling the truth about the way Officer Dana approached. Still a third is that the two officers are in this together. Thus, for the moment at least, Lieutenant Stadler has two police officers to investigate.

65

A Surprise Witness for the Highland Press Case

In his "favorite" pub, as he claims The Toby Jug to be, Wally Birks is not going to stop at the entrance to the washroom alcove to orient himself on the direction of the "Gents." He'd know which way to turn from habit.

66

The Last Will and Testament
of Albion Mulmur

The poet in Kay makes her sensitive to the way Regina Mulmur treats the harness shop. If Regina had "almost used to live in here" as a little kid, she would surely have been more sensitive to the place than she was.

By itself, however, that is not enough. The convincing clue is the way in which Regina closed the door. She seemed to know instinctively that it needed a good shove to close it because the hinges were worn. If she hadn't been here in twenty years, as she says, then it's not likely she'd have known that. Since the will benefiting her was found here, it's fairly clear to Kay that Regina had paid the shop a recent visit.

67

What Happens in
Scene Three?

It should be reasonably straightforward to conclude that the gunman's fingerprints are now in George Fewster's safe—on the Peacock egg. If George were to be dispatched, as the contract apparently dictates, the safe would surely be opened and the identity of the gunman placed at risk of being revealed. On the other hand, if the gunman does not shoot him, George can simply give the egg and fingerprints to the police at will.

But there is a quid pro quo. If the partner "cannot afford to let George live," he will surely try this again. Thus, if the gunman was to turn his professional skills against the man who hired him in the first place, that danger to George would be removed. At the same time, by doing that, he ensures George's silence, since even though George has not committed any crime by turning his partner's plan back on himself, it would be impossible for George to offer the police some fingerprints without arousing suspicion and provoking investigations.

68

Almost an Ideal Spot for Breakfast

If the house has been empty for the past week while the Melches were in Nassau, the large leaves on the plants facing the east window would have rotated naturally toward the light, i.e., the window, over this period of time, particularly in winter. But the leaves were turned toward the west wall. (As he stood in the doorway, Laurie noticed them turned toward him.) Someone who cares for plants had rotated them—standard procedure in indoor plant care—very recently. Laurie Silverberg assumes, quite logically, that a break-and-enter perpetrator is not likely to have done this. That leaves one very likely suspect.

69

Investigating the Explosion

Because the blast came from inside the house. It must have been set up to look like "Nazi types" were responsible.

Doug Doyle's clue comes from the direction of the swastika and the smear from the sprinkler system. Although swastikas can go both clockwise and counterclockwise, as Doug pointed out, the Nazi party in Germany chose a clockwise rotation. Therefore,

Solutions

if a swastika were to be applied to the inside of a glass door in order to appear as though it had been put on from the outside, the artist (terrorist?) would have done it counterclockwise.

Granted, a careful investigation would certainly reveal which side of the glass held the symbol. However, Marni says that "on first impression" it appears some Nazi types were involved, and that may be all the bombsetter wanted to do. Besides, if the door were sufficiently shattered, a less than utterly precise examination might miss the fact.

Where the scheme broke down was in the smearing by the sprinkler system. The sprinklers must be inside of course, and would have come on after the blast. If the water fell on the markings and smeared them, the door would have to have been blasted outward. That is why Doug is suspicious.

70

Some Uncertainty About the Call at 291 Bristol

Shaun's maternal instincts are readily apparent, so it must seem strange, at the very least, that Paige's parents would go away, leaving her alone in the house, with the burglar alarm not working, especially given the recent stalking incident on the campus.

Moreover, if the man in black was breaking and entering, it seems highly unlikely he would wear jewelry that might jingle.

The strongest doubt of all, though, originates from Paige. If she had just emerged from the shower, the mirror in which she claims to have seen the man in black would have been fogged with vapor.

71
The Case of the
Missing Child

While standing in the doorway, Audrey noticed that, behind the father, the venetian blinds are open. At the other window, the mother is looking out. Both say they have not been in the room since Lexie was put to bed last night. In a bedroom exposed to higher buildings such as the neighboring apartments, it surely would have been natural to draw the blinds. This is especially so in light of the mother's statement that anything, including light, can set Lexie off. It seems the parents have much more explaining to do.

72
A Clever Solution
at the County Fair

The obvious, in the case of homing pigeons: Pincher will have to take the first-prize ribbon off, and then have the judges make their decision again. He will then release the winners of the first prize. Since they are homing pigeons, they will fly home—either to Maxwell Stipple's cote or to Madonna Two Feather's.

73

Even Birdwatchers
Need to Watch Their Backs

The scene Ron sees consists of a path on his left at the edge of McCarston's Lake and one that forks to his right. And, he can see where the two paths rejoin at the foot of the Devil's Torrent.

The path on the right must be the one that hikers and bird-watchers use to go around the lake when there is more water in it (and when the Devil's Torrent really deserves its name).

When the weather turns drier and the lake shrinks in size owing to less water flow, another path will develop because bird-watchers especially will stay to the water's edge where the birds are.

If Jos Poot was killed earlier in the season, and in the water, as is apparently the case, Mrs. Poot could have used water buoyancy to get his body to its hiding place.

74

Two Embassy Cars
Are Missing

Captain Surette enjoys the sun on the back of his neck as he looks down the road to where the embassy cars stopped at the intersection. Since there's only an hour of daylight left, he's looking east. There has been a west wind all day. As embassy cars come toward one, it is only possible to see the front edges of the flags mounted on the front fenders because of the air motion. Even when they stopped, the west wind would have held the flags that way. The first auxiliary trooper, therefore, would not have been able to distinguish which car was flying which flag, and since his report does that, the captain draws an obvious conclusion.

Captain Surette would prefer to locate the car with Sudanese flags first, because the trooper's report implied that the Egyptian one was the principal vehicle. Since there is collusion in this case, the Captain interprets that as a deliberate attempt to mislead pursuers, so he is opting for the opposite.

The Sudanese flag, incidentally, is three horizontal stripes red (top), white and black, with a green triangle based on the hoist. Egypt's flag is similarly striped, but with the national emblem center, in gold.

75

A Most Confusing Robbery

Since both suspects qualify, potentially, Mary-Joan has to rely on the video store owner's account. He said that the robber he shot "took off runnin'" down the alley. The droplets of blood that ended at the dumpster were quite widely spaced, four or five yards apart, the FOS had explained. The spacing would suggest someone who was able to run pretty fast.

The suspect hit in the leg, however, would not have been able to run as quickly, with the result that the droplets would be closer together. Therefore Mary-Joan Westlake is going to arrest Suspect Two, the one with the shoulder wound.

76

Transcript (Copy #1 of 4)

Captain Ransom had the third watch, which begins at 6 P.M. It started to rain on his third round trip (8 P.M.). The collision occurred on the next trip, eight minutes into the return leg from Mississauga Island (9:38 P.M.), so the accident occurred in darkness. However, any municipality that has five ferries running every hour (in high season) has to be a large one: a city. Since running time from Mississauga Island to the city dock is only 17 minutes, the lights of the city must be clearly visible to all inbound craft. If the *Gadabout* were being safely and responsibly handled, the outline of a ship the size of the O.M.S. *Oliver Mowat* would have been clearly detailed against the illumination from the city, and therefore avoidable, whether or not her clearance lights were working.